THE STALKER'S SONG

A Gripping Crime Thriller

Georgia E Brown

S☀CCIONES

ISBN: 9781796445572

Design & formatting by Socciones Editoria Digitale
www.socciones.co.uk

＿OGEMENTS

＿ıde to all the team at Socciones for their
＿ce in producing my first novel.

＿es, I should like to thank Michael Robson,
＿ıoxhall. Thanks, too, to Nigel Harling of
＿Rescue Centre for his technical advice.

＿draft, thanks are due to Eve Seymour, and to
＿ınvaluable help and advice and for undertaking
＿I would also like to thank the following for their
＿ful feedback: Angela Coils, Erryl McLarty, Kath
Blacker and Cathy Jensen.

＿ı Georgia for her technical help and my family and
＿ınstinting support and encouragement throughout the
whole project.

ACKNOWLEDGEMENTS

I would like to express my gratitude to all the team at Socciones for their expertise and diligence in producing my first novel.

For advice on police procedures, I should like to thank Michael Robson, Simon Atkinson and Jo Boxhall. Thanks, too, to Nigel Harling of Patterdale Mountain Rescue Centre for his technical advice.

For editing the very first draft, thanks are due to Eve Seymour, and to Steph Boulton for her invaluable help and advice and for undertaking the final technical edit. I would also like to thank the following for their constructive and helpful feedback: Angela Coils, Erryl McLarty, Kath Blacker and Cathy Jensen.

Finally, thanks to Georgia for her technical help and my family and friends for their unstinting support and encouragement throughout the whole project.

CHAPTER ONE

The man salivated as he watched her, groaning as he rubbed his hand over his groin. She was sitting cross-legged on the pale silk throw which covered her large chesterfield-style bed. He thought the tastefully furnished room reflected her innate elegance, with its huge chandelier dominating the high ceiling and scattering prisms of light around the silvery walls and white French furniture.

It always thrilled him to observe her; his pleasure heightened by the knowledge that she was totally unaware of his scrutiny.

When he first set eyes on her, on his TV screen, he knew he'd found his next target. Idly watching the BBC News one evening, his attention was drawn to the cool, confident blonde being interviewed outside the Albert Hall. She'd been waylaid by a reporter on her way into a CBI Conference, with a question about her opinion of the potential effect of Brexit on the economy. Looking smart, in a well-cut dark blue suit, she radiated class as she turned intelligent green eyes to the camera and articulated her views. He found her confidence appealing, knowing that destroying it would give him indescribable pleasure. He'd punched the air, shouting 'Game On! Let the pursuit begin.'

The power he felt as he secretly spied on her was an enduring aphrodisiac. He knew that he was nearing the point where he needed to possess her, body and soul, but for now the chase was exquisite.

Hearing her chatting animatedly with her step-daughter in Barbados, he was surprised to realise that she was talking about taking a trip out there. As she spoke and gesticulated with her free hand, the loosely-tied, white robe she was wearing parted a little, showing the swell of her pale breasts. When she reached over to take a tissue from a flowery box on the bedside table, her gown opened even further, revealing a glimpse of her nakedness beneath. Desire overwhelmed him and, eyes riveted on her body, he unbuttoned his jeans, pulled the zip down and urgently masturbated, his imagination running wild. When his heart rate had returned to something like normal, he tuned back into her conversation and became aware that she was making firm plans to travel to Barbados.

'I feel ready now, Fiona. I think it could be cathartic for me to spend time in the place where your dad and I were so happy'.

Following the sudden death of her husband, at the end of last year, she'd had some kind of breakdown and he'd watched with incredulity and frustration as she descended into a deep depression, mourning for the old man she'd been married to. She took to drink in her misery, and for a few months was stoned most of the time. He simply couldn't understand why someone like her could care so much for such a boring old man. Of course, friends and family had rallied round to give support. Her daughter even put her university studies on hold and moved back home. Close friends took it in turns to stay with her, and her stepdaughter, Fiona, came over frequently from Barbados to be with her. Unfortunately this meant that she was rarely alone, denying him the perfect opportunity to satisfy his longing.

Now, listening to her conversation, he realised with mounting anticipation that things were about to change. He began whistling the song that had been on his mind since he first met her:

Oh Carol, I am but a fool
Darling I love you, though you treat me cruel
You hurt me, and you make me cry
But if you leave me, I will surely die

CHAPTER TWO

British Airways flight 2155 was cruising at thirty-six thousand feet, en-route to Grantley Adams International Airport, Barbados. The moving map told me we were still a fair way from our destination, as I settled further back into my seat and took a deep breath, trying to calm the knot of anxiety nestling in my stomach.

My thoughts drifted back over the last tumultuous year. Almost unbearable grief, combined with excruciating guilt, had driven me to the brink of a nervous breakdown in the months following Peter's death. If I'd known, when he left me that morning, that I would never see him again, I would have dragged myself from my comatose state, held him to me and never let him go.

I'd stayed out very late the night before, partying with my girlfriends, a long-standing arrangement to say farewell to of one of the girls who was emigrating to New Zealand. We ended up clubbing; drinking into the early hours before getting taxis home. As a consequence, when Peter left early the next morning, I barely opened my eyes, let alone wished him a safe trip or kissed him goodbye. I vaguely remember him planting a light kiss on my head before he left, never to return.

After his death, I sank into utter despair. Unable to cope, I couldn't see any point in getting out of bed in the mornings. On the days I did manage to get up, it was a huge effort just to do the basic things; to shower, get dressed, or eat. With a wave of remorse, I remembered surrendering myself to drink, trying to dull the edge of the pain and the guilt, needing the oblivion that only alcohol could bring.

If it hadn't been for the unwavering support of friends and family, particularly Julia and Fiona, and Pauline, a close friend since childhood, I really don't know how I would ever have come through it. God knows how they stuck with me through the misery, the drinking, the abuse I hurled at everyone. I hated the world and everyone in it. I wanted them to go away and leave me alone. I just wanted to die.

'Mum, you can be as nasty as you want. We're not giving up on you,' Julia told me several times.

'Yes, you don't get rid of us that easily,' my step-daughter, Fiona, chimed in. 'Simon insists that I stay over here 'til you're better, so I'm not going anywhere.'

Slowly, I began to emerge from the depths, getting a bit stronger each day; I knew I'd turned the corner when I went a whole day without a drink, then two, three, a week. My recovery steadily continued to the point where I felt strong enough to make the journey to Barbados. I wanted to stay at our holiday apartment, where we'd had some of our happiest times, in the hope that it would prove cathartic, and give me some peace of mind.

'Cabin Crew, seats for landing.' The voice of the captain brought me back to the present, and the knot of anxiety intensified. Had I made the right decision to stay alone at the holiday home we'd shared together? Should I have listened to Fiona's attempts to get me to stay with her and Simon? I told myself to stop being so negative, that it would be good for me; another step in the healing process.

On disembarking, I stood uncertainly at the exit to the aircraft, before resolutely stepping from the plane and descending the steps. The warm, humid air met me, enveloping me like a cocoon. Walking towards the terminal building, I felt calm, suddenly certain I'd made the right decision to come to the island.

There were no delays at Passport Control and as I entered the Baggage Reclaim area, one of the porters came hurrying towards me, smiling warmly and looking very smart in his red waistcoat.

'Need help with your cases, Ma'm?' he enquired, indicating his trolley.

I agreed, and before too long, my cases arrived and were expertly plucked from the carousel and loaded on to the trolley. As we made our way past Customs, the porter chatted animatedly, welcoming me to Barbados. Pulling the heavy load (I've never learned to travel light) he grinned, showing uneven but startlingly white teeth.

'You can chill now Lady, you is in Barbados.'

Fiona was waiting in the bustling Arrivals Hall, a petite figure, in a brightly coloured summer dress. I was delighted to see her and as we greeted each other with warm hugs, I was surprised to find I had tears in my eyes.

'Hey. What's this?' said Fiona, laughing and wiping a tear away with her thumb.

I grimaced. 'Take no notice of me. I'm just so happy to see you.'

The porter kept up his friendly banter as he loaded the bags into the boot of Fiona's car.

'Well, you two lovely ladies are gonna have just the best time in Barbados,' he said, as he slammed the boot and made sure it was properly closed.

I thanked him with a generous tip, and was treated to another flash of white teeth. Soon, we were driving past sugar cane fields and watching the sky begin to darken as the sun made its descent below the horizon.

'Oh, Fi, it's so wonderful to be here again. It just feels… so right.'

Fiona glanced sideways at me as she drove. She looked very pretty, the deep orange of her sundress complimenting her honeyed skin tone and dark, shiny hair.

'I'm so glad you're here – and you're looking really well. Are you absolutely sure you'll be alright on your own in the apartment? It's not too late to change your mind, you know?'

We were passing the port at Bridgetown, and I could see several huge liners moored there. Later, they would set sail for their various destinations and become visible from the apartment as they left the port, lit up like floating wedding cakes against the dark sky.

'To be honest, I'm even more sure now that I'm here. When I got off the plane, it felt somehow as though I'd come home. You know, I need some time for reflection, Fi. When I think about it, I've hardly had a night on my own since Peter died, what with having the breakdown and everything. If Julia hasn't been with me, you've been there, or Pauline, or other friends. You've all been very kind, but I think I need to learn to stand on my own two feet again.'

'Well, we're not far away if you need us, you stubborn moo!'

'I've never really thanked you properly for coming over so often to help look after me when I... went to pieces. Especially as you had your own grief to deal with.'

'Least I could do, Carol. Dad would have wanted me to look after you. And, in a way, it helped me too, to focus on getting you better. Anyway,' she said, changing down a gear as we approached a queue of traffic, 'it's good that you feel strong enough now to come out here.'

When we reached the apartment, there were two large rum punches waiting for us in the fridge, with a note from the housekeeper, Josie, that simply read 'Enjoy.' We sat on the terrace in the warm evening air, sipping our drinks by the soft glow of the lamps set in the surrounding low stone wall.

'When is Julia coming out?' Fiona asked, taking a sip of her rum punch. 'Bloody hell, these are strong!' she pulled a face.

'She's coming just before Christmas,' I said, taking a tentative sip of my drink. Josie's rum punches were legendary. 'Tastes like she's used at least a half a bottle of rum in these.' I spluttered.

'Better let you finish mine,' Fiona said, reluctantly pouring some of her drink into my glass. 'Pity I'm driving; it's delicious once you get used to it.'

'Hey, I'm going to be stoned.' I laughed and pushed her hand away.

'Nothing new there then,' she quipped. We finished our drinks and Fiona stood up, ready to leave. 'No need to come up,' she said, as I made to walk with her up the steps at the side of the villa. 'You've got your unpacking to do. I'll see you tomorrow.' A quick peck on my cheek and she was gone.

Once she'd left, I hefted one of the cases on to the bed and got busy. I looked at Peter's wardrobe, where I knew his clothes still hung, untouched. Fiona and I had agreed we would tackle them together, a task I hadn't yet faced back home in England. I opened the wardrobe door and brought out one of the many tops hanging there; a bright emerald green polo shirt. Burying my face in it, I breathed deeply, but couldn't detect anything of Peter now in its aroma, only a faint smell of the washing powder Josie used. I remembered vividly the last time he'd worn it. We'd been visiting the Barbados Wildlife Reserve at Farley Hill. Strolling around the grounds, we spotted a variety of animals; armadillos, pelicans, deer, but my favourites were the monkeys. I stopped to take a photograph; Peter walking slightly ahead of me. A monkey was keeping pace with him, running along the corrugated roof of a single-storey building beside the path. Suddenly, the monkey launched itself off the roof and on to Peter's back. He got such a fright; screaming like a girl, he started to run. His panama hat flew one way and his sunglasses the other, as he tried to dislodge the monkey. I couldn't move for laughing. I smiled at the memory and, with a small sigh, put the shirt back on its hanger and returned it to the wardrobe, firmly closing the door. *We can deal with that later* I thought.

When I'd finally finished putting my things away, I was suddenly overcome by tiredness, no doubt helped by the effect of the rum punches. After sending Julia a short message to let her know I'd arrived safely, I quickly got ready for bed, sank into the plump downy pillows and pulled a sheet over myself. Sleep came almost immediately.

CHAPTER THREE

He sat in the shadows, watching and waiting. Before too long, he saw the Fiona woman come up from the garden and step into the pool of yellow light cast by the roadside lamp. Quite a pretty little thing, he noted. He watched until she got into her car and drove off, before turning his own car around and heading back to his hotel. 'Not yet, Carol,' he whispered.

Earlier, he'd been at the airport to watch her arrive, needing to be absolutely sure she hadn't changed her mind at the last minute. The touching little scene when she met Fiona, and shed a few tears, made him smile. Soon, he would make sure she shed a lot more.

As he drove, he pictured her settling down for the night. She would be tired after the journey, and would no doubt sleep soundly. His whole body was infused with a delicious sense of anticipation. He could almost taste it. 'Sleep tight, Carol,' he whispered. 'Not long now.'

His fantasies about her were becoming more intense - more violent and sexual, now that gratification was so close. Although he loved the pursuit, the feeling of power that came from silently stalking her, the exhilaration of nearing the end game was pure ecstasy.

Back in his room, he checked her phone, and saw that she'd sent a message to her daughter. 'Hi Jules, Arrived safely. Off to bed now - had one of Josie's rum punches and feeling v sleepy. Fi coming over tomorrow night for catch up. Feels really good being here'.

'Oh, Carol, it's going to feel even better, soon.' As he undressed for bed, he was whistling quietly.

'Oh Carol, I am but a fool...'

CHAPTER FOUR

It was dawn when I woke up, not at all surprised to find that I'd slept for a straight eight hours. Jet-lag always took its toll after the long journey. The eight hour flight from Gatwick wasn't too bad, but the flight from Newcastle to Heathrow, then the transfer to Gatwick added several hours and extra hassle to the journey.

Pulling on a light wrap, I made myself a cup of coffee, and carried it out on to the terrace, where I sat gazing out over the sea. On the horizon, I could see a huge liner making its way slowly towards the port at Bridgetown. I knew it would stay there for the day, leaving its passengers free to roam the island, before setting sail late in the evening for some other exotic location.

Glancing around the terrace, I noticed how beautiful the bougainvillea looked, growing in great profusion up the walls of the villa, creating a stunning cloud of fuchsia. The terrace itself looked neat and tidy, the potted plants all thriving and healthy. Raoul was obviously doing a good job on his weekly visit.

I closed my eyes, took a deep breath of the fragrant air and let the tranquillity of the place seep into my bones. For the first time in a long time, I felt relaxed, almost happy. I thought how strange it was to be bereaved. Since I'd been widowed, I'd felt sort of apart from everyone else, almost in a parallel world. As if life was going on as normal all around me, but I wasn't really part of it. Maybe this break would complete the healing process and help me to fully accept Peter's death and get back into the world again.

'Good morning, Carol.' My reverie was interrupted by Liz's husky drawl. She and Dave were renting the first floor apartment, as they did every year, when they closed down their New York gallery for a month. With beach towels over their arms, they were clearly on their way down to the sea for an early-morning dip. As our regular guests, we'd got to know them quite well and had some good times with them. They made an attractive couple, both tall and slim. Liz was looking good, her deeply tanned body shown off to perfection by a stylish turquoise bikini. Dave's tan was even darker, his light brown hair streaked with sun-bleached highlights.

'Wow, you two are looking well,' I stood up. 'Loving the bikini, Liz.'

'Aw, Carol, we just couldn't believe it when Josie told us about Peter.' Liz's eyes were full of sympathy. 'What a shock. We're so sorry. You must be devastated.' Liz wrapped her arms around me and hugged me tightly. 'How are you handling it all, Poppet?'

'I'm doing ok now, Liz. It hasn't been easy, but... you know, I'm getting there.'

Dave hugged me in turn, muttering how terribly sorry he was about Peter. 'It must have been terrible for you, Carol. So sudden. What a waste... Such a great guy... And so full of life.' He shook his head, sadly, 'Hard to believe he's gone.'

'We're gonna look after you, Poppet,' Liz said, taking my hands. 'We're touring the island with friends today. Staying overnight with them at the Crane Beach,' she explained. 'But we'll be back tomorrow, and we'll get together and spend some time hanging out. We'll have a drink – a toast to Peter. Several in fact.'

'Sounds good, Liz. We'll do that. Look forward to it.'

After they disappeared down the steps to the sea, I finished my coffee, had a quick shower and threw on a white tee shirt and cut off jeans. I grabbed my purse, found the car keys on the hook where they lived in the kitchen and was just about to leave when Josie arrived.

'Hello, my precious,' she bellowed, hugging me. 'How are you copin' my darlin'? God Bless you.'

Josie, a larger than life character, had become like family to us. Peter had called her his 'gem' having found her when he first bought the property. Of indeterminate age, she was full of energy despite her not inconsiderable bulk.

Although we'd spoken several times by phone since Peter's death, this was the first time we'd seen each other and she hugged me warmly, before holding me at arm's length to examine my face.

With tears in her eyes, she asked 'How are you coping, honey, really?' Her tears were threatening to spill over.

'It's been really hard, Josie, but I'm doing ok now. No, please don't cry. You'll set me off and I have to go to the shops. Let's have a coffee when I get back and talk about things then?' I embraced her and kissed her cheek.

'Alright honey,' she said wiping her eyes with the back of her hand. 'Off you go; I'll see you soon.' She patted my hand and bustled off to get started on her chores, her ample derriere swaying as she walked. A painting Peter and I had once bought came to mind; an oil painting by a local artist who specialised in works depicting large-bottomed Caribbean women. The one we'd chosen was of the rear view of a large, beautifully dressed lady, wearing a full-skirted yellow dress and flower-bedecked hat. She was holding the hand of a small child, and they were clearly on their way to the church which could be seen in the near distance. The painting had reminded us both so much of Josie that we just had to buy it.

I headed up the steps at the side of the villa, stopping on the way to watch a tiny humming bird, fascinated as always by how fast its wings moved as it collected nectar from a bright yellow hibiscus, probing with its long beak before whirring off in a cloud of wings.

When the Grand Vitara started first time after such a long time out of use, I breathed a sigh of relief and was soon driving north, towards Holetown, reggae music belting out from the speakers. The road followed the coast and, as I drove I glimpsed patches of turquoise sea to the left, in the gaps between stone-built villas, smart apartment blocks, small hotels and the few remaining chattel houses. Most of the chattel houses were painted in pastel blues or pinks, but I noticed one or two were quite ramshackle, with peeling paint and rusty corrugated iron sheets serving as roofs and fences. There seemed to be quite a bit of building going on at various sites along the route; a good sign that the economy must be picking up, I thought.

Stopping at a zebra crossing to let a group of young schoolchildren cross, I was struck, as always, by how smart they looked in their uniforms of red and grey. I loved the way most of the girls had intricately styled hair, with bunches or tiny plaits all over, tied with bright ribbons. I thought they looked so sweet, holding hands, chattering and laughing as they walked along in pairs. I couldn't help but smile.

Further along, I drove past the Chattel Village, a brightly-painted collection of chattel houses, comprising individual shops, selling everything from floaty kaftans to gourmet delicacies. I made a mental note to call by there on my way back, to get some cheese from the Gourmet Shop.

In the supermarket, I bought fresh, crusty bread, salad ingredients and a few bottles of champagne, as well as some standard provisions and bird of paradise flowers for the apartment. I was looking at the wide variety of tropical fruits and vegetables on display, when I felt a hand touch my arm.

'Hello, Mrs Barrington,' said a deep voice behind me, and I turned to see Raoul standing there, shopping basket in one large hand. 'Just want to tell you how sorry I am 'bout Mr Barrington. Anythin' I can do, you just ask. You know, round the villa and that...'

Raoul was usually a man of very few words and I was touched at his sympathy and offer of help. I thanked him and told him he was doing a great job of looking after the terrace and gardens. He just nodded, and without another word, popped some plantain into his basket, and walked on.

My shopping was stowed in the boot by a young assistant, then I put the aircon on full blast and sat in the car for a minute to ring the Lobster Alive restaurant. Knowing it was a favourite of Fiona's, I ordered freshly-cooked lobster to be delivered to the apartment in time for our supper. When I used to go to the restaurant with Peter, we were always asked to choose a lobster, from a huge tank, where the poor things were kept alive, claws tied. One of the staff would wade in to retrieve the selected creature. I could never bring myself to choose - it made me feel like an executioner, deciding which one would die. Peter used to laugh and call me a softie. One time we were there with Liz and Dave, and Liz told me she always chose an ugly lobster, to make her feel better. I couldn't quite work out the logic of that.

Josie was busy working in the first floor apartment when I got back, so I put away the shopping, changed into a bikini, and made my way down the wooden steps to the rocks and the strip of golden sand beneath the villa. The sun was very hot by then, and it was sheer bliss to submerge myself in the cool water. I swam as far as Paradise Beach, about half a mile, before turning and heading back. The sea was like a millpond, just the way I like it and I floated around for a while, watching a few small crabs scuttling about on the rocks, before emerging from the water, retrieving my towel from a rock, and climbing back up to the villa.

When I walked into the apartment, wrapping the towel around myself, Josie was pottering in the kitchen, and she flicked the switch on the kettle as soon as she saw me. We sat outside, under one of the ecru awnings that made the terrace bearable in the heat of the day, and sipped our coffee. Inevitably, we talked about Peter. Although a year had passed, Josie was still visibly upset at his death; she'd been very fond of him.

'I jest couldn't believe my Peter was dead, honey. Lord, I thought the shock was gonna kill me when Simon told me. Why? Why Peter?' her eyes were filling up with tears again. 'The Lord must a needed him up there. That's the only thing makes any sense,' she said, wiping her eyes with the corner of her apron. 'I pray to the Lord every night for him. And for you too, honey.'

'Thank you, Josie,' I said, trying to swallow the lump in my throat.

'I've known him such a long time, honey. Since Fiona and Jack were babies. He used to come out here on his own, with the little uns. Their mother wouldn't come – wanted to be with her horses. I used to cook for them... he was like a son to me.' Josie's face crumpled and tears ran down her cheeks. She wiped them away, dabbing at her eyes again with her apron. 'I was always telling him to be careful. Never could understand why he felt the need to climb mountains.' She sniffed in indignation before reaching over the table and taking one of my hands in both of hers, 'I was so pleased when you came along, honey. He was so happy, at last.' She squeezed my hand. 'Now, are you going to be alright here on your own?'

'I think so, Josie. I came out here to see if it would help to be here. To be honest, so far it feels good. And Julia's coming out for Christmas, so I won't be on my own for too long.'

'Oh, Julia! My special girl; it'll be so good to see her,' Josie smiled, sitting back. 'How's she doin' at University?' Josie knew Julia had delayed her studies to look after me, and I had to agree with her when she added, 'She's good girl. You know, you're so lucky to have such a lovely daughter.' She took a sip of her coffee. 'And Fiona, too,' added Josie, 'coming over so often to look after you. She told me it helped her to deal with things; she knew her dad would have wanted her to look out for you.'

'I know. They've both been gems. I didn't deserve their help... I was horrible to them. I'm ashamed at the way I went to pieces. I was drinking and everything...'

'Hush honey,' she leaned towards me again and put her hand over mine. 'I know. Simon's told me what's been happening. We all grieve in diff'rent ways and none of us knows how we'll cope until it happens to us.' She patted my hand affectionately. 'I'm just so glad you're here now. It'll do you good, honey. But I thought you might have brought Pauline with you? She would have been good company for you.'

'This is something I just need to do for myself, Josie. In any case Pauline wouldn't have been able to get away. This is the busiest time for the post office, coming up to Christmas. She might come out with me next spring.'

'I think she gets lonely, with her man away so much,' speculated Josie, 'what with her not having any little ones.' When Josie learned that Pauline was unable to have children, she was devastated for her. 'Must be hard for her, especially at Christmas time.'

'She's Julia's godmother you know; she's been very involved with her growing up, so she's been a sort of surrogate mother to her. They're very close.'

We chatted for a few more minutes, then Josie, hauled herself to her feet. 'Well, better get on with me work. Did you say Fiona was coming at six? You two have just the best evenin' together.'

'We will, Josie, don't you worry.' I said to her departing figure.

CHAPTER FIVE

The rest of the day just seemed to fly by, and before I knew it, I was adding slices of mango to a tropical salad to accompany the lobster and crusty fresh bread, singing along to Rod Stewart as I worked. *'If you want my body, and you think I'm sexy, come on sugar...'*

Fiona, always punctual, arrived on the dot of six, having persuaded Simon to give her a lift. He popped in to say a quick 'Hi' before hurrying back to supervise preparations for his restaurant opening at seven. With her car safely at home, Fiona didn't have to worry about drinking and driving, and demolished her first glass of bubbly within minutes, holding out her glass for a refill.

'Just what the doctor ordered,' she said, as we walked out on to the terrace and stood by the rail, looking out over the sea.

'This is the life,' I said. 'Drinking Sundowners and watching a Caribbean sunset. Who could ask for more?' I left unspoken the one thing we'd both ask for if we could; to have Peter there with us.

'I hope we get a green flash,' said Fiona. She was talking about the legendary Green Flash, which it's said brings good luck to anyone lucky enough to see it. Thankfully, there were no clouds to spoil the sunset, and we were able to watch the huge yellow ball as it slipped below the horizon, and see the sky growing pink, orange and purple as it disappeared.

'No green flash tonight,' said Fiona. 'I used to think it was just a legend until I actually saw it for myself. Then I still couldn't believe it. I was totally gobsmacked.'

'Me, too,' I laughed. 'You wonder – *'did I really see that?'* Come on, sit down; let's eat.'

Fiona took a seat at the table on the terrace, and I left her topping up our drinks while I got the lobster and salad from the fridge and collected the warm bread from the oven. We were tucking into the meal, when Fiona announced.

'Jack's here. He's staying with us.'

I stopped chewing, fork in mid-air, unable to hide my surprise. Jack was Fiona's brother and I knew they didn't usually get on together.

Fiona noticed my expression. 'Yeah, I was surprised myself. He just rang out of the blue and said he wanted to come over for an extended break. Told me he needed to get away from the UK. He arrived a couple of days ago and says he'll probably stay over Christmas.'

'Well, that's a turn up for the books,' I said. 'I'm glad now I didn't accept your invitation to stay with you.'

'Oh, come on, he's not that bad.' Fiona bristled, putting down her knife and fork.

'I'm sorry, I know he's your brother, but he's been pretty nasty to me since the day your dad introduced me to him. He blames me for breaking up your parents' marriage. He knew it was over long before I came on the scene, yet he still accused Peter of abandoning your mother for me.' I was indignant.

'I know,' Fi frowned. 'You're right; he knew they both wanted to divorce. He was probably just worried about his inheritance. Oh, he can be such a nasty little shit, sometimes,' she grimaced. 'You know what they say; you can choose your friends, but not your family.'

'True.' I changed the subject. 'By the way, I've started doing some work, from home. Rupert's been really understanding about me being away from the office for so long, but I know he's found it a strain, keeping the business going on his own. Running the Investment Group, as well as everything else.' I took a sip. 'I'm planning to go back full-time after the Christmas break. I've been away far too long; it's time I got a grip.'

'Glad to hear you're ready to get back in the saddle. By the way, what about your properties? Is Steve still looking after them?'

'Yes, he's been sorting most things out for me, maintenance and stuff. Most of the tenants are long-term, and really no bother. A couple of them are a bit more demanding, but luckily they've been pretty quiet of late.' I finished the last morsel of lobster on my plate.

'You know, looking back, I feel ashamed at what I put you and Julia through this year. I used to think I was a strong person - heaven knows, I had to be, to deal with my ex. But honestly, to just go to pieces like that. You'd think I was the only person ever to be bereaved. Before then, I thought people who had breakdowns were just being weak or self-indulgent, but my goodness, I know differently now. I had no control whatsoever over what was happening to me. It was scary.'

'Stop beating yourself up about it, Carol. Grief affects different people in different ways. You couldn't help having a breakdown – and anyway, you're better now, and that's all that matters,' she said, echoing the sentiments Josie had expressed.

The evening flew, and all too soon it was time for Fiona to leave. I walked with her up the steps to street level, to wait with her until her taxi came. The shrubbery was alive with the raucous noise of tree frogs singing their repetitive song, competing with the cicadas to see who could make the loudest racket.

'I've only once actually seen a tree frog,' I told Fiona. 'In Corfu. It was sitting on the branch of a tree, in broad daylight. It was incredible; small and bright green. Looked just like a tiny Kermit.'

'Really? You're lucky. You hear them all the time, but they're elusive little buggers when you try to find them.' she complained.

We reached the road and sat on the garden wall, chatting, under the light of the street lamp. It wasn't long before her taxi arrived and, as it was moving off, she shouted through the open window.

'See you tomorrow. Don't forget your bikini. And, don't worry, Jack's planning to go out for the day.'

I waved her off, amused to notice the hem of her skirt trailing on the road, caught in the door of the cab. *Typical Fiona.* I thought. Turning away, I set off back down the steps.

CHAPTER SIX

He made his way cautiously along the beach, keeping to the shadows as much as possible, avoiding the pools of light thrown on to the sand from the lamps on the cliff top terraces and gardens. Dressed in dark clothing, to be as inconspicuous as possible, he checked out the villas built into the side of the cliff.

He'd enjoyed spying on her today, watching her as she came down the steps in front of the villa, looking fantastic in a red, skimpy bikini. He'd kept his binoculars trained on her as she swam towards Paradise beach, noting that she wasn't a very accomplished swimmer. It took her ages to reach the beach, using a very amateurish breast stroke, keeping her face out of the water as she swam.

Earlier, he'd followed her into the supermarket, fascinated by her pert bottom, encased in tight white jeans. He noticed the looks she got from both men and women as she sauntered around; lust from the men, envy from the women.

Suddenly he heard Carol's tinkling laughter, and looking up, spotted the two women, one dark-haired, the other blonde, coming out of the apartment. He watched as they made their way across the terrace. Carol was wearing a white fitted top with a long flowered skirt. The outfit showed her curves off to perfection.

By the light of the garden lamps, they began to climb the uneven stone steps at the side of the villa, both holding up their hems to avoid tripping. He knew the steps led up to street level at the front of the house. Spotting the open patio door, he thought to himself, Perfect, just perfect.

Without hesitating, he scrambled over the rocks at the base of the cliff and climbed the rough wooden steps. After vaulting over a gate set into the low wall at the edge of the terrace, he hurried towards the open door. As he passed the table, he noticed the two champagne flutes and the remains of the meal. Spotting an empty Bollinger bottle, he thought to himself, *The ladies have obviously had a cosy evening.* Smiling in delicious anticipation, he slipped inside the apartment and found himself in a large, simply-furnished open-plan room.

After taking a quick look around the apartment - it was quite spacious, with a huge bedroom, complete with super-king-size bed, and a rather magnificent marble bathroom – he returned to the main room and concealed himself behind the shutters to await Carol's return.

CHAPTER SEVEN

The perfume of the bougainvillea was strong in the night air and I breathed in deeply, savouring the heady scent. I'd really enjoyed Fiona's visit, despite the brief discussion about Jack. She'd been on pretty good form, telling the most outrageous jokes in her own inimitable way.

Once I reached the terrace again, I stood for a long time by the whitewashed wall looking out over the dark mass of the sea, watching the lights of the fishing boats bobbing in the distance. Nestling beneath a small crescent moon, Venus hung so low and bright, I almost felt I could reach up and pluck it from the sky.

My thoughts strayed to occasions when the sea got rough and huge swells brought waves crashing on to the rocks below the villa. At those times, plumes of spray would drench the terrace. Peter and I would stand by the wall and just watch the drama of the elements, laughing when the spray from a particularly big wave rained on us. Then at night, we'd lie entwined in bed, listening to the sea pounding in the hollows under the rock beneath the house, feeling snug and cosy in our cocoon. The high seas sometimes lasted for days on end, but once the novelty wore off, we longed for the waves to calm down again so we could swim safely once more.

Oh, well, enough reminiscing for one night, I thought to myself. Then with a deep sigh, I turned away from the sea. After clearing the dishes from the table and putting them in the dishwasher, I picked up the empty bottles and dropped them into the recycling bin.

Before locking up, I looked around the lovely open plan living room with its whitewashed walls and simple rattan sofas, scattered with jewel-coloured cushions, and thought how lucky I was to have this gem of a place; a bittersweet thought now that Peter wasn't around to share it.

Oh God, Peter, I wish you could be here, I thought, with a sharp pang of longing, as I plumped up the cushions. Then, with another sigh, I went through to the kitchen and poured myself a glass of filtered water from a jug in the fridge.

Taking the glass through to the bedroom, I put it on the bedside table and switched on the reading lamp. Hitching my skirt up bit and slipping off my sandals, I climbed onto the bed and propped myself up against the pillows, to Whatsapp Julia at home in cold old England. It would be the middle of the night at home, so I knew I couldn't ring her, but I was suddenly longing to hear her voice. I contented myself by writing the message - told her I missed her and how much I was looking forward to her coming out at Christmas and that I'd booked a table at the Cliff for Christmas Day, where Fiona and Simon would be joining us. I wondered vaguely what Jack would be doing and fervently hoped he'd made other arrangements. I pressed 'send' after adding 'love you darling' then swung my legs over the side of the bed, plugged in my phone to charge overnight, and headed for the bathroom.

I pushed the bathroom door open, groping for the light pull. Even before the door swung back, a sixth sense told me something was wrong. My hand froze in mid-air, as I stood, rooted to the spot, gasping in shock. A man was standing there, unmoving, his large silhouette clearly outlined against the window. As I stood, momentarily transfixed with fear, he spoke in a quiet voice.

'Hello Carol, I've waited a long time for this.'

With a moan of terror, in blind panic, I turned to flee. I hadn't got very far when I felt his arms come round me from behind and a large hand was clamped over my mouth. I was struggling, kicking and trying to scream. He was too strong. He was big, much taller than me and solidly built. We were in the hall, just outside the doorway to the bathroom and he pushed me harshly into the wall. Pulling my head back with the hand still held over my mouth, he shoved his considerable body weight against me, winding me. My chest was hurting badly as I gasped for breath.

Oh God was he going to kill me? My heart was thudding wildly and the noise of my laboured breathing was loud in my ears. My lungs felt as though they were on fire.

I felt his mouth against my ear and could smell beer on his breath, mingled with an aftershave I recognised but couldn't recall the name of.

'There's no-one around to hear you. Now be quiet and calm down, I'm not going to hurt you... just take it easy.' His voice was soothing and vaguely familiar and after a few moments I stopped struggling, alert to what he was going to do next.

'I'm going to take my hand off your mouth. If you promise not to scream when I do?' I nodded and he eased his body weight off me a little and removed his hand. His arms were still tightly around me.

'You're hurting me...' I gasped. 'Who are you? What do you want?'

'I want you. Come with me.' Gripping my arms tightly, he steered me forcefully ahead of him, across the hall, towards the bedroom door. My breathing was still laboured, my mind in turmoil. I was desperately trying to think of how I could get away from him. I knew there was no-one in the apartment above, remembering that Liz and Dave weren't coming back until tomorrow. There was little chance of anyone hearing me. The doors and shutters were all locked and I knew that even if I got free, I wouldn't have time to unlock any of them before he was upon me again. I realised with dread that I'd unwittingly locked myself in with him.

'Who are you?' I asked again, trying to plant my feet on the tiled floor, to slow our progress. 'How do you know my name?' The pain in my arms was intense in his strong grip. I tried in vain to twist my head around to see his face. He didn't reply.

'Why are you doing this?' I was whimpering in pain and fear. We were getting closer to the bedroom.

Still holding me tightly, he propelled me through the doorway and flung me, face down, on to the bed. His fingers digging cruelly into my arms once more, I felt his weight on my back as he climbed on to the bed and straddled me. *This can't be happening. Please don't let this happen.*

'I've wanted you since the day I first saw you, Carol,' he was astride me, pinning me down, whispering into my ear. I remembered the aftershave, it was Davidoff. 'You're mine.'

'No!' I screamed. 'I... I don't even know who you are. Why are you saying these things? Why me?' I was desperately trying to identify the voice. It was familiar, but I just couldn't place it.

Bizarrely, he started singing, his lips pressed against my ear:

'*Oh Carol, I am but a fool. Darling I love you though you treat me cruel...* But that's not right Carol, is it? Unfortunately for you, I'm the cruel one.' With that, he bit my ear lobe, hard, and laughed. I screamed in pain and he suddenly flipped me over, so that I was on my back and able to see him. Still astride me, he put one hand over my mouth, pinning my arms down with his other arm and his bodyweight. He was heavy, and I could barely breathe. His face was in mine and the smell of beer was nauseous.

'Naughty, naughty. You promised you wouldn't scream, Carol,' he said in a sing-song voice. I could see his face then, and recognised him at last. I was astonished.

'You? But I don't understand...'

He was smiling down at me. *Oh God, I think he's mad.*

He removed his hand from my mouth again and grasped my left arm in his strong grip. He now had me pinned down by both arms and his body was heavy on top of me.

'I've been planning this for a long time. Since I first saw you. I've been watching you, waiting for the right time. Let me tell you what I have planned. I have to hurt you; I'm going to...' he began to describe in graphic detail what turned him on.

'No!' I yelled. 'Stop this now!' My instincts told me to try not to let him see how scared I was, and I tried to sound assertive. 'Don't you dare do this. Get off me. Now. Get out.' I was struggling, trying to get my arms free.

'Bitch,' he shouted. Then without warning, he punched me hard in the mouth. It felt like an explosion in my face and I could taste blood. I was shouting and thrashing about, trying to break free, trying to knee him in the groin. He punched me again, shouting,

'Bitch! Shut the fuck up!'

Realising he was out of control and that I was in grave danger, I stopped struggling. I told myself *Don't fight it. Just get through this, and stay alive. Do whatever he wants... Don't antagonise him...* I found myself praying *Please, God, help me to stay alive.* I lay there, hurting, terrified, but determined to passively endure what was happening.

At that moment, I thought I heard a noise from the apartment above, and with the possibility of being rescued, I screamed again, at the top of my voice, and renewed my efforts to get him off me. He heard the noise too, and quickly smothered my screams, stuffing the corner of a pillow into my mouth.

'You fucking cow,' he said quietly. Then he leant over me, his weight pinning me down, as he stretched his arm towards the bedside table. Suddenly, there was excruciating pain and a flash of light in my head and everything went black.

CHAPTER EIGHT

Why did she make me do that? he spat furiously, immersing himself in the sea, rubbing frantically at his clothes, his body, his hair, trying to erase all traces of her blood. The bitch had tried to fight him off, screaming and struggling... just like the last one. What was wrong with her for God's sake? It was all her fault. In the end, she'd left him with no choice but to finish her off.

The weight of the stone turtle she kept on the bedside table was considerable, and he'd used all his strength to lift it high and bring it down forcefully on to her head. Blood spurted everywhere from a gaping wound on the side of her head. He was certain he'd killed her, although he didn't hang around to make sure. He needed to get out of the apartment quickly, in case the noise he'd heard meant someone had returned upstairs. He crept through to the living room, unlocked and slid open the patio door without making a sound, and listened for a while... nothing. He swiftly and silently crossed the terrace, jumped over the gate and soon found himself on the beach.

Once he reached the safety of the dark sea, he looked back at the villa but could see no lights showing, other than through the faint crack around the shutters in Carol's bedroom. It seemed that no-one had returned upstairs after all. Thinking of her gorgeous body, he felt cold fury - what a fucking waste! Stupid fucking bitch! Having watched her and wanted her for so long, it was now all over, leaving him feeling cheated and frustrated.

Splashing around, chest-deep in the salty water, he continued scrubbing at his head and body in an attempt to remove every trace of her blood. Suddenly, a voice called out in the darkness, asking him if he was alright. Realising there must be a fishing boat nearby, he ignored the voice and turned, swimming away from it as fast as he could. He was

31

a powerful swimmer and kept going for quite some time, staying parallel to the coast. He eventually emerged from the sea, wiping his face with his hands. In the balmy night air, he walked along the coast for a long time until his clothes had dried enough to allow him to return to where he was staying without attracting undue attention.

CHAPTER NINE

When Carol failed to arrive at three as arranged, Simon wasn't surprised. After all, they both knew she wasn't the most punctual person in the world, and Simon had often remarked that she would be late for her own funeral. After checking there were a couple of bottles of sauvignon chilling in the fridge, he watched Fiona as she added a vase of freshly cut Bird of Paradise flowers to the table on the terrace and stood back to admire her handiwork. She always liked the table to look pretty.

As four o'clock came and went, and Carol's phone continued to go unanswered, Fiona became worried and voiced her concern to Simon.

'She should be here by now, Simon? It's getting far too late for lunch. And it's strange she's not answering her phone; it just keeps going to voicemail.'

Simon looked up from the newspaper he was trying to read, and rolled his eyes. 'Oh, she'll be here soon, full of apologies. Something must have held her up,' he growled. 'You know what she's like. Totally unreliable as far as timekeeping goes.' He went back to his paper.

However, by four thirty, even Simon was beginning to think it odd. He gave another big sigh. 'I'll give her another half hour. If she's not here by then, I'll drive over and see what's keeping her. Ok? At this rate, I won't have bloody time to eat anything. I'll be too busy with the prep for tonight.' He frowned, running his hand through his short, wiry hair.

After thirty minutes or so, with still no word from Carol, he jumped to his feet with an audible groan, grabbed his car keys from the console table and stomped from the room, muttering under his breath, 'Damn the woman. I'd better go and see what's happened.'

Simon was in a temper. He worked long hours in his restaurant and treasured the few hours leisure time he managed to take. He supposed he could have let Fiona find out what was keeping Carol, but he knew she liked to fuss with the food, making sure everything was just perfect. She'd prepared coconut shrimp for the first course, which had to be cooked at the last minute.

He drove as fast as he could in the busy traffic, and after half an hour or so, parked on the roadside above Carol's villa and made his way down the steps in the side garden. It was another very hot day, and as he descended, Simon could see the turquoise bay beyond the terrace below and wished he had time for a quick dip before going back. The Caribbean Sea had never looked more inviting.

He reached the bottom of the steps and as he crossed the patio, he noticed that the sliding door was slightly open. Calling Carol's name, he knocked on the glass, and when there was no response, slid the door further open. As he did so, he noticed some brownish stuff on the white wooden door frame and wondered vaguely what it could be.

The living room was quiet and empty. No sign of Carol. He called out to her again but still there was no response. Feeling uneasy, he made his way tentatively along the short passageway leading to her bedroom, calling out to her as he went.

'Carol, are you there? It's Simon.' Still no response. *Strange* he thought. He knocked on the bedroom door, which was slightly ajar, then pushed it slowly open, a strong feeling of trepidation making the hairs on the back of his neck stand up. The room was in semi-darkness.

Nothing could have prepared him for the sight that greeted him as he entered the dim room. His eyes were still adjusting from the bright sunlight outside, and at first he couldn't take in the carnage before him. As his vision cleared, however, he gasped in disbelief, his mind refusing to accept what his eyes could see.

Carol was lying on the bed, motionless. She was on her back, arms by her sides, her top ripped and pulled up, exposing the bloodied white skin of her midriff and breasts. Blood seemed to be everywhere; on the bedcover and pillows and even splashed up the wall behind the bed. The whole scene was garishly lit by the dim glow of the bedside light. He steeled himself to look at her face and recoiled. The corner of one of the blood-soaked pillows was jammed into her mouth. Around it, her face was swollen and discoloured, drenched in dark blood. She was unrecognisable. Her hair, normally a soft blonde, was matted and dark with blood, almost black. He noticed a metallic smell in the air and was aware of the swish swish of the overhead fan. She looked lifeless and with dread he approached the bed, pulled the pillow out of her mouth and picked up one of her bloodied arms, feeling the wrist for a pulse.

'Carol... Carol, can you hear me? It's Simon.' There was no response, but he thought he could feel a faint pulse. Remembering the first aid training he'd had years ago, he put her into the recovery position, pulling her limp body on to its side and making sure she wasn't choking on her tongue. He'd never seen so much blood. He turned then, and hurried from the room, stumbling along the passageway and back through the living room, onto the terrace, where he knew he could get a signal. He took his mobile from his pocket and tried to key in 211, but his hands were shaking so violently, it took three attempts to hit the right buttons.

'Emergency. Which service please?'

'Ambulance... Something terrible's happened... a woman's been attacked... she's in a bad way. I think she's still alive... Please come quickly.' He could hear his panic reflected in his voice.

'Slow down, sir. Can you give me the address please?'

Realising he'd been gabbling, Simon took a deep breath and made an effort to speak calmly as he gave the address to the operator.

'An ambulance is on its way, sir. Is the patient conscious?'

'No. I thought she was dead at first... but I think I felt a pulse... she's covered in blood. She's got a head wound. I've put her in the recovery position.'

'Ok, sir. The emergency services will be with you in a few minutes. They're on their way now,' she repeated. 'Stay calm and look out for them please.'

He staggered up to street level and slumped on to the garden wall, to await their arrival. Everything seemed surreal to him, as though it was happening in a dream. With a sinking heart, he rang Fiona. As soon as she answered, he spoke quickly, attempting to make his voice sound reasonably normal.

'Fi. Listen, something dreadful's happened. Carol's been attacked. She's in a bad way. I'm waiting for the ambulance now.' He became aware of the sound of wailing sirens in the distance.

'Attacked? Oh my God. How bad is she?' Fiona sounded frantic.

'They're here now, darling. I have to go. I'll ring you back as soon as I can.' He ended the call before she could ask for any further details, then jumped up to flag down the ambulance. The noise of the sirens was now all-pervading and he thought how incongruous the sound was on such a gloriously sunny day. There were two ambulances, followed by a police car. More seemed to be on the way, judging by the sound of sirens in the distance.

'She's down here,' Simon told them, indicating the steps. He quickly led two police officers and four paramedics down the steps, barely registering the unintelligible noises and bursts of static from their radios. They reached the terrace and he pointed to the doors to the apartment.

'She's in there. In the bedroom. On the right.' He couldn't face going back inside and sat down heavily on one of the chairs around the table. A sandy-haired man of around thirty-five came over to him and sat down in the chair opposite Simon.

'Can you tell me who the victim is, sir? And exactly what happened?' he asked, brushing his hair off his forehead before taking out a notebook. 'I'm DI Phillips, James Phillips.'

Simon, looking down at his shaking, bloodstained hands, made a visible effort to pull himself together. Taking a deep breath, he told the DI about coming to check on Carol when she failed to turn up for lunch. He explained that Carol was Fiona's step-mother and they'd been expecting her at around one o'clock. They'd become concerned as time went on and Carol didn't turn up and didn't answer their calls.

Just then, there was a commotion as the ambulance men backed out of the doors with Carol on a stretcher.

'She's still alive. We're taking her to the Queen Elizabeth Hospital in Bridgetown,' one of them called as they hurried by with their patient, manoeuvring the stretcher so they could keep it level while they climbed the steps, shouting instructions to each other.

'Thank God,' said Simon. Then he dropped his head into his hands and began to sob. The officer waited patiently for the storm of emotion to pass, before asking Simon if he was able to continue with his account.

Simon nodded, then quietly related the events leading up to his discovery of Carol.

'I couldn't take in what I was seeing when I looked into the bedroom. She was lying on the bed...'

'How far into the room did you go?' the DI asked. 'Did you touch the victim?'

'Yes. I... I thought she was dead at first. I felt for a pulse... There was a faint one... and then I put her in the recovery position.' Simon spread out his bloodied hands to show the officer. 'The corner of a pillow was stuffed into her mouth... I removed that. I've never seen so much blood.'

Another man came over to them. Bajan. Very tall. Simon estimated about six feet four or five. He carried an air of authority about him, which hinted at strength and competence.

'This is Simon Barker, Sir.' said the DI, rising to his feet. 'He found the victim. His wife is the victim's step-daughter.'

'DCI Brown,' the man said, in a deep, rumbling voice. 'I won't shake your hand, if you don't mind,' he gestured to Simon's bloodstained hands. 'Must have been pretty bad, finding her like that?'

Simon looked down at his still trembling hands. 'Terrible. How the fuck could anyone do that to another human being?' His shock was turning to anger.

'That's what we intend to find out, sir. I'll leave you to finish giving your statement – and then you'll need to get cleaned up.'

The terrace became a hive of activity as the crime scene was cordoned off with blue tape, awaiting the arrival of the forensics team.

'I think we're done for now, but we'll need to speak to you again. And your wife, sir,' the DI told Simon. 'We'll need her statement too.'

Simon nodded, anxious to get moving. 'We'll be at the hospital. I need to call her now and tell her to go straight there.'

CHAPTER TEN

Fiona came hurrying into the bustling Accident & Emergency department a few minutes after Simon arrived. She ran to him and clutched his arms, looking up at him, her eyes searching his for any sign of reassurance.

'How is she?'

Simon noticed all the tan seemed to have faded from her face, which now looked white and drawn. He guided her to a chair, then sat beside her, his arm around her shoulders.

'I don't know exactly, darling... She's pretty bad...' his voice tailed off.

'Simon. You're scaring me... How bad is it?' People were staring and she realised she had raised her voice.

He looked at her, a bleak expression on his face. 'She's in a bad way, darling. But at least she's still alive. I thought she was dead... when I found her on the bed... there was blood everywhere. There's a huge wound on the side of her head – she must have been hit with something.'

'Oh God. But why?.. I was just with her... Why would anyone do that? Oh dear God, she's not going die, is she?'

He took her hand. 'I don't know, darling,' he said gently. 'I don't know anything yet. She's with the doctors now. They've said they'll come and see us... when they know more...'

Just then, a nurse approached, smiling sympathetically, and asked them to go with her. Ushering them into a small room, just down the corridor, she indicated two easy chairs.

'You'll be more comfortable waiting in here. It's a bit more private. I'll get you both a cup of coffee and as soon as we know more, someone will come to see you.' She rustled out of the room, and Simon looked around. It was basically a white, clinical room, but an effort had been made to make it more welcoming. On the walls, there were a couple of prints of tropical flowers, and bright yellow cushions adorned the two Green leather chairs and small settee, matching the curtains, which had been tied back from the small window. *A room to receive bad news in,* he thought.

'We'll have to ring Julia...'

'Let's wait 'til we know just how bad it is,' Simon gently interrupted, taking one of the chairs, 'no point in giving her half a story. We'll ring once we've seen the doctor.'

'You're right... Oh, Simon, I just can't believe this is happening.' Fiona sank into the other chair and put her head in her hands.

'I had to wash her blood off my hands,' said Simon quietly, staring at his hands. He went on to describe in more detail what he'd seen when he walked into the bedroom. 'I've never seen so much blood, Fi. You wouldn't think you could lose that much and still be alive.'

Fiona stared at him. 'But, why? Why would anyone do that to Carol? It's horrific. Oh, God, she must have been so scared.' She began to weep and Simon got up, knelt in front of her, and put his arms around her.

During the next long hour, they talked through what had happened, going round in circles trying to make sense of it.

'We'll have to let Pauline know,' Fiona said, '... and Carol's brother in Australia. Pauline might have his number.'

Eventually, the doctor arrived; they jumped up as he came through the door. As he searched his face for any clue about how bad things were, Simon thought he looked ridiculously young, like a young boy wearing a white coat, stethoscope round his neck, playing pretend doctors and nurses.

The doctor held out his hand. 'I'm Dr. Marshall,' he said, in a surprisingly mature voice. 'Please, sit down.' They resumed their seats and the doctor took the settee.

'I'm afraid the patient – Mrs Barrington - is very seriously injured. Her skull is fractured in two places, and we think there may be some bleeding in the brain. She hasn't regained consciousness as yet, but in any event, we're putting her in an induced coma, to give her brain time to recover. We're still doing tests, but if a bleed is confirmed, the situation will be critical. We need to monitor her closely over the coming hours. Does she have any other relatives who should be informed?'

'She has a daughter, in England. We'll call her.' Fiona began to cry quietly.

'She should get here as soon as possible,' the doctor said. 'Meanwhile, I'll let you know as soon as I have any further information.'

After he left, Fiona, tears still streaming down her face, took her phone from her handbag and held it out to Simon. 'Will you call her? I... just can't.'

Taking the phone from her, Simon squeezed her shoulder before selecting Julia's number.

'Julia, It's Simon. Can you hear me?' he could hear a lot of noise in the background. Rock music, and a cacophony of voices. There was clearly a party in progress.

'Simon? My favourite brother in law. It's Simon, everyone,' she shouted to the room in general. Simon heard shrieking and whooping.

'Julia, I need to speak to you. Turn the music off... Julia, TURN THE MUSIC OFF.' He could hear her yelling to her boyfriend to turn the sound off, and shouting to her friends to be quiet.

'Julia, sweetheart, I'm afraid I've got some bad news,' he said. 'It's about your mum. She's been hurt.'

'Mum...? What...'

Simon interrupted and went on to tell her what had happened, adding, 'We're at the QE hospital in Bridgetown.'

Julia shouted 'No' over and over, then began to sob. Simon could hear her becoming hysterical. Then her boyfriend's voice came on the phone.

'Simon? What's happened? What's wrong?'

Simon brought him up to speed and told him, 'Oliver, you need to get her on a flight over here straight away. We'll be staying at the hospital until she gets here.'

Julia, recovered enough to take the phone back from Oliver, came back on the line. 'Mum is going to be alright, isn't she?' she asked in a tremulous voice.

40

'She's very seriously ill, sweetheart. The doctors are assessing the extent of the damage, to see if there's any bleeding in the brain. We're just hoping and praying that's not the case.'

'Bleeding in the brain?' Julia repeated in a strangled voice.

'Let's just wait and see, angel. We have to hope for the best.'

'I see,' she said in a small voice.

Simon passed the phone to Fiona, after she indicated she wanted to speak to Julia.

'It's Fiona, Julia, I'm so sorry, darling. Listen... no, I know it's not fair after what your mum's already been through this year. Listen, darling, just get here as soon as you can. The next flights won't be til the morning. Book the early one and text to let us know you're on it. Simon will meet you at the airport. Your mum is in very good hands - try to stay strong, for her, sweetheart. We'll stay with her 'til you get here.'

A few minutes later, the door opened and Simon looked up to see DI Phillips enter, brushing his sandy hair out of his eyes. He looked tired and a bit dishevelled.

'Hello again, Mr. Barker. Mrs. Barker?' he enquired, turning to Fiona.

'Yes?' Fiona responded, looking at the proffered warrant card.

'This is the policeman I spoke to this afternoon, Fiona,' Simon explained.

'DI James Phillips,' he said, extending his hand to Fiona. 'I'd like to ask you a few questions, if you don't mind?'

'We've just been on the phone to Carol's daughter,' interjected Simon. 'She's getting the early flight over here tomorrow.'

James nodded, brushing his hair off his face. 'That's good.' He parked himself on the settee and took out his notebook. 'In the course of our enquiries we need to rule out anyone on the island who is known to Carol Barrington. We're examining her mobile phone and computer to find her contacts, but wondered if either of you is aware of anyone she knows or has contact with when she's here?'

'Well, she and my dad knew quite a few people. Just let me think...' began Fiona.

'If you can give us some time, we'll see who we can come up with,' suggested Simon.

'Of course. If you could do it as soon as possible? Give the list to DC Lynn Sands, if you don't mind. She's stationed outside the intensive care department. Now, Mrs. Barker, can you go through Carol's movements for me, since she arrived? As far as you know them.'

'Well...' began Fiona, 'she arrived on Thursday. I picked her up from the airport at about five thirty and drove her to the villa... We had a drink, on the terrace, talked for a while, and then I left.'

'What time did you leave?'

'It was about eight o'clock. Carol was tired. I left her to unpack. She said she was going to have an early night. We agreed to meet the following night - last night.' She paused to pull herself together, before continuing. 'I went there at six. We had a meal and a few glasses of champagne. There was a lot to catch up on; it was a great night. I'd pre-booked a taxi for eleven thirty. Carol waved me off.'

'She walked up to street level with you? Did you notice if she locked the door to the apartment before going up the stairs with you?'

'I don't remember... but I don't think so...' Fiona's hand flew to her mouth, as the implication of the question sank in. 'Do you think someone got in then?'

'It's a possibility. Now, are you aware of Carol speaking to anyone in the short time she was here? Did she mention who she'd seen that day?'

'Just Josie, her housekeeper... oh, and the couple who were renting the apartment above Carol's. She told me she saw them going for an early morning swim and they chatted. She went shopping that morning; I don't know if she bumped into anyone she knew then.'

'Did you notice anyone around when you were with Carol that evening? In a nearby villa, or on the beach for example?'

'Let me think... we ate on the terrace... I noticed a young couple on the top balcony of the villa next door. Like us, they'd been watching the sunset. I don't recall seeing anyone else... Oh, yes, there was the lobster delivery man. He dropped the lobster off at around six thirty. From Lobster Alive.'

DI Phillips made a note before looking at each of them in turn. 'And can either of you think of anyone who could have a grudge against

Carol? Know anyone who dislikes her? Has she ever expressed any concerns about anyone?'

'No, no. Not at all,' said Fiona. 'I can't think of anyone. She's a lovely person...'

'Your brother isn't her greatest fan, darling,' Simon observed.

'You're not suggesting my brother...' Fiona sounded incredulous.

'No, of course not. I'm just trying to think of anyone who dislikes her.'

'What's this?' the DI asked, looking from one to the other.

'My brother resents Carol because he thinks she broke up my parents' marriage. She didn't, but he's always blamed her. But, for God's sake, he doesn't hate her – he's not violent. He could never hurt anyone.' She glared at Simon.

'Is your brother on the island?'

'Yes, he's staying with us, but...'

'I'll take his details and we'll have a word with him. Just to rule him out of our enquiries,' the DI said, taking out his notebook. 'Thank you, Mrs. Barker, you've been very helpful. If you could leave your list with DC Sands? As soon as you can, please. I'd be grateful. By the way, he said, turning to Simon, 'Where were you last night?'

'What? I was in my restaurant all night, until about twelve. Then we all had a drink after it closed. We usually do that after a busy night.'

'Who do you mean by 'we all'?' asked the DI. 'Were you there, Mrs Barker?'

'Yes, I helped to clear up when I got back from Carol's. Then we both had a couple of drinks with the staff. We must have finished at about one.'

'Well, thank you both. You've been very helpful,' the DI said, rising and tucking his notebook into his pocket.

'No problem,' said Simon. 'We'll be here all night, if you need us again.'

After the DI left, Fiona rounded on Simon with fury. 'Why the hell did you have to bring my brother into it?'

'Fi, it just slipped out. I didn't mean anything by it. Of course I don't think for one second that Jack could have done it.'

'They're going to interview him now. How could you?' she was almost crying with fury and actually stamped her foot.

'Oh, come on, darling. They'll be interviewing everyone. He's got nothing to hide, so there's nothing to worry about. Look, it's getting late. It's been a long day. Let's see what facilities are available, if any. We should both try to get some sleep.' He tried to put his arm around Fiona's shoulders, but she angrily shrugged him off.

'Fuck off,' she spat, and stomped ahead of him out of the room.

CHAPTER ELEVEN

Not far from the hospital, at the Barbados Police Headquarters in Bridgetown, the SIO, DCI Louis Brown called a briefing meeting for eleven o'clock that night. He'd hastily put together a strong team; several officers had been contacted at home and drafted in, including some uniforms. All leave had been cancelled until further notice. The 20-strong team was assembled in the Major Incident Room, at the back of the station building.

Sitting on the corner of a desk, one ankle resting on the other knee, the DCI had already begun to address the assembled team, when DI James Phillips came hurrying through the door.

'So glad you could join us, James,' he said, stroking his chin. 'Not putting you out, are we?' Everyone laughed and James shrugged as all eyes turned towards him.

'Sorry, boss. Just come from the hospital.'

'I've asked you all here at this late hour to summarise the situation in the Carol Barrington case. I think all of you are aware now of the serious attack on this lady, a thirty-seven year old woman from England. He indicated a photograph, obtained from Carol's passport, on the white board behind him. The attack took place at her holiday home at Batts Rock and we urgently need to find the perpetrator. It's important that we keep up the momentum.

The victim is in intensive care in the QE. She hasn't woken up yet – and is unlikely to for some time, if at all. She's being put into a medically induced coma to protect her brain. The hospital has advised us that her skull is fractured in two places, and she has concussion. They fear she may also have a bleed on the brain, and if that is the case, this could well turn into a murder enquiry.' He looked around at the sea of faces and saw that he had their full attention. 'We've got two DC's stationed at the hospital; they'll let us know when we get the go-ahead to interview the victim, if and when she regains consciousness. We'll see then if she knows who her assailant is.' Turning to DI Phillips, he asked 'Anybody see anything, James?'

James, who had been leading the team of PCs conducting house to house enquiries, said 'We've spoken this evening to the occupants of all the neighbouring properties. Nobody saw or heard anything out of the ordinary. A young couple staying at the house next door, noticed the two women on the terrace, watching the sunset. They then went out, and returned at about two o'clock, went straight to bed and didn't hear or see anything. The people renting the first floor apartment, Elizabeth and David Henderson, were away overnight, staying at the Crane Beach on the south-east coast – we sent someone down there to check and their friends and staff, all corroborate this. The Hendersons didn't return until...' he consulted his notebook 'six o'clock this evening.

We also spoke to the housekeeper, Josie Wark. She last saw the victim yesterday. She only works four days a week and Saturday's one of her days off, otherwise she would have found Carol herself, this morning. She was extremely upset. She doesn't know of anyone who could have done this, and is not aware of Carol having seen anyone since she arrived on the island, other than her step-daughter and the couple from the upstairs apartment.

I've spoken again to Simon Barker, the step-daughter's husband, who found the victim, and also his wife, Fiona. Simon mentioned that Fiona's brother, Jack Barrington, has a grudge against the victim. Apparently he resents Carol for splitting up his parents, as he sees it. He's on the island, staying with the Barkers. I've arranged for him to come into the station first thing in the morning.'

'Simon Barker volunteered this information?' the DCI asked.

'He did. And his wife was furious, I can tell you,' he grimaced. 'Of course, she doesn't believe her brother could have done it. The Barkers are putting together a list of the names of anyone on the island known to the victim.'

'Yes, DC Sands has just emailed the list through,' said the DCI. 'About twenty five names on it. I want them all checked out, together with all the contacts in her phone and tablet. Who, if any, of those contacts is currently on the island? Have any of them left the island today? See if any have any previous. If you find anything significant, I want to be advised immediately.

I want her text messages examined and her ipad analysed. See if there's anything that may be of interest on there. I want all this done overnight, if I can have some volunteers?' A sea of hands went up. 'Thank you. Now, are there any questions, or anything to add?'

'I can see if any of my informants have anything. I've got a very reliable contact,' DC David Morgan spoke up.

'Do that, Dave,' he said, standing up and looking around the room. 'I'll get an update in the morning.'

DCI Brown left the room and general chatter broke out amongst the team. As the door was closing, he overheard one of them speculating about the bad publicity that would ensue, particularly if the vic died. He couldn't agree more; the murder of a tourist would definitely not be good news for the economy of the island. He decided to try for a complete press embargo on this case until progress had been made.

CHAPTER TWELVE

On the outskirts of Holetown, DC David Morgan pulled the unmarked car into a secluded lay-by just off a remote country road, and switched off the lights. He waited, listening to the wind rustling the sugar cane leaves. Before long, the passenger door was opened and a young dreadlocked Rastafarian slipped into the passenger seat. As always, he smelt strongly of cannabis.

'Well, Moses, what have you got for me?'

'Aint got nothin' man. 'Cept, no way a local done this. Got everyone checkin' but no names comin' up. Word is, it's a visitor.'

'Not a local? You sure about that?'

'Never steered you wrong before. This is so big, man, word woulda got back straight away. Take it from me, he's not from here. We woulda known by now.'

'Is there anything else?'

'No man. But still checkin. Anything more comes up, you'll be the first to know.' Moses put his hand out for the small roll of dollars DC Morgan proffered, before opening the door and melting away into the darkness.

CHAPTER THIRTEEN

The following morning, DCI Louis Brown was ready for business by six, having snatched a couple of hours sleep on the sofa in his office. *Just as well I'm single now* he thought, as he grabbed a coffee from the machine in the corridor, before wandering through to the MIR, where those who'd stayed behind were still at their desks, bleary-eyed.

'Any luck?' he asked, stroking his newly-shaved chin with one hand, cup of coffee in the other. He could swear he could already feel new stubble coming through.

Eddie, one of the support team looked up. 'We've found a couple of people on the victim's contact list who live in England, and are in Barbados now. One of them is Jack Barrington, who we already know about.'

'We're interviewing him later this morning,' said the DCI.

'The other is Sir Ralph McIntyre Brown. He has a villa near Sandy Lane Golf Club. He comes out to Barbados every year, but not usually as early as November. There was a third, one of her tenants, but he returned to the UK two days prior to the attack.'

'Good work, Eddie. We'll follow up on this McIntyre Brown. Anything from the phone or ipad?'

'Nothing of any interest in the text messages, sir. In one of the victim's emails to her step-daughter, sent more than a year ago, she mentions feeling stalked by her ex-husband, Saul Harrison. We've checked, and there's no record of him entering Barbados. But he's known to us – conviction in the UK for GBH about fifteen years ago. Ex-SAS.'

'Interesting. Find out what you can about him. What about the names the Barkers' supplied?'

'We spread them amongst the team,' Eddie said, turning to a fair-haired young man seated on his right.

The young DC spoke up. 'One of those on my list, Tony Meadon, is in England. I've checked, and can confirm he's been there for a week, so he's ruled out. Another, Julien Roberts, was hosting a party in his villa. I've spoken to his wife, who corroborates this, but I'm also going to speak to a couple of the guests, to be sure. The third, Jason Jones, was in his restaurant all night, then drinking with friends until the early hours. A few members of staff have confirmed this, so I believe we can rule him out. The fourth is one of us, and he was on duty that night – DS Jacob Smith. I've got two more to check on.' He turned to a young constable sitting near the end of the table. 'Marilyn?'

The PC studied her notes. 'Of those on my list, Damien Errington was in the QE hospital, all night, following a fall at his villa. Hospital staff have confirmed this. The second, Dale Arnold, is a doctor, at the same hospital, and was on duty that night. Again, confirmed by staff. The last two are both pilots., Paul Bostock was on St Lucia that night and Edward Bates was, and still is, in the States. All confirmed, so all four can be ruled out of the enquiry. I've got a further three to check up on.'

A civilian support worker was next. 'I had the gardener on my list, one Raol Alleyne, age twenty-three. He says he was at home, alone, that night. No-one to corroborate this. Lives alone, on the outskirts of Prospect. He's been the gardener there for four years. No previous. Said he bumped into Mrs Barrington in the supermarket that morning. Just said hello and sorry for her loss. I'll keep him on my list, see what I can find. The other four all checked out, with cast iron alibis.'

A young, Bajan PC reported next. 'I had six on my list; four have checked out, no problem. One, Aidan Pearson, is a guy they used for small DIY jobs, I haven't been able to track him down yet. He's not at home and not answering his phone, but I'll keep on it. The last one, Margaret Miller, I still need to speak to.'

'Thank you. Good work, all of you. Now, I want those of you who've been here all night, to go home and get a few hours rest, once you've done your paperwork. And thanks again for your dedication.'

Bumping into DI Phillips as he left the office, the DCI brought him up to date with what the team had unearthed during the night.

'Get in touch with this McIntyre Brown and set up an interview for later this morning.'

'Will do. Jack Barrington's coming in at nine. That'll give me time to give Sir Ralph a call right away.'

'We'll both see Barrington,' the DCI said. 'Let's see what his grudge is and what he's got to say for himself.'

CHAPTER FOURTEEN

'Jack Barrington?' asked DCI Louis Brown, coming through the door of the interview room, balancing a couple of files and a cup of coffee. From his seat at the far side of a small table in the centre of the room, Jack nodded. The DCI pushed the door to, with his hip, and plonked the files on the desk, placing his steaming coffee alongside.

'DCI Brown,' Louis said, extending his right hand. Jack hesitated, looking a little nonplussed at the sight of the huge black policeman towering over him, before grudgingly leaning forward and shaking his hand. *Limp, sweaty handshake* noted the DCI.

'Thanks for coming in. Did DI Phillips explain what we wanted to ask you about?' The DCI took a seat opposite Jack.

'He said it was to do with the attack on Carol Barrington. Dunno what it's got to do with me,' he replied, somewhat belligerently, eyes downcast. 'He asked if I would come voluntarily into the station to give a statement. So, here I am.'

'Can I offer you anything to drink?'

Jack shook his head, just as DI Phillips came through the door and sat himself down next to his boss. The DI put a note in front of Louis, *Meeting with McIntyre-Brown 1.00pm Yacht Club.*

'Morning, Jack. DI James Phillips.' They shook hands. 'We spoke on the phone. You found us alright, then?'

'Everybody knows where the police station is,' said Jack, in a sullen tone, looking down at the desk.

Clever shite thought Louis, observing him. Young-looking for twenty-nine, slightly built with a mass of dark brown, unkempt hair. He had an unhealthy pallor, despite having been in Barbados for nearly four weeks.

He obviously didn't spend much time in the sun. Judging by his body language, he certainly wasn't happy to be talking to the police, and he was having great difficulty making eye contact.

'Jack,' said DCI Brown, 'we'd just like to ask you a few questions. You are not under arrest and are free to leave anytime you want to, ok?'

'Ok.'

DCI Brown continued. 'On the night that your stepmother…'

'My late father's wife,' Jack interrupted, looking up at last. 'She's no mother of mine, step or otherwise.'

'Alright; your late father's wife. Can you tell us where you were on the night Carol Barrington was attacked? That would be the night before last.'

'I was out on the town,' said Jack, shortly

'We need to know a bit more than that - where you went, who you saw and what you did that night.'

'Am I a suspect then?'

'No, you are not a suspect. At this stage, we're simply trying to eliminate people from our enquiry. Now, would it be true to say that you're not the biggest fan of Carol Barrington?'

'It would,' Jack said with a sneer.

'And why would that be?' asked James. Louis could tell he was resisting the urge to reach over the table and shake the unhelpful little shit.

'I can't stand her. But for god's sake I would never attack her. And as for raping her, that's gross.' Jack pulled a face.

'What makes you think she was raped?' asked the DI, looking up sharply.

'Well… I assumed. That's what everyone's saying. Wasn't she?'

The DI ignored the question. 'What's your history with her? Why do you dislike her?'

'She split my parents up. She's just a gold-digging tramp.'

'Gold-digging? Why do you say that?'

'He was a lot older than her. She had to have been after his money. She made sure he didn't give me any more cash once she'd got her claws into him. Wanted him to make me stand on my own two feet.'

'I can see that wouldn't go down too well,' said the DI, with irony. 'So, let's go through what you actually did on the night in question. In your own words.'

'Since I got your phone call last night, I've been thinking, trying to piece the night together. I thought you would ask about it. I left my sister's place about nine,' he said. 'The trouble is, I got stoned quite quickly. After I left Fi's place, I caught the bus into Holetown and scored some drugs straight away.'

'What did you take?' asked the DCI, leaning forward.

'Just weed, but it was bloody strong stuff. Let's see... I remember watching a transvestite show at Ragamuffin's 'cos one of the 'ladies' made a fool of me. She didn't like me smoking at the table and the stupid bitch stopped her Shirley Bassey act and came over to my table. *Oh look folks, he's smoking!* she announced to the whole fucking room. Then she actually took the cigarette out of my mouth and ground it out in the ashtray. Everyone was laughing. I wasn't going to put up with shit from an old tranny like that, so I left.'

'What time was that?'

'I don't know. I suppose you could check with Ragamuffin's to see what time the show was on. I think it would be about half past ten.'

'What did you do then?'

'I hung around for a while in the main street. There were a lot of people there. You know what it's like in Holetown. Real party atmosphere. I was drinking, smoking weed and people watching... I think I can remember having a burger at some point, but I don't know where I got it from. I've got no memory of getting back to Fiona's. I must have got a taxi, I suppose. The next thing I remember is waking up at about midday the next day. That's when I found out what had happened to Carol Barrington.'

'How did you feel when you were told?'

'I thought it was karma.'

In response to prompting from DI Phillips, Jack confirmed he'd been alone in Holetown. 'I spoke to a few people, as you do, but I don't remember seeing anyone I knew.'

'Is there anyone that could confirm your whereabouts that night?' asked DI Phillips.'

'I told you, I didn't see anyone I knew. I suppose the staff at Ragamuffins might remember their star turn humiliating me.'

'Hmm...' said DCI Brown. 'So, no-one can vouch for you. Did you speak to Fiona or Simon when you got back to the restaurant?'

'I've told you I can't even remember getting back.'

'And you think you got a taxi home?'

'I must have done. It's a bloody long walk. One of the taxi drivers might remember taking me. I think they keep records? Are you going to charge me then? Do I need a solicitor?'

'No, we're just trying to establish the facts at this stage, Jack. However, we'd like you to voluntarily give a DNA sample. Do you have any objection to that?'

'Cool. I've got nothing to hide.'

'Thank you.' The DCI turned to the DI, 'James, can you arrange that before Jack leaves?' Turning back to Jack he said 'We might need to speak with you again. We'll let you know if you need your solicitor present.' With that, the interview was over.

Once the DNA swab had been taken, Jack left the station, after confirming that he was not planning to return to the UK for a month or so. From the window, Louis watched him lean against the wall of the station, light a cigarette with trembling hands and inhale deeply before crossing the road to the nearest bar.

'Check with the taxi drivers to see who took him home, and at what time,' the DCI instructed James.

'Already on to it, boss.'

CHAPTER FIFTEEN

DCI Louis Brown and DI James Phillips made their way past the sleek, black yacht moored at the quayside. *Very nice* thought the DI. As the manager led them through the open-air restaurant, he noticed the sumptuous buffet set out under the vaulted wooden canopy of the Barbados Yacht Club. There was an array of beautifully presented dishes. He saw grilled lobster, crayfish, caviar, poached salmon and langoustines, all nestled in crushed ice. In the carnivorous section, there was a huge side of roast beef, and barbequed suckling pig, alongside an array of salads, vegetables, pasta, rice, even Yorkshire puddings.

'How the other half live,' muttered James, under his breath. 'I've just realised, I'm starving.' As if on cue, his stomach rumbled, loudly, reminding him that he hadn't eaten since his granola several hours ago.

'Keep your mind on the job, Phillips,' Louis replied in mock severity.

They followed the black-suited Manager through to the farthest end of the open air restaurant, past the swimming pool set back on the terrace, to the table where Sir Ralph McIntyre-Brown was swirling his after lunch drink in a huge brandy glass. The DCI introduced himself and his colleague, before apologising for interrupting his lunch. Sir Ralph, he noted, was a man of about sixty five, of distinguished appearance, tall, with silver streaks in his once dark hair. Dressed casually, but immaculately, in a white Gant short-sleeved shirt and navy blue knee-length shorts, he had a military bearing with a hint of self-assured arrogance that the super-rich seemed to acquire.

'Not at all, not at all. Just finished. May I offer you a drink?'

'No thank you sir, we'd just like to ask you a few questions if you don't mind. It shouldn't take long. Don't want to make you late for the Polo.'

When the DI had telephoned Sir Ralph at his home, earlier that morning, he'd been given the choice of catching up with him either at the Yacht Club or at the Polo match being held that afternoon at Holders. Louis thought James had wisely chosen the former, as he knew it would be difficult to hold a private conversation during a polo match.

He'd once been to Holders, in an official capacity, so he knew how well attended the polo games were, and how noisy. He remembered a colourful, well-dressed crowd, floating around with pre-match glasses of bubbly. The compere giving a witty running commentary, while the teams battled it out on the field. He'd been intrigued to see the ladies gleefully carrying out the age-old tradition of stomping on the divots at half-time. Each time fresh horses were mounted, and a new chukka commenced, there was much whooping and encouragement from the crowd. A quiet conversation would have been out of the question.

'What's this about, officer? I'm intrigued. Your colleague wouldn't give me any details on the phone.' Sir Ralph had resumed his seat and gestured for them to sit on the chairs opposite the low table that held his brandy glass.

'First of all, sir,' said the DCI, pulling a chair further away from the table to make room for his long legs, 'I believe you come over to Barbados every year, to stay at your villa. Is that correct?' Sir Ralph confirmed that it was. 'I understand you usually come in January and stay until around the end of March or the beginning of April, would that be right?'

'Yes, that's quite correct.'

'Can you tell me why you decided to come here in November this time?'

'Certainly. My wife and I decided we'd like to spend Christmas out here for a change. Why do you ask?'

Ignoring the question, DCI Brown went on. 'It's concerning the events of the evening of the twenty-ninth of November, the night before last. Can you tell me where you were that evening sir?'

'The night before last?' he slowly repeated, obviously casting his mind back. 'That's when that poor woman was attacked? Terrible business. Left for dead, I heard. Is that what this is about?'

'We're making some routine enquiries, sir. If you could just tell me where you were that night, and who you were with?'

'Well, let's see,' he frowned and took a sip of his brandy. 'I had a business meeting in Holetown, at seven thirty. It went on for about an hour, then I went straight home. Umm... I must have got back at around nine. Yes, I'm pretty sure that's correct. Everyone was talking about the attack the next day – word spreads quickly around this island – and I remember discussing it with my wife then.' He scratched the side of his nose with an index finger.

'I'll need the name or names of who your meeting was with sir? How did you get to Holetown and back? Did you drive?'

'Of course. And, yes, I took my car.'

'Will your wife corroborate what you have said about the time you arrived home?'

'I should think so. But look, Officer, what is all this about? You surely can't possibly think I had anything to do with it?'

'Do you know a lady called Carol Barrington, Sir?'

Sir Ralph looked startled. 'Carol? Of course. She runs our investment club in the UK. In fact, I introduced my friend Peter to her; the man she married. I was deeply saddened by Peter's death last year. But, why? Surely to God it wasn't Carol who was attacked?' he looked astonished.

Either he's genuine or a bloody good actor thought DCI Brown.

'I'm not at liberty to disclose the name of the victim, sir.'

'It has to be her. That's why you're asking the question. I had no idea she was on the island!' he exclaimed. 'We would have invited her over. Oh my god! Poor Carol! How is she now? We heard that the woman who'd been attacked is in intensive care? But her name wasn't released. We had no idea who it was. We all assumed it was a tourist who'd rented the apartment. I just cannot believe it was Carol'. He seemed to be genuinely distraught.

'Can you tell me when you last saw Carol Barrington?'

'Yes,' he spoke slowly. 'It was at Peter's funeral, last year. Poor girl, they'd been so happy together and then in the blink of an eye he was gone. She was absolutely distraught. And now this...'

'Well, thank you sir. We won't take up any more of your time just now, but we might need to speak to you again in due course. Just routine, you understand. Do you have any plans to leave the island in the near future?'

Sir Ralph said that he wasn't planning to return to the UK until April at the earliest. He then confirmed that his wife would be at home if they wished to speak with her.

'We're on our way to speak to her now,' said James, rising to his feet. 'Oh, one more thing, sir, would you be prepared to supply a DNA sample? We're taking samples from every male interviewed in this case.'

'I really would rather not, if you don't mind. You've already indicated that I'm not a suspect, so I don't see the point.'

'It helps in eliminating people from our enquiries, sir. But it's entirely voluntary, so...'

Sir Ralph interrupted, with a note of finality. 'In that case, I will not be volunteering.'

'Very well, sir.' James turned to leave.

'Thank you for your time,' said the DCI, extending his hand. 'We'll no doubt be in touch.'

Driving towards Sandy Lane Golf Club, Louis glanced at James, behind the wheel.

'What did you make of him?' he asked, adjusting his Foster Grants.

'Bit bloody arrogant,' said James, glancing in the rear view mirror as they approached a roundabout. 'Strange, him not wanting to give a DNA sample. Could be hiding something. But, I think he was genuinely surprised when you mentioned Carol Barrington.' He brushed his hair off his face.

'Hmm... well, let's see what his wife has to say. By the way, you need to get that bloody hair cut.' Louis grinned.

CHAPTER SIXTEEN

The villa was enormous, with ochre-painted exterior stonework. A large portico to the front was supported by six tall, Doric-style columns, beneath which an imposing granite-topped dining table was surrounded by twenty ladder-back chairs. Directly in front of the portico, a wide patio led to an Olympic size swimming pool, complete with whitewashed changing rooms to one side.

The DCI looked around the sumptuous reception room into which they'd been shown by a young Bajan girl. She'd met them at the front door after buzzing them through the impressive, gilded wrought iron gates fronting the property.

It was cool inside the villa, after the scorching sun on the portico. The marble-tiled, open-plan reception area was vast, and appeared to take up most of the ground floor. In the centre was a wide, ornately carved, highly-polished oak staircase, sweeping in elegant curves to both right and left, from a central landing at first-floor level. This housed two tall white marble statues of naked women, flanked by luxuriant potted palms. In the reception area were several separate groupings of furniture, more palms and yet more statues, including two very large gilded elephants, all strategically placed to break up the vast room. Louis thought it looked just like a hotel reception area, not at all homely, and he decided that he much preferred his cosy house in St Michael.

As he was taking in the opulence, which he thought was actually quite vulgar, a mature, extremely elegant lady appeared, making her way down the staircase. Her jet black hair was tied back from her pale, oval and rather angular face. He estimated her age at about sixty, but these days it was getting harder to tell.

'Lady McIntyre-Brown?' he asked, walking towards her, hand extended. 'DCI Brown. And this is my colleague, DI James Phillips.

Thank you for agreeing to see us.'

She took his proffered hand, unsmiling. He apologised for the intrusion and asked if she could spare them a few minutes. On behalf of both of them, he declined the refreshments she offered after inviting them to sit on one of the many elegant sofas.

'Lady McIntyre-Brown, we're making some routine enquiries about an incident that took place two nights ago, when a woman was attacked in her apartment, near Prospect.'

'Oh yes? I was having dinner with friends that night, not too far from where it happened. Why do you want to speak to me about it?'

'We're just making a few initial enquiries. Where were you having dinner?'

'I was with a group of my girlfriends, at the Sandy Lane hotel.'

'And what time did you leave?'

'Let's see... my driver brought me home at about 11.45pm. I always like to be home before midnight. At my age you see, one needs one's beauty sleep,' she grimaced. 'But why are you asking these questions officer?'

'As I said, just routine enquiries. We're talking to a number of people who may be able to help. Can you recall whether or not your husband was at home when you returned?'

She frowned, 'My husband? Let me think... he'd gone out to a business meeting earlier in the evening. I assumed he was home, although I didn't actually see him. He may have been in bed already or he may have come in later, I'm really not sure. We have separate sleeping arrangements, you see. I went straight to bed when I got in – I'd had rather a lot to drink, I'm afraid. My husband should remember, why not ask him?'

'We are talking to him,' he assured her. 'Tell me, does your maid stay overnight?'

'She does, yes. Do you need to speak with her?'

He nodded. 'Please.'

She left the room and he heard her calling out for the maid. Before long, she came back with the girl, who she introduced as Lucy.

The girl stood with her hands clasped in front of her and the DCI noted they were trembling.

'No need to be nervous, Lucy,' he said. 'I just want to ask you a couple of questions. Ok?' The girl nodded. 'You know the night the lady was attacked, two nights ago, near Prospect?'

'Oh yessir, I sure do. Ma cousin is a maid at the house next door. She tol' me 'bout it yesterday. We were so shocked at what happened. She was interviewed by the police too.'

'Do you recall what time Sir Ralph came in that night?'

'Yessir. It was about nine o'clock. He'd been to a business meeting. I poured him a whisky. I know just how he likes it; half and half, whisky and water, two ice cubes, slice of lemon.' A hint of pride in her voice. 'Then I chatted to him for a while - he always asks about my day and how my mum is – she's sick you see. Then I went to bed. That would be about ten o'clock. I have to be up early.'

Lucy went on to explain that as her room was in an annexe at the back of the property, she hadn't heard Lady McIntyre-Brown coming home. DCI Brown thanked her and she scampered from the room. He then turned again to Lady McIntyre-Brown.

'Oh, one last question for now. I understand that you and your husband normally come out to Barbados in January each year, but this year time you came in November. Why was that?'

'Well, Ralph decided that he would like to spend Christmas out here for a change. Normally, we spend Christmas at home in England with all the family, but Ralph said he fancied a quiet time for once. I must admit I wasn't too happy about it, but he was adamant and wouldn't budge. I love spending time with my children and grandchildren, but I'm afraid my husband is getting old and grizzly and the noise of the grandchildren annoys him these days.'

'Thank you so much for your time. We may need to ask further questions in due course. Oh, and I'll need to speak to your driver; is he around?'

'He's not here at the moment. Can I give you his number?'

As they left, a few minutes later, James voiced his thoughts.

'Aren't some people strange? All the money in the world, yet no warmth or companionship in that house. Looks to me like Sir Ralph gets more affection and attention from the maid than from that cold fish. Separate bedrooms – what's that all about? No, give me my lovely cuddly Deanne, any time. She might give me a hard time now and then, but she's one red-hot chilli-pepper.'

CHAPTER SEVENTEEN

After leaving the villa behind, James rang the McIntyre-Browns' driver and arranged for them to call in at his house, on the way back to Bridgetown. Before long, they pulled up outside a neat chattel house, painted in the palest turquoise, with brilliant white window frames and door. Brightly coloured flowers trailed from well tended window boxes and spilled over the tubs beside the front porch. James knocked on the door, which was soon opened a fraction by a solemn little boy, who studied them with huge brown eyes, as he peeped around the door.

'Hello. Is your father in?' asked James, smiling down at him.

Without a word, the boy darted back into the house and soon a man came to the door. Of average height and quite lean, his well-developed muscles were evident in his bulging biceps.

'Come in, gentlemen. Elvis Hanson,' he said, extending his hand. After, shaking their hands, he led the way along a short passageway, into a small but very neat room. He indicated two easy chairs, both with brightly-coloured throws over their backs, and then sat himself down on a small two-seater sofa, opposite. 'How can I help you?'

'We're making some routine enquiries and would just like to ask you a couple of questions about the night before last,' the DCI said.

'The night that lady was attacked?' he asked, looking directly at Louis.

'That's right. Can you tell us your movements on that night?'

'Yes of course. I was on duty, working for the McIntyre-Browns. I drove Lady Arabella to Sandy Lane at seven thirty, then picked her up again at eleven forty-five.'

'What did you do in between?'

'I came home to relax for a while before it was time to pick her up again.'

'Did you see Sir Ralph at all?'

He hesitated, looking down, suddenly uncomfortable. 'Well, I know he had a meeting earlier in the evening. He drove himself there and back in the Porsche... then I got a call from him, just after ten o'clock, asking if I could take him back into Holetown. He asked me not to mention it to his wife.'

'Where did you drop him off?'

'At the Lime Grove Centre. I've no idea where he was going.'

'Did you pick him up again, later?' asked the DI.

'No, he said he'd probably get a taxi. Wasn't sure how long he'd be.'

'Has he ever done that before?' asked James. 'Asked you to keep his movements from his wife?'

'No, never. I was a bit puzzled, but you don't ask the boss for explanations.'

'Well, thank you, Mr Hanson. We won't keep you any longer. You've been very helpful.'

Back in the car, on the way back to the station, James took a call from the officer on duty at the crime scene, who told him that two fishermen were there with him. They wanted to report something suspicious they'd seen on the night Carol Barrington was killed.

'I'm with the DCI now, just hold on.' He looked at Louis and raised his eyebrows in query Louis nodded. 'We're only five minutes away, so we'll swing round and come to speak with them. Keep them with you.' He glanced at the DCI. 'Here we go again, boss.'

They found the two men sitting at a small table in the street-level garden, sipping coke. The older of the two, with grizzly grey hair and weatherbeaten face, stood up politely, as they approached. He held out his hand.

James took it. 'DI James Phillips. You must be the fishermen?

'Yeah, man. The other copper asked us to wait here.'

'This is DCI Brown,' James introduced Louis.

'Leroy Bates,' the man said, shaking DCI Brown's hand. 'And this is my son, Lloyd.' Lloyd, who'd remained in his chair, nodded in greeting.

'My colleague told me you saw someone in the water?' asked Louis, looking at the older man. 'Can you tell us what happened?' He pulled out a chair. 'Let's all sit down.'

Once they were settled, Leroy spoke, 'We're in the boat just offshore here, two nights ago, when we see a man. In the water. He was splashing about a bit at first and we thought he was in trouble. I shouted to him "You alright man?" He didn't answer, just took off in the direction of Holetown. Seemed to be a fast swimmer. Powerful. Didn't really think too much of it. Thought it was probably some crazy tourist. They always doin' stupid things like that. When we heard about the trouble at that villa, we wondered, you know, if it could be connected. Thought we'd better tell you boys about it.'

'What time did you see this man?' asked James.

'It was midnight. I know cos Lloyd here was late getting to the boat, down at Paynes Bay, and I was grumbling we wouldn't get started til midnight. We'd just got in position, when we saw him.'

'And how far away from the swimmer were you?'

'Bout fifteen, twenty metres at most. We could see him in the lights from the shore.'

'Can you describe him?'

'Ah man, we only saw him in the water. Couldn't really see much. He had dark hair, shortish. Seemed to be powerfully built. Coulda been white; definitely not black anyway. Light-skinned. Seemed to be wearing some kinda vest.'

'Could you see the colour of the vest?'

'Pretty sure it was black. Dark, anyway.'

'Would either of you be able to recognise him again?' asked the DCI.

'Nah. We didn't see his face properly – did we Lloyd?' he said, looking at his son, who shook his head.

Turning to the second man, DI Phillips asked 'Do you have anything to add to what your father's just told us?'

'No. Wish I'd taken more notice now. Would've gone after the bastard if we'd known. We was more interested in findin the fish.'

'Did you catch any fish then?'

'Yeah man, we had a good night. He must of brought us luck.' he laughed.

CHAPTER EIGHTEEN

He'd called a meeting for six and most of the team were gathered in the large Briefing Room as DCI Louis Brown entered, at exactly six o'clock. A hush fell over the room which had been alive with ribald banter before his entry.

He perched himself on the corner of a desk, outstretched legs crossed at the ankle. Absentmindedly rubbing his chin with one hand, he cleared his throat before announcing, 'Just a brief update, everyone. DI Phillips has some information for us. James?'

James got to his feet, brushing his unruly sandy hair from his eyes, and gave a summary of the interview with Sir Ralph. By way of amusement, he described the lavish buffet at the Yacht Club, to get the team salivating.

'Get on with it,' Louis told him.

James told them Sir Ralph had seemed genuinely shocked when he worked out the identity of the victim. However, he had been unable to establish a solid alibi for the night in question. He'd said he'd been at home after an early-evening business meeting in Holetown, and Lady McIntyre had assumed her husband was in bed when she returned from a dinner at eleven forty-five, but hadn't actually seen him. Their maid confirmed that Sir Ralph had come home at around nine o'clock, and was still up when she went off to bed at ten.

'So far, so good,' continued James. 'We then interviewed their driver, Elvis, who told us that he'd driven Lady McIntyre to the Sandy Lane Hotel at seven, and then, later, he drove Sir Ralph back into Holetown. Just after ten. Elvis hadn't mentioned this to Lady Arabella, as Sir Ralph had asked him to keep it to himself. He didn't know where Sir Ralph was going; he dropped him off just outside the Lime Grove Centre in Holetown.

He's to be formally interviewed again tomorrow. He's coming down to the station with his solicitor,' the DI added, taking a sip of water.

'We also had a chat with two fishermen, who came forward to tell us about a man they'd seen in the sea,' said James, again pushing his stray locks off his face. He went on to summarise the interview with the fishermen. 'So, if that was our man, we could be looking for a light-skinned, male, powerful build, short, dark hair, possibly wearing a black vest.'

'Thanks, James. How did you get on with your informant, Dave?' asked the DCI, turning to DC David Morgan.

Dave gave the gist of his conversation with his contact, and added 'The information he's given in the past has always been accurate.'

'Interesting,' said the DCI. 'If it's a visitor, we have to consider the possibility that it could be someone known to the victim. Did someone follow her out here? Or was it a random attack by someone who noticed an open door? Right, let's continue with the interviews. Sooner we find the perp, the better. Thanks everyone. That's it for now. Make sure the board's updated.'

CHAPTER NINETEEN

At a few minutes before midnight, DCI Brown took a call from Ron Fisher, the Duty Sergeant on night shift. Louis had been in a deep sleep and was not pleased to be woken by the shrill sound of his phone. He answered shortly, 'Brown.'

'Sorry to bother you at home, sir. Thought you might want to know. One of the off-duty PC's arrested a man tonight. He happened to be passing a house, near Prospect, and heard a woman screaming. She'd been assaulted by an intruder. He caught her assailant as he tried to run away. The perp is one Leroy Barrow. He's got form for rape. Just got out six months ago. Coming so soon after the assault on Carol Barrington, I thought you would want to be kept informed.'

'Get him into the Interview Room, and I want DI Phillips there too,' barked the DCI. 'I'll be there in twenty minutes.'

'I've already called him, sir. He's on his way in.'

Brown bumped into Phillips in the corridor and they went into the Interview Room together. The interview got underway and Leroy Barrow, who was accompanied by the duty solicitor appointed to represent him, immediately admitted to being in the house in question.

'I only broke into that house cos I was runnin short a splifs and needed some dollars.' He put his hands out, palms up, in an open gesture, intended to illustrate his innocence. 'I didn't hurt that lady, man, only pushed her outa my way when she tried to stop me leaving with the dollars. Didn't expect to bump into any of you lot as I'm leavin.'

Leroy was young and cocky and trying to give a good impression of being guilty of nothing worse than getting money for drugs.

'You pushed her so hard she fell and broke her arm. That's assault, Leroy,' interjected DI Phillips.

'Aww man, I didn't mean her no harm.'

Barrow seemed to realise he wasn't going to be able to talk his way out of this one and he asked for a few minutes alone with the duty solicitor. When they reconvened, his solicitor informed them his client would plead guilty to breaking and entering but not to assault, as the victim's fall was an accident.

DCI Brown instructed his Duty Sergeant to formally charge Barrow with both offences.

After Leroy had been taken down to the cells, Louis and James discussed the possibility of there being a connection between the assault and the attack on Carol Barrington.

'There's no evidence. Nothing to tie him to the attack on Carol Barrington,' said James. 'But I think it would be prudent to question him about it.'

'I agree. I didn't want to confuse the two issues tonight. We'll get him remanded tomorrow, and then find out what his movements were on the night Carol Barrington was attacked.'

CHAPTER TWENTY

The following morning, through his office window, Louis caught sight of Sir Ralph and, presumably, his solicitor as they approached the station. Sir Ralph looked worried, as well he might. He'd been asked to come to the police headquarters to answer further questions, this time under caution. They made an odd-looking couple as they walked along Roebuck Street, in the bright sunlight.

The contrast in height was almost comical. Sir Ralph, at about six two, immaculate in fawn coloured chinos, white shirt and brown tie, towered above the other man, who was all of five feet three on tiptoe, and scruffy to boot, his greasy hair curling around his shoulders, touching the collar of his ill-fitting brown jacket.

Louis and James left them to cool for a while, before entering the interview room and introducing themselves. Sir Ralph's solicitor was standing, his back to them, gazing out of the window. Sir Ralph was already seated at the table in the middle of the small, bare room. James had deliberately selected this small, stuffy room, where the air-conditioning was suspect at the best of times.

The solicitor turned and approached them, hand outstretched. 'Clive Pickersgill,' he said, shaking their hands heartily. The DCI approved of the firm handshake, and the way Pickersgill easily maintained eye contact.

'Nice room,' Pickersgill added wryly, glancing around. James suppressed a grin. This man was sharper than he looked.

Once the four were seated at the small, rectangular table, DI Phillips offered refreshments. Sir Ralph asked for a glass of water. The tape was switched on and DI Phillips then read out the caution.

'Now, sir,' began the DCI, once the caution was out of the way, 'when we last spoke, you will recall we discussed your movements on the night of the twenty-ninth of November. Would you mind telling me again what you did that evening and night?' DCI Brown put some paperwork on the desk and looked enquiringly at Sir Ralph.

'Certainly. As I told you, I had a business meeting in Holetown early in the evening, which finished at around eight thirty pm I then I drove straight home, arriving at approximately nine.' He sounded rather pompous.

'And then?' asked Louis.

'I had a couple of whiskies, chatted to Lucy for a while, then read the papers and went off to bed. I believe Lucy has confirmed this. I thought I'd seen my wife, as I mentioned when you first asked me, but she has reminded me that I was in bed by the time she arrived home at 11.45pm and, as we have separate sleeping arrangements, I didn't see her until the next morning.'

The DCI looked through the papers in front of him, from which he produced a sheet of paper.

'Unfortunately, we have a problem with your account. You weren't in bed when your wife came home, were you? I have here a statement from your driver, Elvis, who tells us that, later that evening, he took you back into Holetown,' he consulted the paper in his hand. 'At around ten o'clock.'

Sir Ralph turned to look at his lawyer, who hastily asked for a few minutes alone with his client. It was clear this was news to him. DI Phillips stopped the tape and showed them to a separate room. On their return, the tape was switched back on and the interview resumed.

'My driver did take me into Holetown. I'm sorry I misled you. It was foolish of me, Officer... but I didn't want my wife to find out. It's rather delicate you see, I was meeting my, er... friend in a club there. We stayed for a couple of hours before going to a villa in Westmoreland where my friend lives. Eventually, I got a taxi home in the early hours of the morning, around five.'

DI Phillips interrupted. 'As I'm sure you know, it's a serious business, lying to us and wasting our time. Now, we need the name and address of your friend and details of the club you visited.'

Sir Ralph hesitated, looking extremely uncomfortable, perspiration beginning to stand out on his forehead.

'I'm afraid I cannot disclose the name of my friend. It's a high profile person, very well known on the island, and indeed internationally.'

DI Phillips spoke quietly. 'I don't care how well known she is. Don't you realise how much trouble you're in? If you don't tell us and we can't corroborate your story, you will become a prime suspect in the attempted murder of Carol Barrington. You know her; you were in the vicinity; you lied about your whereabouts, and on top of all this, for no good reason that we know of, you've refused to give a DNA sample. It's not looking so good for you is it? Protecting your girlfriend might seem chivalrous to you, but to me it's foolish and dangerous. Now for the last time, who is she?'

Sir Ralph glanced at his lawyer, who nodded almost imperceptibly, before looking at the DI.

'Can you give my client your categoric assurance that the information he is about to reveal will not be made public in any way?' Clive Pickersgill said quietly. Sir Ralph was now wiping his forehead with a handkerchief.

'Obviously, we'll need to speak with this lady and if, as a result of our enquiries, we can rule out your client as a suspect, there'll be no need to disclose information to any third party. If not... we wouldn't be able to give any assurances.'

Sir Ralph lowered his head and in very subdued tones said 'It's not a lady. It's Sir Gordon Peterson, aide to the British High Commissioner to Barbados. I would appreciate your absolute discretion when you speak to him. He's going to be very upset at being identified.'

The DCI kept a poker face. 'And what is the nature of your relationship with Sir Gordon?' he asked.

'He's my... friend,' replied Sir Ralph, unable to meet the DCI's gaze.

'Just your friend, Sir Ralph? Why would you need to keep that from your wife? Is your relationship of a sexual nature?'

Sir Ralph lowered his head, 'Yes' he whispered.

'And the club you went to with him?'

'The Blue Monkey,' he almost whispered, wiping his brow again with his hanky.

A well-known gay club thought Louis. 'Thank you, Sir Ralph. That will be all for now, but we'll need to speak to you again in due course.'

Once they'd gone, Louis and James looked at each other.

'Fucking hell,' exclaimed James. 'I didn't see that coming.'

'Me neither. Of course, this must be kept in the strictest confidence. Not a word to anyone. I need to take this to the Chief.'

'Yes sir. I understand. My lips are sealed.'

'They'd better be,' said Louis as he left and headed straight for the Chief Superintendent's office. He knocked and waited for Chief Superintendant Frank Williamson to respond, before entering the office.

'Sir. Got something you should know. This is dynamite. Sir Ralph McIntyre Brown has only been having a relationship with Sir Gordon Peterson, aide to the British High Commissioner. That's where he was when Carol Barrington was attacked. Who'd have thought it? McIntyre-Brown wants to rely on him to corroborate his whereabouts.'

'Bloody hell, Louis. Keep this under your hat. We can't let this get out. I'll speak with Sir Gordon personally, but don't hold your breath, he's never going to admit this.'

The next day, Sir Ralph was once again in the interview room, Clive at his side. DCI Brown thanked them for coming in again. Louis could tell by looking at Sir Ralph that he hadn't slept at all. He looked dreadful.

'I'm afraid Sir Gordon Peterson cannot corroborate your account, Sir Ralph. He denies seeing you that night. He admits to having met you in the past, but denies having any kind of relationship with you. He reminded us that he's a happily married man, with four children. He's absolutely outraged at the suggestion that he would be involved in any sleazy behaviour.'

Sir Ralph groaned and slumped in his seat, putting his head in his hands. 'I should have known he would deny it. He's lying of course, you must know that?'

'Unfortunately for you, Sir Ralph, lying or not, he's protected by diplomatic immunity. We can't touch him. The only way you can clear yourself now is to submit a DNA sample. And if you continue to refuse to do so, the only conclusion we could come to is that you are afraid there will be a match with DNA taken at the crime scene.'

Sir Ralph's face crumpled and, for a second, Louis thought he was going to cry, but he pulled himself together, sat up straight in his chair and said in clipped tones 'I will agree to provide a sample for DNA analysis on the condition that no details of it are revealed to any third parties. The truth is, I'm HIV positive and I don't want my wife or anyone else to know this.'

'Ah, I see, Sir... and did you make Sir Gordon Peterson aware of that fact, I wonder?' It was a rhetorical question and there was no response from Sir Ralph, who looked totally defeated.

After swabs had been taken, DCI Brown told them, 'It'll take a few days for the DNA results to be processed, but they'll be here well before you plan to leave the island, so for now that will be all and you're free to go.'

CHAPTER TWENTY-ONE

Once Leroy Barrow had been brought back to the station from the Magistrate's Court, DCI Brown told him he was to be interviewed, under caution, in relation to another offence and advised him to have his solicitor present. He declined.

'I aint done nothing else. Why would I need a solicitor?'

Cocky little bugger thought the DCI, *just been remanded for trial and still full of himself.*

The interview was conducted in the same small, stuffy room in the back of the police station. For the record, James gave the names of those present, DCI Louis Brown along with DI James Phillips and the interviewee, Leroy Barrow. He got Barrow to confirm that he'd refused legal representation.

'Now, Leroy, can you tell us where you were on the night of twenty ninth of November? Just to jog your memory, that's the night a woman was attacked and badly injured. Up the coast from Holetown,' the DI began.

Leroy, who had been sitting back in his chair, nonchalantly inspecting his fingernails, looked up sharply and sat up straighter.

'That white woman? I heard 'bout that. Hell man, that wasn't me. I remember that night I was down the coast, shaggin' that sweet little thing lives in the blue chattel house. Everybody talkin' bout that girl; she can bonk and she don't care who with. Why would I need a white woman? I had a good evenin', couple a splifs and a bonk. Man, I don't need me no white woman!'

'Obviously we'll need to check with the girl, to see if she can corroborate your story. What time did you leave?'

'I can't remember, man. I had a few cans and splifs. Prob'ly 'bout midnight I s'pose'

'Then what did you do?'

'Hell man, I dunno. S'pose I must've walked home. Yeah, I just went home, it's not far.'

'Leroy, you've got form for rape and assault. We've got your DNA on file and we'll be comparing it with DNA taken from the crime scene. You admit you were in the vicinity of the attack. If it was you, the DNA will prove it. So, if you did it, it'll be better for you if you come clean now rather than later.' DCI Brown was pressing the matter. Leroy's angelic act did not match his record, which included the assault and rape of a young girl when he was only nineteen, for which he'd served just four years, getting out six months ago. During that assault, he'd hit the victim over the head with a heavy vase.

'I'm tellin' you, man. It wasn't me. I never touched no white woman. I told you what I done to the other lady, just pushed her outa my way. But the white woman? No way.'

'Well, we're still investigating and looking for further evidence. Failing that, the DNA will prove it one way or another.' He turned to DI Phillips, 'Hand him back to the Duty Sergeant.'

CHAPTER TWENTY-TWO

That afternoon, Simon collected Julia from Grantley Adams. With only hand luggage, she was one of the first passengers to clear customs, and he soon caught sight of her, hurrying through, head bent. She looked up and his heart went out to her. In place of the vivacious and flamboyant young girl he'd last seen, there was a white-faced ghost. As soon as she spotted Simon, she ran to him and threw herself into his arms. She was trembling.

'How is she now? Is she any better?' she spoke rapidly, her voice frantic.

Simon hugged her, took her bag and guided her to where his car was parked. Keeping his arm around her, he explained as they walked.

'She's no worse, Julia. She's still unconscious, but the doctor's told us they've put her into a medically-induced coma for now, to give her time to heal. They're still carrying out tests, so we don't know the extent of the damage just yet.'

'How could anyone attack my mum?' she asked, her lips quivering. 'She doesn't deserve this... especially after all she's been through.'

On the journey to the hospital, Simon, as gently as he could, went through the whole story. Julia, shocked at the detail, was trying, and failing, to hold back tears. 'Oh... how could anyone do that to her...? How could they?'

'I really don't know, sweetheart. It's beyond me.'

'She's not going to die, is she?'

Simon looked at her, sitting in the passenger seat like a little lost soul. She looked so much like her mother, the same blonde hair, same upturned nose. She was plainly dressed in a pair of blue jeans with a blue and white striped tee-shirt and white trainers, a far cry from her usual style. He was more used to seeing her in bright, gaudy outfits with lots of beads and scarves in her hair – like a new-age hippie. He supposed being an art student had some influence on her choice of clothes. Or maybe it was the other way round.

'She's seriously ill, Julia. If it's confirmed that there's bleeding on the brain, it could go either way. But the test results aren't through yet, so we just have to hope for the best.'

Julia gave a strangled sob, then sat in silence, *no doubt coming to terms with what she's going to encounter at the hospital,* Simon thought.

Simon rang ahead to say they were on their way, and Fiona met them at the main door of the hospital. Julia rushed to her and clung to her, sobbing. When the sobs had subsided somewhat, Fiona told her the doctors would allow them to see her mum for a few minutes. She took Julia's arm and they all made their way to the IC Department. Simon could see the fear in Julia's face, and wondered how she would cope with seeing her mother.

After disinfecting their hands and donning protective clothing, they were shown to the bed by a nurse.

'Now, don't be alarmed,' the nurse warned. 'There are lots of tubes and equipment, but it's all to help her get better. She's being kept in an induced coma, for now, so she won't wake up. I'll leave you with her for a minute, but please don't touch her, not even her hand. I'll just be over there,' she indicated the nursing station on the other side of the room and walked away, leaving them by the bed.

When she looked towards the bed, Julia's hand flew to her mouth. 'That's not her,' she yelled. 'That's not my mother. Nurse...' Julia's voice rose in hysteria. 'What have they done to her?'

Propped up on pillows, Carol's face was discoloured, grotesquely swollen and looked misshapen. A ventilation tube was strapped to her face, her chest moving up and down as it noisily breathed for her. Her eyes were closed and most of her head was swathed in bandages, startlingly white against her bruised skin. Tubes and wires seemed to be everywhere.

Hearing the commotion, the nurse hurried back to the bed, where Fiona was trying to calm Julia. Between them, they led her away from the bed, to the other side of the room.

'Is your mother Carol Barrington?' the nurse quietly asked Julia. When she nodded, the nurse continued. 'Then that is your mother. There's a lot of swelling and bruising just now and that's what makes it hard to recognise her. At the moment. It will go down in time.' Her voice was soothing and Simon was relieved to see it was beginning to have a calming effect on Julia. She turned to Fiona and buried her face in her chest, sobbing loudly.

Simon thanked the nurse and ushered them both out of the room. 'She's in the best hands, Julia. Come on, we'll leave her for now and see if we can speak to a doctor. Find out if there's any more news.'

The doctor confirmed that Carol was stable, though still critical. Test results were still awaited. 'We're hoping to get some results in the morning,' he told them.

Fiona insisted that the overwrought Julia go home with her for a few precious hours sleep, and Simon volunteered to stay at the hospital, where they had a visitor bed near the intensive care unit. He promised to ring if there was any change during the night.

CHAPTER TWENTY-THREE

Sometimes I could feel people washing me, which was irritating. It was too intimate. Through a fog, I could hear someone talking. I became aware of someone holding my hand. Nothing made sense. I wanted to open my eyes, but couldn't. With a fleeting feeling of panic I realised I couldn't move.

The first time I briefly woke, with an anguished blink, I made a feeble attempt to pull a tube out of my mouth. It was hurting my throat. The tube was replaced and I could hear soothing words before drifting back to darkness.

Then, I was more awake, feeling woozy, with severe pain in my head. I began to panic, again trying to pull the tube out of my throat. The nurses calmed me and told me they were giving me morphine for the pain. After that, time seemed to come and go. Chunks of time when I was awake, then disjointed times, with different people around the bed. One time, I thought I was in a hotel room in London, with my friend, Pauline, but Julia was there.

'Why are you here?' I asked Julia. 'You should be at Uni.'

'I flew here to be with you, mum, as soon as I heard.'

'Don't be silly. You always drive to London. Why would you fly?'

They told me afterwards, some of the other funny things I was saying in my morphine-induced delirium. The pattern on the curtains in the room kept taking different shapes. One minute there were dogs playing on the beach, the next horses jumping over fences. The morphine took away all the pain, and all the anxiety about the tube, which at some stage was removed.

The nurses told me the morphine was being slowly withdrawn, and during a very woozy journey back to reality, I began to feel pain and discomfort. My throat was raw, where the tube had been. I couldn't move my head without the most excruciating pain, and realised that my head was bandaged. I began to tentatively feel around my face and head and then became aware of dressings on my breasts, shoulders and arms.

Everything seemed disjointed. At one stage I remember waking up in the most terrible panic. Nightmares crowded in on me. I dreamed I was being suffocated and was fighting for my life. The nurses told me later that I was thrashing around so violently they had to hold me down to prevent me from hurting myself.

There seemed to be an endless stream of people, coming and going. Fiona, Julia, Simon, Josie, and nurses and doctors assuring me I was safe now. Sounds and smells of hospital, hands gently washing me and Julia, and Fiona holding my hands. One nurse, who told me her name was Wanda, was particularly kind to me. Born and bred in Barbados, she had a lovely, engaging personality, as so many of the locals had.

Waking up, one morning, I became aware of someone singing quietly, on the other side of my room.

'Oh, Carol, I am but a fool...'

'No,' I shouted, alarmed. 'No. Stop.'

'Oh, you're back with us Carol?' the nurse asked brightly. It was Wanda. 'Don't you like my voice then?'

'The song...don't sing that song.' My heart was racing and I felt panic building up. Wanda, detecting the distress in my voice, came over to the bed and took my wrist in her hand, feeling my rapid pulse.

'It's me, Wanda. What is it, Carol? What's wrong?'

'I don't know...the song... don't sing that song.' My breath was coming in big gulps.

'I won't sing it any more if it bothers you, honey,' she said gently, again patting my hand in reassurance. 'Calm down now. Take some deep breaths... that's better.'

The panic receded. 'My head hurts, Wanda. Everything's so strange. Do you know why I'm here?'

'Don't worry, honey. The doctor will prescribe something for your head. He's on his rounds now, so he'll be here soon. After that, if he agrees you're up to it, the police need to speak with you. I'm sure they'll tell you what's happened to you.'

'The police?'

'Yes, they've been on duty outside since you were brought in. I'll let them know you're awake,' she turned to leave. 'But they won't be able to see you until Doctor Gibson gives the go-ahead.'

'Wanda?' She turned back. 'How long have I been here?'

'You were brought in with serious head injuries, six days ago.'

'Six days?' I closed my eyes, wearily. It was too much to take in.

'The police will explain everything, when Doctor Gibson thinks you're well enough to see them. Try not to worry.' She gave me one of her beaming smiles, dimples forming in her plump cheeks.

I must have dozed off again, because I woke with a start when the doctor strode into the room.

'Good Morning, Carol. Sorry to startle you. I'm Dr Gibson. It's good to see you properly awake. How're you feeling today?' Raising his rather bushy eyebrows, he looked at me over his reading glasses.

'Hello, doctor. I'm... fuzzy... my head hurts.'

He bent over me and examined my head, gently easing the dressing aside, just above my left ear, then felt around the wound with his fingertips. I winced.

'Sorry. Being as gentle as I can. It's healing well. Scarring should be minimal and in any case, it'll be largely covered by your hair.' He smiled, a reassuring smile that lit up his face displaying a small gap between his two front teeth.

'When you were first brought in, with blunt force trauma injury to your head, we feared there may have been some bleeding around the brain. We've carried out tests and have been monitoring you carefully. Thankfully, the tests have shown there's no bleeding and the initial swelling is reducing. Your skull is fractured in two places, and you've had concussion. We kept you sedated for a while, to rest your brain and help it to heal. However, we're confident now that you'll make a full recovery. You've been very lucky, in a sense. It could have been so much worse after suffering such a blow. Now,' he said, raising his eyebrows again, 'Wanda's told me you have some memory loss?'

'I... I can't remember anything. I don't know what's happened to me. I remember... I was with Fiona... saw her off in a taxi... went back down the steps... I … I can't remember anything after that. Next thing was… being in here with tubes and drips.'

He took the chair beside my bed and leaned towards me, his hands folded in his lap. I caught a faint trace of something spicy, perhaps cologne. 'The police will explain everything to you about what has happened,' he said gently. 'You suffered a massive blow to your head. You needed time to allow your brain to heal. There's almost always some confusion when you first wake up properly from an induced medical coma. Don't get upset about it, just try to relax and get better. Easier said than done, I know. From a medical point of view we're very pleased with your progress; but of course we understand you will feel confused. You will need to come to terms with what has happened, in due course.' He sat back in the chair.

'Your memory should come back, in time, probably gradually. There's no guarantee, but try not to worry about it for now. Best to just concentrate on getting better. I'll get Wanda to give you some tablets for your headache.'

He turned to Wanda, and gave her some instructions. I hadn't noticed her come into the room. 'Now,' he said, turning back to face me, 'the police are waiting to speak with you. They'll explain everything. But, only if you feel up to talking to them?'

'Yes... I need to know... I don't want to wait any longer to find out what on earth has happened to me.'

They both left, and Wanda returned a minute later. 'Take these now,' she said, with a smile, handing me two yellow tablets and a small beaker. 'They'll deal with the headache. They'll also make you drowsy, so I'll tell the police not to stay too long.'

CHAPTER TWENTY-FOUR

I looked up as a very tall, Bajan man came through the door, wearing an open-neck white shirt and grey chinos. His face could only be described as beautiful. Long sooty lashes framed mesmerising brown eyes.

'Hello, Mrs Barrington,' he said, in a very deep voice. 'I'm DCI Louis Brown with the Barbados police and this is my colleague, DC Lynn Sands,' he indicated a petite woman who had followed him into the room. She looked to be somewhere in her thirties, with straight, glossy black hair and gentle brown eyes that studied me from beneath her fringe. She nodded to me in acknowledgement.

'The doctor thinks you may be up to answering a few questions, Mrs. Barrington. Will that be alright? We won't keep you long.' His voice was deep brown velvet.

He took the chair by the bed and his colleague collected another from the corridor. I suddenly felt scared at the thought of what I might hear.

'Now, Carol,' he began, stroking his chin with his right hand. 'Is it alright to call you Carol?' I nodded and he continued. 'Please call me Louis. And this is Lynn. Can you tell me what you remember about the night you were attacked?' he studied my face as he spoke.

'Attacked?' I repeated, my mouth falling open in surprise. 'I thought I'd had some kind of accident... I didn't know I'd been attacked?'

'I'm sorry. I thought you'd been told. Didn't the staff tell you? Or your family?'

'No... they said the police would.' It was hard to take in.

'I see. Well, I'm afraid that you were assaulted. Six nights ago. Can you tell me what you remember about that night?'

'I can't remember anything... Who would attack me?.. Why?' I spoke slowly, trying to make sense of the disturbing news.

'That's what we're trying to find out,' he leant towards me, speaking softly. 'We know from your doctor that some memory loss is quite normal after a blow to the head. Let's see what you do remember. Do you recall seeing Fiona into her taxi?'

'Yes...' I could picture Fiona waving from the taxi. 'Her dress was trailing on the ground.'

'You can remember her dress trailing? That's good,' interjected Lynn. 'Can you see it in your mind?'

'Yes...'

'That's good. So, you clearly remember her leaving in a taxi. Right. Now, take your time, can you remember what you did next?'

'I... went back down the steps... It was dark... I had to be careful.'

'Careful?'

'Not to fall.'

'Can you remember what happened when you reached the bottom of the steps?' Lynn asked gently.

'No...nothing... I don't remember getting to the bottom... just waking up in here.'

'Do you recall if you saw anyone else when you were seeing Fiona off, or on your way down the steps?' asked Louis.

'No... no, I don't remember seeing anyone at all.'

'And you didn't invite anyone in? A friend, perhaps?'

'No... there was no-one there...' I was puzzled at the question. 'Why..?'

'It's just that sometimes people are attacked by someone who knows them,' he explained. 'When you went back into your apartment, did you lock the doors?'

'I will have done... I always lock up before I go to bed.'

'What about when you left to walk Fiona up to street level, did you lock the doors behind you then?'

I hesitated. 'Well... no... I don't think so... I didn't think... I was only going to be a few minutes...'

'It's possible that someone could have entered the apartment then. There was no sign of a forced entry and the doors were found unlocked the next day.'

'So, you think I could have... locked myself in with the person who attacked me?' It was dawning on me that someone must have already been inside when I locked up. A chilling thought. My head was throbbing and I felt sick.

'Look, I can see you're very tired, now. We'll have more questions to ask you, but they can wait until tomorrow,' he said, rubbing his chin. 'Your doctor warned us not to stay too long, so we'll leave you to rest for now. You've done very well.' He got to his feet.

'No. Please. Before you go... I want to know what happened? All I know is I'm hurting all over. I've got a fractured skull... I've got bruises and sores over my body... What exactly has happened to me?'

'I think we should leave the details 'til you're a bit stronger, Carol,' Lynn said.

'No,' I shouted, feeling frantic. 'I need to know now. Please. Have you any idea what it's like, lying here, like this, and not have a clue about what's happened?'

They exchanged glances, and Louis nodded to Lynn, almost imperceptibly. They were both on their feet, ready to leave, but Lynn now took the chair Louis had vacated and pulled it closer to the bed.

'Alright. I'll tell you what we know so far,' she said, clasping her hands together. 'We got a call from Simon to say someone had been hurt.'

'Simon?'

'Yes. Apparently, when you failed to turn up for lunch at Fiona and Simon's house, they got worried.' Lynn went on to explain about Simon finding me. 'There was a lot of blood. He thought you were dead until he found a faint pulse. He made a 211 call and we responded within five minutes. The paramedics brought you immediately to this hospital. You were hit over the head with a stone turtle – we found it on the floor beside the bed.'

'Was... was I raped?' I had to know.

'The doctors found no evidence of rape. You were badly beaten, and bitten on your shoulders, arms and breasts, but there was no evidence to suggest you were raped.'

'Thank God... oh, thank God.' It was such a relief to hear that. My cheeks felt wet and I realised I was crying.

Lynn patted my hand. 'Carol, can you think of anyone who would do this to you?'

'No,' I whispered. It was all too much to take in. 'Why would anyone do this to anyone? Oh, my head... sorry...' My head felt as though it was going to explode.

'Ok. You've done very well. Rest now. We'll speak again tomorrow. You try to get some sleep. I'll ask the nurse to come in.'

They left then and I lay back, exhausted, my headache becoming unbearable. *Why* I asked myself, *Why would anyone do this to me?* Wanda came in then, and fussed around, adjusting my pillows, tucking the sheets around me and generally making me more comfortable. I sank gratefully into the pillows.

'Wanda, I was attacked. I didn't know.'

'I know you were, honey. We thought it best to let the police tell you. But we're taking good care of you now. Time to sleep. The pills should take effect soon.'

CHAPTER TWENTY-FIVE

His flight home wasn't scheduled for another week, so although he was bereft now that Carol was gone, he decided to act like any other tourist and see a bit of the island before going back home. That day, he'd driven to the very north of the island, near North Point, to see the Animal Flower Cave. The brochure described it as the only accessible sea cave on the island and explained that its name derives from the sea anemones found in the pools of the cave.

On the drive up there, he'd taken several wrong turnings, signposts being few and far between in the interior of Barbados, and one sugar cane field looking very much like another. Once he finally found the place, he was well impressed with the spectacular views of the Atlantic, seen through openings in the rock. The openings, in turn, were stunningly reflected in the pools inside the caves, some of which were deep enough to swim in. He'd had a bite to eat at the open-air buffet there. His favourite Bajan dish was on the menu - jerk chicken, which he'd had with macaroni cheese and ochra. Tasty.

Finally back in his hotel room, after again getting lost several times on the return journey, he opened his laptop and decided to look at the latest news back home in the UK. Scrolling through the headlines, an article caught his eye. What? He sat up straight and stared at the screen in astonishment. He re-read the headline, from the 'Evening Chronicle', the local rag in Newcastle.

Local businesswoman attacked and left for dead in Barbados.

An unnamed North East businesswoman, who we understand is from the Newcastle area, has been viciously attacked in her holiday home in Barbados. The Barbados police are questioning

a local man but no charges have yet been brought in connection with the incident. The victim was taken to hospital in Bridgetown where she is understood to be in a critical condition.

He was stunned, his mind racing in confusion. If she's alive, they'll be looking for me; she must have given them my name. Why are they questioning a local man? He needed to find out what was going on. He'd stopped monitoring Carol's computer once he believed her to be dead, but now he logged on and checked it out, and her mobile... there was no activity, nothing.

He decided to check Fiona's computer, and eventually found what he was looking for. An email, dated three days ago, from Fiona to her mother in the UK, which he read avidly.

'Just wanted to give you an update on Carol's condition. It's awful to see her looking so damaged and fragile. She's still unconscious and the doctors have told us they've put her in an induced medical coma to allow her brain time to heal. Apparently, there is some swelling of the brain, but thankfully they don't think there's any bleeding. They'll keep her in the coma until the swelling has reduced. Poor Julia, all she does is cry and we're doing our best to comfort her. It's a terrible time and we're all praying Carol pulls through.'

He jumped up, pacing the hotel room, running his hands through his hair. The frustration and rage he felt, after their last encounter, was still with him. A vision came to him of her lying on the bed, blood welling from the gaping hole in her head, her breasts littered with livid bite marks. The memory brought a stirring in his loins. He had been so sure she was dead; he was having difficulty getting his head around the fact that she was still alive.

His inner voice cautioned him to forget Carol Barrington. Why not just disappear? Get away while you can, it said to him. Before she wakes up. He silenced the voice. He knew he'd never be able to just walk away and forget about her. She was all he'd thought about, dreamed and fantasised about, for nearly two years. She'd been his full time focus for so long, and now that he knew she was still alive, he was incapable of leaving her behind. She was his.

Sitting back at his computer, he logged on to the internet and began to research the Barbados press. There was no mention anywhere of the attack, and he realised there must be a local press embargo on the story.

Not good for tourism he supposed. Next, he would work on hacking into the Queen Elizabeth Hospital in Bridgetown, to see what he could find out about their patient.

CHAPTER TWENTY-SIX

I woke the next morning with the sun shining through brightly patterned curtains. For a moment I felt happy, before remembering where I was, and why. I could hear a rattling noise and Wanda came bustling into the room, pushing a small trolley.

She was her usual chirpy self. 'Good Morning, Carol. How are you feeling this morning?'

'I'm feeling a lot better today,' I said, sitting up. 'I've slept well. I don't know what was in those pills you gave me, but they really knocked me out.' I yawned.

She set about taking my blood pressure and temperature, before examining the wound on my head. 'You're doing well. Dr Gibson is pleased with you. Your head is healing nicely. I can remove the dressing now.' She gently touched the left side of my face, then began to work on the dressing.

'I see from your notes that you're a widow, honey? You are far too young to be widowed, girl. What happened?' she looked at me with curiosity.

'He died... in a climbing accident; a year ago...'

'Oh, that's awful, honey. Such a shame. What was he like?' she was busy putting all her paraphernalia back on the trolley.

I thought for a moment. 'He was thoughtful, kind. Funny too – we used to laugh a lot together. It was a second marriage for both of us and we both felt we'd found our soul-mate at last... I adored him...' My eyes filled, tears threatening to spill over. 'Oh, I wish he was here with me now,' my voice broke.

'There, there, honey. I didn't mean to upset you. There aint no justice in this life. You lose your poor husband, and now this happens to you.' Wanda sounded indignant. 'It's just not fair.'

She peered closely at my head. 'Anyway, I'm pleased to tell you, your head wound is looking good. No infection at all. Should heal nicely.' She patted my shoulder again. 'Now, are you ok? Those police officers are here again. Do you feel like seeing them?'

I nodded, and with that, she was gone, the creaking and rattling of the trolley becoming fainter as she went down the corridor.

Before long, Lynn came through the door, carrying a black leather briefcase, which she plonked on the floor as she took the chair by the bed. She seemed to be on her own this time.

'Hi, how are you feeling today?' she asked, straightening her skirt. 'You look a lot brighter than you did yesterday.'

'I've been trying to process what you told me. I know what's happened to me; of course I do. Yet somehow it just doesn't feel real. I think because I can't remember it, it feels almost like it happened to someone else, and I'm just an on-looker. Does that make sense?'

Lynn looked thoughtful. 'Yes, I suppose it does. No doubt it'll seem real enough when your memory starts to return.' She took a notebook out of her pocket, and crossed one slim leg over the other. 'Now, before I tell you how the investigation's going, can you give me some background on yourself. Your work, for example. What do you do for a living?'

I told her briefly about the Management Consultancy I ran jointly with Rupert, a former colleague. 'We also run an investment group where we introduce wealthy business people to entrepreneurs looking for investment in their businesses. Oh, and also I have a property portfolio that I manage myself – twelve properties.'

She raised her eyebrows.

'Seven properties were included in my divorce settlement and I've added to them gradually since then – they're my pension fund,' I said by way of explanation.

'And I understand you're a widow?'

'Yes, my husband, my second husband, was killed in a climbing accident, just over a year ago now.'

'That's tough. Sorry to hear that. What about children?'

'You've met my daughter, Julia. She's from my first marriage. Peter and I didn't have any between us. Fiona and Jack are Peter's from his first marriage. We'd only been together three years...'

'I see,' she uncrossed her legs. 'Let me tell you where we are in the investigation. We've been looking through your mobile phone and made a list of all your contacts. We're checking if anyone known to you in England, was in Barbados at the time of the attack. Don't look alarmed. This is standard procedure. In addition, from Fiona, Simon and Julia, we've got some names of people you know in Barbados, and we're checking on them. I'd like you to go through the list, when you're up to it, to see if we've missed anyone out.' She fished in her briefcase and pulled out a thin folder, which she held out to me.

'Can you leave it with me? I just can't think straight at the moment.' I took the file and put it on the bed.

'Of course. But if you do think of any other names, you must let me know without delay. As a matter of interest, we have someone in custody on another matter, who's been interviewed in connection with this case. We don't have any evidence to support his involvement at this stage, so we're keeping an open mind. DNA taken at the scene is being processed. Results are expected in the next couple of days, so we'll know more then.' She crossed her legs again.

'We have established that Sir Ralph McIntyre-Brown and his wife are on the island. Can you tell me how you know them?'

'Ralph? He's one of the investors I mentioned – one of the wealthy business people. It was through him that I met Peter; when Ralph brought him along to join the investment group.'

'When did you last see Sir Ralph?'

'Well, I haven't been going to the meetings for some time. After Peter died, last year, I had a breakdown and haven't been able to work much since. It must have been at Peter's funeral, the last time I saw him - last December. I think he was there with his wife.'

'Did you know he was on the island?'

'No, but I know he has a holiday home here. I think he comes out every year.'

'Has he ever shown any interest in you?'

'Sexually, you mean? Well, no... he's quite proper, actually. A bit old-fashioned.'

'Can you think of anyone who has ever made you feel uncomfortable? Paid you unwanted attention? Or anyone who could have a grudge? Anyone you might have upset at any time, maybe inadvertently? At work? Your Investment Group? Turned down some entrepreneurs? That sort of thing. Could anyone have a grudge against you? Is there a disgruntled former lover in your past? A tenant with a grudge? Have a good think about it and let me know if you come up with any names?'

'I'll try, but I'm sure it won't be anyone I know who attacked me.'

'Hmmm. You'd be surprised how often people are attacked by someone who knows them,' was her response, as she bent down and retrieved a book from her briefcase. 'Would you mind looking at these photographs to see if you recognise any of the faces?' she said, holding out an album.

My heart sank. 'Well... I'm not sure... You know I can't remember anything.' I suddenly felt agitated.

'Don't worry. If you don't recognise any of them, that's fine. Just look at each one, if you don't mind. It's a long shot, but maybe one of the photographs will jog your memory?'

'Well... I can try.' I took the file from her, and started to leaf through the pictures, examining all of the faces carefully. Most were of local, dark-skinned young men. I reached the last page and closed the file. Handing it back to Lynn, I shook my head. 'Sorry. I've never seen any of those men before.'

'Don't worry. We knew it was a long shot.' She put the file back in her briefcase.

'What's he like, this man you have in custody?'

She zipped up the briefcase and put it back on the floor. 'I can't comment on that. Tell me about your former husband. How long is it since you divorced?'

'It's about eight years, now.' My fingers found my scar.

'Do you keep in touch?'

'Not really. But he came to the house a few months ago, when I was ill. I was in bed and didn't want to see him. Fiona spoke to him. He told her he was worried about me after Peter's death and just wanted to know I was ok. I told her to send him away.'

'Did you think that odd? That he would come to your house?'

'Not really. He's a strange sort of character. He only lives a few streets away. I've noticed him parked at the end of my street a few times over the years. I once challenged him about it, a long time ago now, and he said he just wanted to see that I was alright. I don't think that's happened so much since I got together with Peter.'

'That sounds odd behaviour, like stalking. You mentioned that you thought he was stalking you...' Lynn checked her notes. 'In an email to Fiona. Dated two years ago?'

'Did I? Oh, yes, that was after I last noticed him parked in the street. I was annoyed, but not really worried. Has someone been reading all my emails, then?' I was a bit taken aback.

'We had to get on with the investigation while you were unconscious. We couldn't wait for you to wake up, so we searched for anything that could possibly help us to find the perpetrator,' she explained. 'Tell me about your marriage. Why you split up,' she asked.

'Well... I was young when we got married – seventeen - just out of school and pregnant with Julia. He was older, controlling, always putting me down; didn't want me to change. He objected to me going to college, and university. Then when I registered with an Agency and accepted a job, he was apoplectic. That was the beginning of the end.'

'What led to the final break, then?'

'Things just got worse. At work, I was respected. At home, I was still treated as inferior. The arguments escalated and Saul's moods became erratic. I told him I wanted to separate. One minute he would tell me to fuck off, he didn't need me. The next, he would threaten to kill himself if I ever left him.'

'Emotional blackmail,' interjected Lynn.

I nodded. 'Just when I thought I'd never escape without a lot of trouble, he suddenly agreed to let me go. He bought me out of my share of our house. We'd built up the property portfolio together, and he agreed to share this equally too – that's how I ended up with properties.'

'Was he ever violent towards you?'

'Not physically. The hurt he inflicted was all emotional.'

'Do you think he'd be capable of hurting you, physically?'

'Do you mean, do I think he could have attacked me? No. I know he's an oddball, but I don't honestly think he would do me any harm. I really don't believe he would be capable of anything like that.'

'Well, with a conviction for GBH, he clearly is capable of violence.'

I was puzzled. 'What conviction?'

Her brown eyes widened in surprise. 'Weren't you aware of his criminal record when you married him?'

'No... when? I mean, what did he do?'

'It was a long time ago. You'll have to ask him about the details. If we don't find the perpetrator here, we'll no doubt want to interview him in due course, if only to rule him out.'

'In England?'

'If necessary. If our enquiries lead us to believe your assailant could be over there. The UK police won't have any jurisdiction to investigate a crime carried out abroad,' she explained. 'Were there any other men, before you met Peter?'

'No-one of any importance. I went out with a couple of guys, but nothing came of that. I can barely remember their names. Oh, this is exhausting.' I held my head. 'Why can't I remember more about who attacked me? It's so frustrating.' I felt overwhelmed. My head was aching again.

'It's early days, yet, Carol. Give yourself time.' She got to her feet and picked up her briefcase. 'See if you can recall any more names. I'll come to see you again tomorrow, but if you remember any in the meantime, give me a ring.' She handed me a card. 'The sooner we eliminate people, the better.'

She walked towards the door, then turned. 'Oh, by the way, you may be aware there are a couple of police constables stationed outside the ward? It's standard procedure when someone has been attacked and the perpetrator hasn't been apprehended. Nothing to worry about.'

CHAPTER TWENTY-SEVEN

The next day, when Wanda came into my room, I asked her to bring me a mirror.

'You've been putting me off for a few days, but I really want to have a look at the damage. Honestly, I feel strong enough to face it now.'

Wanda nodded. 'Ok. A mirror it is. Bear with me for a minute.' She left the room but was soon back with a gilt, hand-held mirror. 'Now, before I let you look,' she said, holding the mirror behind her back, 'I want you to understand that you are not a pretty sight, at the moment. You won't be winning no beauty contests for a while, Ok? But there's nothing to worry about. Everything will get back to normal, as you continue to heal. Ok?' She continued to hide the mirror out of my reach, until I acknowledged what she'd said.

'I understand.' Feeling a little apprehensive, I held out my hand and took the proffered mirror. I thought I was prepared for anything, but couldn't help letting out an involuntary gasp as I saw my reflection. Nestled amongst a mass of purple, green and yellow bruising, two black eyes looked back at me. The left side of my head looked odd; swollen and misshapen. When I tilted my head to the right, I could see that my hair had been shaved in a large area behind my left temple. A myriad of black stitches stood out luridly against the white skin there.

'Oh,' I whispered, holding my fingertips gingerly to the wound. 'There's a dent in my head. And all those stitches. God, he must have hit me very hard.' I was horrified to think how close to death I had been. 'Whoever did this intended to kill me.' My stomach turned over at the thought.

'Don't think like that, Carol. Everything is healing well. The dent is filling out nicely and should disappear altogether before too long. You've got thirty-two stitches in that wound, honey, but once they're out and your hair grows back, there'll be no scarring visible. So don't worry, girl.' She smiled, taking the mirror off me, and adroitly changed the subject.

'So, where did you meet Peter?'

Truth be told, I felt so chastened by what the mirror had shown me, and the implications of it, that all I wanted to do at that moment, was to be left alone so I could curl into a ball and hide under the bedcovers. It took a huge effort to register Wanda's question and respond to her. I knew she was changing the subject, trying to take my mind off my injuries. She was good at that.

'At work. Someone brought him along to join a group I was running. I thought I was immune to men, but he changed all that. Before that, I'd been married to a controlling and domineering man, and it was so refreshing to be... treated nicely.'

Wanda squeezed my hand. 'It must have been devastating to lose him.'

I nodded. 'It was so sudden. No time to say goodbye.' A pang of intense longing came over me, unbidden, a physical pain.

Just then, the door opened and Lynn came striding in. 'Excuse me, not interrupting, am I? Just want a few minutes with Carol.'

'I was just leaving,' said Wanda getting up. 'We'll talk later,' she said softly, patting my hand again.

Lynn sat down. 'How are you today? You look bit pale. Are you ok?'

With an effort I pulled myself together. 'I've just seen myself in the mirror... what a mess. God, he really intended to kill me, didn't he?'

'Not necessarily,' Lynn said, gently. 'There was only one blow.' She continued in her usual brisk manner. 'Did you come up with any other names for me?'

'I think you've got them all. Everyone's in my phone list. Have you spoken to any of them yet?'

'We're checking on their movements and some interviews are under way now. I'll let you know if anything significant arises. Now,' she said, leaning forward, 'Is your memory of that night coming back at all?'

'No... It's still a complete blank. The doctor says it might come back gradually or even not return at all.' I could see she was disappointed.

'Don't be concerned about it. I wanted to let you know, the DNA results are through now. We've ruled out the man I mentioned, who we have in custody.'

My heart sank. Up until then, I hadn't realised how much I was hoping he would be charged. Now I knew my attacker was still out there, I was suddenly filled with a sense of dread and foreboding.

I could hear dejection in my voice. 'So, what happens now?'

'We continue the investigation. We're doing everything we can to find the person that did this to you. It's a small island, and we're confident we'll find him.'

CHAPTER TWENTY-EIGHT

Two days later, I was sitting on top of the bedcovers, chatting with Julia, who was telling me how upset Josie was about the attack, when Doctor Gibson came in to see me. He stood by the bed, smiling broadly, looking pleased with himself, and I looked at him enquiringly.

'Well, Carol, good news. You're progressing well. You should be well enough to be discharged in the next couple of days or so. With some provisos, I'm happy to let you fly home to England.'

'Oh, that IS good news. I so want to go home.' I felt relief, albeit heavily tinged with anxiety about what might lie ahead. 'What are the conditions?'

'Firstly, I want a nurse to accompany you on the flight to the UK. To keep an eye on you. And the second condition is that as soon as you arrive in Newcastle, I want you taken straight to the RVI for a day or so. We need to be absolutely certain you've withstood the journey without any adverse effects.'

'That sounds fair enough,' I said. 'I just want to get away from what's happened here and try to put it all behind me.'

When Fiona learned that I was to be discharged, she told me that she was coming home with me. 'I've talked it over with Simon, and we both feel that I should be with you, for a while. Just until you are back on your feet and fully recovered. I'm not needed here – the restaurant is over-staffed as it is.'

The day before we left, DCI Brown came to see me again. I was sitting on the bed, checking my phone, when he walked in. He stood by the window, blocking out most of the sunlight, head tilted up, stroking his chin, absentmindedly.

'We'll be liaising closely with the police in Newcastle, keeping them informed of the progress of the investigation,' he began.

'How's it going?' I interrupted.

'I'm afraid we're not in a position to make an arrest at present. The DNA results have ruled out a number of potential suspects. But, the investigation is very much active and we're determined to find your assailant.' He took a seat near the end of the bed, straddling the chair, backwards, his large eyes concentrating on me. 'Carol, we need to know the minute your memory returns, as hopefully it will. The Newcastle police have told us they're appointing a Family Liaison Officer to you, once you're back home, so tell the officer as soon as you remember anything. Anything at all. Ok?'

'Yes of course. Lynn said you'd want to interview my ex-husband?'

'Quite possibly. We may need to speak to a number of people in the UK, in due course. Rest assured, we're doing all we can. Just so you know, once we do charge someone, it's likely to be necessary for you to come back to Barbados to give evidence.'

I nodded. I thought that might be the case, but I dreaded the thought of it.

CHAPTER TWENTY-NINE

We were preparing to leave for the airport; Julia was packing a few last minute things into a holdall she'd brought in for me, Fiona was busy checking the locker to make sure nothing had been missed.

Dr Gibson popped in to say farewell. 'Safe journey,' he said, shaking my hand, with both of his. 'Just want to wish you all the best for the future. And I hope you'll come back to visit this little island of ours again, some day?'

'We'll see,' I said, pretty sure that I'd never come back. I was sad to acknowledge to myself that this lovely place had now been spoiled for me forever. 'Thank you for all you've done for me.' I was feeling shaky and a bit disorientated, filled with mounting apprehension about the journey ahead of me.

'I've prescribed some strong sedatives, to help with the journey. Wanda will make sure you take them. You'll probably sleep for most of it.'

My flagging spirits were bolstered by the warmth from the various staff members who came to shake my hand or hug me and wish me well. Some even brought little gifts.

'They all think you've been a great patient, honey,' Wanda told me. 'Especially considering what you've been through.'

It felt strange to be going home, and although I really wanted to be back in Jesmond, I felt nervous and vulnerable, leaving the safety of the hospital and the reassuring presence of the staff. And so sad to be leaving Barbados in this way, all the happy memories shattered.

I noticed many curious looks as I was pushed through the airport in a wheelchair. Although my head was healing well, it was still a mess, attracting attention and making me feel self-conscious. It was a relief to get settled into my seat, and before long, I fell into a sound sleep, no doubt thanks to the sedatives.

Once we'd landed at Gatwick Airport early the following morning, we were taken by ambulance to Heathrow. Coming out of the airport in yet another wheelchair, I drank in the freezing cold air, so glad to be back in the UK. In the executive lounge, waiting for the connecting flight to Newcastle, I was disorientated and still rather woozy. Wanda fussed around, checking I was alright. I noticed Fiona and Julia looked tired, and realised what a strain all this must be on them too.

'You two look rough...' I began.

Fiona laughed. 'Well, thanks. You don't look too chipper yourself, babe.' We all laughed and the mood lightened considerably.

On arrival at Newcastle, I felt a huge sense of relief to be back home, even though it felt even colder there than in London. The broad Geordie accent of the attendant who helped me into a wheelchair was balm to my ears. But the relief at finally arriving home was suddenly shattered. As I was being wheeled through the terminal to the waiting ambulance, we were surrounded by a noisy bunch of reporters. Microphones were pushed under my nose and a babble of voices fired questions from all directions. I couldn't believe it. I wasn't aware I was news. How did they know when I'd be travelling home? And as a victim of a sex crime, surely I had a right to anonymity? Fiona and Julia were like tigresses, defending me, shouting at the reporters and physically pushing them away. It was a huge relief when the ambulance doors were closed and we had relative privacy. Julia sat close up beside me in the ambulance, and did her best to calm me as I sat shaking and crying.

They were clearly expecting me at the hospital; I was wheeled straight through to a private room, by the ambulance men, as if I were a VIP. Two nurses fussed around me, making sure I was comfortable, and I drank in the warming, familiar Geordie accents.

'The consultant will be here to see you soon,' said a petite blonde nurse.

I looked at my surroundings. Pastel blue walls formed the backdrop for a couple of attractive seascapes. Two striped blue and fawn over-stuffed chairs were arranged to one side, in front of a small, cream-painted coffee table, matching the bedside table. The large picture window, framed by dark blue drapes, looked out on to a neat garden, with walkways and benches. I imagined it would be lovely in the summer, with all the rose bushes in full bloom.

'This is a bit of all right, Mum,' Julia said, nosing around. 'Not like a hospital room at all. Look, there's an en-suite through here.'

I sank gratefully on to the single bed, closing my eyes for a second. There was a brief knock on the door, which opened to admit a middle-aged man, with short, dark hair, heavily streaked with white. He wore dark-framed glasses and a brown checked jacket.

'Mrs Barrington? I'm pleased to see you got here in one piece. I'm Ian Campbell, your consultant,' he held out his hand, peering at me over the rim of his glasses. 'How was your journey?'

I told him it was fine, that I'd slept most of the way.

'Dr Gibson has given me a full report and I'm very sorry to hear about everything you've been through. We're going to keep you here for a day or two; just under observation and to do some tests, check that everything's ok after the journey. Alright? For now, though, you need to rest. Get settled in and I'll come to see you again later.'

Although I'd slept for most of the flight over the Atlantic, I still felt exhausted after the long journey, and soon burrowed under the covers and slipped into oblivion.

It was about six in the evening when I woke up, to find a nurse by the bed with a welcome cup of tea. Wanda came and stayed with me for a while before it was time for her to leave. She was to stay overnight in a nearby hotel before catching an early flight to London, on the first leg of her journey home. I felt quite emotional at her departure, and said a tearful goodbye. She'd been there for me at my lowest ebb, and I felt a close bond with her.

'Honey, you're a strong lady. You will get over this, I just know it. I'm gonna keep in touch with you, to see how you're getting along.'

Not long after she left, there was a knock on the door and a woman of about forty, with bright red hair and heavy make-up, came into the room. She was accompanied by a younger woman.

'Hello, Carol. I'm DCI Patsy Mayne,' she said, briskly. 'This is DC Gayle Jones.' The younger woman smiled.

'The police in Barbados have been liaising with us about your case and now that you're back in the UK we're appointing Gayle here to be your Family Liaison Officer. I think the Barbados police mentioned this to you?'

I nodded. 'Yes, they did.'

Gayle smiled again, and I noticed she was attractive in a natural, no nonsense sort of way, with very short blonde hair emphasising her high cheekbones. About thirty-ish.

'The role of an FLO is to offer you support,' explained Gayle, playing with a filigree silver locket at her throat. 'And, I'll be acting as liaison between you and the police, both in Newcastle and Barbados. The Barbados police will keep us informed of any developments in their investigation, and of course we,' she looked towards DCI Mayne, 'will make them aware if anything changes at this end. Does that sound ok to you?'

I nodded. 'I've still got no memory of what happened to me.'

'So I understand. But the doctors say your memory could return, in time. Let's just see how things go. Now,' she said, sitting down on one of the chairs by the bed, 'your daughter's told me about the reporters at the airport. I don't want you to worry about it, I'll deal with them. I'm afraid your assault attracted quite a bit of local interest. Even, national. There've been articles in the papers and on TV.'

'How did they know I'd be on that plane?'

'They have their methods, unfortunately. They're like vultures once they get their claws into a story.'

'I don't want any publicity, I just want to get back to normal and get on with my life. Surely, they're not allowed to name me?'

DCI Mayne cut in. 'No, they're not allowed to identify victims of sexual assault. Or give information that could lead to you being identified. Unfortunately, other than identifying you, they will print any salacious detail they can get their hands on. Leave them to Gayle,' she said. 'She'll deal with them. She's good at that sort of thing.'

Gayle got to her feet. 'I'll pop in to see you again tomorrow, and every day for as long as necessary. In the meantime, if you need to speak to me about anything, just give me a call.' She handed me a card. 'My number's on there.'

The next morning, Mr. Campbell came to see me again. He reminded me very much of my late father; the same dark-rimmed glasses, the short greying hair and genuine smile.

'How are things today Carol?' he enquired, 'You certainly look a lot better.'

'I'm feeling much better, thanks. I think I must have been a bit jet-lagged yesterday.'

'Well, I'm pleased to tell you that you're recovering nicely. All the tests so far are satisfactory and your blood pressure is good. I'd say you've withstood the journey very well. I'd like to keep an eye on you for one more night, but I think we can safely let you go home tomorrow. However, I need you to promise me that, once you're home, you'll get plenty of rest. It's really important, to complete your recovery.'

'Oh, I will. It'll be a relief just to get home.'

Mr Campbell pulled a chair up, close to the bed, sat down and looked at me, with a serious expression.

'You're very fortunate that no permanent damage has been sustained to your head. I know you're still getting headaches, and some dizziness and this may continue for some time, but just take the painkillers as prescribed, when you need them. And it's really important that you don't miss any of your hospital appointments – we need to keep a close eye on you. With head injuries, on-going care and checks are really important. Remember, if you're worried about anything, just ring the hospital and we'll bring you straight in.'

'I understand,' I said, nodding.

'In time, your memory of the events of that night should return, but there's a possibility that it won't. It's possible you will never remember exactly what happened. It's different in every case. I don't want you to worry about it. Just wait and see what happens and try not to be anxious about it.' I nodded.

'Your other injuries are healing well. There was some infection, from the bites, but that's well under control. Make sure you complete the course of antibiotics and get plenty of rest. I expect you to make a full physical recovery in time. However, the emotional and psychological trauma is a different matter. Coming so closely on the heels of your earlier breakdown, after your husband's death, I'm concerned about your mental state, so I'm referring you to a psychiatrist and a counsellor as an urgent case.'

I was a bit caught off guard. 'Oh, I didn't realise you knew about that.'

'I've got your full medical history here. It would be difficult to make a valid assessment without it.'

'Well, I'm absolutely determined there's no way I'm going to go down that spiral again. It was the suddenness and the finality of Peter's death that hit me so hard. I think I'm normally a strong person. But I'd lost my soul-mate, and life just didn't seem worth living. This is different. I'm determined to deal with this head on. But, I'll be happy to see the psychiatrist and counsellor; I know I'll need some help.'

The, by now familiar, feeling of dread came over me again at the thought of leaving the sanctuary of the hospital. Of course I wanted to go home, but I was filled with trepidation about how things were going to work out. *Why oh why can't they find the person who attacked me?* I knew I would never be able to relax again until he was caught.

CHAPTER THIRTY

Driving home the following morning, Gayle at the wheel, I could see a bunch of people milling around the gates to my house.

'What the...' I began.

'They're reporters, Mum,' Julia's voice came from the back seat. 'They've been hanging around since you got back. I didn't tell you - I didn't want to worry you.'

I was dismayed. As Gayle slowed to turn into the drive, they surrounded the car, waving and shouting, banging on the window.

'Fucking reporters,' she muttered, driving slowly on. 'Excuse my French.'

'How the hell did they know I'd be coming home today?' Like sheep, they followed the car up the drive and as I tried to open the car door, they jostled to get near me, thrusting microphones under my nose, yelling questions. *Like a pack of wolves* I thought.

'How does it feel to be back home, Carol?'

'Are you ever going back to Barbados?'

'Who do you think attacked you?'

'Stay in the car. Close the door,' instructed Gayle. She got out, pushing bodies out of her way and used all her authority to round up the mob and order them back outside the gates. She promised to go back out and speak to them as soon as I was safely inside.

'Bloody animals,' she muttered, opening my door and ushering me in through the front door. 'Not my favourite people.'

I found Fiona and Pauline waiting for me inside; they fussed around as I sank on to a settee, shaking. Gayle went back outside to deal with the pack. Fiona went into the kitchen to make some coffee. Pauline hugged me like she would never let me go.

'It's so good to have you back home. We've all been so worried about you,' she said, indicating a pile of get well cards stacked on a side table. 'I was all set to come out to Barbados when I heard what had happened. I was trying to arrange a relief sub-postmaster to cover for me. But then Fiona told me you were out of the woods and making a good recovery. I've never been so relieved in all my life.' She hugged me again. 'I couldn't bear to lose my best friend.'

Just then, the front door slammed and Gayle came striding into the sitting room. 'I've made it perfectly clear that you won't be speaking to them. They're well aware they can't name you. I've given them a brief statement, so they've got something to print tomorrow and that's all they're getting for now. They're not allowed to come on to your property, so if they bother you after I've left, I want you to call me straight away. Ok?' I nodded and she went on. 'Purely as a precaution, and partly because of all the media attention, we're going to install some basic security equipment in the house. It's standard procedure, when a victim is in the spotlight, as you are. It should only be for a few days. I'm going to leave you now, give you a chance to settle in, but I'll be back later today with the technicians.'

True to her word, that afternoon, Gayle returned with two technicians who set to work installing panic alarms and setting up a direct line to the police station.

'If you're worried about anything at all, just activate the panic alarm and someone will be here within a few minutes. You've got my mobile number, too. Please don't hesitate to ring me if you have any questions, or are worried about anything.'

CHAPTER THIRTY-ONE

Julia came tentatively into my bedroom the next morning, carrying an armful of newspapers.

'Mum, are you sure you want to see these?' she asked, dropping the pile onto the bed. I had insisted that she get all the papers, much against her better judgement.

'You can't protect me from them, sweetheart. I need to see them.'

The headlines read ***Attack Victim returns from Barbados, Woman Returns to NE after Barbados Attack*** and in the less salubrious papers ***Back in the UK Attractive Widow Assaulted and Left for Dead in Island Paradise.***

I groaned when I read them. 'Bloody hell. I hate the way reporters try to milk the most emotional impact out of every situation. I hate being the focus of their attention.'

'At least they can't name you, Mum. No-one knows it's you they're talking about.' Julia tried to sound upbeat.

HE knows, though. I thought. *HE knows I'm back home now.* A terrifying thought.

Later, Gayle called in on her promised daily visit. This time she brought someone with her.

'Carol, this is Linda Wright of Victim Support. We always liaise with Victim Support in cases of violent crime. They offer a lot of help to victims and their families.' Gayle said, by way of explanation.

'Hello Carol,' Linda held out her hand. 'Nice to meet you.' Her handshake was firm, her gaze direct and friendly.

I studied her as we shook hands. She looked to be in her late forties.

Small and round, she had an open face, with an upturned mouth, rosy cheeks and wide blue eyes. I instinctively knew we'd get on well.

'I'm a trained counsellor with Victim Support,' she told me. 'We're not part of the police, but we do work closely with them. We're an independent charity, set up to help victims of violent crime. My role is to give you emotional and practical support. In other words, I'm here for you, whatever.'

'What kind of support?' I asked, intrigued, warming to her.

'Well, on the practical side, I can take you for all your hospital and other appointments. I can also help to keep any persistent reporters at bay. However, my most important role is to act as a sounding board for you and to be there for you, day or night. You need to know I'll always be on your side, Carol, no matter what.' She spoke in a soft Scottish brogue.

'That's good to know.' I meant it. It was a comforting thought.

'There's no further news from Barbados for now,' Gayle said, getting to her feet. 'I'll leave you and Linda to get acquainted. See you tomorrow.'

As I'd suspected, I found Linda a warm, empathetic person, a pre-requisite in her role, I supposed. I learned, in time, that she'd been raped at knifepoint, as a teenager, and it was that experience that ultimately led to her training as a counsellor and joining Victim Support.

We talked through what had happened to me.

'Feelings of shame and thinking that somehow you're to blame, are quite natural after what's happened to you, Carol, but I'm here to make sure you know that no fault whatsoever lies with you,' she told me.

'I don't know what I feel, Linda. I'm so full of mixed emotions. I'm horrified when I think of what happened, but I almost feel that it happened to someone else, not me. If that makes sense? Even though I was so badly hurt, it doesn't seem quite real. My Counsellor thinks I may be in some kind of shock. The psychiatrist suggested that because I've no memory of what took place, my mind hasn't yet fully registered the horror.'

'Well, if it does in the future, we'll face it together then.' Her tone was emphatic.

'I hoped the Barbados police had the attacker in custody, but they haven't – he's been ruled out. It's really scary, knowing that he's still out there. And all this publicity,' I indicated all the papers now lying on the coffee table, 'means he knows I'm back home. I'm scared, Linda.'

'Well, you're not facing this alone, dear. We're all here for you. In all likelihood, the person responsible is in Barbados and won't even see these newspapers, so try not to get too worked up about them.'

'Linda, would you have a word with Julia? She won't listen to me. Before I was attacked, she'd planned to spend a few days in Leeds with her friends and her boyfriend, before Christmas. Now, she thinks she needs to stay here with me. But she doesn't. She's put enough of her life on hold. I want her to go and enjoy herself. I've got plenty of support. Fiona's here most of the time, and Pauline comes most evenings after work. Then there's you and Gayle. I want Julia to be with her friends, having fun, a normal student life. She should go, and come back in time for Christmas. There's no point in her hanging around here. I'm fine now, but she won't listen to me.'

'Och, I'd be delighted to. You just leave her to me. I'll soon sort Julia out.' I smiled to myself at Linda's self-confidence. She seemed the sort who wouldn't let anything beat her and I felt safer when she was around.

I suspect it was with some relief that Julia made arrangements to return to Leeds, after Linda had spoken with her. I don't know what Linda said, but thankfully, it worked. I heard Julia on the phone to Oliver, excitedly making plans. The following day, before she left, she made me promise I would call her if I needed her. Both Linda and Gayle assured her they were available at any time, and she mustn't hesitate to call one or both of them if she needed to talk.

The relief I felt after Julia left, surprised me. I hadn't realised what a strain it had been, trying to be cheerful all the time in front of her. Now, I felt free to give in to my feelings, if I needed to. It was a cold, miserable day, when she left, and afterwards, when I was alone, I sat down at the bottom of the stairs and just howled. That's how Linda found me.

'It's good to be able to let go, when you need to, Carol,' Linda told me. 'Get it all out.'

Later, after the storm of emotion was over, I did feel calmer, but a bit embarrassed that Linda had witnessed it.

'That's what I'm here for. You're bound to have bouts like that. You've been through a hell of an ordeal and your emotions will be all over the place. But, you're a strong person – look how you got over your breakdown after losing Peter. You'll get through this, too.'

We walked through to the kitchen and I made some coffee. 'I feel so guilty about Peter. I think about it all the time, Linda.' She gave me an enquiring look and I told her about my hangover and not even saying goodbye or wishing him luck when he left. I started to cry again.

'Now you listen to me, Carol Barrington,' she said in the sternest voice I'd ever heard her use. 'Everyone feels guilty about something when someone close to them dies. So you had fun with your friends and had too much to drink? So what? He knows you loved him. A hangover is hardly the crime of the century. You said he kissed you on the head before he left? – that's what you should be remembering, not torturing yourself with feelings of guilt. It's not your fault that he died. You should remember all the good times with him. From what Fiona's told me, you brought him immense happiness after years of being in a miserable relationship – so think about that, instead of finding things to feel guilty about.'

Her words helped tremendously and in the weeks to come would prove a turning point in how I thought about Peter – instead of letting the guilt override all the good memories, I realised I had the power to put it to one side, where it belonged, and concentrate on the good things.

'I really must lose some weight,' commented, Linda, helping herself to a ginger snap and dunking it in her coffee. 'These don't count,' she said when she saw me looking. 'They're only about sixty calories,' she laughed. 'Tell me what happened.'

'Peter left early in the morning. He was picking up his mate, Charlie, Pauline's husband, and driving to the Lake District to meet up with the rest of their hiking group. They were doing a fund-raising challenge for charity; climbing Helvellyn.

The police came to the door that evening. They told me Peter had fallen on the descent. A Mountain Rescue helicopter had been scrambled, but paramedics had declared him dead at the scene.'

A deep breath, and I continued. 'I wouldn't believe it at first. I kept telling them they'd made a mistake, but of course they hadn't. It turned out the accident happened at a place called The Chimney. Charlie told me it's a well-known, tricky descent. The Patterdale Mountain Rescue team, recovered his body and took him to their headquarters overnight. Ready for transfer to the morgue at Carlisle, the next morning.'

'Did you have to go over there?' asked Linda, reaching for another biscuit.

'Yes. I had to identify his body. I needed to. I couldn't really believe he was dead until I'd seen for myself. Pauline drove me to Patterdale early the next morning. I remember it was still dark and freezing cold when we set off. All the way there, a voice in my head kept telling me there could have been a mistake and it might not turn out to be Peter after all.'

'I can understand that – clinging on to hope.'

'The journey was surreal. I remember dawn broke just as we reached Alston. After that, the view was breathtaking. Going down the hairpin bends, I could see the hills, all glowing pink, and I remember thinking, *How can there be so much beauty around when Peter's not here to see it? How can things go on as normal?* When we got near Patterdale, I suddenly saw Helvellyn ahead. It was like being physically punched, to see the mountain where he died.'

'God, that must have been awful,' Linda sympathised.

I nodded. 'When I saw the Mountain Rescue Centre, it looked so innocuous. Just a low building, nestling against the trees. Bathed in sunshine. I thought, *My Peter's body's lying in there.* I didn't want to go in. I didn't want my last hope taken away from me. A policeman took me into a small, bare room. I remember white walls and a patterned lino floor. Peter's body was lying on a narrow bed, covered with a white sheet. I couldn't bring myself to go near the bed, at first. I felt light-headed. Thought I was going to pass out. The policeman was kind. Told me to take my time, there was no hurry. Eventually, I went to the bed, and the policemen pulled the sheet back, and I looked at Peter.' I stopped.

'Go on, Carol,' said Linda quietly, putting her hand over mine.

'I'd been warned his face was badly damaged. But I still got a shock. It was such a mess. He looked nothing like the gorgeous man who'd left only the day before.' She squeezed my hand.

'It was heart-breaking, Linda. He was so cold. I wanted to climb on the

116

bed. Wrap myself round him. Warm him up. I told him over and over how sorry I was for not saying goodbye and how much I loved him. I could hardly bear to leave him there, alone. Eventually, I tucked the sheet more closely around his neck and kissed him one last time. When I left him there, I felt that my own life was over, too.'

'So sad, Carol. Here,' she said, handing me a tissue, wiping her own eyes at the same time.

'Charlie told us none of the team was with him when he fell; they'd all gone ahead. He was the last man and it wasn't until he didn't turn up at the rendezvous point that they realised something was wrong. By then it was too late.' I sniffed and wiped my eyes again.

'After the funeral, I was in a really bad way. Fiona stayed with me for a few months. She was a gem. Julia took time off Uni. Pauline was here, when she wasn't working - Charlie's away most of the time, working in Qatar, so she often stays here overnight. All my other girlfriends tried to help, calling in to see me, but very often I just sent them away. I didn't want to talk to people.' I stopped.

'Go on,' encouraged Linda. 'It's good for you to talk about it.'

'I was so depressed I couldn't get out of bed in the mornings. I just wanted to die and be with Peter. I would lie in bed, breathing in the scent of him from his clothes and his pillow. I honestly think, if I hadn't had Julia to live for, I would have ended my life then. I just couldn't see any point in going on. I started drinking heavily. Several bottles of wine a day. And vodka. I was completely out of control. I can see now that I really put Julia and Fiona through hell. Pauline too... But I just couldn't help myself.' Linda nodded,

'Looking back, I'm really ashamed of how weak I was. After all, people lose loved ones all the time, but they don't all give in to despair, like I did. But, I really couldn't help it. I had absolutely no control at all. It was frightening.'

'There's no need to be ashamed of anything. The whole point is, you really couldn't help it. And the important thing is, you got over it.' She covered my hand with hers. 'And you'll get over this too.'

'It's the unknown I'm scared of now, Linda. Who attacked me? Why? I wish the Barbados police could find who did it, so I can move on.'

CHAPTER THIRTY-TWO

On her way down the A1(M), Julia was looking forward to seeing Ollie and catching up with her friends. It would be so good to get back to normality. *Thank God for Fiona and Linda,* she thought, feeling guilty at her relief at getting away from the house. She loved her mother dearly, but the strain of it all was getting to her, too. There was nothing she could do or say to make things any better and, anyway, her guilt was assuaged by knowing she'd left her mum in good hands.

When she arrived at Oliver's place on the outskirts of Leeds, he must have spotted her from his window and rushed down the stairs from his first floor flat, because as soon as she stepped out of the car, he was there, sweeping her off her feet.

'Hi Babe. Missed you so much.' He showered her with kisses before swinging her round and round until she was dizzy. 'Come on, let's get your bag upstairs, hun.' He grabbed her holdall with one hand and put the other arm around her, nibbling her ear as they walked. 'We've got a few hours to kill, before we meet the others,' he told her as they walked up the stairs to the flat. 'I wonder how we can pass the time?'

Later, happy and sated, they lay in each other's arms, knowing they should start showering, both too lazy to move. Eventually, Ollie swung his legs over the side of the bed.

'Ok, lazybones, time to make a move. I'll shower first.'

She watched him as he crossed the room, admiring his rippling muscles. 'Mmm... lovely bum,' she observed, picking up her phone to WhatsApp the other girls. 'Oh, damn,' she cursed. 'Low battery.' Looking around, she found a charger and plugged the phone into the nearest socket. Spotting Oliver's phone on the bedside table, she picked it up, propped herself up on the pillows, and in no time was chatting with her flatmate, firming up on plans for that evening. Oh, it was good to be back in circulation.

He was taking ages in the shower. *What on earth does he do in there?* she wondered, impatiently. For something to do, she began to scroll through the photos on his phone. There were dozens of her and as she went through them she smiled, remembering the various places they'd been taken. She swiped to the next photograph, and froze, puzzled. It was a picture of her mother, lying in a skimpy bikini, by a swimming pool. She remembered it being taken two years ago on a holiday in Menorca. What was Oliver doing with a photo of her mum? She scrolled further, and was appalled to find more pictures of her mum. *What?*

She heard the bathroom door open, and watched as he came into the room, stark naked, towelling his hair, water dripping from his elbows.

'Why have you got pictures of my mum on your phone, Ollie?' she asked in a deceptively quiet voice. 'And where did you get them?'

'Oh,' he stopped dead, flushing, the hands drying his hair, frozen. 'It's nothing, Julia, honestly.'

'Go on.'

'I downloaded them from your phone. Look, it's nothing. It's just a lads' thing.'

'A lads' thing? What do you mean?'

'It's just a laugh. A few of us have got this sort of club – the MILF club and we just share a few pics amongst us.'

'M.I.L.F?' she spelled out, slowly. 'I don't fucking believe this. Mothers I'd Like to Fuck?'

'Yeah. You know what lads are like. There's no harm in it.'

She lost it. 'NO HARM in it?' she jumped up, yelling. 'My mother's just recovering from a horrific attack and you're sharing fucking pictures of her, in her fucking bikini, with your fucking mates. For a LAUGH?'

'Babe...'

'How long has this been going on?' she demanded. 'HOW LONG?' She was shaking with rage.

'I dunno, a few months... Most of the term.'

'The police are still looking for her attacker. They'll be very interested in this little group of yours.'

'Oh come on, babe... that's stupid.'

'Shut up,' she screamed. 'Just shut the fuck up.'

After hastily dressing, she grabbed her holdall, and began stuffing in the few things she'd already unpacked. 'You fucking moron. Dunno what the hell I ever saw in you.' She unplugged her phone and put it in her pocket.

He grabbed her arm. 'Don't go, babe. Let's talk this through.'

She snatched her arm away. 'Don't touch me,' she hissed through her teeth, heading for the door.

'Julia, please...'

'Consider yourself dumped. The police will be in touch.' She slammed the door as hard as she could on the way out and raced down the stairs.

Driving to see her friends in Halls, she could barely see where she was going for the tears in her eyes. Half way there, she pulled into a lay-by, switched off the engine and keyed in Gayle's number.

CHAPTER THIRTY-THREE

Two days after Julia left, I woke up suddenly in the early hours of the morning. I sat bolt upright in the dark, a feeling of terror overwhelming me. My heart was beating rapidly, my breathing laboured. My mind was reeling.

Oh my God. He was in the bathroom. Oh God... Talking to myself and fumbling for the bedside light, I screamed out for Fiona. She came stumbling in from the bedroom next door, pushing her hair out of her eyes.

'What is it? What's wrong?' She hurried towards me, looking puzzled. In panic, I grabbed her arm, shaking her, unwittingly digging my nails into her wrist.

'I saw him, Fiona! He was in the bathroom. I SAW him. He KNEW me. He said my name,' my voice was rising in hysteria. I shook her again. 'How could he know my name?'

'What? Have you had a nightmare?' she looked confused.

'NO.' I shouted. 'Not a nightmare. It was real. Oh God, he was there, standing in the dark, waiting for me...' My breath was coming in short gasps, making my chest ache. 'It was a flashback,' I gasped. 'My memory's coming back.'

'Bloody hell. Look, first you need to calm down. Hush. You're safe now. Come on; deep breaths. Breathe slowly.' Extricating her arm from my grip, Fiona put her hands on my shoulders, breathing slowly with me. 'In... and out... in...'

I did as she said and my breathing slowed a bit. 'It definitely wasn't a dream,' I gasped. 'I remember going into the bathroom and he was there. A dark shape. Waiting for me. I can't see his face... but he knew me, he knew my name! How could he know my name? I can hear his voice saying *"Hello Carol, I've waited a long time for this."'* My heart was thudding rapidly and I took a few more deep breaths, before continuing.

'He was well-spoken, very English. It wasn't a local man.' I felt panic building up again. 'Why would someone who knows me attack me?' I was shaking and shouting hysterically, my voice rising further, 'Who would do that to me?'

Fiona's arms were around me, holding me tightly until I'd quietened down a little. 'Try to stay calm. I'm going to ring Gayle.' She picked up my mobile from the bedside table.

My chest felt tight and I felt light-headed. I made myself sit on the side of the bed and take deep breaths, trying to stem the overwhelming feeling of terror building up inside me.

Fiona had got through to Gayle. 'I'm sorry to ring you in the middle of the night, but Carol's in a state. She's having flashbacks. She remembers the man who attacked her was in the bathroom and he knew her name.' Fiona listened for a few seconds, before putting the phone down. 'She's coming straight over. She said just try to keep calm 'til she gets here.'

Gayle, arrived within half an hour or so, looking pale and tired in hastily pulled on jeans and sweater, under her navy parka.

'It's bloody freezing,' she complained, wrapping her arms around herself. We were in the sitting room by then, huddled in front of the gas fire, both wrapped in warm dressing gowns. Gayle listened carefully as I told her what had happened.

'Could you see his face?' she asked, taking notes.

'No... just the silhouette. But I heard his voice. He sounded well-spoken... He knew me, knew my name...How does he know my name?' my voice was rising again.

'Describe exactly what you can remember. What sort of build is he?'

As I pictured the scene in my mind, I felt again the wave of pure terror that must have hit me when I'd entered the bathroom. My heart began to race again, my hands shaking.

'He was big... at least six feet, probably more. And broad... Powerfully built.'

'And his voice? Does it sound like anyone you know?'

'It seems familiar; I can hear it, but I just can't place it...'

'What exactly did he say?' Gayle's voice was calm, professional, whereas I wanted to scream.

I could hear him in my head, clear as a bell. 'He said "Hello, Carol, I've waited a long time for this." He's English.'

'It's possible this could have been a bad dream. How sure are you that it's a real memory of the attack?'

'I know it wasn't a dream. It was a flashback. I heard him. I saw him.' I was agitated. She *had* to believe me.

'We'll certainly treat this as a genuine memory and inform the Barbados police immediately. They'll take it from there.'

'But, won't you investigate over here, too?' I asked. 'He knows me. He could even live nearby... you've got to find him.' There was urgency in my voice.

'We don't have jurisdiction to investigate the attack itself, Carol. The crime was committed in Barbados. Of course, we'll give every assistance to the Barbados police. In all likelihood, they'll send their own officers over here to investigate further.'

'I'm scared, Gayle. Really scared. How did he know me? Surely this means it wasn't a random attack, carried out by some local person? He was English. He knew me. He must have targeted me.' I could feel hysteria rising in me again at this sinister thought.

'Rest assured, Carol, if anything happens over here, we'll be straight on to it. Meanwhile, try to stay calm. I'll let you know what the Barbados police intend to do.' She stood up to leave. 'It'll be late morning before I come back to you, because of the time difference.'

After Gayle left, Fiona insisted we both go back to bed and try to get a few more hours rest. It was still the middle of the night. She got into my king-size bed with me, and was soon fast asleep. But sleep wouldn't come to me. I lay in a state of terror for the rest of the night, curled into a ball, convinced there was someone out there who was watching me.

CHAPTER THIRTY-FOUR

Early the following morning, at Fiona's insistence, we drove down to Whitley Bay to walk on the beach. It had been raining during the night and walking in the Dene, which I loved to do, would have been a muddy affair. I was feeling washed-out but restless after the previous night, so the idea of getting some fresh air appealed. And, as Fiona reminded me, Linda was forever emphasising how important exercise is in the healing process, so she was on a mission to ensure I had a long walk each day.

I'd been brought up in Whitley Bay and over the last thirty years or so, had witnessed the deterioration of the town centre and sea front. Once a thriving seaside town, it had gone the way of many such places, following the growth of foreign holidays. My mother used to tell me about the halcyon days of the town, when the beach was teeming all summer with thousands of holiday makers, the sand dotted with square green tents and striped deck chairs. Shuggy boats, roundabouts and donkey rides were just some of the attractions for children. All gone, now. But, thanks to lottery funding, re-generation was, somewhat belatedly underway, with the refurbishment of the promenade and The Dome, a well-known iconic landmark. At last, things were beginning to look up for the town.

Normally, the beauty of the North East coast, from Tynemouth, through to Cullercoats, Whitley Bay, and right up to Bamburgh and the Farne Islands, teamed with the spectacular countryside of Northumberland, filled me with a deep sense of gratitude that such unspoilt wonders were on my doorstep, but that day much darker thoughts were swirling around in my head.

The morning was dry and sunny, with a light but sharp breeze coming off the sea. The tide was on its way out, revealing many rock pools, and I could smell the salty tang of seaweed. I breathed in deeply, savouring the smells of my childhood. Although cold, it was quite a lovely day for mid December and walking by the sea would have been pleasant, but for the sense of doom hanging over me. I found myself checking behind, every so often, to make sure there was nobody following us. *God, I'm getting paranoid.*

At first, as if by common consent, we walked in silence, each lost in our own thoughts, our fleece-lined jackets keeping the cold wind at bay. We headed for St Mary's Island, with its tall, picturesque lighthouse. The island always brought back fond memories of the past, of idyllic days spent there with a close friend, when we were young, but today I barely noticed it. I was mentally scanning through the names of people I knew, seeking some clue as to who could have wished to harm me, trying to put a face to the voice.

After a while, I turned to Fiona 'You believe me, don't you Fi? You don't think I was just having a bad dream, do you?'

Fiona bit her lip, shaking her head. 'Of course I believe you. I saw the state you were in last night when you shouted for me. But, I don't understand why you think he's here? If you're right about him being English, isn't it equally possible, more likely really, that it's someone from here, who knows you, but lives in Barbados? Otherwise, this person would have had to follow you out to Barbados, and I don't really think that's likely, do you?'

'I just don't know. I'm going mad trying to work things out. All I'm certain of is, it was definitely a flashback. He knows me; he knew I'd be there. The words he said, *I've waited a long time for this*, mean he must have planned it. And he's definitely English. I just have the strongest feeling that he's from here. I wish I could see his face! Why can I hear his voice, yet not recognise it? It's so frustrating.'

'Do you think it might help to talk things through with Linda? I think we should call her when we get back.'

'Yes, and hopefully there might be some word from Barbados.'

We were silent for a while, watching a golden retriever frolicking on the sand. He ran into the sea, then lay down flat in the water, a look of ecstasy on his face as the waves washed over him. You could almost hear him sigh with pleasure. The North Sea in December is freezing, so he obviously didn't feel the cold. He came out of the sea and bounded towards us, nudging the pocket of my jacket for non-existent treats, before shaking himself, spraying us with water and sand.

'Thanks, mate,' cried Fiona, laughing and brushing water and sand from her trousers.

'I've been thinking,' I resumed our conversation, 'I wonder if it might be a good idea to hire a private detective? He could actively investigate over here, where the UK police can't. Might be worth a try? If he comes up with anything concrete, he could pass it on to the police here, for them to pass on to Barbados. What do you think?' I asked, turning to look at Fiona.

'Actually, I've been thinking along the same lines myself. Unless the Barbados police send people over right away.'

We climbed the steps from the beach to the cliff top, the exertion making me slightly breathless. 'Doing nothing is just not an option. I've got to do something… I'll speak to Gayle this afternoon and see what she thinks. I'm also thinking of going to see a hypnotherapist to see if my memory can be recovered that way.'

'Oh, I've read about that going horribly wrong,' Fiona frowned. 'Be careful. I think they sometimes dredge up memories that are not actually there?'

'Anything's worth a try. I refuse to just do nothing and wait for him to attack me again. I'm going to get a Mace spray on the internet. And I'm going to carry a knife everywhere I go.'

'Carol!' exclaimed Fiona. 'You can't do that. It's against the law.'

'I don't care. If I have to defend myself, I'm going to be prepared.' Fear made me defiant.

Fiona shook her head in disagreement, but didn't say any more on the subject. We reached the causeway, on either side of which, families were exploring the newly-revealed rock pools, looking for crabs and other creatures. Every so often a child shrieked in delight when they caught something alive in their fishing net. I breathed in deeply, again, savouring the evocative smells.

As we approached the island, I showed Fiona the cottage where I used to stay, with my friend. 'That's the window of the bedroom where I used to sleep,' I said, pointing to the dormer window on the right of the red shingle roof of the cottage. 'I used to lie in bed, watching the light from the lighthouse sweeping past, like a searchlight. Pity the cottage has new owners now, or we could have had a look round it – it's a quaint old building.'

We contented ourselves by making a circuit of the small island, inadvertently startling a few seals basking on the rocks. They quickly scampered back into the sea, when they caught sight of us. A few other visitors were wandering around, chatting, laughing, enjoying the sunny morning, seemingly without a care in the world. I envied them.

As we started back over the causeway, I returned to our conversation. 'I keep wondering, how did the attacker know I would be in Barbados? How did he know I'd be by myself? Something just doesn't add up.'

'I'm with you there. The flashbacks have opened up a whole new can of worms.'

We retraced our steps along the promenade and back down on to the beach again. Gulls swooped and screeched overhead, so loud at times that conversation was almost impossible, and we walked in silence for a while. We came across the golden retriever again; he was a real beauty with a very pale, almost white, coat and big black eyes. He greeted us like long lost friends, wagging his tail and nudging us, sniffing our pockets again, still hopeful of getting something to nibble. I squatted down and gave him a cuddle, lost for a few seconds in the comforting warmth of his soft, albeit wet, fur.

I was deep in thought, as we walked on. Was it possible that someone went to the trouble of deliberately following me out to Barbados with the intention of attacking me? Who would do that? And why? I wasn't aware of having any enemies; why on earth would anyone want to target me? Yet, it had to have been planned. What else could *I've waited a long time for this* mean? It was a chilling thought, and I felt a tight knot of fear grip my stomach. I desperately hoped I was wrong, but a voice in the back of my head was telling me I was right, and I'd learned to trust my instincts over the years.

CHAPTER THIRTY-FIVE

On her way to see the DCI, Gayle was deep in thought. She'd got to know Carol quite well, and knew her to be level-headed and sensible. What if she was right? If her attacker had a 'cultured English accent' and also knew Carol's name, then it was entirely possible he lived in the UK. On the other hand, she reasoned, he could equally be an ex-pat, living in Barbados.

'What are your thoughts, Gayle?' asked DCI Patsy Mayne, once Gayle had relayed the details.

'Well, Carol Barrington's a credible person,' she began, playing with her locket. 'She's in no doubt that it's her memory returning. Based on the accent she remembers, and the fact that her assailant knew her, she's convinced her attacker lives here in the UK. She wants us to investigate over here. I've explained about lack of jurisdiction, but told her we'll work closely with Barbados.'

'It's the only course of action we can take for now. I'll give DCI Brown a call right away. Let's see what they've got to say. They'll probably send some of their people over here.' She picked up the phone.

Later, Gayle visited Carol again and brought her up to date. 'They're sending a couple of officers over, immediately. They'll be here within the next two days.'

'Thank goodness,' said Carol, playing with a tendril of hair, twirling it round her finger, before tucking it behind her ear. 'Actually, Gayle I was going to suggest that I hired a private detective to investigate over here... but if the Barbados police are coming over, I don't suppose there's anything to be gained?'

Gayle was clearly not impressed, and answered quite sharply.

'Nothing at all. In any event, a private detective would only get in the way of the investigation. I can't see that anything useful would be achieved by hiring one. And it could potentially do a lot of harm. The Barbados police are carrying out a thorough investigation. There's really no need for anyone else to be involved.'

'Well, thank God they're coming over. I need to know something is being done here,' Carol paused before continuing. 'I'm also thinking of seeing a hypnotherapist, to see if my full memory can be recovered by that method. What do you think?'

Gayle sighed. 'Again, not a good idea. It can be a very risky thing to do. On top of that, any 'evidence' found under hypnosis would be most unlikely to be accepted by a court of law. It would be strongly objected to by the defence. On balance, I think it would do more harm than good.'

'Well, I need to do something positive, Gayle. I refuse to cower in the corner, just waiting for him to get me.' Carol sounded obstinate.

Gayle hoped Carol wouldn't take her idea of seeing a hypnotherapist any further, but suspected she might. She'd developed a liking for Carol, admiring her strength in dealing with the attack, and her determination now not to sit back and be a victim. Having gone to pieces when she lost Peter, she seemed to have gained some inner strength that was helping her to cope now, with what, after all, would have completely demolished most people. Gayle hypothesised that because Carol had ultimately come through the worst thing that could happen to her - losing Peter - she had somehow gained the ability to deal with anything else life threw at her. *I should have been a psychologist* she thought.

CHAPTER THIRTY-SIX

'Dusty? Hi, it's Tim. How are you?' Tim had christened me Dusty years ago, when he found out my maiden name had been Miller.

'Tim! How lovely to hear from you. I'm good thanks, what about you?' I was so pleased to hear his familiar voice.

Tim had kept in touch, and visited me fairly regularly since Peter died. He and Peter had been like brothers, and Tim was devastated at his loss. He told me he still suffered nightmares about that day on Helvellyn. As leader of the hiking group, he felt an overwhelming sense of responsibility for Peter's death. Charlie had said much the same thing, and I told Tim what I'd told him, that neither of them was to blame. There was nothing anyone could have done to prevent it. The group had collectively agreed to descend Helvellyn by the more difficult route over Striding Edge, as opposed to the less exposed Swirral Edge. They were all experienced hill walkers and wanted to take the more challenging route. Tim could not have foreseen that Peter would lose his footing on the infamous Chimney descent and plunge off the ridge to his death.

'Will you be in this evening? I thought I might pop by to see how you're doing, on my way back from the office. About eighteen hundred hours – I mean six o'clock?'

'Yeah, I'll be here. Look forward to seeing you.'

He arrived on the dot of six and I remembered Peter telling me that Tim was the most punctual person in the world, probably due to the twelve years he spent in the Royal Air Force. A very tall man, he stood about six feet four, with short brown hair, slightly peppered with grey strands. Always smart, this time he was wearing a beautifully cut pale grey suit with a crisp white shirt and red tie. He was quite handsome, with aquiline features, and despite having left the RAF some ten years or so ago, still had a military bearing.

He seemed quite emotional to see me. We hadn't met up since the events in Barbados, although he'd phoned and sent flowers. He hugged me warmly, then stood back to examine my face, tentatively tracing the still livid scars with one finger, concern written all over his face.

'You poor thing, Dusty. I just can't believe what shit you've been through this past year or so. It's more than most people could stand. How on earth are you coping with it all?' He looked shaken at the sight of me.

'Oh, I'm getting by. Come and have a seat and I'll get us a drink.' I poured two large G&T's and we sat for a while, by the garden windows, catching up on things. Tim told me the group had resumed their regular hikes once again, after a long gap following Peter's accident, when they hadn't had the heart to go on meeting up every two weeks as though nothing had changed. A couple of members had moved away or dropped out for other reasons, but most of 'Team Ryan' was intact, he told me.

'We're planning another fundraiser in three weeks. Snowdonia, this time, but it won't be the same without Peter. He was such a character, larger than life; he's a real miss.'

'He would want the group to carry on, Tim. The fundraising's for such a good cause. It's been over a year now, although sometimes I still can't believe he's gone. When I wake up in the morning, just for a few seconds I feel happy, then it all comes flooding back…' To my surprise, my bottom lip was trembling and Tim jumped up and came to sit beside me. He took my hands in his.

'You've been through such a lot. It's just not bloody fair. As if losing Peter wasn't bad enough, some bloody maniac attacks you just as you're putting your life back together! How are you really coping? The truth now.' He looked at me intently.

His face was full of concern and suddenly, unbidden, I started to cry. *I can deal with anything except sympathy and kindness* I thought. Then, I took a deep breath and words just poured out of me. I told him about the flashbacks; my belief that the attacker knew me, and spoke perfect English; my fear that he might come back to finish the job.

Tim looked quite shaken, and put his arms around me, holding me to him until I'd calmed down, I fished a tissue from my sleeve, and wiped my eyes, then blew my nose.

'What have the police got to say about all this? Surely they can offer you some protection?' he asked, sitting back, playing with the signet ring he always wore on his right hand.

'Some officers are coming over from Barbados. It's their case, so the hands of the UK police are tied, apparently - lack of jurisdiction. But, the police here have put some security measures in place. They decided to do that when I was discharged from the RVI, because my case attracted so much media interest. You should have seen all the reporters hanging around outside.' I took a sip of my drink. 'They're going to keep the security in place until things are resolved. I've got a couple of panic buttons, with a direct line to the police, and I already have security lights and cameras in place at both the front and back of the house.'

'Well, that's something,' Tim pursed his lips, sounding relieved. 'They must be taking this threat very seriously. They don't use expensive manpower for nothing.'

'Yes, they're giving me a lot of support. They've assigned an FLO - a Family Liaison Officer to look after me; Gayle. She's a great help. She comes to see me every day and I can contact her any time. Also, Linda comes most days. She's a counsellor with Victim Support and she's lovely. Pauline often stays, and Fiona's staying with me for as long as I need her, so I'm not on my own. Julia was here, but thankfully we persuaded her to go and spend some time with her friends.'

'How is she coping with all this?'

'She's better for being away from things for a while. It's been so hard on her.'

'And where's Fiona? It's ages since I've seen her?'

'She's gone to see her mother. She'll be back soon.'

'I'm glad to hear she's staying with you. I don't like to think of you on your own, especially now.'

'I've made an appointment to see a hypnotherapist tomorrow, to see if my memory can be recovered that way.' I told Tim. 'Gayle's advised against it, she says any evidence gathered that way would be inadmissible. But I think it's worth a try. If I do remember who did it, I'm sure enough evidence will be found to take him to court. I need to know who did this to me. Pauline's going with me.'

'Really?' Tim's eyebrows shot up. 'Well, let's hope it produces some results. You must let me know. And you are aware that if there's anything at all I can do to help, you just have to ask.'

With that, he gave me a huge hug and a peck on the cheek and took his leave.

Soon after I'd shown him out, Fiona returned, grumbling about her mother, as usual.

'She always picks fault with me. I don't know what's wrong with her. Tonight, she's blaming me for Jack staying in Barbados for so long. Like, Hello? How's that my fault? I'm not even there. Oh, she does irritate me. Can you wonder I don't want to stay with her?'

'Well, do you feel better for getting that off your chest?' I asked, laughing, and she began to laugh too. 'Time for another G and T.'

CHAPTER THIRTY-SEVEN

The man made his way stealthily through the trees. Enough light filtered through the overhead branches from a nearly-full moon to aid his progress. He knew he was taking a big risk, with Fiona still there with her, but he couldn't wait. Her full memory could return at any time, and then she would be lost to him forever. Since finding out that she was still alive, she had been all he could think of. Thoughts of her were all-consuming.

Dressed in black, he felt like a commando on manoeuvres, as he crept through the trees at the back of the houses. At the thought of seeing Carol again, he felt a surge of adrenalin.

Soon, peering through the bushes, he could see the house, set back about fifty feet from the fence. The lights were still on, so they hadn't gone to bed yet. Cautiously he made his way up the side fence, where the trees and shrubs provided the thickest cover. His plan was to scale the fence then hide in the shrubs until all the lights were out and the house quiet. He would leave it an hour before making his move. Then he would break in through the side door, into the garage and then into the house. He had chloroform to deal with Fiona, but Carol he was planning to take his time with. He got a hard-on just thinking about her.

That morning, when Carol and Fiona were on the beach, he'd paid a visit to the house and disabled the security light at the back, so he was confident he wouldn't trigger the motion sensor. With no nosy neighbours to worry about, it had been almost too easy to scale the fence, get into her garden and work on the lights, undisturbed. He'd worn a plastic mask of an old man's face, just in case he was caught on camera, but he was pretty certain he'd avoided it.

This time, wearing his black balaclava, he peered over the fence. Through the shrubbery he could see the two women, sitting in the conservatory. Carol was using her hands, in that way she had, to emphasise a point she was making. He hoped they'd be going off to bed soon. It was past their usual bedtime. After watching them for a few minutes, he decided to get into position. Confident he couldn't be seen in the darkness, he scaled the fence, intending to wait in the dense shrubbery on the other side. Suddenly, he heard a click and the garden was lit up, as bright as daylight.

SHIT. He froze, then scrambled back the way he'd come, hoping they hadn't seen him. Hurrying back through the trees, tripping over roots in his haste, he retraced his steps to the street and the safety of the car, pulling off his balaclava as he went. On reaching the street, he slowed down to a walking pace, inwardly cursing. I must have missed a second security light. I'm getting careless in my old age. Shit, shit, shit.

CHAPTER THIRTY-EIGHT

We were sipping our drinks. Adele's 21 was streaming loudly and Fiona was singing her heart out.

'*Never mind, I'll find someone like you,*' she warbled. '*I wish nothing but the best for youoo...*' Suddenly the floodlight came on outside, lighting up the garden as bright as day. Fiona swore and jumped to her feet, eyes like saucers, pointing into the garden.

'Bloody hell,' she yelled. 'I'm sure I saw someone... in the bushes..'

'Where?' I leapt to my feet, peering into the garden. 'Are you sure? I can't see anything?'

'There,' she said, pointing to the shrubbery on the right hand side of the garden. 'I'm sure I saw something move. I think I saw a figure.'

'Could it have been an animal? We've got a lot of foxes around here.' I studied the bushes, desperately hoping it was only an animal.

'Well, I definitely saw movement.' She pointed to the bushes again, her hand shaking.

I reached for my mobile and hit the key to connect with the special number the police had given me to guarantee a rapid response. Within five minutes, two officers were checking the garden and searching around the dene, only to confirm that the intruder, if indeed there had been one, was long gone.

'No sign of anyone, love. No footprints, nothing. Could've been a fox. Let's have a look at the CCTV.' We moved into the sitting room to watch the footage. The screen showed some movement of the shrubbery near the side fence, but there was no clear image and it was impossible to tell whether it was an animal or a person.

Worryingly, though, the security men told me they'd discovered that it looked as though the cable to one of the security lights had possibly been tampered with.

Gayle arrived a little later, having been alerted by her colleagues, and joined us in the sitting room. Taking out her notebook, she asked Fiona to describe exactly what she'd seen. Fiona, still a bit shaken, repeated what she'd told me.

'So, you can't be sure it was a person?' Gayle probed.

'Well, I assumed it was. The light came on and I saw movement in the bushes.'

Gayle went into the hall to speak with her boss on her mobile, then came back into the sitting room.

'Right, Carol. It may be nothing, but as a precaution, this is what we propose to do now. We're going to assume that there may be a threat, because of the possible tampering of the security light. So, we're going to have someone check the security lights around the house every day, starting tomorrow. If it was an intruder, he's probably been scared off for now and may lie low for a while, but if he's planning to come back, we'll know about it in advance.'

'Oh, heavens.' I was a bit taken-aback.

'We'll get the checks in place and monitor the situation thereafter. Are you ok with that?'

'Yes… but… what happens if the lights are tampered with again?'

'We'll put a plan of action in place if that happens. In the meanwhile, you've still got the panic alarms and you know the number to call in the event that you need to. These are just precautions. It might all be for nothing,' Gayle said. 'It could have been a fox or something else in the undergrowth. Animals are always triggering security lights – and damaging cables for that matter. But, better safe than sorry.'

CHAPTER THIRTY-NINE

He watched and listened as they all talked things through after his little mishap. The Fiona woman hadn't actually seen him, and no-one was sure that it wasn't an animal that had triggered the motion sensor. He was kicking himself for missing the second security light. It wasn't like him to be so careless. He would lay low for a while, then take care of the lights properly. Meanwhile, he would monitor the cameras round the clock to ensure they weren't on to him. He couldn't be sure what was being said away from the conservatory – if only the fucking camera in the sitting room hadn't fucking packed up. He banged his hand down, hard, on to his desk, in frustration.

The Victim Support woman, Linda, was a frequent visitor, calling to see Carol almost every day, it seemed. Oh they did have some cosy little chats together. Linda was very good at drawing people out. He was fascinated by all the emotion she drew out of Carol, how she got her to bare her soul about her fears, and how much she still missed her husband. He was still none the wiser as to why she'd chosen to marry such an old man. True, he was very rich, but she wasn't doing too badly herself, so she didn't really need his money. He would never understand how she could throw herself away on him.

Most of the chatting seemed to take place in the Garden Room (as Carol called it; to him it was a Conservatory) and he was relieved the camera in there was still working. With the one in the sitting room no longer operational, his eavesdropping would have been up the spout if that one hadn't been in place.

He watched as the FLO came and went each day, but didn't catch any further mention of his last aborted visit. All seemed to be quiet on the western front, and he decided it would soon be safe to pay a return visit.

He was amused when he heard that the Barbados police were on their way over. Good luck to them, he thought to himself. Bring it on.

CHAPTER FORTY

Early the following morning, I got a call from DCI Louis Brown. He and DI Phillips had arrived at Gatwick, from Barbados, and were on their way to Heathrow to catch their connecting flight to Newcastle.

'We'll need to catch up with the Newcastle guys first,' he said in his deep voice. 'Then we'll need a few hours rest. Could we meet up early evening, say six-ish? We'll come to your house if that's ok?'

Later that afternoon, I drove to Whickham, with Pauline, to keep my appointment with the hypnotherapist. I was filled with trepidation as we approached his consulting rooms, which were located above a solicitor's office, just off the main road. I was sick with nerves at the thought of identifying my attacker, and gripped Pauline's arm as we walked.

We located the correct entrance from a brass plaque at the side of the doorway, which proclaimed *A E Blacker, CMH MPNLP*. After climbing a set of steep, rather narrow stairs, we found ourselves in a small, brightly lit reception area where I gave my name to an elderly lady, sporting a purple curly perm. In a soft Geordie accent, she asked us to take a seat while she buzzed through to let Mr Blacker know his patient had arrived. Moments later a door was opened on the far side of the room and Mr. Blacker emerged.

'Good afternoon, ladies,' he greeted us with a beatific smile. I saw a portly, late middle-aged gentleman with round, pink cheeks above a grey and white streaked beard. I thought he looked rather like a garden gnome as he ushered us through into a large, airy room.

He invited Pauline to sit in a chair in a corner of the room, and said he was quite happy for her to remain to observe the session. His friendly and reassuring manner was soothing and I began to feel I was in good hands and relaxed a little.

It was all very strange. After the preliminaries, during which I gave him the background and told him what I wanted to achieve, most of which we'd gone through on the phone when I first made the appointment, he asked me to take a seat in a reclining dentist-type chair.

Once settled in the chair, I looked around the rather dull room. Drab sage green walls were the backdrop for a couple of grey filing cabinets, next to which stood a lovely antique oak desk, eighteenth century if I wasn't mistaken, with leather inlay on the top and carved legs. I met Pauline's gaze and she stuck her tongue out at me, trying to make me giggle to lighten the mood. It worked.

Mr Blacker sat himself down in a low, burgundy leather chair, next to me.

'No need to be nervous,' he said in his mellifluous tones, noticing my shaky hands. 'You've come to me for help, so let's see what we can do.' Smiling reassuringly, he asked me to close my eyes and relax back into the chair, which I did.

In a quiet, soothing voice, he took me right back to my birth, telling me to be proud of my enormous achievement in being conceived in the first place He told me the sperm that helped make me was the fastest swimmer out of millions of sperm, all competing for the same egg. So, against all the odds, I had been born.

'That means we're all born winners,' he told me. 'We've beaten all the odds and we're here.' His voice held a note of joy at this wonder.

I was vaguely aware of being in the present, in his room, and of Pauline sitting quietly in the corner, yet I wasn't there completely. My mind was going to strange places. He gradually brought me forward, in stages, through my life until we reached the events in Barbados. I talked about waving Fiona off, then going back down the steps, then standing by the sea wall, watching the moon and the fishing boats bobbing in the sea. Then... feelings of agitation and panic... I knew I was lashing out but couldn't control myself... then I found myself returning to the present. I could hear Mr Blacker's soothing voice, waking me, reassuring me. His gentle, professional manner had the effect of quickly banishing my agitation, and soon my heartbeat returned to normal.

'We can try again in a few days, if you want to, Carol,' he told me, once I was calm and fully awake. 'But I don't think it's going to work for you. Sometimes the brain doesn't want you to remember something because it's too traumatic for you to deal with. My honest opinion is that you should let things take their course. If your memory is to return, it will do so in its own time. And if it never returns, so be it.'

I felt despondent and disappointed, yet, paradoxically, relieved that I didn't have to face the truth just yet. Pauline held my arm as we returned to the car.

'That was so frightening, watching you. Everything was fine until you got to the part where you were standing at the sea wall. Then you got very upset. You were screaming and thrashing about, obviously terrified.' Pauline stopped walking and turned to face me, 'Please tell me you're not going to try again.'

'Screaming? I didn't realise. But the feeling of terror was so awful. I don't want to go through that again. So, I think I'll take his advice and leave it alone.'

'Phew. Thank God for that,' Pauline wiped her brow with a dramatic gesture. 'I couldn't go through that again. Now let's just get you home. I think we could both do with a strong cup of coffee.'

Just after six, a white Nissan crunched up the drive, and I watched from the window as DCI Brown unfurled his long legs as he emerged from the car, and stood up to his full, impressive height. Wearing a dark short overcoat, a striped scarf around his neck, he looked good. I felt a frisson of interest, the first since Peter.

'Hello, Carol,' said Louis, when I answered the door. 'Good to see you looking well. I think you've met DI James Phillips?'

'Of course. Hi James. Please come in.' I opened the door wide and felt the icy blast of the December air rush in. 'Cold enough for you both?' I asked as I led them through to the sitting room. Fiona had taken the opportunity to go out with Pauline and a few other girlfriends. I would have liked to have joined them; have a normal night with the girls, for once. It felt like ages since I'd had fun.

'I must say, you're looking a lot better than you did the last time we saw you,' said the DI. 'How are you coping?'

'Well, I'll cope much better once you've caught whoever did this to me,' I touched the scar on my face, flinching slightly at the feel of it. I noticed Louis staring at me and caught a fleeting glimpse of something - compassion? interest? pass briefly across his face.

'Well, that's what we intend to do,' said the DI. 'Do you mind if we ask you some more questions?'

'Would you like coffee before we start?'

Once we were seated, with steaming mugs of coffee in front of us, DCI Brown spoke. 'The team at Newcastle have kept us up to date with events over here. So, can you tell us about your flashbacks, Carol? We understand you've had two now?'

I explained about the first flashback, which had woken me up. 'And then it happened again, when I was walking on the beach, the same flashback. I could suddenly see the silhouette of a man in the bathroom in the villa. It was terrifying.' I went on to describe it in detail.

'So you still can't see him, or recognise his voice?'

'No. I wish I could. Against Gayle's advice, I saw a hypnotherapist today, but it didn't help. Too traumatic. I freaked out and the hypnotherapist had to bring me out of it straight away. So, I'm no further forward I'm afraid.' I saw them exchange a glance, before the DCI spoke.

'Hypnotherapy doesn't always work, and I'm with Gayle on this one. It can be quite a dangerous thing to do. I hope you're not going to try again?' He sounded quite stern.

'Well, I thought it was worth a try,' I said, feeling like a naughty schoolgirl.

'Going back to the flashbacks,' the DCI began, subtly changing the subject. 'If they're accurate, the perpetrator is quite tall, well-built and English-speaking. We're planning to interview a number of people from your contact list whilst we're over here, and we'll be asking everyone for voluntary DNA samples. The local boys are going to help us. It's looking more than likely that the perpetrator was not local to Barbados, which backs up your belief that it's someone from England.

We've now ruled out most of the people interviewed in Barbados. We believe it's possible that you were followed out there, perhaps by someone using a false passport.'

'Your former husband sounds a strange character,' said the DI. 'Is there any possibility, in your mind, that it could be him?'

'I didn't think him capable of violence like that. But, Gayle's told me he has a conviction for GBH, from way back. I wasn't aware of that.'

'That apart, he is ex-SAS. He can hardly be sweetness and light. Anyway, he's the first on our list to interview. What about your business partner, Rupert, what's he like?' he pushed his hair out of his eyes.

'Well... he's gay, so he certainly wouldn't be interested in me, sexually.'

The DCI took over, 'You've had some time now to think about all of this, Carol. Has anything new occurred to you? Is there anyone at all that you are remotely concerned about? Anyone who has ever made you feel uncomfortable?' he raised his chin, stroking it with his right hand.

'The only person I know who hates me is Jack, Fiona's brother. But you've ruled him out. I really can't think of anyone else – and I think about it all the time, believe me.'

'There's something else we'd like to check. If the perpetrator did follow you out to Barbados... and that's still a big 'if', how would he know you were going to be there? We've asked the Newcastle police to check your house for bugs, including your computer and phone. We could be dealing with a stalker here, so best to be thorough. Technicians will be here in the morning to do a sweep.'

'You think my house might be bugged?' Such a possibility hadn't occurred to me and I was aghast.

'It's just a precaution,' said Louis, putting his hand up, palm forward. 'Just something we need to rule out, so don't panic.' His deep voice was reassuring.

'We've been briefed on what happened last night, when the security light was triggered. There's no evidence right now to connect that with the events in Barbados, so the local police are dealing with it, but obviously we're liaising very closely with them. The security arrangements they've put in place should keep you safe until things are resolved.'

After they left, I found myself feeling even more apprehensive and fearful than before. Was I being stalked? Was someone watching my every move? I felt sick with fear and prayed that they would find him soon.

CHAPTER FORTY-ONE

I sat nursing a plastic cup of hot coffee, hardly able to believe what I was hearing. Fiona was beside me, both of us sitting opposite Detective Superintendent Mike Jensen in his office, at Newcastle Central Police Station. On the left were the two detectives from Barbados. Gayle, who was seated next to the Superintendent, was fiddling, nervously I thought, with her locket. DCI Patsy Mayne was next to her, her red hair glinting in a shaft of sunlight coming through the window behind her. A man I didn't recognise was next to Patsy.

Gayle had phoned me when I was out walking with Fi, and asked if we would call by the station on our way back home. It seemed an unusual request, as Gayle usually came to me, but we complied, curious as to why we'd been summoned.

Earlier, police technicians had turned up at the house to search for bugs. We'd gone for our walk, leaving them to it, and I wondered if that's what this was about. But, I wasn't expecting the bombshell that DS Jensen tossed into my lap.

'I'm afraid I have something unsettling to tell you,' he said, looking at me steadily over the top of dark-rimmed reading glasses. There was a pause. 'Our technicians have found hidden cameras in your house. Highly sophisticated equipment, clearly planted by somebody who knows what they're doing.'

'What..? Where..?' I exchanged a horrified glance with Fiona.

'In the conservatory and in the sitting room, although they believe that particular one has malfunctioned. Also, in your bedroom, and in the bathroom.' He studied me over the top of his glasses.

I was stunned. 'What? My God, he's been watching us? Even in the bathroom?' I put my coffee on the desk, my hands shaking. 'How did he get into the house to put them there? How long have they been there? Oh God...' I felt violated, thinking of all that he must have seen. 'He must be sick.'

'I know this is an awful shock for you, Mrs Barrington. I'm afraid it looks as though we could be dealing with a stalker here.' He paused, no doubt to let his words sink in, before continuing. 'Richard here – sorry, I haven't introduced you. This is Richard Smith, a criminal psychologist who assists us with certain cases.'

I looked at the tall, thin man, who nodded at me, noting the side parting in his short dark hair, and rimless glasses. He reminded me very much of Jacob Rees-Mogg, and spoke in the same cultured tones.

'We've been discussing this case,' continued the Superintendent, 'examining events to date and it's Richard's professional opinion that the assault in Barbados was most likely carried out by the same person who planted the surveillance equipment in your home. It has the hallmarks of a predatory stalker.'

'But,' I interrupted, 'surely I'd know if I was being stalked? Nobody's made contact...'

'Not this kind of stalker, Mrs Barrington,' Richard Smith interrupted. 'This type is a sexual predator, often going after complete strangers, or casual acquaintances. He's the most dangerous type.'

I looked at him, aghast.

'Predatory Stalkers research their victims, sometimes over a long period of time, before making their carefully planned move. The stalking is foreplay to them, giving them a sense of control and power over the victim. The goal is the sexual attack.

It's the violent sexual fantasies that they engage in while researching, planning and following the victim that really gets them off, as they prepare for the ultimate thrill – the sexual assault itself. He can take delight in the details, deciding how long to prolong the suspense, rehearsing the attack, fantasising about the victim's response. This breed of stalker is particularly dangerous when spurned.'

I was feeling numb and having difficulty getting my head around it. I realised Richard Smith was still speaking to me.

'The predatory stalker is usually a wolf in sheep's clothing; when caught he is often proclaimed by those who knew him as the least likely of perpetrators. Friends are left stunned and disbelieving.'

'But... are you sure? Isn't all this supposition?' I was floundering.

'As I said, this situation has all the hallmarks.' He sounded pompous. 'We can only be absolutely certain once he's caught.'

'But...' I began.

'We're going to work with Louis and James here to resolve this case,' the Superintendent said, putting his elbows on the desk and leaning towards me. 'The stalking and planting of surveillance equipment is taking place here, so we will investigate. Once the culprit is apprehended, and there's evidence linking him to Barbados, which we fully expect to find, he'll be extradited there to face trial.'

Sitting back in his chair, he continued, 'Your computer and mobile will probably also have been compromised. They're working on your computer right now, and if you let me have your phone, we'll get that checked too.'

I felt almost paralysed with fright at the thought of someone preying on me, watching me. It was too much to take in. I got my phone out of my pocket, and slowly handed it over. 'But, why? Why me?'

Rees-Mogg lookalike replied. 'There'll be no emotional attachment to you. He won't be in love with you, or anything like that. For reasons of his own, he has selected you, but for him it's all about his need for dominance and control, and the gratification of sadistic sexual desires.'

I shuddered. 'How sure are you about the link between the surveillance and the attack in Barbados?'

He explained the rationale. 'The assault in Barbados was a sadistic, sexual attack, probably interrupted, as no actual rape took place. The assailant would be enraged at not being able to fulfil his fantasy and that may have triggered the brutal end to the attack. Now that surveillance equipment has been found in your home, it is obvious that someone is watching you; following your every move. And may have been doing so for a long time. The flashbacks you've been experiencing - the words he used – "Hello Carol, I've waited a long time for this" all add up to the likelihood of one very dangerous Predator Stalker being responsible. In my view, the chances of two separate people doing these things to one person is so remote as to be discountable.'

Gripped with intense fear, I opened my mouth to speak, but no words came out. I tried again. 'So what happens next?'

'With your permission,' the Superintendent replied, 'we want to leave the surveillance equipment in place for the time being. We don't want to alert him yet to the fact that we know about it. It might give us the opportunity to feed him false information, which could help to trap him. I know it's a lot to ask, Carol, but we'd like you to carry on as normal. As if the cameras weren't there. I think we could disable the one in the bathroom – it'll seem that it's just malfunctioned, like the one in the sitting room, if that helps?'

'I can't take all this in,' I whispered, looking at Fiona.

'Me, neither.' she whispered, shaking her head.

'We'll be with you every step of the way, to help you through this,' Gayle offered. That was some comfort, but not much.

We made our way home in a daze, both of us trying to process the devastating information we'd just been given.

The next couple of weeks were very difficult for us, to put it mildly. Fiona and I tried to act as normal as possible, and anything we didn't want overheard, we said to each other away from the areas of the house under surveillance.

It's hard to describe my feelings. When the safety of your own home is compromised, you've got nowhere to run to, to get away from things. Nowhere to hide. I was trying to stay strong, but I was scared every waking minute. I was terrified every time I left the house too, certain I was being followed. It felt as though I was losing my mind. I was living in a state of constant terror, knowing someone evil was out to get me.

CHAPTER FORTY-TWO

'Saul Harrison?' DCI Brown looked at the man who'd answered the door, noting his height and build. 'I'm DCI Brown and this is DI Phillips, Royal Barbados Police. We're making some routine enquiries about a recent incident and would like to ask you a few questions. May we come in?'

Saul shrugged, before grunting his assent and leading them into a fairly large open-plan kitchen/dining room. It was tastefully decorated, but very untidy, with unwashed dishes on most of the surfaces and a pile of clothes on the floor.

'Do you live here on your own?' the DI asked, glancing around.

'Yes,' said Harrison, shortly. 'Is this about what happened to Carol?'

'Why do you suggest that?' the DI asked, sharply.

'My daughter told me what happened to her mother,' he replied calmly, a note of sarcasm in his voice.

'Can you tell us where you were on the night of 29 November?'

'Well, I certainly wasn't in Barbados, if that's what you're asking,' he said in an insolent tone.

'The question was, where were you?' the DCI interjected.

'I was here, at home. Ill. I was in bed for a whole week, hardly able to move. Must have picked up a bug.'

'Did you see a doctor?' asked DI Phillips.

'No. I don't bother much with doctors. It was flu. I knew it would just run its course.' He leaned back against a wall and folded his arms. He didn't invite the officers to sit.

'Can anyone corroborate your whereabouts?' asked the DCI.

'Shouldn't think so. I live by myself. Don't have many visitors. I didn't see anyone at all. Couldn't even be bothered to answer the phone.'

'Mind if we all sit?' said the DCI pulling out a chair and taking a seat at a small, round dining table in the bay window.

After some hesitation, Harrison pulled out the chair opposite. Once they were all seated, the DCI continued.

'How would you describe your relationship with your former wife, Mr. Harrison?' he said, changing tack.

'I don't really have one. I never see her these days.'

'Yet you went round to her house some months ago?' the DCI asked, stroking his chin.

'So?' The insolent tone was back, the arms still folded.

'Why would you do that, if you never see her?'

'She'd lost her husband. She was in a bad way. I was worried about her.' He spoke slowly, as though explaining something to a small child.

'And did you see her?'

'No. She didn't want to see me. She told her stepdaughter to send me away.'

'And how did that make you feel?'

'Sad. Still worried for her. I only wanted to let her know I was here for her if she needed me.'

'Weren't you angry that she wouldn't see you? Didn't you feel small? Resentful?' asked the DI, pushing his hair out of his eyes.

'You need to get that hair cut,' Harrison told him, insolently. 'No, I didn't feel small or resentful. Just sad for her.'

'Why do you sit in your car in her street, watching her?' DCI Brown asked. 'You've been seen on a number of occasions.'

'Look, I still care for her. From time to time, I like to have sight of her, to check that she's ok. Alright?'

'No, not alright, actually. That's abnormal behaviour. Stalker's

149

behaviour.'

'I don't expect you to understand. But that's just the way I am. I'm not stalking her. I don't wish her any harm. The opposite. I just need to satisfy myself that she's alright.'

'You're a former SAS man, aren't you?' asked the DCI.

'What's that got to do with anything?' Harrison glared at the DCI.

'When you were active, did you have access to forged documents? Or at least to contacts who provide such things?'

'It's years since I was in the SAS. I got involved in all sorts of covert activities. Protecting the likes of you. I don't know where you're coming from with this?'

'Do you have access to forged passports?' the DCI persisted, ignoring Harrison's insolent tone.

Harrison raised his voice, banging both hands on the table, making it rattle. 'Oh for fuck's sake. You think I used a forged passport and travelled to Barbados to attack my wife? My former wife,' he corrected himself. 'Why on earth would I do that? I just live a few streets from her. Why the fuck would I need to go to Barbados? Why wouldn't I just attack her here if that's what I was about?'

'Why indeed?' asked the DCI.

'This is bloody ridiculous. I've had enough of this. I'd like you to leave now.' Harrison got to his feet. 'Go on, fuck off.'

'No problem, Mr Harrison, but we may need to speak to you again. If we do, it'll be at the station next time. In any event, we'll need a voluntary DNA swab from you. Do you have any objection to that?'

'Yes, I fucking do. Knowing you lot, you'll fit me up. I'm not giving any fucking sample. The door's there.'

'In that case, you'll be one of our top suspects, Mr Harrison. We'll see ourselves out. We'll be in touch.'

CHAPTER FORTY-THREE

Gayle came every day, as usual, then towards the end of the second week she spoke to us, in the sitting room away from the cameras. Linda was there, too.

'The security people have just advised me that the floodlights have been disabled, sometime today. Both of them. They were ok yesterday. We now think a further visit must be imminent.'

'Oh shit,' I said, a hollow feeling forming in the pit of my stomach.

'We're going to leave them out of action,' Gayle told us, 'and we're putting two men actually inside the house from tonight, as well as a couple outside. I want you and Fiona to keep to your usual routine. Go off to bed at your normal time each night. If you hear anything, any noise or commotion, whatever you do, don't come downstairs. We'll call you when it's safe to do so. Do you understand?'

'Yes… but do you really think he'll come?' I asked. 'Sorry, that's a stupid question. Why else would he disable the lights?'

'We're pretty sure he will, but we don't know when. I can't think of any other reason for disabling the lights. He'll wait a while, to make sure we don't suspect anything. Try not to worry, and make sure you don't mention anything anywhere he can see and hear you. You'll both be safe, as long as you do as we say, and we'll have someone with you all the time.'

Fiona looked at me. A look full of trepidation, no doubt matching my own, and I noticed Linda looked a bit taken aback and heard her questioning Gayle about what might happen.

'Surely Carol doesn't have to stay and endure this, if she doesn't feel up to it? Couldn't she and Fiona go to a hotel 'til all this is over?'

'If that's what...' began Gayle.

'No,' I interrupted. 'I want to see this through. We'll be fine, as long as the police are here. Won't we, Fi?' Although looking pale and apprehensive, Fiona agreed with me.

We spent the evening in a state of nervous apprehension, trying to act as normal as possible. After watching TV for a while, at about ten we moved into the sitting room where we had a nightcap and chatted about what we thought might happen. Would he come? Were we on the verge of finding out who attacked me?

Unsurprisingly, we found sleep hard to come by, nervously waiting to see what would happen, and jumping at every little night sound. Both too scared to sleep alone, Fiona was sharing my bed, and we found comfort in each other's presence. The first night went by uneventfully and the security men left in the morning, saying they would return the next night.

After six nights of this, nerves frayed to shreds, we were beginning to think it was all a mistake and he wasn't going to come.

CHAPTER FORTY-FOUR

He decided to wait to see if his handiwork was discovered, listening and watching every day. When he didn't hear any mention of it during his eavesdropping, he became confident his previous sojourn had gone unnoticed. However, his innate sense of caution told him to let some time go by before he took any further action.

A week passed, and with nothing to arouse his suspicions, he decided to act. It was around eleven and very dark when he entered the Dene. There was a half-moon sending weak light filtering through the densely packed trees, as he picked his way carefully along the narrow track, excited and exhilarated by what he was about to do. He intended to watch the house for a long time before breaking in through the side door, to make sure both the occupants were fast asleep. Piece of cake.

His determination to deal with Carol was stronger than ever. He wanted to subdue her, punish her, hear her whimper, see the fear in her eyes as he took her.

CHAPTER FORTY-FIVE

The strain of waiting was getting to us. By the seventh night, a sense of anti-climax was beginning creep in. Where was he? As I lay in bed beside Fiona, waiting for something to happen, I was gripped with the usual fear, mixed with a growing sense of frustration, Why the fuck didn't he just get it over and done with? My nerves couldn't take much more.

'I can't let you face all this on your own,' Pauline had said, aghast, when I filled her in on the situation. She'd volunteered to stay overnight with us, suggesting she came to the house every night, after work. Gayle vetoed the suggestion, wanting to contain the situation as tightly as possible. She felt a third person in the house would only complicate things, so Pauline had to be content with just having supper with us a couple of times, before going back to her own place.

On the seventh night, Fiona and I kept to our usual routine, as instructed. Going to bed at around eleven thirty, we chatted for a while after carrying out our ablutions, before putting the lights out. All was quiet and eventually I drifted off to sleep.

The sound of an almighty crash brought both of us bolt upright in bed. This was followed by the sound of furniture falling over and voices shouting, scuffling. I didn't dare move or even put the light on. Fiona clung to me in fright. We held each other tightly, as the noises seemed to go on forever. Then a light was switched on downstairs and an officer came upstairs, knocked briefly, and put his head around the bedroom door.

'Would you like to come down now, Miss?'

Before getting out of bed, I put the bedside light on. Fiona's face probably mirrored mine – a mask of fear, pale skin and huge eyes. I reached for my dressing gown and Fiona did the same.

'I'm so scared,' I whispered. 'Who's going to be down there?' My heart was thudding so violently I thought it would burst out of my chest. I was about to find out who had attacked me, and suddenly I was really terrified. For a moment I thought I was going to pass out and felt myself swaying.

'Easy, Carol,' Fiona held on to my arm. 'You ok?'

I nodded. The moment had passed. My knees were shaking as I made my way slowly down the stairs, holding tightly to the banister. Fiona followed closely behind. As I descended, heart in my mouth, I could see several black-clad security men in the dining hall below. One of them was astride a man, who was lying face down on the wooden floor, beside an overturned chair, hands pulled behind his back. As I watched, the police officer straddling him secured handcuffs on his wrists, before getting to his feet.

'Get up,' he barked at the man on the floor, roughly grabbing him by his shoulders and hauling him upright. The intruder had his back to me and when he turned around I gasped in disbelief.

'Saul?' My hand flew to my mouth, which was open in astonishment. My voice came out an octave higher than usual.

'Do you recognise this man?' asked one of the black-clad officers.

'Yes... it's Saul,' I whispered, then added 'My ex-husband.'

Stunned, I couldn't believe what I was seeing. This wasn't making any sense. Surely I would have known if it was Saul who had attacked me in Barbados? Surely I would have recognised his voice, would have remembered it was him? Wouldn't I?

I looked at him and saw his face was blacked up, like a commando. He wouldn't look at me. I screamed 'What are you doing? What the bloody hell are you doing?' He didn't answer me, just kept his head down, staring at the floor and I heard one of the officers begin to read him his rights...

'Saul Harrison, I am arresting you on suspicion of aggravated burglary. You do not have to say anything. But it may harm your defence if you do not mention when questioned something you later rely on in court. Anything you do say may be given in evidence.' Again there was no response from Saul.

I screamed again, 'Why Saul?' I tried to reach him. I wanted to make him look at me and tell me why he was doing this, but one of the officers held me back.

It was all so surreal. This couldn't be happening. Two of the police grabbed an arm each and quickly bundled him out of the door to a waiting police car. The other two officers remained behind to brief us on what had happened.

Gayle arrived. 'This is becoming a habit, rushing over here in the middle of the night,' she said, trying unsuccessfully to sound flippant.

It transpired that one of the officers, who had been waiting in the Dene, had seen a black-clad figure climbing over the back fence just after half past one, and alerted his colleagues inside. It was decided to hold off making an arrest until the intruder had broken into the house. They heard the sound of splintering wood at the side of the house and realised he was gaining entry through the side door of the garage, after which he jemmied the door leading into the short passageway between the garage and the dining room. Between them, the two officers waiting inside had taken him down.

'Gayle, I really can't believe it was Saul who attacked me. I would have known. Surely I would have known?' My voice was rising in anguish.

'We don't know for certain that it was him in Barbados. There's no evidence of that at this stage. I gather, though, from transcripts of your interviews in Barbados that you thought he was stalking you in the past?'

'I wouldn't call it stalking. I know he sometimes parks in my street. But, I don't think he wants to harm me. It's hard for anyone who doesn't know him to understand. He's just an oddball. But I can't believe he'd hurt me.'

'Is that why he brought this along, then?' asked one of the officers, holding up a large evidence bag containing a lethal-looking curved knife, like a small machete.

I looked closely at it. 'My God. He had that?' I was shocked.

'I'm afraid so. Not something someone harmless would carry, in my book.' He set his lips in a thin line.

Gayle steered me, and Fiona, into the sitting room. 'Sit down, you two. You look like ghosts.'

I sank gratefully on to a settee. My mind was incapable of coherent thought. Nothing was making sense to me and I kept seeing the machete.

I became aware of Gayle's voice. 'We'll get a warrant in the morning to search Saul Harrison's house. If, in the course of that we find evidence that links him to Barbados, we'll pass it to the Barbados police. We'll inform them of what's happened tonight. No doubt they'll want to interview him again.'

One of the officers came out of the kitchen just then, carrying a tray holding mugs of steaming tea. Mine was laced with something strong, and I gratefully drank it, trying to stop my hands shaking enough to avoid scalding myself.

'I've got a couple of people coming here,' continued Gayle. 'They should be here any minute, to secure the broken doors for tonight.' She'd no sooner finished speaking, when two men arrived, carrying wood and bags of tools. In no time at all, and after much hammering, the temporary repairs were done.

'Sweet dreams,' quipped one of the men, as they left. 'You'll be safe now.'

Gayle had to leave, but said she'd be in touch in the morning with an update. One of the other officers was to stay with us until the morning, to give us some peace of mind, for which I was very grateful.

When the others had gone, I looked at Fiona, whose face looked almost as white as her dressing gown.

'You look all in, Fi,' I said, and she nodded, too drained to speak. We said goodnight to the security guy, who said he would sleep on the sofa; left all the mess and mugs and went up to bed. Fiona slept soundly, only waking up when the security man popped his head in at around eight in the morning to say he was leaving. I'd lain awake all night, in complete turmoil, my mind going over and over the events of the night and the attack in Barbados. I kept seeing that wicked-looking machete. I was trying to equate the voice I remembered with Saul's voice. Saul's was similar. Could it have been him? Jumbled thoughts went round and round in my head, until I must have eventually fallen asleep in exhaustion.

CHAPTER FORTY-SIX

Detective Superintendent Mike Jensen noted the physique of the man being manhandled into the custody suite, comparing it mentally with the description Carol Barrington had given of her assailant in Barbados. It wasn't his case, of course, but he wondered.

He'd been informed that Saul Harrison hadn't said a word since he was arrested, and had made no comment when the charge was read out to him.

'Take him down,' he told the Duty Sergeant, before turning to DCI Patsy Mayne. 'Leave him alone for a while to reflect on things. Find out what you can about him. We'll get a warrant in the morning to search his house and business premises. Are you taking Gayle into the interview?'

'Yes, as FLO for Carol Barrington, I want her involved.'

The interview commenced. 'Can you confirm, for the record, that you have declined legal representation?' asked DCI Mayne.

He muttered assent, and DCI Mayne continued. 'Would you please tell us why you broke into your former wife's house in the early hours of this morning?'

There was no response.

'Mr Harrison, would you please answer the question,' she said, leaning over the desk towards him. 'There's nothing to be gained by staying silent.'

'What's the point? You won't believe me. So, I might as well save my breath.' Harrison sat back in his chair, and crossed his arms, nonchalantly looking up at the ceiling.

'Try us,' said DCI Mayne. Silence. 'Look, stop messing about. Just explain why you broke into your former wife's house, armed with a knife. It's a simple enough question.'

Harrison took a deep breath, looked her in the eye, and said with a sigh, 'I was following someone.'

'Who?'

'I saw this guy, in her street. He seemed to be watching Carol's house, driving slowly past it. He turned into a side street, the cul de sac at the end of her road. It seemed a bit odd, so I followed him. He parked at the end of the cul de sac, got out of his car and went into the Dene on foot. I thought he was up to no good, so I followed him.'

'Why did you think he was up to no good?' asked the DCI.

'He looked shifty. Just something about him.'

'When did you blacken your face?' The DCI changed tack, slightly.

'As a matter of fact, I always keep some camouflage in the glove compartment. Throwback to the SAS days. It only took two seconds.'

'And the knife? Do you keep that in the glove compartment too?'

'Not usually. I'd been using it earlier in the day to cut some rope and it just happened to be in the car. I took it in case I needed it for self-defence. In case he had a weapon.'

'So, you saw this mystery man, driving slowly past your former wife's house? Would you like to tell us what you were doing in her street?'

'I like to keep an eye on her. I just like to check she's ok, so sometimes I drive through there.'

'You've been divorced for, how long?' asked DCI Mayne, consulting her notes. 'Ah, yes, about eight years? Have you been keeping an eye on your former wife all that time?'

'I knew you wouldn't understand,' he said, spreading his hands, palms up, and shrugging. 'Take it or leave it, it's all the same to me.' Harrison sat back in his chair and once again folded his arms.

'Can you describe the car this man was driving?' asked DC Jones.

'Dark blue BMW; new,' he said confidently.

'And the registration number?'

'I only got part of it... JB18,' Harrison said. 'When I saw him get out of his car, I was suspicious. It was dark in the Dene and I lost sight of him, so I stayed on the track til I got to Carol's house. I had to check he wasn't planning to harm her.'

'What did this man look like? Can you describe him?'

'I never saw his face. He was about the same build and height as me. Dressed in black.'

'What made you think he was planning to harm your ex-wife?'

'A gut feeling. I'm sure I saw his car in her street once before, but it didn't register until I saw it again, driving past. He was peering into her windows.'

'Go on. You blacked up, grabbed a knife and followed this man into the Dene. What happened next?'

'When I reached the back of the house, it was in darkness, but I could see him. He was inside the house, silhouetted against the front windows. I panicked. I had to stop him from getting to her, so I climbed over the fence and broke into the house by the side door.'

'Didn't you stop to wonder how he had got in? Was there any sign of a break-in?'

'It crossed my mind, but I was in a bit of a panic. Needed to get in there quickly. Then I got collared by you lot.'

'And you expect us to believe your story?' asked DCI Mayne.

'You can believe what you like,' he said. 'It's a matter of complete indifference to me. All I know is, there's someone out there who wants to harm Carol. I hope you find the bastard before I do.' He spoke in a matter-of-fact manner, and clearly didn't care whether or not he was believed.

'There was no-one there, but you. This mystery man hadn't broken in and was nowhere to be seen. Not even a footprint. Do you see how it looks to us?'

'I said you wouldn't believe me,' he repeated, crossing his arms again.

The DCI got to her feet. 'You'll be going before the magistrates this morning and we'll be asking for you to be remanded in custody. That's all for now.'

CHAPTER FORTY-SEVEN

Early the next morning, Gayle arrived just as we were finishing breakfast. It was raining heavily; strong gusts of wind driving the rain horizontally. It was drumming against the kitchen window, fat drops chasing each other, in rivulets, down the glass. She came in, wiping her face, looking miserable and dishevelled.

'What's happening now, Gayle? What did he have to say?' I asked her, as soon as she walked into the kitchen. 'I can't believe it was Saul who attacked me. Surely I would know... if it was him... I would have recognised his voice. Heavens, I was married to the man for more than a decade.'

'Hold on, Carol. Whoa...' Gayle said putting her hand out, palm towards me. 'Just let me get my wet jacket off. God, I'm glad to be inside.' She removed her navy parka, which was dripping all over the floor. Fiona took it from her and put it in the warm utility room, to dry off a bit.

'There's no evidence to say that Saul had anything to do with Barbados. We need to keep an open mind at this stage. The Barbados crew are to interview him again, later today. It's their job to look for the evidence. As for last night, Saul claims he was following someone whose car he'd seen driving slowly past your house. Says he was trying to protect you. That he saw someone in the dining room and thought it was the intruder.'

'Really..? Do you believe him? It sounds bizarre, but not unlike him.'

'The fact is, he broke into your house. His face was blacked up and he was carrying a knife. This all suggests pre-meditation. We'll check out his story as far as possible, but he's now been charged with Aggravated Burglary and will be going before the magistrates later today. We want him remanded in custody.'

'Oh. God, I just don't know what to believe.'

'If Saul is telling the truth, then that means the attacker's still out there,' Fiona said in small voice.

'Yes, if he's telling the truth,' agreed Gayle. 'So, we intend to leave the security arrangements in place; the panic alarms, etc. And we'll still have someone call by to check the security lights each day until this is resolved. You'll need to be vigilant, both of you. If you're worried about anything or see anything suspicious, or think you're being followed, you must get in touch without delay.'

'So you really don't think Saul's the predator?' I asked.

'We don't know at this stage. We can't jump to conclusions. We need evidence before we can link him with Barbados. Believe me, the Barbados police will be looking at him even more closely after this.'

CHAPTER FORTY-EIGHT

After Gayle left, I felt restless and unsettled. I needed to be busy, to do something other than go mad, thinking everything through and getting nowhere. The weather was foul and a walk was out of the question, so I suggested to Fiona that we tackle the job we'd been putting off; sorting out Peter's things. She readily agreed and I realised she, too, needed something to do.

'Just suppose. What if it turns out that Saul is the person who attacked you? How would you feel?' Fiona asked, placing a tee-shirt on the pile for the charity shop.

'Well, after last night, I'm beginning to think anything's possible. I mean, carrying a bloody machete...'

'And getting blacked up and breaking into your house. What do you think would've happened if the police hadn't been here?'

'I don't know. I just don't bloody know. Stop asking me. I just don't know what the fuck the truth is any more.' I dropped my head into my hands.

'Oh, I'm sorry. I don't mean to put any more pressure on you. I just want you to be prepared. The facts all seem to be pointing to him.' Fiona looked contrite.

'I won't believe it til the police prove otherwise,' I said with more conviction than I felt. In truth, my mind was in turmoil.

Dealing with Peter's things was proving a slow and emotional task. Most of his good clothing was to go to charity, a few things to be kept. Whenever a particular sweater or jacket reminded one of us of the last time we saw Peter wearing it, the reminiscences, and the tears, came thick and fast. Even after all this time, faint traces of his aftershave could be detected on some of his shirts and sweaters.

Sitting on the floor, surrounded by heaps of Peter's clothes, Fiona started chatting about what life was like, at home, before her parents' split.

'It was such a relief to me when Dad told me they were splitting up. I mean, I loved them both, but I could see how they were tearing each other apart. And, hell, life's too short. They'd just gone in different directions. Mum lived for her horses, never happier than when she was in the saddle. Dad was much more of a social animal, as you know. Mum no longer wanted to go out anywhere with him, and was always in jodhpurs. Quite honestly, she often smelled of horseshit,' she laughed. 'Still does.'

'Really?' I asked, amused, folding a soft blue cashmere sweater for the charity shop pile.

'It's ironic that Dad's success meant that mum could afford to indulge her passion. Which in turn widened the gulf between them.'

She picked up a multi-striped Ted Baker scarf and put it to her face, inhaling deeply. Her eyes filled with tears. 'I can still smell Dad on this.' The tears spilled over, silver trails running down her cheeks and dampening the scarf.

'Oh sweetheart, is this too much for you?' I said, hugging her. 'I can finish off, if you like.'

'No, we'll do it together,' she sniffed and wiped the tears away with her fingers. 'I'm fine, really.' She managed a tremulous smile.

A bit later, when I was folding one of Peter's jackets, it felt heavy. I checked the pockets and found an old mobile phone.

'Look what I've found,' I said, holding it aloft. 'We'll have to see what's on this.' I tried to switch it on, but was disappointed to find the battery was flat. Of course it was. 'I'll put it on charge and we'll look later, once it has enough power. Shouldn't take long.' I went through to my bedroom, where I found a lead that fitted. I was intrigued about what it might contain. Maybe some photographs, so far unseen? I felt the old familiar pang of longing for Peter. What I wouldn't give to see him just one more time; to hold him, to feel his arms around me.

'Right,' I said briskly, pulling myself together and going back into the dressing room, 'We're nearly finished here. Another half hour should just about do it. And then we'll look at the phone.'

Later, over a glass of prosecco, we sat side by side on the settee in the sitting room, excited to find out what was on Peter's mobile. What a trip down memory lane. The hundreds of photographs we found kept us engrossed for the next hour, evoking smiles, laughter and a few more poignant tears. We came across one that Peter had taken of the hiking group.

'Who do you think that is?' I asked Fiona, pointing to one of the team. He was standing at the end of a line up, next to Peter. 'It looks just like one of my tenants, but it can't be.'

'I don't know who it is,' she said, frowning at the screen, and chewing a nail. 'Apart from my dad, the only other members I know are Pauline's husband, whatsisname. And Tim, of course. I know a lot of them were at the funeral, but I can't remember all the faces.'

'Hmm... I thought I knew all the team...'

That night, I had an uneasy feeling and couldn't get to sleep. I got up, retrieved the phone and studied the photograph again. It looked so like my tenant, Dan Smithson. Surely, it couldn't be. Peter would have mentioned if one of my tenants had joined the group. But, of course, as they'd never met each other, Peter wouldn't have known it was my tenant, unless Dan had told him. Could Dan have joined the group, unaware that my husband was a member? Quite possibly. Why did I feel so unsettled?

I must have drifted off because I woke suddenly, at around four in the morning, trying to clarify my thoughts. What if... what if Dan Smithson was my attacker? What if he'd joined the group to get close to Peter? What if Peter's death wasn't an accident? What if he'd killed him and was now coming after me? My mind was working overtime and I was breathing hard, fighting panic. Calm down I told myself. This is just middle of the night thinking. How could I make sense of this? *Tim*, I suddenly thought. *Tim will know*. I decided to ring him first thing in the morning.

CHAPTER FORTY-NINE

'Thanks for coming, Tim,' I said. Now that he was here, I realised in the cold light of day how ridiculous I was going to sound.

'How are things Dusty?' he asked, smiling warmly and giving me a peck on the cheek. As always, he looked immaculate, in a dark blue suit, white shirt and multi-coloured striped tie.

First, I brought him up to date with all the recent events since I last saw him. From the discovery of the bugging devices and cameras, the possibility of a predatory stalker, to Saul breaking in. He was incredulous.

'My God. The whole situation is enough to drive you out of your mind. Cameras? In your own home? And Saul? Do you think it was him who attacked you in Barbados?'

'Before last night, I would have categorically said 'no'. Now, I just don't know. The Barbados police are interviewing him again, today. I'm tired of trying to make sense of things. But there's something I want you to help me with, Tim.'

'Oh yes?' he looked at me, eyebrows raised.

I told him about finding the phone in Peter's pocket and coming across pictures of the hiking group. I showed him the photograph with the man I was concerned about, and pointed him out.

'Look, the man there, next to Peter.' The man I was pointing out was well-built, about forty, wearing a black woollen hat and dark blue jacket. 'Who is he? I thought I knew all the group members, but I don't remember seeing this guy before.'

Tim took the phone from me and peered at the screen. 'That's Terry Archer. He joined the group about two years ago. Nice chap, got on well with everyone; lived in Hexham. Why do you ask?'

I hesitated, 'Well... I'm almost sure that photograph is of one of my tenants. But that's not his name; it's Dan Smithson. And he lives in South Shields, not Hexham.'

'Wouldn't Peter have known if he was one of your tenants?' Tim said, clearly wondering where I was coming from. He handed the phone back to me.

'No, Peter never met the tenants. I manage the properties myself. Peter never got involved.'

Tim frowned, looking puzzled. 'Dusty, I'm not sure what you're suggesting? How can it possibly be your tenant? The photograph's a bit fuzzy. Isn't it more likely there's just a resemblance?'

Realising how foolish I sounded, I said 'You're probably right, Tim. I'm no doubt just being paranoid. But as soon as I saw that photograph I felt sure it was Dan Smithson. I'm really on edge just now, imagining all sorts of things.'

'Not surprisingly,' said Tim.

'Look, I'll be honest with you. My mind is going into overdrive. I couldn't sleep last night. What if... what if that IS a photograph of Dan Smithson? What if... he joined the group using a different name? To get rid of Peter?'

'What? Come on, Carol, I really don't think...'

'Hear me out, Tim,' I persisted. 'What if he's my attacker? He gets Peter out of the way to get to me? Then he seizes his chance and follows me to Barbados?'

'This is preposterous. All you've got is a fuzzy photograph and all of a sudden, the guy's a murderer and a stalker?'

'Just bear with me for a minute. Is this Terry Archer still a member of the group?'

'No. He left the area about six months ago. I think he said he was moving to London.'

'Well Dan Smithson is still a tenant in South Shields. He rents one of my flats in Marine Park in South Shields.'

'Have you discussed any of this with Gayle?'

'Not yet, but I don't think there's much point. There's no evidence. The police wouldn't act on a fuzzy photo, with nothing else but my hunch. I was hoping... hoping you might go to see Dan Smithson, just to check? After all, you know Terry Archer personally, so you're the best person to check if they're one and the same person.'

'Dusty, I have to say I think you're being paranoid. It's hardly surprising, with all you're going through. But I think you need to keep a sense of proportion.' Disappointment must have been written all over my face.

Tim put his hand up, 'Please don't look like that. To put your mind at rest, I'll call there on some pretext or other and speak with your tenant. Just to check that he and Terry Archer are not the same person. I think you're mad, but I don't want you to be worrying unnecessarily. You've got enough on your plate.'

I was surprised, but pleased 'Oh Tim, thank you.' I hugged him. 'I'm so grateful. I'm sorry in advance if I'm wasting your time. If it's any consolation, Fiona thinks I'm crackers, too.'

Fiona came in just then, and after she and Tim had mutually agreed that I was losing my marbles, we spent the next hour or so bringing Tim up to date with everything. We went into more depth about the events of two nights ago. He didn't seem to be able to make any more sense of it than we could.

Later, after Tim left, Fiona told me she thought it was kind of him to indulge me.

'I think Tim's got the hots for you, Carol.' I threw the tea-towel at her. 'Methinks the lady doth protest too much,' she laughed.

'It's nothing like that, Fi. He's just such a nice man.'

CHAPTER FIFTY

DCI Louis Brown, together with DI James Phillips, listened to Patsy Mayne's summary of the search of Saul Harrison's house. They were meeting in her office at Newcastle Central Police Station, prior to their second interview with Saul Harrison. Louis looked around, unimpressed with the drab walls and furniture.

'The search revealed an unlicensed shotgun, hidden in the back of a wardrobe, together with a small stock of ammunition and camouflage materials,' the DCI told him. 'But, we thought you might be interested in these,' she said, handing over an evidence bag of documents. 'There's a recently-renewed passport, and a British Airways return ticket to Barbados'. She pointed at the bag. 'Departure date of twenty-sixth of November. Not quite sure what it means,' she shrugged. 'The tickets are unused.'

'Thanks, Patsy,' the DCI said, taking the evidence bag. 'Appreciate all your help. We'll see what explanation he has for this lot.'

After Harrison confirmed once again that he had declined legal representation, the DCI began questioning him. Without preamble, he got down to business. 'So, you were planning a trip to Barbados, Saul?'

'Found the ticket, have you?' Harrison said, studiously examining his fingernails.

'A ticket to co-incide with when your former wife would be there. Why didn't you use it?'

'I was ill. I told you. Couldn't even get out of bed, never mind get on a plane,' he went on examining his nails.

'Why did you buy the ticket in the first place?' asked DI Phillips.

'You won't believe me,' he sighed and looked up at DI Phillips. 'I

169

knew from Julia that Carol was going to be on her own out there. I was concerned for her. I wanted to be nearby in case she needed me.'

'Let me tell you my theory,' said DI Phillips. 'You've been stalking your wife. That's not in dispute. You've told us about sitting outside her house and watching her. You were obsessed by her and after her husband died, you went to her house to see her. But she rebuffed you. You got into her house, covertly - not difficult for you with your skill set. In her absence, you installed surveillance equipment. You found out she was going to Barbados and you knew she'd be on her own. That's when you bought your airline ticket. But then, you had second thoughts. Decided it was silly to use your own name. Too traceable. So, through your contacts you obtained a false passport. Am I correct so far?' he asked, looking at Harrison, There was no response. 'You carried out a reconnaissance, from the beach, and took your opportunity to get into her apartment when she left to see her step daughter into her taxi.

I don't think your plan was to kill her, but when she rebuffed you again and fought back, you lost your temper and did this to her.' Slowly, one by one, he laid the crime scene photographs in front of Harrison.

Harrison's face drained of colour as he examined them. He pushed them away, whispering. 'No. No. I couldn't do that to her. I would never hurt her.' He put his head in his hands and began to sob. Eventually, he looked up and, in a strangled voice, told them, 'I still love her. I fucking LOVE her. How could I ever do that to her?' he gestured at the photographs.

'You had the motive; she spurned you. You had the opportunity and no alibi. The means – as a former SAS soldier, you were resourceful. In addition to that, you have a history of stalking her and mentally abusing her during your marriage.' The DI gathered up the photographs as he spoke. 'It doesn't look good.'

'I'll tell you something,' Harrison said, his voice shaky but intense, 'I hope I find the bastard that did that to her, before you do. I know how to deal with fucking scum like that.'

'You won't be able to do much from a police cell. By the way, we're processing the DNA taken after your arrest. Let's see if we have a match with DNA taken at the scene.' The DCI stood to his full height.

Rubbing his chin, he continued. 'We've read the reports of your interview last night. This claim that you were following someone else seems a bit thin. There was no evidence anyone else was around. Not a footprint. Not a shadow. Seems to me, you were trying to finish the job you started in Barbados. I advise you to get yourself a solicitor, because you're going to need a good one.'

CHAPTER FIFTY-ONE

He'd heard tiny noises behind him as he made his way into the Dene, and as a precaution, had slipped off the track and hidden behind a large oak, silently waiting. Sure enough, before long he'd heard footsteps and sensed, rather than saw, a dark shape pass. He'd abandoned his mission and then driven around for a while to see if anything happened.

When, from the safety of his car parked half way up the street, he'd seen someone bundled into the police car outside Carol's house, he was intrigued. Was that her ex? It looked like him. He laughed all the way home. If that was him, the wanker had done him a favour.

But, seriously, they must have been waiting for him. How had they been expecting his visit? Thinking it through, he came to the conclusion that they must have put surveillance in place, following his earlier aborted visit. Also, the fact that he'd heard no mention of anything untoward in his eavesdropping, led him to the conclusion that they could have found his cameras and were playing him. The bastards had set him up.

Assessing the potential damage, he immediately got rid of his car, before hiring another, using an alias. Now there was no link.

It was time for the final push.

CHAPTER FIFTY-TWO

Tim put the address in his Sat Nav and, following the verbal instructions, took the exit for South Shields after leaving the Tyne Tunnel. He pulled into a wide street, lined with cherry trees, bare now in the depths of winter. Drawing up in front of a smart, two-storey block of flats, the voice told him, "Your destination is on your left" and then "You have reached your destination."

Carrying a clipboard, he walked up the path towards a wide, red-painted door, flanked on either side by boxes of winter-flowering pansies. When he pressed the bell, he could hear it echoing within the flat. Before long, the door was opened and he was face to face with a man of around thirty-five. Tim studied him, taking in his build, which bordered on heavy. Dark, curly hair, swarthy skin, sporting a five o'clock shadow.

The man looked at him. 'Can I help you?'

'Dan Smithson?' Tim asked in his measured voice.

'Yes, what can I do for you?' Smithson had a look of polite enquiry on his face.

'I'm Tim Lawrenson. I've just been appointed as your Landlord's agent and wondered if you could spare me a few moments? My apologies, I should have rung you before calling, but I was in the area and took a chance on you being in,' he improvised.

'I see. Good to meet you.' Smithson extended his hand, smiling.

Tim shook his hand. 'Mrs Barrington's asked me to do an initial survey of her property portfolio. Check on the condition of the properties. Find out if any repairs are required. That sort of thing. I wondered if it would be convenient for me to have a look around?'

'Oh. I'm terribly sorry, I'm afraid you've caught me at a bad time. I was just about to go out. I've got an appointment. Any other time, by arrangement, would be fine,' he said, checking his watch.

'Not a problem. Can you just confirm there are no outstanding maintenance issues that you're aware of, at the moment? No? Very well, I'll call soon and arrange a convenient time to do a proper inventory. Sorry to have bothered you.'

'No bother at all. Good to have met you.' They shook hands again, before Tim turned and walked back down the path.

On the drive back through the Tyne Tunnel, Tim was looking forward to putting Carol's mind at rest about Dan Smithson. He could understand why she'd mistaken Terry Archer's photograph for Dan Smithson. There was a resemblance. Similar sort of build, and the same thick, dark, curly hair. Similar features. But he definitely was not Terry Archer.

He reached Jesmond, and before long drew up on the gravelled drive. He'd rung ahead to say he was on his way, and Carol answered the door within seconds of him ringing the bell.

'Were you waiting behind the door?' he asked, amused. He gave her a brief hug and a peck on the cheek as he entered the hallway. 'I've just come from South Shields.' They were walking into the sitting room and she turned to him.

'I know you have. You just told me on the phone. Stop teasing. What did you find out? Is it Terry Archer?'

'You can relax, Dusty,' he said, placing his hands on her shoulders and looking into her eyes. 'Your Mr Smithson is definitely not Terry Archer, so that's one less thing for you to worry about.'

She breathed an audible sigh of relief. 'Thank goodness for that. Tell me exactly what was said.'

'I introduced myself as your agent and asked if I could inspect the property. He was very polite, but said it wasn't convenient. He was going out. I can see why you thought that the photograph of Terry Archer was of him; there's a definite likeness there. Same sort of hair.'

'Oh, what a relief. I feel such a fool. Thank you SO much for checking for me. You must think I'm unhinged. Come to think of it, I probably am.'

He laughed. 'Not at all, darling. Well, maybe just a bit. But at least that puts that fear to bed for you. I'll keep in touch, but if you need anything in the meantime, you know where I am, just call me. I need to get to the office now. Take care.'

He hugged her again, before leaving. 'See you again soon, Dusty.'

CHAPTER FIFTY-THREE

In the office allocated to DCI Brown and DI Phillips, courtesy of Newcastle Central, Gayle was chatting with the two detectives when the door opened and Superintendent Jensen popped his head around it. He entered and plonked himself on the edge of a desk.

'How's the investigation coming along?' he asked. 'Any progress?'

'The evidence is mounting against Saul Harrison,' said DCI Brown, who was sitting on the edge of the desk opposite. 'We're going to put what we've got to the DPP in Barbados if the DNA results are a match. Let's hope they are. That would clinch it.'

'What if the DNA doesn't match?' asked the Superintendant, biting on some hard skin on the side of his finger.

'We hope it does. But if not, we've got circumstantial and will keep digging. If we can place him in Barbados, we're home and dry. He may have travelled on a false passport, maybe via another island, so it's a bit like looking for a needle in a haystack, but the team back home are on it. We know, from the tickets your people found, that he was intending to go to Barbados while his ex-wife was there. We think he changed his mind about using tickets in his own name.'

'If he does turn out to be your perp,' said Gayle, 'the profile of a predatory stalker doesn't quite fit - in that his victim is known to him and professes to be in love with her,'

Louis turned to her. 'I guess these psychiatrists don't always get it right.'

'Well, if you do have enough to charge him,' Mike Jensen said, 'we certainly won't object to extradition. Your case trumps ours. By the way, how're you enjoying the cold weather? Bit of a shock to the system, I should think, after Barbados.'

CHAPTER FIFTY-FOUR

Sitting at the desk in my office at home, I was trying to focus on an email I was composing to a Japanese company relocating to Tyneside in three months time. I was determined to get back to work, and had accepted a new commission with them. Surely, I thought, by then this will all be resolved? I needed the discipline of work. My injuries were practically healed now, and the stronger I got, the more I was going stir-crazy hanging around the house. The terror at being stalked had settled down into a permanent feeling of dread, deep in my belly. True to her word, Gayle kept a close eye on me and I knew help was just the press of a button away, should anything happen.

Although I tried to insist, Fiona refused to leave me and return to Barbados. She confessed that things still weren't too good between her and Simon, since he'd pointed the finger at her brother. An act of treachery she was finding hard to forgive. She had tried to persuade me to go shopping with her at the Metrocentre, a huge shopping mall in Gateshead but although I was tempted, I really needed to work on the new commission.

The phone on the desk rang and I picked it up, impatiently, keen to get back to wording my email. It was Dan Smithson. I groaned inwardly.

'Hi Carol, sorry to bother you, but it's an emergency. Water's pouring into the kitchen from the flat above. It's coming through the light fitting. I'm worried about the electrics and the ceiling's beginning to bulge. I didn't know if it was you I should ring, or your new Agent, but I don't have his number.'

Shit I thought. I was the only person with a key to the first floor flat, currently empty. I would have to go straight over there. I knew from past experience the damage water can do to property. Why oh why hadn't I sorted out a real Managing Agent?

'This is ironic,' Dan continued, 'coming so quickly after his visit. I no sooner tell him that everything is hunky-dory, when this happens.'

'I'll deal with it,' I said quickly. 'Tim is away at the moment,' I improvised. 'I've got a spare key to the upstairs flat,' I got up from the desk, 'I'll call a plumber and come straight over.'

'I've already called him. I hope that's ok? I still have his number from when he installed the new boiler.'

'Right.' I reluctantly closed my laptop. 'I'll leave now and be there in about half an hour.' I put my phone down and hurried to the bedroom to change into my boots and put on a warm jacket. I scribbled a quick note for Fiona, leaving it on the hall table. Just then, Pauline turned up, and insisted on coming with me once I'd outlined the problem.

'Have you run it by Gayle? she asked. 'You know she's warned you to be extra vigilant and to let her know if you're meeting anyone.'

'But... oh, I suppose you're right. This is awful, having to be wary of practically everyone I know.' In my hurry to get over there and prevent the ceiling caving in, I'd momentarily overlooked the need to be cautious. I picked up my phone and got through to Gayle and explained the situation.

'I'll have to go over there, Gayle. The upstairs flat is empty just now, and I'm the only one with a key. The last time one of my tenants had a water leak from the premises above, it ended up with the ceiling coming down. Cost a fortune. Huge insurance claim. Pauline's going with me. I'm sure everything will be ok.'

'Well, just to err on the side of caution, I'm going to ask a couple of the South Shields lads to accompany you. They'll meet you at the flat. Better safe than sorry, although in the light of recent events, I'm not sure you are in any further danger. Give me the address.'

'What do you mean?'

'Actually, I was planning to come to see you later today. I understand the Barbados officers are close to charging Saul Harrison with the attack on you in Barbados. Some fresh information has come to light, which has convinced them he could be responsible, although their enquiries are still on-going. I'll talk it through with you when I see you later.'

I was dismayed. So, it looked as though it might be Saul after all. I felt sick. After that bizarre night, a week ago, when Saul was arrested, things had been very quiet at home. An uneasy peace had settled over the house. The security paraphernalia had been left in place, as had the surveillance cameras. The security lights continued to be checked daily. Saul was still in custody. Gayle told me he'd been interrogated about the events in Barbados, and had no alibi for a few days either side of the attack. He claimed he was ill and in bed for almost a week, but didn't have anyone who could corroborate this. Everything seemed to be in limbo. Now, it looked as though he was going to be charged with attacking me.

'Are you still there, Carol?' Gayle's voice came over the phone.

'Yes, I'm here. Just trying to take it in.' I shook my head.

CHAPTER FIFTY-FIVE

On the drive to South Shields, I talked things through with Pauline. We'd been friends for a long time, since school, and she'd known Saul for as long as I had.

'Do you really think Saul's capable of doing that to me?' I asked her.

She took a deep breath. 'I wouldn't have said so,' she said, slowly. 'But... I'm not really surprised, if that makes sense? There was always a dark side to him. Sinister, even. I used to hate the way he treated you. Always putting you down. Making everything your fault. He could be an absolute shit.' She glanced at me. 'And if the police are going to charge him, they must be pretty sure he did it,' she added.

'I never realised you felt that way about him. I mean, I knew you didn't like him much, but still... I wonder what new evidence they've found?'

We drove in silence for a while, in the dimness of the Tyne Tunnel, each lost in our own thoughts.

'What's this tenant like?' Pauline asked, as we exited the tunnel.

'Well, I've always found Dan to be a decent guy. Likeable. But a bloody nuisance. Always wanting something done at the flat. I've kept meaning to appoint a managing agent, to keep him out of my hair. I bloody wish I had. Still, it's hardly his fault this time.'

After taking the eastbound slip road, I turned the car in the direction of South Shields town centre.

'I feel a bit ashamed, and stupid, that I suspected him of being a murderer.' I glanced at Pauline, and pulled a face.

'And a stalker,' she laughed. 'Seriously, though, there's so much turmoil in your life just now, I think you'd suspect even the Pope of being a murderer, if he was in the vicinity.'

'I would not,' I said, indignantly. 'He doesn't speak good English.'

'Is this guy married?' she asked, as I slowed the car to turn into the tree-lined road towards the flats.

'No, single. I'm not sure if he's been married, but he's got two kids. He works from home as some kind of IT consultant. That's why he needs a two-bedroom flat. He uses the second bedroom as an office, and it doubles as a bedroom for his girls when they visit.'

I parked on the road outside the flat, and looked around. There was no sign of the police, so we sat in the car for a few minutes, waiting. Dan must have seen us from his window, and came to the front door.

'Is that him? Mmm... looks a bit of alright,' muttered Pauline. 'I wouldn't say no.'

'Hey, don't forget you're a married woman,' I joked. 'Let's just go in. He must be wondering why we're just sitting here while his ceiling's in danger of collapsing. The police won't be long, I'm sure.'

We walked up the short path to the front door. The tubs flanking either side of the step were brimming with winter-flowering pansies, and looked glorious. Dan was on the doorstep and greeted us with a friendly smile.

'Hi, this is a friend, Pauline. Pauline, Dan.' I looked at him as they shook hands. He looked different; his dark curls were gone, replaced with a very short style. His hair even looked lighter.

'Been having your hair cut? Suits you. Makes you look younger.'

He preened, running a hand over his head, apparently pleased at the compliment. 'It was starting to thin a bit. Thought I needed a change. Come on through. The plumber hasn't arrived yet, but he should be here any minute.'

As we followed him along the hallway, towards the lounge, I noticed how clean and tidy the place looked, though almost bare. The photographs of his two girls, and a couple of vividly-coloured abstract paintings, usually on the walls in the hall, were missing.

'Where have all the photographs and paintings gone?' I asked, gesturing to the walls.

He turned to me, 'Oh, I'm going to emulsion the walls. Just getting the place cleared to start decorating. I take it that's ok? I mean, I'm using the same colours, just freshening it all up, really.'

'No, that's fine.' I followed him into the pristine living room, and again registered bare walls. 'You decorating in here, too?' I asked.

'Yeah, doing the whole place up.'

We walked into the kitchen. Near a pair of step ladders, was a half-full bucket of water on the floor, directly beneath the light fitting. Big fat drops were plopping into it quite rapidly.

'That's the third bucket,' Dan pointed out. 'I've had to push a hole in the plaster, to stop the whole ceiling coming down,' he explained, looking up.

I followed his gaze. 'Well, you did the right thing. But what a mess. I'd better get upstairs and see what's causing it. No sign of the plumber yet?'

'No, he said he'd be straight here. You go on up. I'll give him another call first.' He picked up his phone.

Key in hand, I stepped out of the front door and looked around. Still no sign of the police. *So much for back up* I thought, letting myself into the door to the first floor flat. I ran up the stairs, heading for the kitchen, which I knew was directly above where the water was coming through. I couldn't see anything untoward. I crouched to look under the sink unit. No leaking pipes that I could see. I thought *Shit, it must be coming from a pipe under the floorboards.* I heard a noise behind me and looked up to find Dan had followed me up.

'Can't see anything obvious under here,' I told him.

'Let me take a look.' He got down on all fours to examine the pipework under the sink.

'No, you're right,' he said, getting to his feet and wiping the dust from his knees. 'Let's pull the washing machine out, check the pipes at the back,' he suggested. Together we shuffled the machine out, but the floor behind was dry and the pipe looked intact.

'What time's the plumber getting here?' I asked him. 'Doesn't he know it's an emergency?'

'He's been stuck in traffic. There's been a big accident on the main road apparently, but he's on his way now. We'll just have to wait for him to find the leak. There's nothing obvious here. Must be under the floorboards. We need to turn off the stop cock. Do know where it is? I didn't see it under the sink... I'll just have another look.' He got down on his hands and knees and stuck his head into the cupboard. 'Oh, here it is,' his muffled voice informed me from the depths of the cupboard. 'It's a bit stiff... oh that's it, it's turning.'

He backed out of the cupboard, a triumphant look on his face. 'That should stop it til the plumber gets here.'

I thanked him for his help and as we made our way back down the stairs, I asked 'Where's Pauline?'

'Oh, she asked if it was ok to use the bathroom.'

'How are your girls?' I asked, as we made our way back down the stairs.

'Oh they're great,' he said, his face lighting up as he talked about them. 'Jessica's going to be thirteen next week. Can't believe she's going to be a teenager.'

Before following him back into the ground floor flat, I looked again to see if the police had arrived, but there was still no sign of them. I wondered if they'd been caught up in the same accident that was holding up the plumber – that would explain them not showing up.

We made our way down the hall, through the living room and into the kitchen again. The water was still plopping loudly into the bucket, but less frequently. There was no sign of Pauline and I was wondering what was keeping her so long in the bathroom.

'Coffee while we wait?' Dan asked, opening one of the kitchen wall cupboards.

'Yeah, that would be good, thanks,' I said. 'I'm just going to see what's keeping Pauline.'

I turned to head for the bathroom, when my hair was suddenly grabbed from behind in a painful grip, and my head forcefully jerked back. It was so sudden and unexpected, I had no time to react. A foul-smelling pad was clamped over my nose and mouth and I found myself choking, struggling to breathe. I fought to get free with every ounce of strength I possessed, kicking and elbowing, but my vision blurred, I began to feel woozy and realised I was losing consciousness. Just before I passed out,

I noticed a pool of bright red blood on the cream floor tiles, spreading out from behind the kitchen island.

CHAPTER FIFTY-SIX

I became aware of movement and pain and couldn't work out what was happening. My head was throbbing and I felt sick. Trying to put my hand to my head, I realised my hands were tied behind my back.

Suddenly I was thrown against something and realised I was in the boot of a moving car. There was something stuffed into my mouth, which felt incredibly dry. *Oh God* I thought in mounting panic, *I can't breathe.* I felt myself starting to hyperventilate. I've always been a bit claustrophobic, and this was my worst nightmare come true. I could feel my heart rate escalating alarmingly, and my breath was coming in shallow gasps, through the gag. *Keep calm* I told myself, *keep calm... you need to deal with this.* I tried to control my breathing; deep breath in through the nose, hold it for a count of seven, then slowly release it through the mouth, *in......hold.......out.*

Gradually, my heart rate slowed, and I tried to take stock. My ankles were hurting and I realised they too were tightly bound. *Oh shit.*

I remembered an article I'd recently read about what to do if you ever find yourself locked in the boot of a car. What the hell did it say? Try to kick out the tail lights and put your hand through to attract attention? Where the hell were the tail lights? I couldn't see a damn thing. I didn't remember any advice about what to do if your hands and feet were bound. *Where's he taking me?* I thought. *What's he planning to do? What's this all about?*

My hands touched on something warm behind me. Exploring with my fingers, I found another hand. Pauline was in there with me... I grasped her fingers and tried to call her name, but only managed a pathetic grunt through the gag. There was no responding pressure from her fingers... *Oh Pauline, please be alright. Please don't let him have hurt you too badly.* I remembered the blood spreading out on the floor. *Oh God.*

I tried to turn myself over to face Pauline and after an exhausting struggle, managed to heave myself around, claustrophobia forgotten in the desperate need to help my friend. I wanted to touch her, to try to assess how badly injured she was, but unable to use my hands, all I could do was put my face close to hers to check if she was breathing. I couldn't see her in the dark. There was no sound from her, and I couldn't detect any breathing.

'No, No, No.' I tried to scream. 'Oh God, please no.' Panic, shock, terror built up inside me until I thought I was going to pass out. I could barely breathe; I couldn't release the scream inside that was threatening to choke me. *Oh God, please, please, please make her breathe. Don't let her be dead.* I could hear whimpering and keening noises and realised that they were coming from me. My face was lying in something sticky, and there was a strange metallic smell. I realised I must be lying in Pauline's blood.

I don't know how long I lay there, helpless to help Pauline. Hours seemed to pass. I wouldn't accept that she was dead at first, but as time passed, I could feel her body cooling and I knew. My mind became numb and I seemed to float away, no longer trapped in the boot of a car, but watching myself from somewhere above, clinging to the body of my dearest friend. This couldn't be happening. Everything was surreal.

Eventually, a long time later, the motion suddenly stopped and all was quiet. I felt the car dip, and then rise, as he got out. This was followed by a low rumbling noise, like a roller-shutter door moving. Then the car briefly moved again before coming to a halt. Another low rumble. Suddenly the boot was opened and he was standing there, silhouetted against the blinding light of a fluorescent fitting above his head. He fiddled with the bindings on my ankles, then grabbed my arm and roughly hauled me out of the boot.

Excruciating pain shot through my numb legs and ankles, and I staggered and would have fallen but for his iron grip on my upper arm. We were in a garage and I registered bare brick walls and a steel roller-shutter door, before being pushed unceremoniously through a doorway, into a small galley kitchen. He then manhandled me into a sparsely furnished sitting room, with a chintzy settee and one armchair.

He threw me into the chair, then bent over me and savagely ripped the tape and gag from my face. It hurt like hell, but it was such a relief to be able to breathe properly and I took some big gulps of air.

'Pauline?' I sobbed. 'Why?'

'Shouldn't have brought her with you, should you?' he laughed. 'It was just meant to be you. Pure improvisation, getting rid of her. Thought I did rather well, seeing as I wasn't expecting you to have company. I had an iron bar there just in case you proved troublesome. Came in handy.'

He was looming over me and suddenly I remembered this happening before. *Of course,* I thought, as the realisation hit me.

'It was you,' I whispered. 'In Barbados.'

'Oh how perceptive of you, Carol. I knew you were bright.'

CHAPTER FIFTY-SEVEN

Gayle called in to see Carol, as she did most days. Fiona answered the door and ushered her in.

'Carol's not in just now. She left me a note. She's gone to see a tenant in South Shields. Can I get you a drink?'

'Isn't she back yet?' Gayle asked, sharply, following Fiona into the sitting room.

'Well, no. I've just got in. I don't know what time she went. Why? Is there a problem? Pauline's with her.'

'Just a minute.' Gayle took out her phone and walked into the hallway to make a call. Fiona could hear the urgency in her voice as she yelled at someone down the phone. She came back into the sitting room, looking agitated, the phone at her ear.

'Carol's not answering her phone. Have you got Pauline's number?'

'She could be driving; I don't think she's got hands-free in her car... I'll get Pauline for you.' Fiona keyed in Pauline's number, which just rang out before going to voicemail. 'She's not answering either. Gayle you're worrying me. What's wrong?'

'I arranged for some police cover for Carol, as a precaution. But they were involved in an accident on their way, and didn't get there in time. Do you know who the tenant is? Do you have his number?'

'Well, no, but Carol keeps files on the properties, in the office. I'll just see if I can find that one.'

After a minute or so, Fiona returned with a red file in her hands, the spine labelled *SOUTH SHIELDS*. She handed it to Gayle.

Inside the file, there were two sections, with dividers indicating

Ground Floor and *First Floor* It obviously had to be the tenant in the ground floor flat that Carol had gone to see, and looking inside, Gayle found the tenant's name, Dan Smithson, together with a telephone number. She was just about to call him, when a small photograph fell out of the file on to the floor. Fiona, who was looking over her shoulder, picked up the photo and looked at it.

'Oh, is that him?' she asked, looking at a sandy-haired, plump-ish man, smiling for the camera. 'Strange. He's nothing like the man in the other photo that Carol was so worried about.'

'What other photo? What are you talking about, Fiona?'

Fiona explained about Carol finding the photograph on Peter's phone and getting Tim Lawrenson to check him out.

'Tim put her mind at ease,' she said. 'He told her the tenant is definitely not Terry Archer. He did say there was a resemblance, but I can't see it, if that's the tenant in the photo.'

'Who is Terry Archer? Can I see this other photograph?' Gayle's tone was urgent.

'According to Tim, Terry Archer is the name of the man in the photograph Carol found on Peter's phone,' Fiona explained, scrolling through to find the picture. 'That's him,' she said, handing the phone to Gayle.

Gayle studied the photograph closely, then went very still. 'And Carol thought this was her tenant?'

'Yes, she was really worried. Her mind was all over the place. She had it in her head that he'd joined the hiking group to get at Peter, before coming for her.'

'And she never thought to mention this to me?'

'Well, she asked Tim to check him out first, because Tim's the leader of the hiking group. He knows the man in the photo. She knew Tim was the only person who could absolutely confirm that her tenant is not the man in the photo.'

Gayle muttered something unintelligible before going into the hall again and making a call to DCI Mayne.

'Boss, I'm concerned for Carol Barrington's safety, and her friend, Pauline. They went to see one of Carol's tenants in South Shields about

189

three hours ago and haven't returned. Their phones are just ringing out. I arranged back up, as a precaution, but it never arrived, because of an accident en route.' Gayle was pacing up and down the hallway.

'I've just been shown a photograph of a man Carol thought was her tenant. You know I never forget a face. Well, I'm certain it's a man I interviewed some time ago, in London, called Justin Green. One of Justin Green's students at University College London, was beaten and raped in her own flat. She later died of her injuries. Her flat had been bugged. We interviewed Green as a person of interest, but he had a cast iron alibi and was therefore never treated as a suspect. But, I always had my suspicions - there was something about him that didn't ring true.'

'Go on,' encouraged Patsy.

'If I'm right, then Justin Green is living under an assumed name, as Carol's tenant. He also used the name Terry Archer to join the hiking group that Carol's deceased husband was a member of. I'll explain the situation fully when I see you, but I believe they're in grave danger. I want to go over to South Shields, without delay to check things out. I'll need some back up.'

'How certain are you that the man in the photograph on the phone is Justin Green? Could you not be mistaken? You're making a lot of assumptions, based on your recollection.' The DCI was playing devil's advocate.

'I've got no doubt at all. I'll never forget his face.' Her voice betrayed her agitation. She wanted to get over to South Shields right away.

'Ok, Gayle. We'll go with it. But if you're wrong, you could have egg on your face.'

'I'll take that chance, boss.'

'Right. I'll request assistance from South Shields; get a couple of their lads to go there now. And I'm on my way, too.'

'I hope they're more efficient than those morons were this morning. They didn't even report back to let me know they'd been in an accident. That left Carol totally exposed. I'm leaving now.'

Fiona was on her feet, waiting for Gayle to go back into the room. 'What's going on?'

'I just need to check something out. Can't say much more at the moment. I'll keep in touch and let you know what's happening. Try not to worry.' And with that she was gone, leaving Fiona very worried.

Driving through the Tyne Tunnel, Gayle thought back to the case in London. A young girl had been raped and beaten in her flat, and died later without regaining consciousness. The assailant had stuffed her knickers into her mouth to gag her, before assaulting her. Justin Green had been interviewed in the course of the enquiries and there had been something about him that hadn't rung true with Gayle. He was the victim's lecturer at college, where she was studying electronics. The girl had been for a quick drink with friends after class one night, before returning to her first floor flat, where she was attacked. Justin Green had been interviewed as a general suspect, but had provided a solid alibi for that night.

Gayle had left London soon after, for personal reasons, whilst the investigation was in progress, so didn't have any further involvement with the case. She'd kept in touch with a colleague on the force however, and knew that the perpetrator had never been found. That was five years ago.

When she arrived at the flat in South Shields, a squad car was already there, waiting. She quickly outlined the situation to the two young DC's, then knocked at the door. When there was no response, she used the key that had been in Carol's file. The door opened into a wide hallway. A spacious bedroom led off the hall to the left, a smaller bedroom and separate bathroom to the right. The living room was straight ahead. It was a large room, with a high ceiling. A spacious, modern kitchen was accessed through a door on the far side of the room.

The flat was tastefully furnished and was very tidy, but it soon became obvious, as they looked around, that it wasn't being lived in. There were no clothes in the wardrobe, no food in the fridge or cupboards, and the waste bins and wheelie bin were all empty. The kitchen ceiling was damaged around the light fitting, and tiny drops of water were still coming through, dripping into an overflowing bucket.

Gayle also had with her the key to the first floor flat, so they went up there next. Notes in Carol's file indicated that the flat was currently unoccupied, so she wasn't surprised to find it empty. She quickly looked around, but couldn't see any sign of where the water might be coming from. More importantly, neither was there any sign of Carol or Pauline.

Gayle had just gone back down the stairs, when DCI Patsy Mayne arrived. She quickly brought her up to speed and explained in more detail about the photographs, showing her the one she'd found in the file and the one on the mobile phone.

'So, if Carol Barrington thought the guy in the photograph on the phone was her tenant, then whose picture was in the file? They couldn't be less alike. Yet, this Tim Lawrenson told her he thought there was a resemblance after meeting the tenant. Something isn't adding up here. Gayle, how certain are you that the photograph on the phone is of Justin Green?' she asked.

'One hundred per cent. I never forget a face. It's definitely him.'

'And Tim Lawrenson knows him as Terry Archer? We need to speak with this Tim, urgently.'

'I'll see if I can get a contact number from Fiona.'

'And you're sure Carol and Pauline went into the flat? Couldn't they have gone somewhere else, shopping or something, when the police didn't turn up?'

'It's possible, but I'm sure Carol would have rung me. If only to complain about the police not turning up. And why aren't they answering their phones now? I'm really uneasy about this.'

'Right, we'll ask around to see if the neighbours have seen anything unusual. Circulate the details of Carol's car and see what that brings up. And get Tim Lawrenson to go to the station in Newcastle. We'll interview him as soon as we get back.'

Just then, a young PC came to the door of the ground floor flat.

'Ma'am? Something you need to see here.' Gayle followed the DCI and the constable into the kitchen. He walked round to the far side of the central island, where he pointed to some fresh-looking stains on the tongue and groove woodwork. 'This looks like blood, ma'am. Still wet. Looks like someone's tried to clean it up, but has missed the bit in the grooves.'

'Oh,' Gayle exclaimed, involuntarily. 'How did we miss that?'

DCI Mayne squatted down to take a closer look. 'Right, this is now a crime scene. Gayle, get forensics here. Robin, man the door. You know the drill – nobody to enter until forensics arrive.'

Two Detective Sergeants, and eight uniformed lads from Newcastle were drafted in, and door to door enquiries were swiftly under-way. The initial response didn't produce anyone who recognised the photograph from the file. No-one seemed to know much about who had lived at number 27. Gayle spoke to an elderly lady, who lived in a bungalow to the rear of the block of flats. The lady said her bedroom window looked on to the garage door at the back of number twenty-seven. She told Gayle she'd often seen a large, dark-blue car being driven into the garage. Unfortunately, as the car had tinted windows and the garage door was operated by remote control, she never actually saw the driver, and so couldn't give a description or recognise him from either photograph.

It was now late afternoon, and after Gayle had checked again that neither Carol nor Pauline had returned home, nor been in touch with Fiona, the conclusion was reached that this could be a double abduction and a possible assault. DCI Mayne got the Superintendent on the phone and brought him up to speed.

'Right, Mayne. I'll be SIO on this. First briefing in the Major Incident Room in, say, an hour and a half.'

On her way to the station, for the briefing, Gayle detoured to bring Fiona up to date. She omitted to mention the bloodstains. Fiona was shocked to learn that Carol and Pauline were missing, but Gayle was unable to give her any details. She knew that in any possible kidnap situation, information is tightly controlled and always at the discretion of the Senior Investigating Officer.

'Oh God, what do you think's happened to them?' Fiona asked, searching Gayle's face. 'Where can they be? I'll have to let Julia know. Give her more bad news about her mother. When will it all end?' She looked very worried and began pacing about, running her hands through her short hair, making it stick up. 'Pauline's husband is working away in Qatar... I don't know how to contact him.'

'Come and sit down, Fiona.' Gayle steered her to a chair. 'We'll advise everyone who needs to know. I'm going to ring Julia myself now and arrange for her to come straight home. We'll have someone drive her up. I want you to keep her here, with you, until we get things resolved. Will you do that? You have my number. Let me know immediately if you hear anything from Carol or Pauline. I'll let you know as soon as we have some news. In the meanwhile, apart from discussing this with Julia, you can't tell anyone else what's happening. It's absolutely vital, in a potential abduction, that information is tightly contained.'

'I understand.' Fiona's face had lost all colour.

'I'm arranging for an officer to stay with you. She's on her way now. And it shouldn't be too long before Julia gets here.'

In the car, Gayle got Julia on the phone and explained what had happened.

When Julia went into panic mode, crying and shouting, Gayle felt the need to be firm. 'Julia. Calm Down. I'm arranging for an officer to collect you to bring you home. I want you to stay with Fiona until I contact you again. Do you understand? We're doing all we can to find your mum.' Once she had established that Julia understood her instructions, she hung up before Julia could ask for more details.

Gayle had to keep an open mind until they could establish exactly what had happened, but she feared the worst. She was pretty certain that Justin Green had abducted Carol and would probably kill her, if he hadn't already done so. A chilling thought crossed her mind. If she hadn't seen that photograph, and if she hadn't been on that case in London five years earlier, the team now wouldn't know who they were looking for. At least now they had a name, and a face.

CHAPTER FIFTY-EIGHT

I was slumped in the chair, shivering. 'But why? Why me?'

'You've no idea, have you Carol?' he was leaning over me, his face in mine, smelling of Davidoff aftershave. 'From the moment I saw you on TV, I knew I had to have you.'

'TV?' I couldn't think what he was talking about.

'There you were, outside the Albert Hall. All business-like and aloof in your blue suit. Cool and confident.' He grinned and took a seat on the settee, spreading his arms wide, hands on the back of it. 'I needed to shatter that confidence.'

The penny dropped. I couldn't believe it. I'd been interviewed by the BBC for all of two minutes, a couple of years ago, on my way into a business conference. Something about my opinion on the economy.

'I wanted to see you subdued and whimpering, so I tracked you down,' he grinned, pleased with himself. 'Found you were a landlord. I kept an eye on your portfolio and rented the first property that became available. When you came to interview me for the tenancy, I thought *Wow she's even better in real life'*. He crossed his legs and settled back further into the settee, preparing to expand on his theme. 'I've enjoyed watching you; fantasising about what I'm going to do to you.' He licked his lips. 'Couldn't make my move while you were with that old man. Then after he'd gone, you were never alone. What with your breakdown and everything. How could you have a breakdown over an old man like him, when you could have me?'

My heart stopped. Suddenly I knew. 'That WAS you in the photograph, wasn't it?' I asked quietly. 'You joined the hiking group.'

He jumped up and loomed over me again, one hand on each arm of the chair, his face in mine. 'What photo?' he demanded. 'What fucking photograph are you talking about?' He was red in the face, screaming at me.

'On Peter's phone. A photo of the hiking group.'

'Trust fucking Peter to have a fucking photo.' I could see him thinking, making the connection. 'So that's why you sent your new 'Agent' over...'

'But... Tim said it wasn't you...'

'Tim.' He spat out his name, as he stood up. 'I'm smarter than all your knights in shining armour.' He smiled at me, a smile of pure malice. 'Thought he'd recognise Terry Archer? The only trouble with that is, it wasn't me who answered the door,' he laughed heartily. 'It was my brother.'

Oh, Tim, that's why you didn't recognise him. 'Did you kill Peter?' I asked quietly. I had to know, yet I didn't want to know.

He was still laughing as he sat back down on the settee. 'It was like taking candy from a baby.'

'You murdered him? You murdered Peter?' A wave of anguish coursed through my body. Painful. Overwhelming. I felt as though I'd been punched hard in my stomach.

'Yes, naive little Carol, I murdered your beloved husband. And I enjoyed it. It was almost too easy. Waited til he was just about to descend the Chimney, then one hefty push and he was gone.' He mimed pushing someone, laughing.

A wail of fury erupted from me. 'You bastard. You evil, fucking bastard.' I jumped up, screaming, struggling against the bonds on my wrists, wanting to kill him with my bare hands, but only managing to kick out at him.

He got to his feet, took a step towards me, and pushed me violently back into the chair. I felt a stinging blow on the side of my head. Putting his face in mine once more, he pulled a pet lip and in a mock-hurt voice said, 'You must have known you were better off without that old man dragging you down?'

My mind was reeling. The shock of knowing he'd murdered Peter added to my terror. He was already a double murderer and that realisation brought with it the certain knowledge that he would kill me too.

I tried to marshal my thoughts. *We shouldn't have gone into the flat before the police arrived. Will Gayle know by now that we didn't have an escort? Will she be looking for us? It'll be too late. She won't know where to look...*

I had to keep him talking. Try to work out how I could possibly get away from him. 'How did you know I'd be in Barbados?' I asked, already knowing the answer.

'Oh Carol, there's nothing about you that I don't know. Didn't you know I was watching your every move?' Without waiting for an answer, he went on. 'I've listened to your phone conversations; all your little chats and emails with Fiona and Julia. I've watched you crying yourself to sleep over that old man...'

He resumed his seat on the settee. 'Pouring your heart out to that Linda. "He was my soul-mate," he mimicked. 'And as for the Barbados police. Those fools were never going to find me entering Barbados. As if I'd travel as Dan Smithson... give me some credit.'

My mind was trying to process everything. It felt like a knife in my heart to know that Peter had been murdered, but I couldn't let myself think about that now. Nor could I think about Pauline's poor body lying in the boot of the car. If I dwelt on them, I'd go to pieces completely and I knew that if I was to stand any chance of survival I needed a cool head. I'd have to deal with those things later; for now I needed to keep my emotions in check. I had to concentrate on finding a way to survive.

'It was great fun finding out that ex of yours had been arrested. Never laughed so much in my life. What a moron! Thinks he's still in the SAS,' he laughed scornfully. 'Another little knight in shining armour. Well, just look where that's got him. Actually, he's lucky he's in prison, safe from my attentions.' Warming to his theme again, he went on, 'What you don't seem to have grasped, Carol, is that I'm cleverer than all your other admirers. I'm always one step ahead, of them, and the police.'

My wrists were on fire and I had cramps in my arms. 'Please, could you untie my wrists? They're really hurting... I promise I won't try to get away.'

He gave me a withering look and I thought he was going to refuse, but he got up from the chair and pulled a knife from his back pocket. For a heart-stopping moment I thought he was going to stab me, but he roughly yanked me by the shoulder, turned me sideways, then sawed at the tape around my wrists. Relief was mixed with intense pain as I rubbed my sore wrists and felt the circulation returning to my numb hands, arms and aching shoulders. He leant over me again and put the tip of the knife against my throat.

'Do anything stupid and I'll slit your throat,' he said, almost casually, and I didn't doubt him. He resumed his seat on the sofa and went on, 'While you were in the cupboard, I took your car to an old, disused garage, down by the docks. They won't find it. And they won't have a clue where to start looking for you.'

In the cupboard? 'But they know I was coming to see you.'

'Really? They'll find the flat empty; obviously not lived in for some time. Once they start to suspect something's happened to you, they won't know where to start looking. There's no way they can trace you to this place. They don't know my real name; they'll be trying to trace Dan Smithson, who doesn't exist. You're the only person who knew me by that name. Ah, and I remembered you took a picture of me when I first took up the tenancy, so I took the liberty of removing it from your file when I was in your house. And replacing it with another. He looked pleased with himself. 'You see, I think of everything. There are no photographs of Dan Smithson for anyone to find. Neat, eh?'

'There's the one on Peter's phone.'

'Well, let's think about that, Carol.' He got to his feet, pacing about the small room. I could see he was thinking through the implications of the police possibly having his photograph. 'Best case scenario, the police don't make any connection between Dan Smithson and the photo on the phone. Even if they know you thought the guy in the photo was your tenant from South Shields, Tim will tell them that it's not. They'll find the substitute photo I put in your file and be looking for a chubby, ginger bloke. Worst case scenario, they decide the picture on the phone IS of your tenant, and they circulate it. That could possibly bring up my real name. But, look at me now. I look nothing like I did. No-one seeing me now would recognise me as Justin Green. And I'll be long gone by the time they work anything out, anyway.'

He continued with his diatribe. 'I got rid of my car after I realised that macho ex of yours had probably seen it. Got a replacement using another alias, so there's no link there. I rented this place a couple of months ago. We're very remote, high up on the moors. There's no-one around for miles.' He smiled at me again, a cold grimace.

'I took risks to get to you, Carol, knowing your memory was coming back. I couldn't have you telling your 'friend' Gayle, all about me.'

'But I didn't remember. I didn't know who you were,' I protested.

'Too risky, Carol. You could've remembered any minute. Anyway, it's too late now. Pity really that I hadn't finished you off that night in Barbados. It would've saved me an awful lot of trouble. Then again, I wouldn't have had all the fun I've had watching your feeble efforts to come to terms with things and try to work out what happened to you. Or the fun we're going to have now.' The chilling smile again; he was enjoying himself.

'Whatever. Here's the plan now. We're going to have some fun. Lots of fun, together. You'll enjoy it; well some of it, and then it'll be time to say goodbye. When it gets dark, we're going to go for a little drive on the moors. There's no-one around, so don't go thinking you're going to get any help. I've been busy. I've prepared a nice little place for you. It took some digging in this cold; the ground was bloody hard. It'll have to hold two of you now, of course. Friends forever,' he laughed. 'Means I'll have to haul your bloody friend's body over the moor, of course. Fucking nuisance.

I hope you appreciate all the effort I've put in just for you? You'll never be found. There'll be no reason for anyone to ever start looking around here. You'll just disappear off the face of the earth.' He smiled again, spreading his arms wide, palms up, delighted with his ingenuity.

CHAPTER FIFTY-NINE

As the realisation sank in that he really was planning to kill me, I felt faint, my guts churning in fear. *Oh God, Julia will never know what happened to me.*

'I can see you sitting there wondering how to save yourself Carol. But you can't. If you try to get away, believe you me you won't succeed.'

'What's wrong with you that you feel the need to kill me?'

'Oh, Carol, Carol. Please spare me the psychoanalysis.'

'What about your children? You'll lose them forever if you go to prison.'

'Children? What children?' he laughed.

'Your girls. Jessica... The photos on your wall...'

He laughed even harder. 'You are so gullible. I've got no kids or ex-partner living around the corner.'

'Well, why...?'

'To make me seem like a regular guy, Carol. Someone you'd trust and rent your flat out to. Made me seem like less of a loner, less of a weirdo. And it worked, didn't it?'

I didn't respond. Changing tack again, he suddenly jumped up, put his face a few inches from mine again, and bellowed at me.

'Have you any idea how long it took me to wash your blood off? I was in the sea for bloody ages. Then I had to walk for fucking miles to dry off! And then to find you were still alive! My God, I had a wobble then.' He was yelling at me and seeing him ranting and getting more incoherent, I realised that he was becoming even more unstable. The thought was chilling. *I'm going to die at the hands of this madman.* With a cry of rage, I launched myself at him, kicking him and trying to gouge his eyes out, raking his face with my nails.

'You evil bastard,' I screamed. He held me off easily, laughing, then grabbed one of my wrists, turned me round and twisted my arm hard up my back. The pain was excruciating and I cried out.

'Scream all you want, Carol, there's nobody to hear you. Oh, I do love it when you're mad. Now, this way,' he said, shoving me ahead of him. He propelled me out of the sitting room, into the tiny hall. With my wrist still held firmly in his grip, he pushed me forward, up the stairs. When I stumbled, he slammed his knee into my back and yelled, 'Bitch... keep moving.' We reached the upper landing and he pushed me straight ahead, into a bedroom. 'I've had fun preparing this for you, Carol.'

I looked around and saw a neat, lightly-furnished bedroom. I couldn't see anything out of the ordinary. In the middle of the far wall, there was a double bed, covered with a white bedspread. The only other furniture in the room was a small pine chest of drawers and two matching bedside tables. Then I noticed the manacles attached to the wall behind the bed.

'No,' I said quietly. 'You don't need those... Please...'

'Oh I love it when you beg. But trust me, they'll add to the fun.' He had the knife in his hand again. He yanked on my arm turning me to face him and put the point of the knife under my chin. 'Take your clothes off.'

Slowly, reluctantly, I removed my jacket, then hesitated.

He waved the knife. 'Keep going.' His eyes were boring into me.

I had no choice but to do as he said. Soon, I stood there, in my underwear, cold and quivering with fright and nerves.

'That'll do,' he said. Putting the knife on the bed, he threw me down on my back, climbed over me and quickly got one wrist shackled, then the other. My strength was no match for his and though I struggled and scratched and kicked and tried to bite him, he easily overpowered me.

Once my hands were secured, he tied cord around each ankle, and secured them to the legs at the base of the bed. Totally vulnerable and exposed, I'd never felt such helpless despair and fear in my life. With the knife in his hand, he climbed on to the bed and came towards me and I thought *Just stab me. Get it over with.* I felt eerily calm.

After that, everything was pain. Soon, I ceased feeling the blows. My mind disconnected from my body and it was almost as though I was floating above watching this happening to someone else. His perversion was sickening and the only way I could endure it was to take my mind away from that place and float off to oblivion. I tuned out, no longer hearing his grunts and profanities. Time meant nothing and I've no idea how long I was in that dreamlike state, hovering above my body, feeling and hearing nothing.

Then, abruptly, it was over and he got up off the bed, panting heavily and wiping sweat and blood from his face. 'Did you enjoy that, bitch? I did.' The maniacal grin again.

I slowly, reluctantly, came back to reality. 'I need to use the bathroom.' My voice came in a hoarse whisper. I wanted to scrub his filth off me.

'Not a chance, babe. It's nearly dark enough now. Time to take your final journey. But first, something for you to think about on the way. He sat on the bed, as if we were about to have a cosy chat, and watched my reaction closely when he began to speak.

'I've not only been watching you, Carol, I've been spying on your very lovely daughter... oh, yes, I've got great plans for Julia. She's just like a younger version of you. Perhaps she'll have the sense to be nicer to me than her mother was.'

I screamed 'No' and struggled against my bonds. With the back of his hand, he hit me hard in the face.

'I like her nice little flat in Leeds. Very cosy. Oh, and what a delectable body she's got! Don't you think the young have it all? With their smooth skin and tight little pussies. She has no idea how lovely she is. But, I'll delight in telling her, as I...'

I became aware of a noise, a haunting, keening sound that came from the depths of despair and realised it was coming from me. He punched me hard in the side of my head. I must have briefly passed out, because the next thing I became aware of was him screaming at me to get dressed. The manacles had been removed, but even so, I struggled to get my clothes on. I was in a daze and shaking so much it was a struggle to pull on my boots. Whimpering noises were coming from me, unbidden. He propelled me down the stairs, half pushed, half dragged me through the kitchen and into the garage.

'You get to be with your friend again,' he said, in a chirpy voice. Then, holding my arms in a painful grip, he pushed me head-first into the open boot of the car, scooped my legs up and threw me in. I had a brief glimpse of Pauline's lifeless face, before he slammed the boot closed and all was dark. The horror was almost more than I could bear.

I felt the car reverse a few metres before coming to a halt again and then I heard the roller-shutter door being closed. He was back in the driving seat and the car was rocking on the uneven road. I was being tossed about, bumping into Pauline's body, stiff and unyielding now. *Oh Pauline... Pauline...* I was in a living nightmare, moaning in terror.

CHAPTER SIXTY

Tim Lawrenson was in DCI Patsy Mayne's office when Gayle got back to the Station and there was a message for her to go straight there. Mayne introduced them and Gayle took a seat.

'Mr Lawrenson has just arrived. I've explained that we need him to clarify certain things. Would you like to proceed?'

'Mr Lawrenson,' Gayle said, turning to him, noticing his smart appearance, and aquiline features. 'You're a friend of Carol Barrington. Can you tell us, please, why you visited her tenant, Dan Smithson, in South Shields?' She looked at him, chin tilted up, waiting for his response.

Tim looked puzzled. 'Can I ask why you're asking me this? Has something happened?'

'We can't tell you anything further at the moment, I'm afraid,' said Gayle, rather brusquely. 'Could you just answer the question please?'

Tim looked worried, but gave a clear account of Carol asking him to check out her tenant after becoming worried about a photograph she'd found on her late husband's phone.

'I knew the photo was of Terry Archer, one of the hiking group, but Carol was adamant it was her tenant. I thought she was being paranoid, but I agreed to check him out just to put her mind at rest.' His direct gaze was upon Gayle.

'What happened when you got there?' the DCI interjected.

'I posed as her newly-appointed agent when Dan Smithson came to the door. He was not Terry Archer. I could see some resemblance; the same dark, wiry hair. We chatted for a few minutes about the condition of the property. I found him quite a charming fellow. Then I left. I went to see

Carol and told her she was mistaken.'

'Would you please look at this photograph,' said Gayle, putting the photograph from Carol's file, on the table. 'Do you know this man?'

Tim looked carefully at the chubby face and reddish hair before shaking his head. 'No. I've never seen this man before.'

'Mr Lawrenson, could you have been mistaken about Terry Archer not being Dan Smithson?' Gayle asked.

'Absolutely not,' Tim said briskly, looking directly at her with his intelligent, blue eyes. 'I got to know Terry Archer very well during the time he was a member of the hiking club. It was not Terry who answered the door.'

'Thank you, Mr Lawrenson. You've been very helpful. We may need to speak with you again. If we do, we'll be in touch.' DCI Mayne rose to her feet.

'Has something happened to Carol?' asked Tim, frowning. 'Please, you have to tell me.'

'I'm afraid we're not at liberty to disclose anything at the moment, sir. We'll be in touch.'

'But... is she alright? Why are you asking these questions?' he demanded, his habitual controlled manner deserting him.

'I'm sorry, there's nothing further we can tell you at present.'

'Bollocks. Surely you can tell me if Carol is alright?'

'I'm sorry, sir, but we can't give you any information at the moment,' DCI Mayne said, firmly. Relenting a little, she added, 'When we're in a position to give out further information, we'll be in touch with you.'

'Come on,' he pleaded, 'you can't leave me worried sick like this. You must be able to tell me what's happened. I'm not leaving here until you do.' He resumed his seat and crossed his arms.

'Look,' said Gayle, 'we know how worried you are. But you must understand that there are circumstances in which we are not at liberty to give out any information. - when an investigation is at a sensitive and critical stage. As an ex officer, I'm sure you'll understand.'

'We will let you know, as soon as we are at liberty to disclose information,' said the DCI. 'That's a promise.'

After Tim left, still very unsettled and unhappy, the DCI and Gayle discussed the interview.

'I think the photograph in Carol's file of the chubby red-haired man, was put there to mislead us. Green could have placed it there when he broke in to plant surveillance equipment,' offered Gayle.

'What's your view as to why Lawrenson is certain Dan Smithson is not Terry Archer?' asked the DCI.

'I can only think that it wasn't Dan Smithson who answered the door. He could have sent someone else to the door, knowing Lawrenson would recognise him and his cover would be blown. I think we should check if a Terry Archer travelled to Barbados.'

'We'll make a fully-fledged detective out of you yet, DC Jones,' said Patsy. 'I think your theories could be spot on.' She held the door open. 'I know you're up for promotion. I'll put in a good word for you.' She glanced at her watch. 'Time for the briefing.'

Just before Detective Superintendent Mike Jensen entered and addressed the hastily-assembled team of twenty, Gayle had a quick word with DCI Brown, suggesting he check on Terry Archer entering Barbados,

'Right,' the Super began, 'we now believe that Carol Barrington and her friend, Pauline Bradley have been abducted, from a flat in South Shields, and at least one of them is possibly injured. Let me sum up the situation so far. Some of you know from the initial briefing that Carol Barrington was attacked and critically injured on November 29 last year, in her holiday home in Barbados. At first, she had no memory of the attack, but then got flashbacks that indicated her assailant knew her and was English. The Barbados police have now ruled out everyone interviewed so far in Barbados. Two of their officers are over here, continuing enquiries.' He turned to where the two were sitting. 'This is DCI Louis Brown, and DI James Phillips. We're working together on this case, for now.

From Carol Barrington's former husband, who is currently in custody, we have a partial number plate and a description of the car possibly being used by the abductor. It's still being traced.

This morning, DC Gayle Jones, the FLO on this case, went to see Carol Barrington,' he turned to Gayle. 'Can you tell us what happened, Gayle?'

'Sir. Carol Barrington rang me at nine this morning to tell me she needed to visit a tenant in South Shields and was taking her friend, Pauline Bradley with her. She indicated their photographs on the white board behind her. As a precaution, I arranged for a couple of the South Shields lads to meet her at the property.'

Gayle went on to detail her conversation with Fiona, and produced the phone with the photograph. 'I recognised this man as Justin Green, someone I interviewed five years ago in connection with a rape and murder in the Wimbledon area. He had a cast iron alibi and therefore wasn't in the frame. But my hunch at the time was that he was somehow connected. He was a lecturer at University College London and the victim was one of his students. She'd gone home to her flat near the college, where she was badly beaten and raped. She died soon after being taken to hospital. Mid-case, I moved up to Newcastle and had no further involvement, but I know the perpetrator was never found.' She had their full attention.

'Any questions so far?' the Super asked. When they shook their heads, Gayle went on to summarise the events of the day, then continued.

'Fresh bloodstains were found in the kitchen of Dan Smithson's flat, out of sight behind the island. Forensics say there has been an attempt to clean up the blood; traces have been found over a large patch of floor. The assailant missed the bits we found. Samples were analysed and compared to Carol and Pauline's medical records for blood type. The blood is possibly that of Pauline Bradley. Neither of the women have returned home, or been seen since they left Jesmond at around nine this morning.'

'Just to clarify things,' interrupted DI Kris Hunter. 'You're saying you believe Dan Smithson, the tenant, is Justin Green, who also uses the pseudonym Terry Archer?'

'Yes, that's right. He used the name Terry Archer to join the hiking group, possibly to dispose of Carol's husband who died in a climbing accident last year, but this is supposition at this stage.

We got the Met to check their records of the attack in Wimbledon, five years earlier, looking for any information on Justin Green, but because he was never an active suspect, there was little information on file, and no photographs. A check on the address he'd given at the time, showed he'd long since moved on and no-one could be found who knew of his whereabouts. They promised to trace his family and give us the details as soon as possible.'

Chief Superintendent Jensen got to his feet. 'It's imperative we find this Justin Green as soon as possible. I'll deal with the media on this; no other information is to be given out. This has to be tightly controlled. Right everyone, we need to find this man, and fast. Let's get to work.'

He assigned some of the team to the job of delving into records, checking on NI databases, credit cards, trying to pick up Justin Green's trail and that of his aliases. Others were despatched to South Shields to do more house to house enquiries; CCTV footage was to be checked, around the area of the incident and wider, looking for Carol Barrington's car. Saul Harrison was to be shown the photograph to see if he recognised him as the man he claimed was watching Carol, and to see if he could recall any further details of the car.

'Gayle, as soon as the information's come through from the Met, I'd like you to follow up with Justin Green's family. Take Georgia with you.'

'Yes, sir.' She turned to DC Georgia Green, a bright girl who had only been with the department for six months but was already showing promise. Before she had a chance to speak, the Office Manager, Wendy, interrupted.

'The Met have just emailed the details. There's a mother, and a brother, both living in London.' She handed Gayle a note of the details.

'Thanks Wendy. Can you get someone to book our flights as soon as possible, please, and we'll need to stay in London overnight. Book us an early flight back tomorrow?'

DCI Louis Brown answered his mobile. He listened in silence before thanking the caller and announcing 'Terry Archer flew to Barbados on the twenty-sixth of November and returned on fourth of December.'

'Yess,' cried Gayle, I was right.' It felt good to be vindicated, but she took no pleasure from knowing that Carol and Pauline were without doubt in grave danger.

'Good work, Gayle.' Praise indeed, from the Super.

CHAPTER SIXTY-ONE

Wendy got them on the five o'clock flight to Heathrow, meaning they had to leave straight away. Once on board, Georgia kept up her incessant chatter, with bits of office gossip and rather lurid details of her sex life with her current boyfriend.

After a while, Gayle tuned out. She thought back to the unresolved case involving the attack and murder of the student, and her gut feeling that Justin Green was involved. At the time, she was living with her partner of three years, and they were happy, or so she thought.

As a rookie PC then, she was finding the case quite harrowing. One day she was sent home early with a particularly severe migraine.

She walked in on her partner, naked, on his knees on the rug in front of the log burner, with another woman. They were so engrossed, they didn't even realise she was there until she screamed at them. Yelling with hurt and rage, she kicked him between his legs and he rolled away clutching himself in agony. Out of her mind with fury and hurt, she started kicking the woman in the head and body, before her partner recovered enough to pull her away.

The woman turned out to be a DCI in the Met. Gayle had seriously assaulted a senior officer, causing actual bodily harm. In the end, they came to an understanding. Gayle would immediately put in for a transfer, out of the area. In return, the DCI would not press charges. This had the double advantage of saving both the DCI's marriage and Gayle's career.

'So you screw my partner behind my back, and I'm the one who has to leave?' Gayle had said, bitterly. But she knew when she was beaten, and left London soon afterwards for Newcastle, where she moved back in with her mother.

The worst part for her was leaving in the middle of such a serious investigation. Now, she had a chance to finish the job. She wanted, more than anything in the world, to find Green before he could kill again. She tuned back into the present with a jolt, as the wheels of the aircraft thudded on to the tarmac.

Once they'd disembarked, she switched on her phone and received an update from the office on how the team was progressing. It wasn't encouraging. She explained to Georgia as they walked.

'The car that Saul Harrison saw, the dark blue BMW, has been traced to a car hire firm. They confirmed it was rented by a Terry Archer, but so far there's no trace of it. There's no record of any car registered to either Justin Green or Dan Smithson.' They reached Arrivals, and headed for the BA desk, where the Met had left a set of keys to a car they'd arranged to put at their disposal.

Gayle continued. 'The uniformed officers despatched to South Shields reported nothing unusual seen by any of the neighbours interviewed so far. There was no CCTV to the rear of the flats - which was presumably where he must have had a car ready to take Carol away. It would have been easy for him to bundle someone into the car, unseen, if it was parked in the yard, especially as there was no-one in the flat above to witness anything.'

'What about the front of the building? Any cameras there?' asked Georgia, as they headed for the car park.

'The cameras at the front only picked up the rear of Carol's car, but the rest of the car was obscured by trees. The team said it was frustrating to see it being driven off within ten minutes of being parked there, with no clear view of the driver.'

'Assuming Green took the car, I wonder what he did with it. And where were Carol and Pauline at that time? They must have been left in the flat when he disposed of the car, if the rear doors and boot were visible in the CCTV footage?' Georgia said.

'I wonder if he'd already killed them? Or disabled them in some way?' Gayle speculated. 'The team are examining traffic camera footage in the vicinity of the flat to see if the car's journey can be tracked.'

'And presumably hoping to catch his route back to the flat,' Georgia added.

They located the car and Gayle wasted no time in heading for Wimbledon to see Justin Green's elderly mother, Maud Wilkinson. She lived in a nursing home, which they eventually found, hidden away down a side street off Wimbledon Common. Gayle was grateful to whoever had invented satellite navigation systems. Without it, she thought they'd have had great difficulty finding The Cedars, in the dark.

It was gone seven when they arrived, and, as they made their way across a poorly-lit car park, Gayle hoped the residents hadn't yet retired for the night. She'd phoned ahead and made the manager aware they were on their way, so she presumed Mrs Wilkinson would have been kept up in any event.

They were eventually admitted into the building after pressing the bell and waiting for what seemed like ages for someone to come to the door. The Manager, a slim lady of medium height, neat in a fitted, blue dress, introduced herself and asked them to call her Marianne. She had a warm smile, and Gayle got the impression she'd be kind to her charges.

'It's coming up to bedtime for the residents,' Marianne told them, 'so Mrs Wilkinson's quite tired, and on top of that, she's not a well lady. I understand that your questions can't wait until tomorrow morning, but can I ask that you try not to tire her too much?'

'Of course. We won't keep her too long,' Gayle assured her.

They followed Marianne through to the residents' lounge, where a number of elderly people were seated in a wide semi-circle, either asleep with their heads slumped on their chests, or watching Emmerdale, which was blaring out from the TV. Gayle thought it quite depressing and hoped fervently that she didn't end up in a place like this, no matter how kind the staff.

Marianne pointed out a frail-looking lady, sitting in a wheelchair near the window, staring into space. Her knees were covered by a pink woollen blanket which she was clutching with thin, bony fingers. She looked up as Marianne put her hand on her shoulder and bent to speak to her.

'Maud, these are the two ladies I told you about. They want to speak with you. Is that alright? I'll just take you through to next door, so you can talk in private. They want to ask you a few questions. Nothing to worry about. They've come down from Newcastle just to see you, so be nice to them.'

There was no response from Maud. Turning to Gayle, as she grasped the wheelchair handles, Marianne whispered 'She can be quite obtuse and bad-tempered at times, so try not to upset her.' She walked ahead of them, steering the wheelchair through wide double doors that led into an adjoining, smaller room, with pale walls and parquet flooring. She tucked Mrs Wilkinson's blanket snugly around her before turning to leave.

'I'll just be out here, if you need me,' she added, before closing the double doors behind her.

Gayle made the introductions and asked Maud if she minded answering a few questions. She looked confused, but nodded her assent and Georgia pulled a couple of dining chairs nearer to the wheelchair.

'Mrs Wilkinson, can you tell us when you last saw your son, Justin?'

She may have looked frail, but when she replied, Gayle was amazed to hear a surprisingly firm voice with a strong cockney accent.

'Haven't seen him for years. Not since he inherited his father's money. Never gave me a farthing... I'm his old mum, and he couldn't even spare a penny for me. Always was a selfish little bastard. Never visited me since I come in here, not once.' She set her mouth in a thin, hard line; she looked angry and her tone held more than a touch of bitterness.

'So, do you have any idea where he could be now?' Gayle asked her.

With a withering stare, she replied, 'None at all. I've just told you, I haven't seen him for years.'

'Why did Justin leave the area, Mrs Wilkinson, do you know?'

'He was always a closed book. We was never close. His father didn't hang around long after he was born. He was something big in the city, you see, and someone common like me wasn't good enough for him. But, give him his due, he provided for Justin and kept in touch with him.' She had a faraway look in her eyes as she went down memory lane.

'I married Chris Wilkinson when Justin was eight. From the start, Justin took a dislike to Chris, and made life as difficult as he could for us all. He was a sly little shit. Always causing trouble.'

Gayle tried to interrupt, but Mrs Wilkinson continued her monologue, unabated.

'A year later, along come his half-brother, Rob. Justin's behaviour got worse. The last straw came on Rob's second birthday. Justin took his new puppy into the back yard and beat and kicked it so hard, the poor thing had to be put to sleep. I couldn't take no more. That's when Justin's father sent him to boarding school, down in Kent. Much to our relief. He was a bright kid. Had an aptitude for computers. And electronics. After finishing school, he went to Glasgow University - did electronic engineering. Became a lecturer at University College, London. By then he was living in the city centre and we never saw him.'

'And do you know why he moved north, Mrs Wilkinson?' Gayle prompted her, thinking she was surprisingly talkative for a tired, sick old lady. She needed her to get to the point.

'I'm coming to that. I never knew why he moved north. Never did tell us why. He was the educated one of the family and we always knew we weren't good enough for him; just like his father in that respect. It was around the time his dad died and left him the money that he moved away.' She closed her eyes, and rested her head on the back of her chair.

Gayle thought she'd dozed off, but she suddenly opened her eyes and said 'His brother's a different kettle of fish; he's a good boy. Comes to see me when he can. Loves his old mum. He's a good boy; nothing like Justin.' She picked abstractedly at the pink blanket.

'Ah yes, his brother. Rob, isn't it? Is he in touch with Justin, do you know?'

'He might be, but if he is, he never mentions it to me. He knows it upsets me to hear his name.' She paused. 'How do you know Rob then?'

'I was involved with the case about five years ago when one of Justin's students was murdered, do you remember that? Rob told us he was with Justin on the night of the attack.'

She looked up sharply. 'They never told me much about it,' she said defensively, worrying the blanket again. 'Nasty business from what little I knew.' Gayle wondered then if she'd harboured any suspicions at the time.

'Different boys... different fathers.' Mrs Wilkinson muttered, her fingers working away at a loose thread. She seemed to lose interest then and closed her eyes, resting her head again.

'Thank you so much for your time Mrs Wilkinson, you've been very helpful.' Gayle turned and impulsively patted her shoulder.

'Goodbye Mrs Wilkinson,' said Georgia. There was no response.

'What did you make of that?' Gayle asked Georgia as they headed for the car.

'Well, I thought she looked uncomfortable when you mentioned the attack on the student, and the alibi given by his brother.'

'Mmm... yes, so did I. Let's see what Rob has to say, shall we?'

CHAPTER SIXTY-TWO

Rob Wilkinson ran a fruit stall in Covent Garden, and was known locally as 'Rob the Fruit'. Gayle and Georgia went straight from the care home to his Edwardian semi in Putney, where he lived with his wife and two daughters. His mother had told them Rob didn't go out much at night, so Gayle hoped to catch him at home. He looked surprised when they showed their warrant cards, clearly wondering what two police officers were doing on his doorstep, but courteously invited them in.

He led them into the lounge, an elegant room, with a high ceiling, tall sash windows and delft rack around the pale yellow walls, with blue willow plates. Despite its grandeur, the room had a cosy feel, with a bright blue long-pile rug and toning cushions on the plush velvet settees. Gayle noticed a large box of toys in one corner. There weren't any children in sight, but she noticed a few photos of two little girls of about six and four. Both had Rob's dark, corkscrew curls. Rob's wife, a petite blonde lady with a warm smile, offered to make them some coffee.

Gayle studied Rob as she placed her briefcase on the floor. She could see a resemblance between the two brothers, both had thick, dark, quite curly hair and were about the same height, but Rob was more wiry; less stocky.

'We need to ask you a few questions, Rob. About your brother. We need to find him urgently. Do you know where he is?' she asked as soon as his wife had left the room. Rob took an armchair and invited them to sit opposite, on one of the settees. Rob's wife soon returned, carrying a tray holding a steaming cafetiere, which she placed on the low table in front of them.

'Give it a couple of minutes before pressing the plunger,' she instructed, looking at Rob. 'I need to see to the kids.' Although the coffee smelled good, Gayle was impatient to get on with questioning

Rob.

'To answer your question, I don't know where Justin is now,' said Rob, ignoring his wife's words and pressing the plunger on the cafetiere, and pouring the coffee.

'When did you last see him?' asked Gayle, accepting a small china mug of coffee.

'I saw him last week, actually. I had to go to Newcastle for a friend's funeral and I rang him and arranged to call in at his place in South Shields. First time I've seen him for about three years. We do speak on the phone from time to time, though.'

'What did you talk about?'

'Well, I'd put together a plan to extend my business. I was hopin' Justin would back me, with a loan. He's a cheeky bastard; said he didn't think I had any business acumen and hinted I'd probably spend most of it on drugs. It's not true. I've been clean for years; not that he'd know. Anyway, in the end, he coughed up.'

'Do you mind telling us how much you borrowed?'

'Twenty grand. He transferred it into my bank two days ago.'

Georgia told him, 'We'll need to see that transaction. We're trying to trace your brother, and he just might have left a trail.'

Rob looked slightly startled, but before he could say anything, Gayle asked, 'Did it look as though he was living at the flat when you called in?'

'Well, I think he was still living there, but the place looked bare. No pictures on the walls, bare bookshelves, that sort of thing. When I mentioned it, he said he was in the process of moving out. Out of the area altogether; said he wanted a fresh start. He wouldn't tell me where he was off to. Just said he'd get in touch once he'd settled in.'

'Do you have any idea at all where he might have gone? Anywhere he might have mentioned in the past? Any gut feeling?' Gayle asked.

'No. He never gives anything away.. I know practically nothing about what he gets up to these days.' He took a sip of coffee, the cup rattling against the saucer as his hand shook.

'Why did he move up North in the first place?' Gayle asked. 'Your mother didn't seem to know.' She watched him biting his lower lip.

'I don't really know either. He came into a lot of money when his dad died, so he wasn't tied to his work any more. Why are you asking about him anyway? What's he done?' Rob asked, putting his cup down carefully, trying to control the trembling.

'We need to find him urgently, Rob. If there's any little thing you can tell us that might help? It's really important, could be a matter of life and death,' Gayle said.

'Fuckin' hell. What's happened? You're worryin' me now. What's he done?' Rob was getting agitated, rubbing the back of his neck with one hand.

'We want to talk to him in connection with the abduction of two women. They could be in grave danger. We need to find him quickly.'

He slumped in his seat and put his head in his hands. 'If I knew where he was, I'd tell you, believe me!' he muttered through his fingers. 'I swear I would.' Looking up, he asked, 'Do you really think he's involved?' he looked stricken.

'Yes, we do. Do you know if he has any friends in London? Anyone he keeps in touch with?'

'I wouldn't know. I hardly ever see him, and he tells me nothing. He was always a bit of a loner, though. Never knew him to have any close friends.'

'Did you notice what car he had, when you were up there last week?' asked Georgia.

'Yeah, he had a dark blue BMW, Seven series; a real beauty. I noticed it parked in the yard. Tidy motor.'

'You gave him an alibi five years ago, when one of his students was attacked, did you not?' Gayle asked, changing tack.

He turned to her. 'Yes... yes I did. Why'd you bring that up?'

'Were you covering for him by any chance?'

He shook his head in denial, but couldn't meet her eyes. 'No. Course not. He was with me all night, just like I said.' But his face told a different story.

There wasn't much more to learn from Rob and they stood up to take their leave.

'If you think of anything; anything at all that might help us to find him, please call me straight away.' Gayle handed him her card. 'It might save someone's life.'

He nodded, taking the card. 'I will.'

Once back in the car, Gayle asked 'Well, Georgia?'

'Judging by his manner, I suspect, he gave his brother a false alibi five years ago. If so, he must be bitterly regretting it now. If his brother has killed Carol or Pauline, he's going to have a lot to answer for. He'll end up doing time himself.'

'If he did, he deserves to rot in hell,' said Gayle. 'But, I believe him when he says he doesn't know where his brother is now. I think he would tell us in a heartbeat, if he knew.'

'He must be wetting himself, wondering what his brother's done now,' said Georgia.

The office had booked them into the Ramada, near Gatwick, for the night. As there'd been no time to pack an overnight bag before they left, neither of them even had a toothbrush. The concierge at the hotel was very accommodating, however, when they told him of their plight, and made him aware they were police officers. He produced toothbrushes and a few extra toiletries. After putting them in their room, they made their way down to the bar for a much-needed beer.

'Cheers. Now that really is what the doctor ordered,' said Georgia. 'Did I tell you about the gadget Mikey got me from Anne Summers...'

'Cheers,' Gayle interrupted. 'No, and I don't want to know, thanks. We'd better go up to the room - Crimewatch will be on soon. We'll get something to eat from room service.'

Inspector Mike Jensen was to appear on Crimewatch. Gayle knew they'd be showing a blown-up version of the photograph from Peter's phone, and was hopeful it might elicit a good response. They settled down on their beds to watch.

'We're looking for this man in connection with the disappearance of two women. If you see him, do not approach him. Call this number or dial 999. I repeat do not approach him.' The photograph appeared on the screen and was held there for some time.

After the programme, Gayle rang the DCI to report on the interviews with Justin Green's mother and half-brother.

'I'm afraid, we're no further forward, Boss. Neither the mother nor the brother has any idea where he is now.'

'Ok. The Super's getting the team together for an update at nine thirty in the morning. Will you make it?'

'We'll be there. We're booked on the early flight.'

After a quick bite, eaten cross-legged on their beds, Gayle was ready to turn in. It had been a long day. She took a quick shower, rinsed her undies through, and put them to dry on the radiator overnight. She could always finish them off with the hairdryer in the morning, if necessary.

'I can see you're miles away, Gayle,' Georgia said as she lifted the crisp white duvet and slipped into bed. 'You think they're already dead, don't you?'

'I've got no doubt he'll kill them both, if he hasn't already. When he's finished with Carol, of course. He'll probably view Pauline as collateral damage.'

'Hey, Gayle, don't let this get to you. That's the trouble with being FLO, you get too close to people.'

'It's not that. I know how to stay detached. But I want to get to him in time, if we can. After everything Carol's been through, if that bastard kills her, there's no fucking justice.'

Gayle was surprised to find that Georgia snored like a freight train and put her pillow over her head to drown out the awful racket. *It should be her head I'm putting a pillow over,* she thought grumpily. She couldn't sleep, despite being so tired, and not just because of the snoring. It was hard to relax, knowing that Carol was in grave danger from a man she felt she should have somehow stopped, five years ago.

Towards dawn, despite the snoring, and her jumbled thoughts, Gayle managed to snatch an hour's sleep, through sheer exhaustion, before waking, bleary-eyed, ready to start another long day.

A young constable from the Met picked them up at the hotel, to drive them to the airport. Gayle noticed him eyeing up Georgia, and she could see by the covert flirtatious looks Georgia kept giving him that there was an attraction between them. She smiled and thought to herself that didn't bode well for Mikey.

She rang the DCI on the way to the airport, to find out what the Crimewatch response had been, hoping something concrete had resulted from the publicity. Patsy told her there'd been a huge response; sightings had been reported from John O'Groats to Land's End. Many leads were being followed up, but so far nothing substantial to go on.

CHAPTER SIXTY-THREE

He hadn't re-tied my hands and I started frantically feeling around in the dark, trying to find how to get to the tail lights. I located one and kicked at it, but couldn't hit it hard enough to break it. I started screaming for help, in the vain hope that someone was around to hear me. I knew it was useless, and eventually gave up. I concentrated on trying to find something, anything, to defend myself with, to no avail. I thought if I could lift the floor of the boot, I might find some tools there, but I couldn't get any leverage on it, with the weight of two bodies pressing it down.

Lying in the dark, pressed up against Pauline's body, on my way to almost certain death, I was filled with the deepest fear and despair, terrified for myself, but even more scared for Julia. And heartbroken for Peter and Pauline.

'I'm so sorry, Pauline,' I sobbed. 'It's my fault... I'm so, so sorry...' I found myself praying. 'Oh God, please look after Peter and Pauline. And help me... please, please keep Julia safe... please don't let him get to Julia. Please God, I beg you keep Julia safe.' I felt I was losing my mind.

Before long, the terrain got much rougher; it felt as though he was driving over deep ruts. I was being thrown all over the boot and kept slamming into Pauline's body. The terror of my situation overwhelmed me. I was babbling and praying and sobbing.

'Oh God, please help me! Please, please don't let me die. I don't want to die! Peter I need you to help me. I don't want to die here. They'll never find me. They'll never know what's happened to me. God, please don't let him get to Julia. I love you Julia... stay safe...' I felt a stinging warmth spreading between my legs and realised I'd wet myself. Suddenly, the car came to a halt. I felt the door slam, then the boot was opened, with a rush of freezing air.

'Get out,' he said. It was very dark and I could hardly make out his silhouette against the darkened sky. He grabbed one of my arms and roughly hauled me out, banging the boot lid behind him. 'I'll have to come back for her,' he grumbled. Still painfully gripping my arm with one hand, he pushed me ahead of him, pressing the point of the knife against my back with the other.

'Where are we going?' I whispered, stumbling along in front of him.

'I've told you, Carol. To your final resting place. It's all ready for you. I think you'll like it. In the daylight you'll have lovely views across the moor. Might be a bit of a tight fit with two of you in it, but never mind.' he laughed.

My eyes were becoming accustomed to the dark. By the faint light of a frost-rimmed sliver of moon, which, ironically looked like a hazy smile in the sky, I could make out that we were on a desolate heather-covered moor. There seemed to be patches of gorse and a copse of trees ahead. He pushed me along in front of him over the hard, uneven, ground, steering a path through the prickly heather, in the direction of the copse.

My foot slipped on an icy rut and, as I fell, he momentarily loosened his grip on my arm. Scrambling quickly to my feet, I started running as fast as I could, slipping and sliding on the icy ground.

'You fucking bitch,' he yelled, lunging after me 'You won't get away.'

I kept on running, slipping, nearly falling, my skirt and legs catching on the gorse, my breath coming out in big gasps as the freezing air hit the back of my throat. I didn't waste time turning round, but I could hear him closing on me. I kept on going, frantically trying to get away, trying to outrun him. Then, a painful thud in my lower back jerked my body forward and sent me sprawling to the hard ground, knocking my breath out of me. He straddled me as I lay there face down, in great pain, gasping for breath.

'Nice try, babe. Futile, but a nice try.' He was laughing.

I could feel his hot breath on the back of my neck, as I struggled to get air into my lungs. Bizarrely, he began to nibble my ear, and whisper endearments. He told me I was beautiful, that he loved my body. Then he described in salacious detail what he was going to do to me. He shoved his hand up my skirt, then suddenly recoiled in disgust.

'Ugh. You've wet yourself, you filthy bitch. You stink.'

I was still face-down on the ground, my arms spread-eagled. With my hands I was feeling around on the hard ground, searching for anything that I could use as a weapon. Just as he lifted himself off me, sniffing in disgust, my right hand closed around what felt like a small stick. Grasping it, I twisted my body around and struck out as forcefully as I could towards his face, taking him by surprise. I felt the stick connect with something and heard the knife clatter to the hard ground as he put both hands to his face, screaming in pain.

'My eye! My fucking eye!' He was on his knees, and eased off me a bit as he clutched his face with both hands.

I didn't hesitate. I pulled myself out from beneath him and scrambled to my feet, thanking God I was wearing flat boots. I started to run again. The trees weren't far away now and I headed for them as fast as I could. I kept slipping on the frozen ground and tripping over spiky gorse and heather, expecting to feel his hand grabbing me any second. I didn't dare look back. I could feel the leather of my ankle boots and my skirt being ripped on the shrubbery as I ran. Suddenly, I was in the woods and trying to make my way in complete darkness. I bumped into trees and stumbled over roots, but I just kept going and eventually I could see a faint glimmer of light ahead. Before long, I broke out on the other side of the copse. My breath was coming in loud rasps, my chest burning and painful, and I had to stop, doubled over, until I was able to breathe a bit easier.

Before leaving the cover of the trees, I stood and listened, straining my ears for the slightest sound. I couldn't hear anything, but didn't dare believe that he wasn't following me. I could see another small wood in the distance, and I pressed on towards it, my breath coming in white clouds in the freezing air. When I reached the trees, I ventured a look behind me, expecting to see him coming over the moor, but I couldn't make anything out. I didn't dare relax and I turned and pressed on, once again negotiating a dense wood before reaching open moorland again.

I stumbled on for hours and hours, too scared to stop. My legs and hands were shredded with the gorse and heather; my knees were painful from falling onto the unforgiving ground and my throat was raw from the freezing air, but still I pressed on. Every time I thought of his face, the adrenalin kicked in again and gave me the strength to keep going. I had no idea what direction I was going in, and just hoped I wasn't going round in circles. Eventually the first signs of dawn appeared; an ethereal sky with pink and purple streaks showing through a misty haze. In the growing light I could see some kind of building not far ahead. As I got closer, I could see that it was a barn. By now, utterly exhausted, I staggered towards its high open door and stumbled inside. In the semi-dark, I found a large pile of straw and burrowed into it, trying to hide completely from sight.

CHAPTER SIXTY-FOUR

I awoke from blackness to a gentle voice asking if I was alright. I sat up with a scream of fright to see a man of about sixty, leaning over me. He'd been shaking my arm to wake me and jumped back himself at my reaction.

'Don't be frightened, love. I'm not goin' to 'urt you. This is my barn. I'm a farmer. I live nearby. I just found you 'ere when I came to pick up some equipment. I spotted you asleep in the straw. I've got my jeep outside. You look as if you could do with some 'elp.' He had a kindly face and was looking at me anxiously.

I dragged myself out of my bed of straw and tried to stand up, but staggered and would have fallen if he hadn't caught me. My legs were stiff and sore and the farmer held on to my arm to steady me. I looked down at my shredded skirt, bloodied legs and filthy boots, and realised what a sorry sight I must look.

'Thank God you're here... there's a man... he's coming after me. He's going to kill me! He's going to get my daughter...'

'Come on lass, you're in safe 'ands now. Nobody's goin to 'urt you. Let's get you back to the 'ouse. My wife'll make you a lovely cuppa and get you cleaned up.'

'We need to phone the police! Have you got a mobile?' I found myself clutching his arm, frantically.

'Nay lass, but there's a phone at the 'ouse. You can use that.'

I could have cried at his kindness, as he helped me out of the barn, to his waiting jeep. I was conscious of a sour smell and realised it was coming from me and remembered I'd wet myself. I kept looking around, anxiously, expecting Dan Smithson to materialise and finish what he'd started.

'Where are we?' I asked, once we were moving. I had no idea which direction the car had taken when we left South Shields; we could be almost anywhere.

'We're on North Yorkshire Moors, lass. The most remote part. Nearest village is ten miles away. Where've you come from, love? Nay, you can tell me later, let's get you 'ome to the wife first. My name's Joe, by the way.'

'Mine's Carol, Carol Barrington.'

He drove carefully and slowly over the fields. I think he was trying to spare me as much shaking about as he could. The sky was light now and the sun was a pale yellow in the sky. I wondered how long I'd slept and Joe told me it was nearly noon. I kept looking round, scanning the horizon, expecting to see a figure still coming after me.

Eventually, we drove into a cobbled yard that fronted an old stone farmhouse. With wood-smoke spiralling from its chimney, it looked incongruously peaceful. Strutting hens scattered out of our way, flapping and squawking noisily.

Joe ushered me into the porch and then into a warm, low-ceilinged kitchen, calling out to his wife as he sat me down in an overstuffed armchair beside a flickering log-burning stove. I was desperate to speak to Gayle, and he quickly handed me the phone. I'd memorised her direct line number, and soon she answered.

'Gayle. It's me... Carol.'

'Carol? Carol? What a relief!' Gayle almost sounded emotional. 'Where are you?'

'It was Dan Smithson, Gayle... in Barbados. Pauline's dead... he... he killed her. He's going to go after Julia... he knows where she lives. You've got to protect her!' I could feel panic rising in my throat and knew I was gabbling.

'Slow down, Carol,' Gayle spoke calmly. 'Julia's up here with Fiona. We had her collected from university when we realised you'd been abducted. She's safe; there's an officer with them, but in the light of what you've just told me, I'll strengthen the protection. I'll do it straight away. Just give me a second...' I could hear her giving instructions in the background. 'Right, it's organised. Another officer will be there with them very soon. Don't worry, we'll keep Julia safe. He won't get to her.

226

I promise you. Now tell me where you are.'

The relief of knowing Julia was safe was too much for me. I broke down and couldn't stop sobbing. Joe took the phone from me and I heard him giving the address. They spoke for some time and I heard him explaining how he'd found me in the barn and brought me to the farmhouse. Then he handed the phone back to me again.

'She'd like to have another word, lass. Can you manage to speak now?'

I nodded, wiping my face with the hanky Joe had passed to me.

Gayle's voice sounded sympathetic, yet firm. 'Carol, I'm going to be on my way to see you very soon. I'll pick up Julia and Fiona, on the way. We should be with you in about two hours or so and you can give me the full story then. In the meanwhile, one of my colleagues has just spoken to the North Yorkshire police and they're sending two officers over to stay with you. They should be there within fifteen minutes. They'll arrange to have a doctor take a look at you. Now, can you tell me anything about the car he's using?'

I could hardly bear to think about the car. 'It's... light coloured. Big. I think it's a Peugeot... he's got Pauline's body in the boot...' My voice broke; I was choking back sobs. 'Poor Pauline, she didn't deserve that... he hit her with an iron bar...' The sobs came then, and I couldn't go on. Joe took the phone from me again and went on talking with Gayle

A small, pretty lady with a mass of dark, curly hair had come into the room while I was on the phone and now she rushed over to me, dark eyes registering shock at my appearance.

'Oh you poor, poor thing,' she whispered, stroking my head whilst I sobbed. She stayed with me until the wracking sobs had subsided somewhat, then told me to lie still, she wouldn't be a moment. She turned and hurried from the room.

A few minutes later, she returned, her arms full of blankets and pillows, and I watched through the doorway as she proceeded to make up a bed on a settee in the next room. I glimpsed low beams and the flicker of flames from an open fire.

'I want you to lie here quietly, love,' she said, gently taking my arm and leading me through to the makeshift bed. She helped me to lie down and, tucking a blanket around me, instructed Joe to put the kettle on.

Patting my shoulder, she told me, 'Now you just rest there, and I'll get you a nice cup of tea... I'm Mary, by the way.'

'Thank you,' I whispered, my head sinking on to soft, plump pillows.

Returning with the tea, which she placed on a side table near me, she sat on a stool and looked at me, with concern. 'Listen, love, Joe's told me as much as he knows about what's happened, so I'm not going to ask you any questions. You'll have enough from the police, once they get here. For now, I just want to you rest. Much as I'd like to, I don't think I should try to clean you up. It might be important that the police see you as you are.'

I realised she wanted to be sure we didn't destroy any potential evidence, but I was longing to submerge myself in a hot bath and scrub all the filth off me.

When the police arrived a few minutes later, I was so relieved to see the two officers that the tears came again. I realised I'd still been terrified in case Smithson had seen me with the farmer and might come bursting into the farmhouse at any minute.

'It's all right lass, you're perfectly safe now,' the male policeman quickly reassured me, in a booming baritone. He was huge, tall as well as broad, his bulk seeming to fill the room. His companion was young and pretty, smart in her black uniform. 'I'm DI Bill Davis, and this is PC Rachel Best. We've heard about you Carol, the whole country's been looking for you.'

Rachel sat down on the stool next to me. 'There's a doctor on her way, Carol. How are you feeling?' she asked gently.

'He killed my friend,' I sobbed. 'Pauline... I saw her blood... he put her in the boot of the car... with me... I knew she was dead...' I couldn't go on and Rachel sat, patiently, waiting.

'Where is she now, her body?' she asked, in a gentle voice.

'He left her in the boot of the car... when he took me over the moor... I... I don't know what he's done with her...'

Taking out her notebook and pen, she asked me to tell her everything. 'Take your time and tell me exactly what's happened. Can you do that?'

Haltingly, in fits and starts, commencing with the phone call from Dan Smithson, I went through my ordeal.

'So, you last saw this Dan Smithson on the moor, last night. Do you know what time that would have been?'

'No... it wasn't long after it got dark.'

'Have you any idea if he was badly injured after you struck out at him?'

'I don't know... the stick must have gone into his eye...he screamed 'my eye'. That's how I got away... but I don't know how bad it was.'

She went on to ask for a description of Dan Smithson; what he was wearing, height, build, etc. I described him as best I could, mentioning his newly-cropped and lightened hair.

'Were you raped, Carol?' she asked gently, speaking quietly so only we two could hear. 'The doctor will need to know.'

I nodded and lowered my head. The tears came again.

'I'm so sorry. Why don't you just rest for now, until the doctor gets here? No more questions for the moment.' She patted my shoulder.

In the warmth of the room, I felt myself getting drowsy and must have drifted off to sleep. The next thing I knew, I was being woken by Mary lightly squeezing my shoulder, telling me the doctor was here. After asking everyone to leave the room the doctor turned to me.

'I'm Laura Quayle. How are you feeling, Carol?' Without waiting for an answer, she continued, 'I want to assess your condition, check how serious the damage is. I need to see if any urgent treatment is required, Ok?'

'Yes,' I whispered.

'I understand you've been attacked. The PC has told me that you've been raped as well as beaten,' she said quietly, taking my hand, examining the scratches and scrapes. 'Can you tell me how he beat you? Did he use a weapon?

'No... he punched me. Hard. In my face and stomach. And he bit me... all over. I was tied up...' I started to cry as shame washed over me.

'You'll need a more in-depth examination later. We'll take swabs and samples, to preserve any evidence, check for any STD or pregnancy. I'm afraid that's the usual procedure when someone's been raped. For now, I just want to check the extent of your injuries.' She carefully examined the bruises and bites, scrapes and scratches. There was hardly a part of my body that wasn't hurting.

'STD?' I echoed, as the significance of her words hit me.

'It's routine, in a rape situation. We need to check to make sure nothing's been transmitted.'

'Ugh, I just want to wash him off me... I feel so dirty... filthy.'

'I'm sorry you can't have a bath just yet, but you'll be able to before too much longer. Now, can you tell me where you hurt the most?'

'It's hard to say... all over... I'm very sore down below.' I dropped my head, shame washing over me again. Hot tears scalded my face.

'Carol, you've done nothing wrong. None of this is your fault. You've nothing to be ashamed of. The only person to blame for all of this is your attacker. Not you; not in any way whatsoever. Do you understand?' she spoke firmly.

I nodded, unable to speak.

When the humiliating examination was over, she removed her surgical gloves. 'There's extensive bruising and some tearing. We'll need to carry out an internal examination once we get you to hospital to rule out any internal injury. If necessary, that can be done under anaesthetic, so don't worry,' she tried to reassure me. 'Now, let's get the worst of these other injuries cleaned up.' I lay mute and hurting as she gently swabbed and disinfected the gashes and cuts on my legs and the bites on my body.

'Your legs and hands are badly torn. Gorse is most unforgiving... there, finished for now,' she said, straightening up. 'I want you to rest for a while. I'll come to see you again when you come into the hospital, once the police have spoken with you... And, one further thing,' she said in a stern voice. 'Look at me. Get rid of those feelings of guilt. You've survived a horrific attack; you have every reason to feel proud of yourself. Remember that,' she smiled and patted my arm.

'I'll try,' I said, knowing the shame would live with me for the rest of my life.

CHAPTER SIXTY-FIVE

When her mobile began to ring, the minute she walked into the main office, Gayle, feeling uncharacteristically irritable, through lack of sleep, thought *No bloody peace for the wicked. Can't I even have a cup of coffee?* She didn't recognise the number and answered rather brusquely,

'DC Jones.'

'Gayle... It's me, Carol.'

'Carol? Carol? What a relief.' The relief Gayle felt on hearing Carol's voice was immense. She sank into her seat. 'Where are you?'

Once the call was over, she jumped to her feet in excitement, just as Patsy came through the door.

'Boss, I've got news,' she announced. 'Carol Barrington's safe. She just called me.' She held up her mobile and a cheer went round the office.

Patsy stopped in her tracks, surprised. 'Where is she?'

'In a farmhouse on the North Yorkshire Moors. Unfortunately, Pauline is dead.' Gayle gave the DCI a brief report on her conversation with Carol.

'We need to let the Super know,' the DCI said. 'Come with me, Gayle.'

In the Superintendent's office, Gayle summarised Carol's call and her talk with the farmer, Joe Carter. 'The Yorkshire lads are sending a couple of people over to stay with her,' she concluded.

The office was buzzing when Gayle returned to pass on the Super's message that there would be a team briefing in fifteen minutes. Questions were fired at her from all sides, everyone wanting to know the details.

'Sorry, you'll have to wait for the briefing. I need to let her daughter know she's safe,' said Gayle. She checked the time, before keying in Julia's number. 'Gayle here. Great news, Julia. Your mum's safe. I've just had a phone call from her.' The shriek from Julia could be heard across the office. 'She's in Yorkshire – I can't go into detail just now; I'll explain everything when I see you. I'm leaving the office soon to drive down there. I'll pick both you and Fiona up on the way.'

'But, is she ok? What's she doing in Yorkshire? Why is there a policeman at the house with us?' Julia fired questions at Gayle.

'Julia, your mum is safe. That's all I can tell you for now. I'm just going into a meeting, so I'll bring you up to date when I see you.' She disconnected the call before Julia could ask her anything else.

Chief Superintendent Mike Jensen made his way into the MIR. Standing in front of the white board, he looked around, noting the air of excitement rippling through his team.

'Morning, everyone. I'm sure you'll all have heard the good news by now that Carol Barrington has been found, in North Yorkshire, alive and relatively well. And the bad news; that unfortunately, her friend Pauline Bradley, who went with her to see Dan Smithson, or, to give him his real name, Justin Green, has been killed.

So, this is now a murder enquiry.' He scanned the faces, of the team, noting he had their full attention 'I've been speaking to the Yorkshire constabulary and this is the situation,' he said. 'Carol has confirmed that her abductor is her tenant, who she knows as Dan Smithson. We believe his real name is Justin Green. She says he's the person who attacked her in Barbados, as we suspected. She managed to get away from him last night on the moor, and was found hiding in a barn this morning.' You could have heard a pin drop in the room.

'I'm leaving now, for Yorkshire. We need to get manpower down there immediately to take control of the search for Justin Green, who apparently has the body of Pauline Bradley in the boot of his car. He may be injured. I've spoken with the North Yorks Division; they're happy for us to lead the case, and are offering us every assistance. They've already got a helicopter in the air, and men and dogs on the ground, searching the moor. They've calculated how far Carol could've walked, and drawn up a grid of the initial area to be covered.

We understand Justin Green has changed his appearance. He's now clean-shaven with very short, light-coloured hair. Bit thinner, too. We'll get a new photofit done for Carol to approve. She's also given a description of the car he's using; large, light-coloured, probably a Peugot; no number plate I'm afraid. Unfortunately, the Yorkshire lads have told us she wasn't able to tell them the whereabouts of a cottage she was held in. However, she's given a rough estimate of how long the car journey took from the cottage to the moor, so they can factor that into their calculations. We'll need to draft in some uniforms to get the numbers. Right. Let's get moving.'

Before leaving, the Superintendent took the Barbados officers to one side. 'Looks like your theory of the ex being the perpetrator is up the spout,' he said.

'Yes, quite a turn up for the books,' said the DCI. 'We'll stay with it until the perp's found, but murder now trumps our case. It's all yours from now on.'

'Yep. Extradition's out of the question now,' agreed Detective Superintendant Jensen.

CHAPTER SIXTY-SIX

When she left the station, Gayle rang Julia again to let her know they were on their way, and asked them to be ready to leave. She suggested they pack a bag for Carol, who would be needing a change of clothes and some toiletries.

Georgia chatted animatedly as she drove, surprisingly not about her sex life, but about the case, wondering how Carol had managed to escape.

Before long, they reached Jesmond, and Georgia pulled into the circular gravelled driveway leading to Carol's front door. Julia came running out of the house, her blonde hair, now tinted bright pink, was looking wild. She was flustered and red-faced. Fiona had followed her out and was trying to put her arm around her, telling her to calm down, but Julia rudely shrugged her off.

'Is she alright? Is Mum ok? How can these things keep happening to her?' She was almost hysterical, shaking Gayle's arm and searching her face for answers.

'Let's go into the house for a few minutes and I'll bring you all up to speed with what we know. Ok?' Gayle took Julia's arm and firmly steered her through the front door and along the hall into the kitchen, where she sat her down and told her about receiving the call from Carol.

'You've actually spoken to her?' Julia interrupted, her eyes brimming with unshed tears. 'So she's ok?'

'She's had a very rough time, Julia. But she's safe now, that's the main thing. She's in a farmhouse on the North Yorkshire Moors and is being well taken care of until we get there. She told us the man who took her is one of her tenants, Dan Smithson. He took her to a cottage, then out on to the moor. She managed to get away from him and was found by a farmer this morning, in his barn. He took her to his home. That's where she is now. The local police are with her.'

'Dan Smithson?' said Fiona, slowly, as she put two and two together. 'So, he lured her there by pretending there was an emergency... the water leak?'

'I'm afraid so. We don't have all the details yet, so the sooner we talk to Carol, the better. Now, I'm afraid I have some bad news for you. I'm sorry to have to tell you that Pauline is dead.'

'Pauline?' said Fiona, putting her hand to her mouth. 'Oh my God, no.'

'Aunty Pauline's dead?' shrieked Fiona. 'She can't be. What's he done to her?'

'I know it's a terrible shock for you both,' said Gayle, putting her hand on Julia's arm. 'We don't have any further information at the moment. We'll find out more when we speak to your mother. So I think the sooner we get down there, the better. Come on, let's go.' She put her arm around Julia and steered her towards the front door.

'Does Charlie know?' asked Fiona in a small voice.

'Yes, he's been informed,' said Gayle. 'He's on his way home.'

They piled into the car, Julia with silent tears coursing down her face, Fiona white-faced with shock.

'What about Smithson?' asked Fiona. 'Has he been caught, yet? Why did we need a policeman here with us?'

Gayle eased into the passenger seat and fastened her seat belt, before twisting round to look at Fiona in the back seat. 'He hasn't been found yet,' she said. 'There's a search taking place right now. We're looking for him and his car, as well as the cottage he's been using. Turning to Julia, she said 'Apparently, he made some threats about you, Julia. That's why we had the officers at the house.'

'Bloody hell,' Fiona muttered.

'What threats?' Julia demanded.

'That's all I know for now. No point in speculating. We'll find out more when we speak to your mother.' Gayle turned back to the front and settled into her seat.

Georgia manoeuvred the car out of the drive, heading for the A19. The day was overcast, intermittent showers forecast.

Fiona spoke from the back seat. 'How much can one person go through? Her nightmare started with my dad's death and hasn't stopped since. It's enough to make anyone lose their mind. Thank God she's safe... but poor Pauline.' Gayle could hear her sobbing quietly in the back.

After a while, Gayle noticed Julia had barely said a word since getting into the car. 'Are you ok, Julia?' she asked, twisting round again to look at her. 'You're very quiet.'

'I'm trying to take it all in. I'm just so relieved Mum's ok but I can't bear to think about what she might have gone through. And Aunty Pauline... I can't believe she's dead...' her voice broke.

Fiona put her arms around Julia, and Gayle was pleased to see Julia lean into her.

Soon they were approaching the turn off from the A19 on to the A174. By then, the threatened rain showers had become a reality and the wipers were working overtime to cope with the deluge. Georgia had to concentrate hard on her driving and was hunched forward over the wheel, the rhythmic swish and thud of the wipers loud inside the car.

They took a series of B roads, heading towards Pickering, then turned north. Before long they found themselves on a narrow road, climbing and winding through open moorland. The rain had eased somewhat, but a fine drizzle persisted, and the noise of the wipers seemed to discourage conversation. They were in a valley known as the Hole of Harcum, named by many as the Devil's Punchbowl. As they climbed out of the valley, the moor spread out before them, vast and remote, the landscape becoming more bleak and windswept.

Looking out over the barren moor, and trying to avoid potholes, Georgia said, with feeling, 'God, look how bleak it is up here. She must have been terrified, running all night, not knowing if he was behind her. It's the stuff of nightmares. Thank God she managed to get away from him.'

Gayle gave her a warning frown, glancing to the back seats, hoping her comments hadn't been overheard.

They followed the narrow road as it wound through heather and gorse, splashing through puddles and sending spray in all directions, before turning on to single-track dirt road, leading to the farmhouse. After bumping and jolting for about half a mile, they arrived at their destination exactly two and a half hours after leaving Newcastle. They saw a low two-story stone building before them. It looked rather picturesque, with casement windows, and smoke curling from a huge chimney on the gable. Gayle could imagine how it would look in summer, bathed in sunlight, with the climbing roses that framed the front door, in full bloom. Georgia parked the car in the large cobbled area to the front of the house, scattering the hens roaming freely around.

'Well done, I'm impressed,' said Gayle. 'Looks like you managed to miss all the hens.'

In the kitchen, the two officers introduced themselves and Rachel told them Carol was asleep in the sitting room.

They moved into the adjoining utility room to speak privately. The DI told Gayle that the farmer, Joe Carter told them he'd found Carol Barrington burrowed into a bundle of hay in one of his remote barns, high on the moor, where he'd gone to pick up some equipment. She was terrified when he woke her and kept saying over and over that someone was trying to kill her. When she realised he wanted to help her, she told him she'd got away from 'him' and had run and walked all night long, not daring to stop. She was dishevelled, exhausted, with many cuts and bruises on her legs, hands and face.

'Joe Carter will be here shortly. He's just seeing to some livestock. His wife, Mary, is here. The doctor's examined Carol and confirmed her injuries are not life-threatening. They consist mainly of severe bruising, possible cheekbone fractures, abrasions and bites. She needs to be fully checked over in hospital, but the doc is of the opinion that can wait until after she's been questioned.' He put his notebook back in his pocket.

The DI confirmed that a helicopter was searching the area right then, looking for any sign of Justin Green, and his car, the large light-coloured Peugeot that Carol had described. There were also men on foot, with dogs, combing the area.

'We have confirmation from a local Estate Agent that he let a cottage to a Justin Green a month or so ago. There's a forensic team at the cottage as we speak,' he added. 'There's no sign of Green.'

'Thanks, Bill. We've got a team on their way down. Let's hope we find the bastard soon.'

Rachel brought Gayle up to speed about her interview with Carol and confirmed she'd been beaten and raped. 'She's in the sitting room, now. She's been sleeping on and off. She's clearly traumatised.'

With Georgia, Gayle went back through into the kitchen, where she bumped into the farmer's wife. Gayle saw a kind, open face, with lots of laughter lines, all framed by dark, curly hair, sprinkled with grey. Mary told Gayle that Carol had fallen asleep as soon as the doctor had left. She briefly described how Carol was filthy and covered in bruises, cuts and scratches when she arrived.

'I wanted to clean her up, but thought it best not to, in case it spoiled any evidence... she could do with a bath, mind.'

'Thank you Mary, you did the right thing. I need to talk to her now, and then we'll get her off to hospital for a full check-up. They'll clean her up then, don't worry.'

Just then a tall, ruddy-faced man came into the kitchen.

'This is my husband, Joe. He found Carol in the barn.'

Gayle shook his hand and asked if he would give a statement to Georgia, after they'd seen Carol. Mary picked up the tray of steaming mugs of tea, and headed for the sitting room.

'That poor girl were in a right state, I don't mind telling you. Never seen anyone so scared in all me life,' Joe volunteered. 'At least she's safe now.'

Gayle followed Mary into a cosy room where a blazing log fire radiated warmth from the depths of an inglenook fireplace. Carol looked awful. She was lying on the settee, covered up to her chin with a blue patterned wool blanket. Her face was like parchment, swollen in places, livid bruises forming on her cheeks. Her eyes were closed. Julia was on her knees beside the settee, stroking Carol's hand and talking gently to her. Gayle could hear the relief in her voice as she told her mum how glad she was that she was safe.

Mugs of tea were handed round and Julia and Fiona tried to help Carol to sit up to drink it, but she pushed them away and sank wearily back on to the pillows.

'It's good to see you, Carol. We've been so concerned,' Gayle said, gently touching her hand. Tears welled in Carol's eyes. 'Do you feel up to telling us what happened?' Gayle asked, studying her closely. Her blonde hair looked like a dirty, matted rug, and as well as the bruising and swelling to her face, her lips were cracked and split and her sunken eyes had a haunted look.

'Yes,' she whispered.

'I'll leave you to it,' Mary said, walking to the door. 'Make sure the lass drinks that tea.'

Gayle suggested it would be best if Fiona and Julia went with Mary, but Carol put her hand on Fiona's arm and shook her head.

'Let them stay,' she said quietly. She looked at Fiona, still holding on to her arm. 'I need to tell you something,' she gulped. 'He... he murdered Peter.'

Fiona recoiled in shock. 'My Dad? He murdered my Dad?' her voice rose alarmingly and the colour suddenly drained from her face. Gayle guided her to an easy chair and made her sit down, quietly asking Georgia to add plenty of sugar to Fiona's tea, to combat the shock. 'So... it must have been him... in the photograph? But... Tim said it definitely wasn't.'

'He sent his brother to answer the door,' Carol's voice was barely a whisper.

'So that's the explanation,' said Gayle. 'I wish you'd told me about the photograph, Carol. If you'd mentioned it before you went to South Shields, all this might have been avoided. If I'd seen it, I would have recognised Justin Green and stopped you from putting yourself in danger.'

'Tim said it wasn't ... I thought I was just being paranoid... oh, I've been so stupid...'

'Well, be that as it may. How do you know that Dan Smithson, or to give him his real name, Justin Green, murdered Peter?'

'He told me...' said Carol, in a small voice. 'Said it was like taking candy from a baby.'

Fiona wailed loudly and Julia rushed to put her arms around her.

'Look, I think we all need to take a little time to calm down. I'll give you a few minutes.' Gayle slipped out of the room, and Georgia followed.

'I can't fucking believe this, Georgia. She's an intelligent woman. Why didn't she mention the photograph when she told me she was going to see him? How could she be so bloody stupid?' Gayle was furious.

'Well, playing devil's advocate, she did try to find out whether it was the tenant. No doubt if this Tim had confirmed her suspicions, she would have come straight to you.'

'Right,' said Gayle, taking a deep breath. 'Let's go back in.'

'You ok now, Fiona?' Gayle asked as they walked into the room. Fiona, who was still slumped in the chair, clutching her mug, silently nodded.

Look,' Gayle said gently, taking the stool next to Carol, 'I know you've had a terrible ordeal, but it's really important that I take your statement. Are you able to tell me what happened, from the beginning? I'm so sorry the police failed to turn up at the flat. They were involved in an accident when they were on their way to you.'

'I wondered... where they were. He came to the door, so we went in. I didn't suspect anything... I trusted Tim...'

Gayle nodded, 'I understand.'

'He... he looked different. Even his eyes... I think he's bleached his eyebrows and lashes.'

'That's interesting. We knew about the hair and clean-shaven bit, but not the eyebrows and lashes. We'll get that circulated right away.' She looked at Georgia, who was already on her phone, giving an update to the team.

'Pauline wanted to come with me... I wish she hadn't...' her eyes filled again, and Gayle waited for her to compose herself. She went on, haltingly, describing the full horror of what she'd gone through.

'We've found the cottage. The forensic team are there now,' Gayle told her.

'Was he there? Have they got him?' There was a note of hope in Carol's voice.

'No, we haven't found him yet. We've got teams out right now, searching the moor. They've got a helicopter in the air and teams of men with dogs. They're looking for the car and for him – if he's still out there on foot. Do you feel up to telling me what happened when you got to the cottage?'

Carol looked at Julia, uncertainly.

'I need to hear, Mum. Please.' Julia came to sit on the floor beside the settee and took Carol's hand. 'Please. I need to know what you've been through, so I can help you.'

In a monotone, talking almost as though it had happened to someone else, Carol described her ordeal in the cottage. Julia became more and more visibly upset. She recoiled and started to sob when Carol described what took place in the bedroom, all colour drained from her face.

'He put me in the boot again... with Pauline's body...' Carol's voice was flat. 'I knew he was going to kill me too.'

Julia gave a little scream and Carol squeezed her hand, before going on, haltingly, to tell them how he'd prepared a grave for her, and the threats he'd made about Julia being his next victim. They were all stunned and were silent for a few moments, taking it all in.

'What an evil, evil bastard,' Julia sobbed. 'I want to kill him myself.'

'You and me, both,' muttered Fiona.

'We need to find him - did he mention any particular place to you, Carol? Anywhere he might have been thinking of going to... afterwards?' Gayle asked.

'No... no.'

'How did you manage to get away from him?' Gayle asked gently.

Gayle couldn't help but feel admiration for her as she described her escape.

'You did well, Carol. And you don't know if he was badly injured?'

'No. He screamed out, something about his eyes... put his hands to his face. That's how I got away.' She lay back on the cushions, clearly exhausted.

'Good for you, Mum. I'm proud of you,' Julia smiled through her tears.

'Thank you Carol, you've done very well. I know that was harrowing for you. Now, we need to get you to hospital for a full check-up... we'll need to take swabs.'

'Yes... the doctor explained everything.'

'There's an ambulance on its way. It'll be here soon to take you to Helmsley. Georgia and another officer will go with you. Fiona and Julia too. We'll have two officers with you and Julia at all times, so don't worry about your safety. We need to look after you until Justin Green is found.'

'Find him soon,' said Carol, as paramedics transferred her to a chair, ready to take her to the ambulance.

'We will. One other thing, the photo from the phone is being digitally altered to reflect what you've told us about his appearance now. I'll bring it to the hospital later.'

CHAPTER SIXTY-SEVEN

After an intimate, humiliating and at times painful examination, during which every inch of me was inspected, and swabs, samples and scrapings taken for analysis, and needles stuck into me, I was finally allowed to have a shower. I was so grateful. I'd never in my life felt more dirty or soiled or violated. I scrubbed and scrubbed at myself, until my skin was raw and bleeding in parts, trying to erase all traces of that monster.

I didn't want to leave the shower, and stayed under so long my skin became wrinkled, and still I was frantically rubbing at myself. In the end, two of the nurses came into the cubicle and persuaded me to turn the shower off, before helping me out. They gently dried me and re-applied antiseptic to my wounds before dressing them.

Doctor Quayle came to see me in my room.

'You'll be feeling better for having a shower, I expect?' Without waiting for my response, she continued. 'You've been through such an ordeal, both physically and mentally, that you'll need to be closely monitored. I'll pass my notes to your own GP and she'll keep an eye on you, once you've been discharged from here. You're going to need a lot of support and help, not only from your GP, but from counsellors and psychiatrists, to come to terms with what's happened to you. But for now, you need to sleep.'

She instructed the nurse to give me a pain-killing injection and I felt myself relax. I quickly fell asleep, not opening my eyes until bright sunshine was streaming through orange and lemon curtains. I came to, slowly, and for a few moments, couldn't understand where I was. I looked around at the lemon-coloured walls, and again at the geometric pattern of the curtains, before the penny suddenly dropped and I groaned aloud. The impact of remembering what had happened to me was vicious. I doubled up in agony, bringing my knees up to my chest. I could hear myself wailing.

A nurse hurried into the room, followed closely by Doctor Quayle.

'Carol, it's alright. You're safe now. Everything's going to be alright now.'

'I can't bear it,' I sobbed. 'I just want to go to sleep and never wake up.'

Apparently, Dr. Quayle had been waiting for me to wake up, anticipating the trauma I'd be going through. She sat with me until the wracking sobs subsided.

'That's better. I'd like you to eat some breakfast now. You need something on your stomach. No,' she said as I began to protest, 'I know you won't feel like it, but will you eat a little just for me?'

The nurse brought poached eggs on toast. I reluctantly nibbled on a piece of toast, but could barely swallow a bite.

'Your daughters are waiting to see you. The police officer needs to speak to you, too. I'll send her in first, if that's ok with you?'

Gayle came through the door, looking rather hesitant, not like her usual boisterous self.

'Hello, how are you this morning? You look so much better than yesterday,' she said, studying my face. 'Before we talk, I hate to ask, but would you mind taking a look at this updated picture of Justin Green?' she held out a photograph, which I reluctantly took from her. There he was, looking at me, and I felt a jolt of pure revulsion. 'Is that a good likeness?'

'Yes,' I said, handing back the picture. 'That's exactly what he looks like now.'

'Thanks for that. I know how hard it must be to look at him. We'll get it circulated. We've had search teams out again since first light, scouring the moor, but so far we've drawn a blank. We think now that he must have returned to his car and driven off the moor. Obviously, we're trying to trace the car. We're doing all we can to find him. In the meanwhile, how are you feeling?' she asked, her voice softening.

I felt my eyes fill with tears again. 'If you want the truth, Gayle, I just want to die. I can't bear to think about it. It all keeps washing over me like a big, black wave, crushing me. I really don't know how I'm ever going to come to terms with it. How long do you think it'll be before you find him?'

'Every force in the UK is looking for him. We're watching all the airports and ports. The updated photo will be widely circulated – it'll be on TV, and in all the social media. Appeals are going out to the public to keep a lookout for him. His options will be limited. I'm confident we'll find him soon.'

'I hope so.'

'The thing is, Carol, we need to keep you and Julia safe, until he's found. We work with an Agency that's found a safe house for you. Somewhere he can't find you.'

I let that sink in. 'Oh, what a nightmare. When is all this going to end?' I started to cry. 'Where will this place be? What about Julia's studies? What about Fiona?'

'The most important thing right now is your safety. And Julia's. The Agency has come up with a nice cottage, just by the sea in Cleveland. You'll have to live under assumed names and you won't be able to have contact with friends or family for a while. We know how clever Green is with computer and phone hacking. We can't risk him tracing your whereabouts.'

She studied my face, which must have shown utter despair. 'Fiona can go with you, if that's what you both want, but the same rules will apply to her. She certainly can't stay in your house in Jesmond. And we can't risk Linda keeping in contact. But we'll assign a local Victim Support contact, rape counsellor and psychiatrist, as well as a local FLO. I won't be able to keep in touch directly, but I'll get feedback on how you're doing.'

'I can't take all this in,' I said, weeping again. 'Do I have a choice?'

'This man has shown unbelievable determination to get to you. He's obviously prepared to risk anything. He could have just disappeared after the abortive attempt to kill you in Barbados. No-one knew who he was; he could have resumed living under his real name, quite easily, with no consequences. But, what does he do? Takes great risks to get to you, even when he knows police are involved in looking after you.

The man is extremely dangerous, and we have no reason to believe he's going to stop pursuing you now. And Julia too, from what he told you. We can't force you to go, but if you don't, we can't spare the manpower that would be needed to protect you round the clock. You have to disappear... hopefully not for long.'

'Will I be able to go home first? To collect some things?'

'Yes, we'll take you there after you're discharged. I'm sorry about you having to be cut off from everyone, but it's vital, to keep you safe. Justin Green is a technical expert and capable of hacking into almost anything. We know he'll go on stalking you, and that means he will try every avenue to find you – including following people who know you.' She stood up. 'Fiona and Julia are waiting to come in and see you, so I'll leave you for now.'

They came into the room and I could tell immediately from their demeanour that Gayle had already briefed them on what was to happen. They both gave me hugs, then we looked at each other, almost lost for words. Julia looked bewildered and angry.

'This is surreal. How can one evil bastard cause all this upset?' she demanded. 'They'd better bloody well catch him soon.'

Fiona told me she wanted to come to the safe house with us. It would mean she couldn't visit or contact her mother, but she said she hoped to be able to make her understand. She wanted to see this thing through with me, to the end. I felt incredibly grateful to her. I really didn't know how I would have got through all this without her. Suddenly, I wanted nothing more than to be in my own home again, one last time.

Dr Quayle turned up just then and told me I was to be kept in for one more night, and would be discharged the following day.

'When you leave, you'll need to get lots of rest,' she said, glancing at Fiona and Julia. 'And, of course, as I've already said, you're going to need further counselling and strong support, you too, Julia.

Had life ever looked more bleak?

CHAPTER SIXTY-EIGHT

The team scouring the moors had so far drawn a blank. Gayle had been told that if they were unsuccessful today, the search was to be called off and it would be assumed that Justin Green had been able to return to his car and drive off the moor.

The cottage that had been let to Green was located about twenty miles from the barn where Carol had taken refuge, so the search team had been able to map out a more accurate search area. Gayle was pretty sure by now that they were wasting their time. Her gut feeling was that Justin Green was long gone and could be anywhere by now, which meant of course he couldn't be too badly injured. The estate agent had provided a spare set of keys, and the forensic team were going over the place.

Gayle had found Carol looking a lot better this morning when she'd seen her at the hospital, but to be fair, she thought, she really couldn't have looked any worse than she had yesterday. Her eyes, however, still had that awful, haunted look she'd seen yesterday, and Gayle wondered if it would ever leave her.

The knowledge that she and Julia would need to go to a safe house seemed to hit her really hard. Her nightmare seemed never-ending.

Gayle wondered about why Green had chosen to use his real name when he leased the cottage. However, when she thought it through, she realised that he couldn't have known that she would make the connection between Dan Smithson and Justin Green. It was pure coincidence that she'd worked on the murder case in London five years earlier, and was therefore able to recognise him from the photograph on Peter's phone. He must have thought that once he discarded 'Dan Smithson' there would be nothing to connect him with Justin Green and he'd be home and dry. It was chilling to think that it was such a tenuous link; a million to one chance that had led to her identifying him so quickly.

Gayle and Patsy were billeted at a small guest house not too far from the crime scene; the rest of the team were scattered around the area, all in small bed and breakfast places or, like them, in guest houses. In the small, bright dining room, as they tucked into a dinner of home-cooked roast beef, they discussed the case. Delicious, crispy Yorkshire Pudding, with gravy, was served for the first course, which the owner told them was the traditional way to eat a roast dinner, in Yorkshire.

'In the morning, as soon as she's discharged, we'll take Carol home,' Gayle said, taking a mouthful of pink roast beef. 'Before that, first thing, we'll take a look at the cottage.'

They had some difficulty finding the cottage; the Sat Nav didn't seem to be able to pinpoint its exact location. After a couple of false turns, when it tried to direct them across fields, they eventually arrived outside a plain, two-storey cottage, having found their way more by good luck than good management. It was located at the edge of the vast moor, in an extremely isolated position, and Gayle could see why Green had chosen it. She noticed the square bay window to the front, and the roller shutter door to the garage on the left side of the building, just as Carol had described. The officer on duty outside the cottage looked freezing cold and fed up, but he managed a weak smile and a 'Good Morning' as they disembarked from the car.

DCI Mayne had told Gayle that the team searching the moor had resumed their search at first light and were covering the last segment mapped out as being feasible for Justin Green to have got to on foot. There was still no sign of the car, and it was looking increasingly likely that he'd been able to get back to it, and simply driven off the moor. If so, it was unlikely that Carol had inflicted anything other than a superficial wound.

The forensic lads handed out shoe covers and paper overalls. 'You'll need to put these on.'

'Found anything of interest?' Gayle asked.

'We've bagged and tagged quite a bit of stuff, including the bed sheets. Lots of DNA on there. We've got fingerprints from the manacles and from a broken bottle of Dettol in the bathroom. Looks like he packed in a hurry. There are clothes hanging out of drawers and some dropped on the floor of the wardrobe.'

'What about the broken bottle of antiseptic? What's your take on that?'

'We bagged some discarded bits of cotton wool, soaked in the antiseptic. Looked as though they'd been used to clean a wound. Must have dropped the bottle.'

They made their way upstairs and found themselves on a small, square landing.

The technician followed them up. 'This is where he brought her,' he said, indicating the bedroom door opposite the stairs. 'Judging from the stains and blood on the sheets, she had quite an ordeal, poor girl. Look, spots of blood on the wallpaper here, and on the manacles.' He pointed out the stains.

Georgia looked at the manacles, gleaming dully on the wall behind the king-size bed. 'How terrifying. To be tied up and absolutely bloody helpless,' she whispered to herself.

They went back downstairs. Looking around the ground floor, there was evidence the cottage had been recently lived in; bacon, sausage, tomatoes and the remnants of a pork pie with egg in the middle, were in the fridge. Along with half a pint of fresh milk.

'I wonder where the bastard's gone?' the technician said, walking into the kitchen. 'I hope you get him before he does any further damage. Fuckin' manacles. I'd like to put him in the fuckin' manacles and cut his balls off. Then stuff them down his throat.'

'Ditto,' Gayle said. 'But we've got to catch him first.' She was beginning to feel despondent. It was clear that Justin Green had returned to the cottage, hastily packed and left. 'We've got a nationwide search on our hands.'

'Aye, well good luck with that. The sooner that bastard's found, the better for all of us.'

CHAPTER SIXTY-NINE

By eleven the next morning, once paperwork was sorted and drugs dispensed, I was allowed to leave. Before we left, Dr Quayle came to see me again, and wished me luck.

'You're a strong person, Carol. If anyone can come to terms with the horrific things you've had to endure, it's you. I know you'll receive help and I just want to wish you the best of luck in the future. And remember, no feelings of guilt or shame. What happened to you was not in any way your fault. Keep in touch and let me know how you get on.' With that, she hugged me warmly before turning on her heel and walking away. After a few steps, she turned back and said quietly, 'Don't let him win, Carol.'

On the journey up to Newcastle, we were all subdued. Julia was quietly crying, cuddled into me in the back seat. The knowledge of the horror I'd gone through, was almost too much for her to bear. And it wasn't over yet. She had to move to a new location, leave all her friends behind, abandon her studies yet again. Her whole life was in turmoil, her aunt was dead, and both she and I were in terrible danger. How bad could it get?

For myself, I couldn't begin to think how I could ever come to terms with what had happened. I felt utterly degraded and hopeless. I prayed they would find Justin Green soon, so Julia and I could try to struggle back to some semblance of normality. I knew with certainty that there would be no peace for either of us while that man was walking free, probably still hunting us. I realised with a heavy heart that whatever happened, life would never be the same again for us.

A thought occurred to me. 'Gayle,' I asked, 'can I let Tim know that we have to go away? Not where I'm going, of course, but just that we have to disappear for a while? Otherwise, he won't know what's happened to me and I know he'll be very worried.'

'Tim? Yes, but that's all you can tell him. You or Julia can advise the university, too. Don't use your own phones, I'll give you one to use. No phones or computers for now. He'd have no problem tracing you through your devices. Hopefully, it won't be for too long, and then you can all start to get back to normal.'

Kia was waiting for us when we eventually arrived at the safe house. She greeted us warmly.

'Come on in, you must be exhausted. I'm Kia, your FLO. I'm here to help you settle in. Let me take those.' She took my hastily-packed bags and put them on the small landing at the bottom of the stairs. 'Do you want to look around?'

With no enthusiasm, I traipsed around the house, followed by Julia and Fiona. It was quite small and impersonal. A tiny kitchen, barely big enough to squeeze in the three of us at once, old fashioned, but neat. A decent size lounge, with a small dining room off. The depressing decor was everything I hated – green flock wallpaper and rose coloured shag-pile carpet. Upstairs, three bedrooms and a tiny bathroom This was to be our home for the foreseeable future and it was a bleak thought.

Kia stayed to get us settled in and told us she'd arranged for a doctor and psychiatrist to call the next day. A new Victim Support Counsellor was also to come the next day.

'The house is fitted with sophisticated security systems, so you mustn't worry about your safety,' she told me. 'And let me show you where the panic buttons are. You won't need them, but they're there to make you feel safe. The door has a spy-hole, triple locks and a chain. Never open it without first checking who is there. And if you're in any doubt, don't open it. Tomorrow, I'll go over a few safety issues, but for now I think you should unpack what you need for tonight and get some rest. We've stocked the fridge and cupboards, so you won't starve.'

After she'd gone, with a promise to return in the morning, a wave of despondency came over me. I could see that Julia was deeply upset too. Fiona tried to be cheerful, but I could see her heart wasn't in it. She, too, was facing a period of isolation and must have been feeling pretty disorientated herself.

'Let's just go to bed,' I suggested. 'Things might look better in the morning.'

'Right. I'll make some hot chocolate for us all and bring it up.' Fiona had already checked out the supplies.

Before we'd left the hospital, Dr Quayle prescribed anti-anxiety drugs for both Julia and myself. These were lifesavers and I don't think either of us could have functioned without them. They helped to take the edge off things, albeit causing some drowsiness and feelings of being rather spaced out.

That first night in the safe house, we sat on my bed in our pyjamas, drinking our hot chocolate, and talked for a while. I don't think any of us wanted to be alone, but eventually exhaustion overtook us and with hugs to comfort each other, Julia and Fiona went to their own rooms. Once alone, I wept and wept, wondering how I was ever going to get through this. Eventually, I fell into a troubled sleep, peppered with disturbing dreams.

Each day was an ordeal, something to be got through. Despite the medication, I lived in a constant state of tension and fear. I stared out at the bleak view of the unkempt back garden and barren fields beyond, and the knowledge that Justin Green was out there somewhere filled me with terror. At times it all threatened to overwhelm me. Kia told us that it was alright to go out, for a walk on the beach or to the shops, and reassured us that we were safe from him; that there was no way he could possibly know where we were. But I wasn't convinced. On the odd occasion that we did venture out, mainly at Fiona's insistence, I was paranoid, looking over my shoulder all the time and unsettling the others. Each time, it was an enormous relief to get back to the house and lock the door securely behind us. When the Victim Support Counsellor, a lady named Isabelle, became aware of just how frightened I was, she volunteered to come out with us each time, and this did help to allay my fears a little.

My emotions were all over the place and I started suffering terrible mood swings, over which I had no control. Isabelle took me to see both the doctor and the psychiatrist twice a week, in an endeavour to stabilise me. My medication was adjusted, and somehow we managed to settle down into some sort of routine.

Boredom was a big factor. Julia was fretful about missing her studies, and her friends. Fiona was worried about her mother and was still heartbroken about her father being murdered. The house was a cauldron of volatile emotions. Julia and I had huge rows which usually ended up with us screaming at each other over nothing. Anything could trigger a row, no matter how trivial. Each time it happened, we both felt remorseful afterwards and vowed it wouldn't happen again. Until the next time.

To add to our despondency, Kia was unable to give us any positive information about the investigation. There was no sign of Justin Green, despite a massive nationwide police search. Would they ever find him? Could we be stuck here forever? Surely not.

CHAPTER SEVENTY

Two weeks later, Gayle rang Kia, the acting FLO in Cleveland, for an update on Carol and Julia. Kia told her they were going stir-crazy and that their emotions were all over the place.

'I think Carol is cracking up, quite frankly. And Julia's not far behind her. Fiona's doing her best to keep things as calm as possible, but I think she's fighting a losing battle. Carol and Julia have nearly come to blows a couple of times, and I get the impression they're not normally like this?'

'No, they're not. What help are they getting?' Gayle was concerned. 'I'd hoped they would manage better than this.'

'I've got the doctor seeing them regularly; he's keeping a close eye on them. They're both on tranquilisers. The psychiatrist is also having twice-weekly sessions with them. The Victim Support counsellor, Isabelle, is a gem. She's coming to see them every day until things improve. To be honest, Gayle, I think they could just about cope with the trauma of all that's happened, if they were in their own home. It's being in the safe house that's getting to them. Being cut off from their friends and family. Unable to get on with their lives. They keep asking if any progress has been made in finding Justin Green?'

'Well, as you know, nothing concrete so far. It's a mystery. How can someone whose face is splashed all over the media, just disappear into thin air? We're keeping tabs on his family in London, but so far he's made no contact. He's ditched his mobile phone. He's not using his computer. We don't believe he's gone abroad, definitely not under any of the names he's used so far. We're checking every possible avenue, but so far, zilch, nada, nothing.'

'Carol won't be too happy to hear that.'

'Well, she'll just have to learn to be patient, I'm afraid. It's still early days, and we're fairly confident of finding him soon.' Gayle didn't feel as confident as she made herself sound. It had been two weeks since he went missing, and the longer it went on, with no positive sightings, the less chance there seemed to be of finding him. She knew that it's always better if progress is made whilst an enquiry is new and fresh. The longer it goes on, the less chance of a successful outcome. The situation was less than satisfactory, but the whole team was still working on it and optimism was generally still high. She wished she could talk to Carol; she was sure she would be able to get through to her, but that was out of the question for now.

They were getting a lot of response from the public. Justin Green had so far been seen in Southend, Aberdeen, Pontypridd, North, South, East and West London, Newcastle, Manchester and Leeds. Every lead was followed up, but had led nowhere, so far. Some people had even taken covert photographs of people they thought were Justin Green, but none had turned out to be him. Where was he? Was someone hiding him? If he was on his own, he'd have to emerge sometime, if only to eat.

Hospitals had been checked, but there was no record of anyone attending with an eye injury. There'd been no activity on any credit or debit cards in his name. He was a wealthy man; was his money abroad? How did he access it? A few of the team were working on finding out what his financial arrangements were; trying to get a trace that way. There'd been no confirmed sightings of the car, but CCTV cameras at a petrol station just north of Leeds had picked up a light-coloured Peugeot filling up, in the early hours of the morning following the incident on the moor. The driver was wearing a cap, pulled down low, which obscured his face. The assistant remembered him buying pain killers and a coffee, as well as petrol, but couldn't be sure that it was the same man as in the photograph shown to him. The car number had been circulated but no further sightings of it had been made. Was that Justin Green?

CHAPTER SEVENTY-ONE

Tony and Sandy bumped along the track in their SUV, looking for the right spot. Sandy had opened his fly and had her hand round his shaft, which was now standing up proudly. He tried to push her head down there, but she laughed saying it was too bumpy. She was being thrown all over the place; he would have to wait until they stopped.

By the time he found a suitably sheltered spot, well off the beaten track, he was bursting for it and they quickly scrambled into the back seat, where he pulled off Sandy's jeans and tiny thong and entered her without ceremony. It was a quick, urgent fuck, but very satisfying.

Later, they knew, they would make love again, taking their time and drawing out the sensuous pleasure, but meanwhile they had a picnic to attend to. Sandy had excelled herself, Tony thought, as he watched her unwrap roast chicken breasts, a lovely dressed salad with prawns and avocado and crusty rolls. A couple of bottles of his favourite beer, and a pack of profiteroles completed the repast. He loved these outings with Sandy at weekends – a chance to get away from their respective parents' watchful eyes.

Westlife was playing on the radio. 'We had joy, We had fun, We had seasons in the sun...' he sang, loudly, leaning over and tickling Sandy's ribs.

'Stop it, you fool,' she laughed, 'I'll drop all the food.' She had spread a cloth between them on the back seat, and was putting out the picnic on to two plastic plates. Although it was a sunny March day, it was still too cold to eat outdoors, so the seat was to serve as their picnic table.

They ate their fill, washed down with a bottle of beer each. Sandy was putting the detritus of their meal into a waste bag, when Tony shouted excitedly,

'Look! A red squirrel.' He was pointing up at a nearby spruce.

'Where?... Oh, I see him. Isn't he beautiful?' Sandy was captivated. The squirrel began to move off through the trees. 'Let's follow him.' With that, she quietly opened the back door and climbed out of the car. Tony caught up with her and together they stealthily followed the squirrel.

'Look, he's coming down the tree.' Sandy pointed.

They held their breath as they watched him nimbly descend the trunk and sit on the ground, not far from where they were standing. He sat up and wiped his whiskers with his paws, totally unaware of their presence. He was a beauty, with a huge, bushy red tail. Sandy, leaning forward to get a better view, stepped on a twig, which snapped loudly, spooking the poor thing. He raced back up the trunk and disappeared into the depths of the branches.

'Oops,' said Sandy.

'Right, young lady. Back to the car with you... and when we get there...'

Sandy laughed and ran off with Tony in pursuit. Trying to evade capture, he watched her duck low and push through some low-hanging spruce branches.

'Tony! Tony, come here,' she called, her voice coming from depths of the branches. There was an urgent note to it. He began to push through the branches, just as she emerged. 'There's a car under there,' she said, gesturing to where she'd just come from. 'Strange.'

'Is there anyone in it?' Tony said, pushing through to take a look. There was something odd about this, he thought. The car looked abandoned; the foliage seemed to have grown around it. He peered curiously through one of the back door windows, then cupping his hands around his eyes, he looked closer, puzzled. 'There's someone inside,' he shouted. 'On the back seat.' He knocked on the window, calling 'Are you alright, mate?' When there was no response, he opened the back door and immediately stepped back, gagging as the stench hit him full in the face.

Sandy had come alongside him, 'Oh my god,' she yelled, tugging at Tony's sleeve, turning to run. 'Let's get out of here.'

They turned and ran in panic. In their haste they couldn't find their car.

Sandy kept muttering over and over 'Oh my god, Oh my god,' as they frantically searched for the place they'd left it.

Eventually locating the car, they scrambled inside and Tony retrieved his phone and pressed 999.

'No bloody signal,' he muttered, putting the key into the ignition and revving the engine. 'We need to get out of the forest.' He quickly reversed and turned the car round, before driving at speed back up the rutted track.

'Slow down,' yelled Sandy, 'we'll hit a tree!' She was being shaken all over the front seat, and was frantically trying to fasten her seatbelt. Eventually the car emerged from the trees on to a slightly wider track, then after a few more minutes, on to something resembling a road.

Tony jammed the brakes on and the car screeched to a halt. Sandy, who'd been unable to get her seat belt fastened, was thrown forward and banged her head on the windscreen.

'Tony, for fuck's sake,' she screamed.

'Sorry hun,' his hands were shaking as he picked up his phone again. This time he got a signal and when he was put through to the police, said 'I want to report a body. I've just found a body. In Kielder Forest. It's in a car.'

CHAPTER SEVENTY-TWO

'Sir?' Gayle was hurrying along the corridor. 'Sir?'

Chief Superintendent Jensen, turned enquiringly.

'A car's been found, sir... in Kielder Forest. A large pale grey Peugeot. There's a body in it. And the body of a female in the boot. It's been there for some time according to the local police. They've secured the area. I'm hoping it's Justin Green.'

'It certainly sounds like it. Good. Well, let's hope it's him. That would draw a line under the whole thing. Are forensics there?'

'All in hand, sir. It's DCI Mayne's day off today. I'm on my way up there now to see if I can ID the bodies,' she grimaced. 'Not looking forward to that.'

'Let me know when you get back and I'll call a briefing. It'll be good to put this one to bed.' He walked on, then turned, 'By the way, Gayle' he said, with black humour 'don't forget to take a mask.'

Gayle collected Georgia and together they got into the car and headed for the A1. Her mind was busy, working out the likelihood of it being Green. If, indeed, the body was that of Justin Green, it would bring tremendous relief and closure, to Carol and Julia. Not to mention Charlie, who would finally be able to bury Pauline. And, it would draw a line under the investigation. Case satisfactorily resolved.

'Why do you think he would be in Kielder?' Georgia asked, as they drove along. 'Assuming it's him, of course.'

'I'm just thinking that through. We're not sure it's him yet, but I think it's got to be. Especially with the body of a woman in the boot. If I recognise the body as Justin Green, we'll bring his brother up to do the official ID. We'll let the Yorkshire lads know then. And Barbados. No point in alerting them just yet, in case it's not him.'

'I've never seen a body,' confessed Georgia. 'Will I be able to see him?'

'Well, it's not going to be a good one for you to start with. There's quite a bit of decomposition according to the local team on site. But, hey, if you want to, I don't see why not, as long as you know what you'll be letting yourself in for.'

'Cool. If it does turn out to be Justin Green, I wonder what's happened?'

'My guess is he could have been badly injured when he was stabbed in the eye. Maybe he was in pain and tired and needed to rest. He must have decided to get off the main road and hide in the forest for a while. He would have known Carol would have given a description of the car, and we'd be looking for it.'

The Northern Area police were at the scene, having responded to the 999 call. From the alert circulated after Justin Green disappeared, they quickly realised that the car could be of interest to the team at Central and contacted Newcastle.

'Kielder is enormous,' Gayle told Georgia. 'It's the largest man-made woodland in Europe. About 650 square kilometres of forest. It's mainly conifers, mostly spruce, with some scots pine, larch and douglas-fir thrown in.'

'Just listen to you,' Georgia laughed. 'You sound like my old geography teacher.'

'When I came back to the north-east, I did some research on Kielder. I visited one day and was overwhelmed by the sheer size of it. The forest surrounds Kielder Water, which is the largest man-made reservoir in the UK. There, now you're as wise as me. Come to think of it, what better place to hide a car?'

They were met by a young officer who introduced himself as Constable Chris Stevens. With his blonde hair and ruddy cheeks, he looked all of sixteen. *I'm definitely getting old*, Gayle thought. He suggested they follow his car into the forest, and soon they were bumping along a narrow rutted track, with huge conifers rising on either side. After a few minutes, they could see blue police tape up ahead, and found a small clearing on the left where they parked up.

A DCI greeted them and explained that the body had been found by a young couple, looking for red squirrels.

'Amongst other activities,' she said and grinned. 'Two police constables were first on the scene and they immediately called for support. The duty officer, was next, and he supervised the securing of the scene before contacting me. That's when they found the second body in the boot. The photographer has just finished. SOCO are doing their bit. The bodies are still in situ, in the car, but we need to move them to allow proper examination.' She turned, as a man approached. 'This is David Dawkins, the Divisional Surgeon.'

'Hi, David,' Gayle said. Their paths had crossed on other cases, so they knew one another. Gayle found him to be a jolly sort of person, given the horrible tasks he had to perform.

'Hi Gayle, how're you doing? Hope you haven't eaten recently?' They put on forensic suits and David led them past a tent which had been set up next to where the car was hidden under the trees. 'Once you're happy, we want to move them on to gurneys inside the tent, so I can take a closer look at them. I have to warn you, the bodies are not a pretty sight. There's some decomposition and a lot of maggot activity. In the male body, there appears to be damage to the left eye – that's where the maggots are concentrated.'

'How long...?' Gayle started to ask.

'I would say less than a month. The body's not too badly decomposed, but we've got the winter temperatures to thank for that. Would have been a different story in the summer. The presence of maggots, a large mass, indicates he's not been dead for more than a month. My best guess at this stage would be three to four weeks. From what I can see, lividity suggests that the body hasn't been moved, but I need to take a proper look to be certain. If I'm right, he died where he was found, lying on the back seat of the car. Looks to me as though he could have lain down in the back, maybe for a sleep, or because he wasn't feeling well. Looking at that eye, I would say that could have something to do with the cause of death, but I won't know for sure until I do the autopsy. There's no obvious sign of any other injuries, apart from a few minor scratches on his face.'

They reached the car, and David held the door open so Gayle could look in. She leaned in. Even though she was wearing a mask, the stench in the car was vile and filled her nostrils, seeming to cling to the back of her throat. With trepidation, she looked at the face.

In death, he looked ghastly. His left eye area was swollen, and black, green and blue, with what looked like a large open sore beneath. The sore was heaving with maggots. At first glance, he looked very different from the man she knew as Justin Green. Remembering what Carol had told her about his hair now being very short and light, and his face clean-shaven, she took a closer look. She was pretty sure that underneath all the mess, it was him, but not one hundred percent. However, the injury to the left eye was consistent with what they would expect from Carol's description of what had happened, so all in all, there was little doubt in her mind that it was him.

She turned to Georgia, who was looking ashen, and said 'I think it's Justin Green, but I can't be sure. We'll need his brother to ID him properly.' Georgia turned and fled and Gayle could hear her retching on the far side of the tent. She still hadn't seen her first body, just smelled it, thought Gayle, smiling to herself.

David led Gayle around to the back of the car. 'This one's not much better,' he said. 'There's a large wound to the back of the skull and the maggots are doing their bit there, too.'

It took all her resolve to look into the boot of the car. Pauline was lying on her side, facing outwards. Her eyes were open, staring sightlessly from a face that looked almost untouched. Blackened dried blood had spread underneath her head. Gayle turned away, sickened. 'It's Pauline Bradley.'

'We'll start the PMs this afternoon, as soon as we've got them to the mortuary,' said David. 'I'll do the male first. For now, if you're happy, we'll move them to the tent?' She nodded. 'So you think it's your man?' he asked.

'I'm pretty sure... especially with having Pauline's body in the boot. We'll need to get his brother up to do a formal ID. I'll arrange that straight away?'

He nodded, 'Sooner the better. You attending the PM?'

'Yes, if I can; let me know what time you're starting it.'

As Gayle walked by the tent, the DCI was waiting for her. 'We've recovered his belongings from the car. Amongst his things were two passports, one in the name of Justin Green and the other, Terry Archer. Neither names are on the database – they're not known to us.'

'Justin Green is known to me. Terry Archer is an alias,' Gayle explained. 'I'm pretty sure the body is that of Justin Green; as far as I can tell, with the mess he's in. I hope it bloody well is; he's caused us no end of trouble. What else was in the car?'

'An overnight bag, with a few clothes in it, a laptop and a mobile phone.'

'We'll need to take a look at everything. This guy, and I'm pretty sure it is him, is wanted for murder and attempted murder. One of the crimes took place in Yorkshire; but it's our case, and the North Yorkshire team are assisting us. It's a bit complicated, as the original crime took place in Barbados.'

'Yes, I've heard quite a bit about it. Well, we'll give you every assistance.'

Gayle rang the Met and arranged for someone to pay Rob Wilkinson a visit and make arrangements for him to travel up at once to identify his half-brother. Then she collected a still very shaken Georgia, and they headed back to Newcastle.

'Want to attend the post mortem with me, Georgia?' Gayle asked, mischievously.

She looked shocked 'Only if I have to?'

'No, I'll let you off this time. I think you've seen enough for one day.' Gayle laughed. 'You'll get used to it you know, but that was a bad one for your first body.'

Gayle rang the Inspector on the way back, and gave him an update. By the time they arrived at the station in Newcastle, the Inspector had called the team together in the MIR.

'You've just got time to grab a coffee, Gayle,' DCI Patsy Mayne told her. Patsy had come into the station as soon as she'd heard the news.

When Gayle walked into the incident room, coffee in hand, a sea of faces looked at her expectantly. The excitement in the room was palpable. She knew there'd been a lot of frustration in the team, at the lack of progress following all the activity of searching the moor and the cottage. Since then, they'd drawn a blank. It was just as though Justin

Green had disappeared into thin air.

'Right,' began the Super, 'as I'm sure you all know by now, the Peugeot we've been looking for has been found, hidden in Kielder Forest. There were two bodies in the car, a male on the rear seat and a female in the boot. They appear to have been there for some time. Gayle's been up there, with Georgia. I'll let her tell you what she found.'

Gayle stood up. 'The Peugeot was found by a young couple, Tony and Sandy, in Kielder Forest. They were larking about; Sandy was being chased by Tony and she ducked under some low branches and literally bumped into the car.'

Gayle went on to describe how the young couple had opened the car door when they got no response to knocking on the window. 'As you can imagine, they got quite a shock when they opened the back door and the stench hit them. As soon as they could get a signal, they rang the police. When the police got there, they found a second body in the boot. A woman's.'

She took a sip of coffee, before continuing. 'I went up there with Georgia. According to the pathologist, the bodies have been there for three to four weeks. He was able to arrive at a reasonably accurate estimate, based on the maggot activity on the corpses.'

'Ugh...' the involuntary sound had come from Wendy, who looked embarrassed as everyone laughed at her.

Gayle continued. 'On the male body, the maggots were concentrated in a large mass on an open wound to the left side of the face, around the eye. You'll remember of course that Carol told us she stabbed Justin Green in the left eye with a stick.

I took a look at the corpse and I believe it to be that of Justin Green, but I can't be one hundred percent sure, due to the decomposition and the maggot activity. But everything points to it being him. His half brother, Rob Wilkinson, is on his way up from London to formally ID him. The body in the boot is that of Pauline Bradley. She has a large wound to the back of her head. Post Mortems are being held later this afternoon and I'm planning to go along to observe the one on the male.

We recovered a computer and mobile from the car, along with an overnight bag, and these are with forensics. There were also two passports, one in the name of Justin Green and another in the name of Terry Archer. Both names have been run through the database, but don't show up anywhere. Any questions so far?'

'How sure are you that it's him?' A young D.S., Andy Best, who'd helped co-ordinate the search on the moor, spoke up.

'Pretty sure, but we'll have to wait for formal identification before we can start to celebrate.' There were grins all round.

'Thank you, Gayle. Now, Andy, once forensics are done, I'd like you and Georgia to look through his computer and mobile phone; see if there's anything relevant there. Jane, you check through his overnight bag. Wendy, see if you can get anything from the passports. Once we get the ID and the cause of death, we'll be able to put this case to bed.'

CHAPTER SEVENTY-THREE

David had arranged for the body to be moved to the city mortuary in Newcastle, and by the time Gayle managed to get there, he had the post mortem well underway. She got kitted out in the ante-room and made sure her mask was firmly in place before entering the post mortem suite. David had already done the Y section and she watched as, together with a young female assistant, he carefully removed the yards of slippery intestines, before transferring them to a dish with a resounding plop. She looked at the face. The maggots were gone, and she assumed they'd been scraped off and kept as specimens somewhere. Without the presence of the wriggling mass, she got a better look, but still couldn't be certain it was Justin Green.

She studied the pretty face of David's young assistant and wondered at the appeal of such a profession to a young girl, but hey, each to his own, she thought. She guessed some of her friends thought the same about her choice of career. As a detective, you certainly see the seedier side of life; things most people are only vaguely aware of and, thankfully, rarely experience, she thought.

David was dictating his findings as he went, and she tuned out a bit, as there didn't seem to be anything out of the ordinary, so far. He prised the ribs apart and removed the heart and she knew the next step would be to look at the head. This was the interesting part for Gayle.

After he deftly made the incision to the scalp, she watched in fascination as the scalp was pulled forward, and the facial features collapsed. David put the still-saw to work and began to slice off the top of the skull. Once he'd removed the top, he carefully extracted the brain, examining it closely for any damage.

'There is leakage from a small, shallow puncture to the frontal lobe, with haemorrhage and massive infection,' he dictated. 'The puncture appears to have been made through a transorbital route, via the roof of the orbit, through the left eye, which has a ruptured globe. This leads me to the conclusion that a pointed object penetrated the left eye and broke through the fragile bone in the roof of the orbit, and entered the brain. This injury caused a slow leakage of fluid, leading to infection. Death would be inevitable, but may have taken quite some time to take place. In the meanwhile, the person would have been able to function but would gradually become more and more disorientated and unwell. There would be total loss of sight from the left eye, severe pain in the head and extreme fatigue.'

David was finishing up, leaving the closing and tidying up to his assistant. He and Gayle both left the room, and were removing their scrubs.

'Haven't seen one of those for a long time. Very rare injury,' David said, shrugging on his tweed jacket.

'The victim told us she stabbed at his face with a small stick she'd found on the ground. It was dark, so she couldn't be sure exactly where, but she's sure she made contact because he cried out in pain, clutching his face and yelling about his eye.'

'That would certainly be consistent with my findings. She must have stabbed at him with some force. It's not easy to penetrate the roof of the orbit.'

'Well, thank God she did, or she'd be be lying in her own grave now. She was fighting for her life.'

'I'll be starting on the female body at three pm,' said David.

'I won't be attending that, David. I knew her; I just couldn't take it.'

David nodded, 'I understand. I'll let you have the results as soon as I have them.'

Once back at the office, Gayle went straight to see her boss and gave her the results of the post mortem.

'Right. That fits in with what the victim told us. I'm getting the team together for an update in about...' she consulted her watch 'twenty minutes. There's been a new development... No, wait for the briefing.' She was teasing her, but wouldn't be drawn on what the new development was.

When Gayle walked into the incident room eighteen minutes later, she could feel an undercurrent of excitement; there was a buzz in the room. The team members were all there, waiting for the SIO, and a lot of banter was flying about. They were teasing Wendy about a live sex show she'd gone to see on a recent trip to Amsterdam. She'd just admitted to being picked out of the audience to go on to the stage, where some twerking had taken place.

'It was innocent enough,' she was explaining, 'I kept all my clothes on, honestly! And it was all simulation.'

'You mean all penetration,' quipped one of the PC's (who certainly wasn't PC).

All banter was dropped when the door suddenly swung open and Chief Superintendent Jensen strode into the room. He asked Gayle to report on the findings of the post-mortem, which she did in some detail, and confirmed the cause of death was consistent with what Carol had told them.

'The stick she stabbed at him with must have penetrated his brain, causing leakage of fluid from the brain, eventually leading to death,' she concluded.

'Go Girl,' one of the PC's whispered under his breath, earning a stern look from the Super.

'Thanks, Gayle. Now, I think Andy has some news for us. Andy?'

'Sir.' He told them that when he examined the computer found in the car, he came across material that confirmed Carol's contention that her husband had been murdered by Justin Green.

'There are photographs of Peter Barrington, with captions saying, for example...' Andy was scrolling down the screen 'and I quote, *This fucker's days are numbered* and further on, under a photograph of Team Ryan, *The Team's soon going to be a man down.* Then there's a caption underneath a copy of the coroner's report that reads *Easy peasy. One push and it was all over.*'

'Cocky bastard.' Gayle muttered.

'There are emails between Terry Archer and the captain of the hiking club, Tim Lawrenson,' continued Andy. 'Archer, aka Justin Green, applied to join the hiking club six months before Peter Barrington's 'accident'. Looks like the findings of Barrington's inquest will have to be re-examined.

There are also hundreds of pictures and videos of Carol Barrington on his computer. Many appear to have been recorded in her home. We know of course that he set up cameras in the house, even in the bedroom and bathroom. He's apparently been watching her for more than a year. There are pictures of her in many different locations, on the beach, in an office, shopping, etc. So it looks like he's been stalking her. Without her knowledge. He's been following her every move.'

'Thanks, Andy. Good work. That all fits in with the assessment of the psychologist that we were dealing with a predatory stalker,' the Super said, before turning to Gayle. 'Has the brother identified the body yet?'

'I'll check with David. Rob Wilkinson should have arrived at the mortuary by now.' She picked up her phone. After speaking with David, she put the phone down and turned to the team. 'It's him. Rob's confirmed it's definitely his brother.'

A cheer went round the room and a few high fives, too. The satisfaction of having closure on such a momentous case was obvious. There was still work to do, however. The suspected murder of Peter Barrington would have to be investigated and evidence gathered. Gayle thought to herself, Justin Green had targeted an innocent, unsuspecting woman and her equally unsuspecting husband and completely shattered their lives, murdered the husband, murdered the friend, all in order to act out his perverted and violent sexual fantasies. From what Carol had told them, there was no doubt that had he successfully disposed of her, he would have gone on to attack her daughter.

Over the years, Gayle had learned not to be shocked by anything, but this case had come pretty close.

CHAPTER SEVENTY-FOUR

I was slumped in an uncomfortable armchair, trying to read Dan Brown's *The Davinci Code* but finding it difficult to concentrate. Julia came through from the kitchen.

'Fancy a game of scrabble?' she asked.

Despite myself, I laughed. 'Is this what we've been reduced to? Playing scrabble during the day? Whatever happened to studying and running a business?'

It was three and a half weeks since we'd had to move to the safe house, and it was purgatory. Our lives were on hold. We were incommunicado and felt cut off from everything to do with our normal day to day lives. Added to that, we were trying to come to terms with, and deal with, everything that had happened. To be fair, we were receiving a lot of support, from the doctor, psychiatrist, the new Family Liaison Officer and Victim Support counsellor. Without them, we'd be in real trouble.

In the past, I'd hardly had a cross word with Julia, but since we'd been incarcerated in this house, we were having screaming matches and more than once we nearly came to blows. The most trivial thing could set either of us off. Just the other morning, Julia had used my hairdryer and failed to put it back in my bedroom. The furious and totally unjustified reaction that had evoked from me when, with dripping hair, I couldn't find my dryer, was akin to road rage.

'You selfish little bitch!' I'd screamed at her. 'Typical. No thought for anyone but yourself. Don't borrow my things if you bloody well can't be arsed to put them back.' I'd caught sight of myself in a mirror, as I was screaming at her, brandishing the hair dryer aloft, and was shocked at the twisted fury on my face.

What on earth was happening to us? Fiona was a gem, as always, but I think the strain of it all was getting to her too. Her usual bouncy optimism was missing these days and, as her tan faded, she looked increasingly pale and drawn.

I didn't want Julia to see the tears that I constantly felt perilously close to shedding. All I wanted to do was hide under the duvet, curl up in a ball, and weep. I felt so worthless. Despite remembering what Dr Quayle had instilled in me - that it was not my fault in any way that I'd been raped - I did feel a deep sense of guilt. Had I invited it in any way? What was it about me that made him target me? Did I unknowingly encourage him in any way? Was there anything I could have done to prevent it? What did I do to bring such danger, not only to myself, but to my beloved Peter and Julia and my dearest friend, Pauline? It was all a bitter price to pay for my forgotten two minutes of fame. Whenever I thought about what he said he was going to do to Julia, I went cold. If I hadn't managed to get away from him... I couldn't bear to think about what he would have done to my precious daughter. *Oh why the hell can't they find him? Where is he? Is he nearby?* I was going out of my mind with worry, fear and frustration.

I was torn. If I only had myself to think about, I would take my chances and move back to my house. With sensible security precautions, maybe even hiring a bodyguard, I would have felt reasonably safe from Green. But, I couldn't take a chance on him getting to Julia. No, all things considered, despite the fact that it was driving us mad, we had to stay in the depressing safe house, until he was caught. If only it would happen soon.

Kia, was helpful, but she wasn't Gayle, whom I'd become very fond of. Despite Kia's best efforts, we just couldn't establish the same rapport, and I missed Gayle... I felt myself beginning to tear up again.

'Come on, Mum, snap out of it. We're playing scrabble. Either that, or a walk on the beach. But it's freezing and chucking it down, so I think Scrabble wins, don't you?'

Julia set up the board and, after each taking our seven tiles, we drew a further tile each, to decide who would start. I picked an 'A', so went first. My heart wasn't in it, but for once Fiona and Julia were in light-hearted mood and there was plenty of joking and innuendo.

'Is there such a word as "wank"?' Fiona asked. Julia laughed, but it turned out to be a valid word, and as Fiona put the K on a double letter square, and a triple word square was included, she got a score of 45.

'Wow,' said Julia. 'Who'd have thought a wank was worth so much?'

Despite myself, I laughed. Normally I would have told Julia not to be so crude, but these were not normal times.

We were interrupted by the doorbell chiming and looked at each other nervously. Although we knew there was no way Justin Green could find us there, nevertheless we were always fearful.

'I'll go,' I said. 'It's probably Kia.' I went to the heavily-locked door and peered through the spyhole.

'It's Gayle,' I shouted in disbelief, then quickly unlocked and opened the door. 'Gayle. How lovely to see you.' I impulsively hugged her.

'I have news, she announced,' as we both walked into the sitting room, where Julia and Fiona looked just as surprised to see her as I had. They both jumped up and welcomed her like an old friend, with hugs all round.

'I didn't think you were allowed to come here?' Julia said.

'Well, normally, I wouldn't be. But there's been a development.' She grimaced. 'I think we should all sit down. How are you all doing?' she asked.

'Never mind how we're doing, Gayle. Get on with it. We're dying to hear about this new development,' I said impatiently. I was tingling with anticipation; hoping it was good news, but scared in case it was bad.

'Well, there are two major developments. Firstly, I have to tell you that we've found Justin Green. Or rather, his body. He's dead.'

'His body?' I was astonished. 'He's dead? But how...?' I hadn't yet started to feel the relief that would kick in later. It was such a shock.

'His body was found in his car, hidden in Kielder Forest. The post mortem shows that he died from the wound to his eye...'

I interrupted. 'What...? I killed him? But how... how could he get to Kielder?'

'Let me tell you what happened, and I'll answer your questions later' she said, raising her hand.

Gayle went on to tell us what had happened, from the young lovers

272

finding the car in Kielder Forest, to the results of the post mortem.

'Without treatment, he couldn't possibly have survived,' explained Gayle. 'But he was able to function for a period of time. Piecing the picture together, after you got away from him, we think he drove his car back to the cottage, packed a few things and headed north. According to the coroner, he would have felt progressively unwell and his vision would have gradually worsened. We think he found a secluded place to stop and rest, keeping the car out of sight, possibly not realising that he was dying.'

I began to feel the tension drain away from my body. We were free. He couldn't get to us any more. I looked at Julia, whose mouth was hanging open.

'We're safe. Oh, thank God. We're all safe.' I shouted jubilantly.

They both looked shocked at Gayle's news but were soon smiling with relief. Julia started jumping up and down with excitement, clapping her hands and chanting 'We're safe. We're safe. We can go home.'

'What about Pauline?' I asked quietly. 'Was she still in the boot?'

Gayle nodded. 'Yes, her body was still there. The post mortem showed she died of a massive brain haemorrhage following a blow to the back of the head. The pathologist said death was instantaneous; she won't have suffered at all.'

'Thank God for small mercies. How's Charlie? I feel terrible that I haven't been allowed to contact him.'

'Well, I think now he has Pauline's body to bury, he's coping a bit better. And the fact that she didn't suffer is a big comfort to him. He does understand why you haven't been able to get in touch. But, in any case, all that will change now. It's over.'

Julia, still jumping around the place, wrapped her arms around me. 'Oh, Mum, we're free. We can go home.'

Fiona joined in the hug, 'Group hug,' she shouted. 'Thank God, Thank God. Thank God.'

Gayle watched us, a look of tenderness on her face, if I wasn't mistaken. Then, she clapped her hands, before ushering us towards the stairs. 'Right. Pack your things. I'm taking you all home.'

Throwing clothes into a bag in my bedroom a few minutes later, I had a chance to talk quietly with Gayle, who was sitting on my bed, watching me. 'I'm glad he's dead,' I told her. 'He didn't deserve to live. I'm glad I killed him. I know I would never ever have been able to forgive him. Some people are evil through and through and he's one of them.'

'I can't disagree with that sentiment. Now, come on,' she said, rising from the bed and opening a drawer, 'I'll help you get the rest of your things together. Time to go home.'

CHAPTER SEVENTY-FIVE

Home. We were home at last, and it was so good to be free of the huge cloud of fear that had hung over us for so long. Relief was mixed with apprehension about how we would cope with the future.

Gayle came to see me a couple of days after we'd settled back in. 'I wanted to let you know. Green's half-brother has been charged with perverting the course of justice by giving Green a false alibi in a murder case five years ago. Green's DNA taken from the cottage, matches that found at the murder scene in London, when a young girl was raped and murdered. Without the alibi, Green would have been found out then, and you would have been spared all this.'

'If only,' Julia whispered.

'He's got a lot to answer for,' Gayle said. 'If he hadn't pretended to be Justin Green when Tim called, none of this would have happened. And Pauline would be alive. He's as bad as his brother. He'll pay for it now.'

Over the next few days, Julia and I made some decisions. She agreed to go back to University in a couple of weeks, at my insistence. The only way to put all this behind her is for her to get on with her life. Resume her studies, have fun with her friends. She told me she's not seeing her boyfriend any more, but she wouldn't be drawn on why. I expect there'll soon be another on the horizon. It won't be easy for her to carry on as normal, and she'll continue to need counselling and support for some time, but it will be a good start for her to try to get back to her normal life.

They're re-opening the inquest on Peter, soon, and the verdict will be changed to one of murder. Just for the records. Nothing will bring Peter back. When I told Tim, that Green had murdered Peter, he was incandescent with rage and I think if he'd been able to get his hands on Green at that moment, he would probably have killed him. After he calmed down, he told me he'd always been puzzled by Peter's fall, knowing what a competent climber he was. Now things made terrible sense to him.

Tim took a long time to forgive himself for not sussing out that the person who'd answered the door to him at Dan Smithson's flat, was in fact 'Smithson's' half-brother, Rob Wilkinson. Rob told the police that he'd done as his brother asked, and pretended to be him when the landlord's agent knocked at the door. He'd done so, with no questions asked, in order not to jeopardise a twenty grand loan his brother had agreed to give him. Justin Green had looked out of a window and spotted Tim at the door. Not wanting Tim to recognise him, he persuaded his brother to answer the door and masquerade as him.

As for me, I'm determined not to live as a victim. I've decided that I will learn to live with the memories. The mental scars will fade over time and eventually become barely visible. I refuse to dwell on events or let them dominate me and spoil the rest of my life. I know that I will continue to need help, probably for quite some time, but I also know I'll beat these feelings of wretchedness that ambush me when I least expect it.

The mind is a funny thing. At first, when I learned that I had killed Green, I was glad. But within a couple of days, I began to have nightmares. I see myself stabbing the stick into his eye and I see him lying on the back seat of his car, writhing in agony. Dying the most horrific death. My heart feels heavy with the guilt of knowing that I have killed a man, no matter how much I tell myself that he deserved to die. Nothing eases the heaviness inside me, and those feelings, added to everything else that happened, make me a complex case for the psychiatrists and counsellors.

Simon came over from Barbados for a few days, and eventually persuaded Fiona to go back with him. She's just been the best, sticking with me through all of this and she needs a period of calm tranquillity herself. I hope they find it together.

Charlie came to see me yesterday, but it was a bit awkward. I sense, deep down, he resents me, because it was me who was being stalked, yet I lived, and Pauline died. We hugged and cried together and parted on good terms, but, sadly, I don't think we'll be keeping in close touch.

I've been thinking a lot lately, about the plight of some women in this country and have decided to set up a trust fund to support a network of Womens' Refuge Centres in the north of England. To my delight, Linda has agreed to head it up.

The Centre will be named Sanctuary and will provide safe places, where frightened women can find shelter from predatory men. According to Gayle, I will be shocked by the demand for safe places, there being no shortage of abusive men in the region. Women, apparently, are violated on a daily basis. I want to help every one of them to be able to say 'I won't let him win.'

CHAPTER SEVENTY-SIX

(Two Years Later)

The shrill, insistent ringing of his phone drew Chief Superintendent Jensen reluctantly back into his office with a groan of frustration. He was just about to escape for the weekend and was almost out of the door, when the bloody thing rang.

'Shit,' he muttered. Turning back, he dumped his coat and briefcase on the desk, and snatched up the receiver, 'Yes?'

'Call for you sir,' the receptionist announced. 'Detective Superintendent Fisher, Dallas, Texas.'

'Texas? Put him on.'

'Detective Superintendent Jensen?' a voice asked in a Texan drawl.

'Yes, this is Mike Jensen.'

'Hi, Mike. This is Ben Fisher, Detective Super with Dallas Law Enforcement. Got me some interesting news for you. Courtesy of Interpol, we have a DNA match with a felon you had two years ago. The intriguing thing is, you have him as deceased at that time.'

'Really? Who is it?'

'Guy by the name of Justin Green. Don't know if you remember the case?'

'Green? I remember the case very well. Silly question, but could you be mistaken? Green's body was identified by his brother and there were other indicators that pointed to it definitely being Justin Green.'

'Sorry. No mistake. I'll send over the documentation and a photo

278

straight away. You'll get them on your screen soon.'

'I'd appreciate that. What has this person done over there?'

'Same thing. Rape and murder of a young woman. Her boyfriend walked in on him and gave chase. We had a couple of officers nearby, and between them, they cornered him. Open and shut case.'

'You've got the death penalty in Texas, I believe?'

'We sure do. This guy's gonna get a lethal injection. Guess you guys got some investigating to do over there, to find out who the John Doe is you burned.'

'Indeed we do. I'll arrange to send a couple of officers over to interview Green. See if we can find out whose body was found in his car.'

'Sure thing. We'll give them every assistance.'

'Well, thanks for that, Ben. Much appreciated. Under the circumstances, we won't be seeking extradition. We're happy to let you guys deal with him – unless of course he's found not guilty. Then we'll have him back over here for trial.'

'Mike, there aint a snowflake's chance in hell of him getting out of this one. Mark my words, he'll be on death row in a few months.'

'We'll follow the trial with great interest.'

'I'm sure you will, Mike. You have a good day now.'

Mike slowly put the receiver down, before opening his laptop. He picked up the phone again. 'Ask DCI Mayne and DI Jones to come to my office immediately, please.' *Bloody hell*, he thought, gazing at the DNA data in front of him.

Gayle bumped into Patsy in the corridor, en route to the Super's office.

'Wonder what this is about?' she queried, with a grimace. 'Something tells me my weekend's up the spout.'

'Come in, come in,' the Super shouted, impatiently at Gayle's tentative knock on his door. 'Come over here,' he said, indicating his computer on the desk. 'There's something I want you both to see.'

They gathered in front of the blank screen and, after a bit of fiddling with the mouse, the Superintendent brought up a photograph.

'That's Justin Green,' Gayle immediately volunteered. 'Obviously an old photo, from when his hair was dark and he had a beard.'

'This photograph was taken last week.' He turned and looked from one to the other, 'In Dallas, Texas.'

'What? But it can't have been, sir.'

'I've just had a call from the Dallas Police Department. They arrested him following the rape and murder of a young woman. Interpol has matched his DNA with that of Justin Green.'

'Christ,' exclaimed Patsy.

'Couldn't have put it better myself, Patsy,' the Superintendent remarked.

'But... his brother ID'd the body. The wound to the eye matched Carol Barrington's account...' Gayle was thinking aloud. 'Pauline's body was in the boot... Is it possible he inflicted the *same* wound on someone else? Was he that sick?'

'That's what I want you two to find out,' said the Super. 'And we need to know who the poor sod is that was cremated. Use whoever you need in the office, but not a word to anyone else about this until we know where we are with it. You'll need to go to Dallas to interview Green.'

'The press will have a field day if they get hold of this,' said Patsy.

'Yes, I want to keep it as quiet as possible, for as long as we can. I don't relish the thought of having it splashed all over the papers and social media that the wrong body was burned.'

'Yes sir. Will we extradite him?'

'No. We'll let the State of Texas try him. They've still got the death penalty over there.'

CHAPTER SEVENTY-SEVEN

Gayle followed Patsy into her office. 'This is the last thing I expected. It's surreal.' she said.

'Interpol won't be wrong,' said Patsy. 'There's virtually nil chance of it being a mistake. Let's assume it's him, and look at how he could have done it.'

'So,' Gayle hypothesised, 'he has to have found somebody else, same build, same hair, similar features. How likely is that? Then he would have had to kill him by poking a stick into his eye. His car was well hidden, so maybe he banked on the body being a bit decomposed before being found, to make identification more difficult. I know I wasn't absolutely certain it was him, with all the maggot activity.'

'But his brother had no doubt at all?' Patsy raised her eyebrows.

'Rob Wilkinson's already doing time for giving Green a false alibi, in the case I was working on in London. And we *know* he pretended to be Green, when Tim Lawrenson went to the flat. He's proved he can be bought.'

'Let's start with him. We'll go to London by car in the morning. I'll pick you up at six? I'm afraid you were right about your weekend being up the spout,' Patsy laughed. 'After we've seen him, we'll go straight out to Dallas. Leave the car at Heathrow.'

'Never been to Dallas before,' said Gayle. 'Hope we can make time to do some sightseeing.'

'The only sight you'll be seeing is Justin Green's evil face.'

'Something's just occurred to me, Patsy. Green's hair was almost military, once he'd had it cropped. On the road to Kielder, from Yorkshire, he would pass Catterick garrison. Could he have picked up a soldier on the way, maybe hitch-hiking back to base? Could be, that put the idea into his head to substitute his body for his own?'

'It's a possibility. He had to find him somewhere. We'll check with Catterick. I'm also wondering how he got away from Kielder? It would be quite a walk to get to civilisation. Did he steal a car? We need to check if any were stolen in the area at that time. I'll get a few of the team to start digging.'

'Just one other thing,' Gayle added. 'We need to check if DNA was taken from the body when the PM was done. And, if so, was it compared to Green's known DNA?' She went on to suggest the answer to her own question. 'I don't suppose there was any need to make a comparison, as there didn't appear to be any doubt about the identification of the corpse.'

'There's a lot to check out. See you at six.'

Sleep wouldn't come to Gayle. She tossed and turned all night, thinking things through. Trying to work things out. She found it hard to believe that Justin Green was still alive, but she had to accept that he was. Bleary-eyed and looking far from her best, she tried to look alert when Patsy collected her on the dot of six. However, Patsy's first words when she saw her, 'God, you look rough Gayle,' told her that her attempt had failed.

They were on their way to Belmarsh Category A Prison in Thamesmead, South East London where Rob Wilkinson was serving eight years for perverting the course of justice. The previous year, once Wilkinson had identified his half-brother's body, the Met was informed that he must have lied when he gave an alibi for him five years earlier. The DNA taken from the crime scene in the cottage in Yorkshire, matched that taken five years ago, from the crime scene in London that Gayle had worked on.

Rob Wilkinson had been interviewed by the Met, and before long, had confessed to giving a false alibi. In mitigation, he told the court that he did not know his brother had committed a crime. His brother had told him that on the night in question, he had drunk a lot of whisky at home, and passed out. To avoid becoming a suspect, Justin Green had asked his half-brother to give him the alibi, and Wilkinson had agreed. The judge, whilst taking into account the mitigation put forward, nevertheless took a stern view of the offence. By giving a false alibi, Wilkinson had enabled a murderer to remain free to murder again.

The drive down was fairly uneventful; for once, traffic was light and with no hold-ups, they reached Belmarsh just before noon. They went through the usual prison security procedures before being shown to a small interview room in House Block One, which housed prisoners serving one year or over.

'Hello, Rob,' Patsy said, once the prisoner had been shown into the small, bare room, and seated opposite them on the other side of the desk, in the middle of the room. 'I'm DCI Mayne, and I think you already know DI Jones?'

Without waiting for a response, the DCI got down to business. 'Can you tell us why you identified the body found in Kielder Forest as your half-brother, Justin Green?' she asked.

Rob blustered. 'What do you mean? It *was* my half-brother.'

Patsy changed tack. 'We'd like to take a look at your bank accounts, Rob. Would you have any objection to that?'

'Why..? I mean where are you coming from with all this?'

Patsy put the photograph of Green on the desk in front of Wilkinson. 'Is this your brother?' she asked, quietly.

He looked at the photograph, then back at the DCI. 'Yes, where did you get that?'

'It was taken just a week ago.'

Rob visibly paled, then blustered. 'It can't have been. You know he's been dead for more than two years.'

'But that's just it, Rob,' said Gayle. 'He isn't dead. And you know it. Why did you lie? Did he pay you? Will we find a large sum of money sitting in your bank account?'

Following more denials, Rob eventually caved in, surprisingly easily, and it became clear why, later on when his secret bank account was accessed. He confessed he'd received a phone call from his half-brother, the day after the abduction of Carol Barrington and Pauline Bradley, and in return for three hundred thousand pounds, had agreed to identify the body as Justin Green, should it be discovered.

'Who was it you cremated?' Patsy demanded.

'It was a soldier he'd given a lift to. That's all I know.'

'Do you have a name?' Gayle asked.

'No, I just know he was a soldier he picked up on the road. It wasn't planned. Justin said it was sheer coincidence that they looked alike.'

'Your brother stabbed a sharp object into that soldier's eye, to replicate his own injury. I hope you're proud of yourself, shielding scum like that. You're as bad as he is. You're going to get a hefty term added to your current eight years. You won't be out for a very long time.'

Rob lowered his head for a few seconds, then looked up and asked, 'Where is he now? Where did you get the photograph?'

'He's in prison in Dallas, Texas, charged with the rape and murder of a young woman. Another one whose blood is also on your hands. They have the death penalty in that State, just in case you didn't know.' Gayle took delight in telling him.

There was no response from Rob, who buried his head in his hands.

'He's probably working out how he can get his hands on his brother's fortune,' remarked Gayle as they left.

CHAPTER SEVENTY-EIGHT

Gayle and Patsy were seated at the square, metal table, waiting for Justin Green to be brought into the interview room. Gayle looked around the small, bare room, noting that the furniture, such as it was, was screwed securely to the floor, and the one, small window located high on the wall, heavily barred.

The door was flung open, and Green, dressed in an orange jumpsuit, was brought in by a stern-faced guard, who pushed him into the chair on the opposite side of the table. The guard unlocked the handcuffs holding the prisoner's hands behind his back, before taking up his place, against the door.

'I'm DCI Mayne and I think you've met DI Jones?' began Patsy. 'We'd like to ask you some questions about your activities in the UK.'

'DI Jones? Ah, yes, I remember you. In London. So that's how you knew my real name – it's all falling into place now. You weren't a DI then, just a little rookie. You're obviously going up in the world.'

'We know you paid your brother to ID the body, Justin,' said Gayle.

'A master stroke, don't you think, Gayle? I always fancied you, you know? When you were just a new little DC, so young and innocent.'

'We have evidence that you attacked and killed your student, seven years ago. We have evidence you killed Peter Barrington and Pauline Bradley. We have evidence that you stalked, abducted and attacked Carol Barrington. Who was the man whose body you left in the car, Justin? Your brother tells us it was a soldier.'

'Have you come all this way just to get his name, ladies? What a wasted journey. I didn't need to know his name, I just needed his body,' he laughed. 'I threw his papers in a bin.'

'And you stabbed him in the eye, to make us think it was you,' stated the DCI.

'Ingenious, wasn't it?' he laughed again. 'It worked. If I hadn't been caught over here, you would never have known I'm still alive.'

'Yes, well hopefully not for much longer, Mr Green.' said the DCI.

'Just out of interest, Justin,' began Gayle, 'how did you overpower him? He was the same build as you, and fit.'

'Ha ha. Wouldn't you like to know,' he said, touching his nose. You'll just have to work that one out for yourself.' He sat back, looking smug.

'And how did you get away from Kielder? Out of the forest?'

'Oh come on. Ask some intelligent questions, ladies,' he said, rolling his eyes in mock exasperation. 'Haven't you heard of such a thing as a bike?'

'We must inform you, Mr Green, that unless, by any chance, you are acquitted here in Dallas, we won't be asking for your extradition,' said the DCI. 'We're happy for you to be tried, and hopefully executed, over here. Interview terminated four fifteen pm.'

As they left, they could hear him cheerfully whistling. Gayle thought she recognised the tune and wracked her brains before she remembered. It was an old favourite of her mother's, by Neil Sedaka...

CHAPTER SEVENTY-NINE

I was very pleased to see Gayle at the door, surprised too. It had been a long time. I invited her in and, after a few pleasantries, she suggested we sit down.

'I have some news for you,' she said.

I searched her face, wondering what news she could have. I wasn't prepared for her bombshell.

'Justin Green is still alive.'

I felt as though she'd just thrown a jug of icy water in my face. My head jerked back in shock. 'What..? But... he can't be... How?' I was stunned, unable to string a sentence together. Shaken and upset, I felt the horror flooding back, as a wave of anguish washed over me.

'Just sit quietly for a minute. I know it's a shock. It was to me, too.'

Gayle told me everything, from the Chief Super receiving the phone call from Dalllas, to her interview with Justin Green in his cell. Once my brain had accepted that he was still alive, I was filled with conflicting emotions. I didn't yet feel any immediate relief to know that I hadn't killed him after all, but hoped that as the knowledge seeped into my psyche, my nightmares would stop. The knowledge that he was likely to end up on Death Row was comforting and calmed my panic.

'But... who...?' I began.

Anticipating my question, Gayle interrupted. 'It was a soldier on his way back to Catterick Garrison whose body was in the car. He'd been listed as AWOL when he failed to report for duty. Apparently, it wasn't the first time he'd done that sort of thing, disappeared for a while, so his family wasn't too worried when the Redcaps came to their door. They just assumed he was off on his travels and would eventually turn up.

Now, they have to come to terms with the knowledge that not only will they never see him again, but they don't even have his body to bury.'

'Oh God, that's awful... but... how did he have the same injury?' My voice trailed off as I realised what Green must have done. I felt sick, overwhelmed by the old familiar feelings of horror and revulsion. I groaned and doubled up with the pain that suddenly coursed through my gut. 'Oh my God...'

'Take it easy, Carol.' Gayle put her hand on my arm. 'At least we know he'll never be able to harm anyone again.'

I shook my head, still doubled over. 'I thought I'd come to terms with his evil, but to do that... the poor boy. And then the young girl in Dallas – I can hardly bear to think about her. It's heartbreaking.'

I'm still learning to live with what Green did to me. Knowing he is still breathing on this earth has shaken me to the core, but it helps to know that he'll never be free and that in all likelihood he will have the death penalty to look forward to. Even so, a feeling of being watched has returned and I can't shake it off, hard as I try.

There is little left of the trusting, optimistic person I used to be. He has changed me irrevocably, but I'm still determined to carry on, do whatever good I'm capable of in this world, and come out on top.

Sanctuary is up and running now, and Gayle was right. Although it's true, thank God, that most men are decent, normal, nice people, I nevertheless never cease to be shocked by the sheer numbers of women who are victims of a small number of evil men; raped, gang-raped, beaten, mentally abused, stalked, physically abused, pimped out, imprisoned, enslaved, threatened... the list goes on.

After running Sanctuary for a few months, I decided to devote myself to developing the network, on a full-time basis. Together with Linda and the team, we're gradually expanding the area covered by our network, providing safe spaces and support for as many of these women as possible. Our motto is 'WE WON'T LET THEM WIN.'

THE END

ABOUT THE AUTHOR

Georgia E Brown has used her love of writing to produce The Stalker's Song, her first novel, for Crime/Thriller aficionados.

After a long and successful business career specialising in HR, but also incorporating entrepreneurial ventures such as retail, property development and management consultancy, the author has used her people skills to great advantage in developing the characters in this novel.

Asked to describe Georgia in a few words, her friends came up with (amongst others): hard-working, compassionate, generous, thoughtful, creative, sassy, forgetful, witty, good fun and loyal - and makes great lasagne!

Printed in Great Britain
by Amazon

86169534R00171